downriver drift

downriver drift

TIM BOWLING

HARBOUR PUBLISHING

Published by
HARBOUR PUBLISHING
P.O. Box 219
Madeira Park, BC Canada
V0N 2H0

THE CANADA COUNCIL | LE CONSEIL DES ARTS
FOR THE ARTS | DU CANADA
SINCE 1957 | DEPUIS 1957

Cover design by Martin Nichols, Lionheart Graphics
Cover photograph by Calen Darnell
Printed and bound in Canada

Harbour Publishing acknowledges the financial support of the
Government of Canada through the Book Publishing Industry
Development Program (BPIDP) and the Canada Council for the
Arts, and the Province of British Columbia through the British
Columbia Arts Council, for its publishing activities.

Canadian Cataloguing in Publication Data

Bowling, Tim, 1964–
 Downriver drift

  ISBN 1-55017-220-4

  I. Title.
PS8553.O9044D68 2000   C813'.54   C00-910289-2
PR9199.3.B6358D68 2000

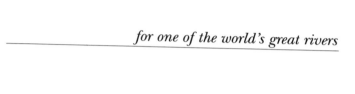

for one of the world's great rivers

ACKNOWLEDGEMENTS

As always, the debt I owe to family and friends extends far beyond their help in literary matters. But for their specific insights, conversation, and support with regards to this book, I wish to thank Jack Hodgins, Theresa Shea, Curtis Gillespie, Russell Thornton, and Sally Ito.

I am grateful, as well, to the editors of *AlbertaViews, Event,* and *Queen's Quarterly* who published excerpts, and to Howard White, Peter Robson, Marisa Alps and everyone at Harbour Publishing for their hard work and enthusiasm.

chapter one

*I*n the middle of a March night, nearly thirty years ago, a heavy fog rolled in off the Gulf of Georgia toward the town of Chilukthan. The mast lights on the gillnetters drifting nearby in the mouth of the Fraser River vanished, along with the stars that mirrored them, followed soon after by the harbour's dim orange lights and the few windowpanes still shining on the long gravel dyke that separated the town from its tides. Quickly, the fog and the dark erased all boundaries between land and water and transformed the distinct world of salt marshes, silt islands, and potato fields into a sudden sameness; only the vague outlines of shapes existed, the ruins of a salmon cannery along the riverbank no different than a swaybacked barn on the edge of town, a fathom of current no deeper than a foot of clayed earth in a backyard garden.

By seven o'clock that morning, the fog was at its heaviest and had stopped moving; it hung over the empty shops and quiet houses clustered around the centre of Chilukthan as if the sky had dropped or the ground had lifted. Certainty became impossible. Was that the ringing of a churchbell or the clanging of a jetty buoy? How close was that stench of rotted fish?

The town slept on. A gull screeched briefly from the roof of a machine shop near the harbour, then fell silent. Its echoing, fractious cry hovered, like the fog, directly over the main street, a quarter mile of small rain-darkened shops, a few skinny Edwardian houses, moss-speckled and listing like ships in a storm, and, just where the street ended at the dyke and harbour, a large vacant lot overgrown with grass and blackberry bushes.

But now the fog had obscured everything. Even the gull's cry, fading in the cavernous white, carried a plaintive, searching note, as if to stress that the unusual nature of the morning made no more sense to the town's winged residents than to anyone else. It was spring, after all, not fall or winter, the usual seasons of heavy fog. Almost petulantly, the gull screeched again, and the echoes followed one another like footsteps into the gloom.

At the far end of the street from the harbour, Joe Meers stood motionless before the door of his butcher shop. He held his right arm out, with the palm of his huge blunt-nailed hand facing up, as though he might be enticing a chickadee or sparrow to light on it. Only when the gull screeched the second time did he shiver and finally lift his gaze from the faint black smudge of the shop key in his hand.

After a few seconds, he slowly lowered his head again, closed his fingers around the key, and stepped closer to the door. With some difficulty, he inserted the key in the lock and turned it.

Once inside the shop, he exhaled deeply, only then realizing that he had been holding his breath. The fog had made him anxious, not because the short walk from his house into town had been dangerous—he knew the route so well he could have walked it safely with his eyes closed—but because nothing disturbed him as much as the arbitrariness of life. Though a man of forty-five, the butcher had an almost childlike need for predictability, for the days to follow one another without any drama that might destroy his emotional calm. And a spring fog was certainly dramatic, and therefore a threat to his belief in the virtues of order and routine. Why, in March, should he even have to think about the simple task of taking his key from his pants pocket and inserting it into the lock?

He flicked on the shop light and the brightness soon dispelled his anxiety. Back in familiar surroundings, next to his glass display case that exhibited cuts of meat, and with his knives hanging on the wall and his storage freezer humming in the back, Joe immediately relaxed. This was his world, neat and small, everything in its place, from the cash register to the weigh scale to the peg where every afternoon at closing he hung a clean smock for the next day's work. Even the faintly antiseptic smell, the lingering result of his efforts to subdue the mingled odours of blood, meat, garlic and spice that accompanied his trade, and of which it was never entirely free, seemed welcoming.

Joe took a deep breath and strode across the clean linoleum floor to hang up his coat and put on his smock. It was still early; he had an hour or perhaps two to prepare for customers. How he relished this time of day! No one to complain about prices or weights, no one to demand his attention, yet still work to be done, a whole day to be set in motion, properly and efficiently.

And Monday mornings were particularly pleasant. To start his week, Joe would select a large, juicy bone for Shamus, the Mawsons' grizzled, bowlegged black lab who arrived regular as clockwork just as the shop opened. This ritual had been taking place for over a year, and the butcher, at first disturbed and perplexed by the dog's scratching at his door, now looked forward to each visit with pleasure.

In his faithful appearances, the arthritic old lab provided a little companionship for Joe, who lived alone and, since the deaths of his parents some years before, had no family. It was a small thing, he realized, but if the dog offered even some slight connection to the warmer domestic life he had not yet ruled out for himself, well, what harm was there in that?

At five after eight, with the fog still thick and the silence of the shop unbroken except by the chopping rhythm of his cleaver, Joe stopped working long enough to lean out the door and listen. He expected to hear the clack of the dog's nails on the sidewalk, but heard only the drip of moisture off the telephone lines. He waited a minute, then gave a soft whistle: "Here Shamus, here boy." The sound of his own voice made him uneasy. It was all wrong, this absence, wrong as the heaviness of the fog. He could not get his mind, or rather his nerves, around it. The shop was open, the week had begun, but the bone had not been collected. Therefore, the shop was not open and the week had not begun after all.

Joe stood in the doorway, rubbing his forehead. Perhaps the dog did not want to venture out in such weather? Yet he had never missed a Monday before, and the weather had often been poor. Joe shrugged and turned back into the shop.

Fifteen minutes later, he stood in the doorway again, irritated with himself but unable to settle down to work without a resolution to the mystery. Ah, this is foolishness, he concluded, yet somehow he could not put the issue out of his mind; it seemed connected to the unusual fog and the anxiety he had felt fumbling with his key.

A foghorn blew mournfully in the distance. Joe pictured a large freighter navigating its way up the mouth of the river, and this image of motion encouraged him to act. Because he disliked the phone and only used it for business reasons, he decided against calling the Mawsons.

Instead, he chose to close the shop briefly and walk to the end of the street. Shamus might just be moving slower in the fog. It would be easy to follow his probable route in reverse, and if the dog was not there, then Joe would simply have to go about his day and wait for an explanation.

The row of neighbouring businesses stretched in a long black outline ahead of him, like a collection of boxcars junked on a siding. He passed the dull gleam in the windows of the five-and-dime and the hardware store, but saw no one inside. Most of the other shops were in darkness.

Every few steps, he stopped and whistled, half-expecting Shamus to respond or to appear, but no bark greeted him and only the dripping whiteness swirled around his legs. The town was oddly silent. Eight o'clock had come and gone, yet there was little sound or motion beyond the occasional passing car and sweep of headlights. Joe kept whistling just to remind himself of his own presence. The familiar landscape seemed almost foreign; he saw the same buildings as usual, the same sidewalk, the same telephone poles, but the fog had given them a curious new vitality, so that they seemed to be moving toward him even as he was approaching them.

By the time he reached the end of the street, his anxiety had returned. He peered into the vacant lot and shouted "Shamus! Here boy!" and was about to turn back when he heard a weak bark. He shouted again, but this time heard only the echo of his own voice. Had he imagined the bark? He stepped a few paces into the wet grass and listened. Nothing. And yet . . .

He continued on, straining to hear something other than his own breath and the swish of his legs against the grass. Once into the lot, he decided that he might as well cross it. If the dog hadn't appeared by then, he likely hadn't left the Mawsons' yard at all, since they lived on the first street on the far side of the lot.

Joe sighed, resigned to the change in his routine the fog had ushered in, but impatient to be back at work. He found the firmer ground of the dirt path and increased his pace, striding so quickly that he did not see the black shape in front of him until he had stumbled over it.

Getting up, he felt a sharp pain in his knee, but the whimpering just behind him soon commanded his full attention. He knelt over the dog, aware of the whumping noise of a tail striking the ground.

"Shamus, here fella, what's the matter, boy? Couldn't make it this morning?"

The lab, panting heavily, pushed its muzzle into Joe's hand. A rank smell of soaked fur and urine rose from the ground. Joe removed a blackberry bramble stuck to the dog's ear and picked a few burrs off his dull and grizzled coat.

Gently, he stroked the dog's head as he spoke to him, then stood, backed away a step, and called him to come. Shamus whimpered, barked weakly, and shuffled a few inches forward on his paws. "That's all right, fella," Joe said. He stepped forward, laid his coat on the ground, then very carefully rolled the old lab onto it. This wasn't easy; Shamus weighed almost fifty pounds and even a small amount of motion made him yelp.

Eventually, the butcher bundled the dog up and lifted him in his arms. More carefully than before, he continued through the lot toward the dyke, speaking soothingly and feeling the warmth and heavy heartbeat against his smock. "Hang on, old friend, hang on," he whispered, as much to himself as to the animal in his arms.

The dog began to rasp just as Joe emerged from the lot and passed the government wharf. Another freighter sounded off the river, two long, bass-deep calls of warning to smaller vessels. Joe passed under the sound, his attention tuned to the dog's laboured breathing. "Please, old fella," he whispered again. "Just hang on till I get you home."

But the dog was a dead weight by the time the butcher reached his destination. He could feel the extra heaviness in his muscles, or at least imagined he could. He stood at the top of the Mawsons' gravel driveway, staring down at the single white bulb burning over the side door of the house, and felt as though he'd emerged from his storage room, a chunk of beef in his arms, the hoar still on it, and his breath cold on his lips.

He didn't know what to do next. Should he lay Shamus in the side yard and let the family find him there? That way, he could avoid their grief and the death would remain a private matter. But perhaps they'd like to know that the dog did not die alone? Or would they be upset that someone else, a butcher no less, had been present at the end?

Joe scowled at the house. The muscles in his arms were sore and the pain in his knee had increased, yet he could not make a decision. The dog was dead, that much was certain, so why couldn't he just knock on the door and tell the family? It maddened him, this hesitation that he always felt whenever his routine had been altered. Why could he never accept change? Yes, yes, the day could have been like any other, but here he was now, a dead dog in his arms, his knee aching, and his shop closed when it should be open. Why could he not simply do what he knew to be necessary?

But footsteps and voices stopped him before he started down the driveway. They came from the direction of the dyke, faint at first, then firmer, definite. Relieved, Joe waited for the speakers to appear.

The thin beam of a flashlight wavered toward him. Someone spoke, a man's voice: "That was Smitty at the towhead. He was going to make another set. Maybe he's just wanting one to eat or . . ." The footsteps stopped abruptly, but not before Joe made out two figures in the gloom.

After a pause, the same deep voice broke the silence, louder this time: "Who is it? Who's there?" The flashlight bobbed quickly over Joe. He took a deep breath and plunged back into the world.

"It's Joe Meers," he answered.

There was another pause, some hurried whispers, and Joe heard his name repeated, then the word "butcher."

"Mr. Meers? What are you doing out in this mess?" The figures moved close enough for Joe to recognize them. As he suspected, they belonged to Vic Mawson and one of his sons, Corbett, a young man in his early twenties. The butcher did not know the family well. Mrs. Mawson had been into his shop on occasion, but the others he knew only by hearsay and by glimpsing them around town. The father and his two sons were salmon fishermen. Joe couldn't remember ever speaking to them before, or to the young daughter he'd seen with them. He must have exchanged pleasantries with Mrs. Mawson a few times, but he had no memory for small talk. With a start, he realized that he had probably spoken more words to the dog than to the rest of the family combined.

As if following his thoughts, the flashlight focused on the black weight in Joe's arms.

"Shamus? What's the matter . . . Dad, that's Shamus!"

The father nodded slowly, as though the scene was something he'd been expecting. The fog unwrapped from his body like gauze bandages, revealing a short, slight man in his late forties who wore a black skullcap pulled tight over his forehead, a thick, down-filled hunting vest, and a pair of old gumboots cracked up the sides as though made of dry clay. With the index finger of his left hand, he held a small salmon, a jack spring. A stem-thin trickle of blood ran down its silver length and very slowly dripped onto the pavement, like part of the moist air that had turned dark red. In his right hand, he held the flashlight, the beam of which now pointed at the ground.

Joe sensed the man's discomfort—was it fatigue or just the strangeness of the meeting?—and looked down, the rank musk of wet fur wafting stronger into his nostrils. When he looked up again, Vic had not moved, but Corbett, a half-foot taller than his father, had come up beside him.

Finally, Vic uttered a single word: "Dead?"

Joe nodded. "I found him in the lot by the wharf. He . . ." Embarrassed, he didn't know whether he should tell the whole story, admit that the dog had died in his arms. "I . . . I fell over him."

The younger man stepped forward, causing Joe to shift his weight so quickly that his knee, stiff from being locked in one place, almost buckled.

"Shamus, hey boy," Corbett said gently, one hand reaching out to stroke the dewed fur. Joe noticed the pearls of moisture on the young man's sideburns, and the way his large green eyes peered out from under his bangs.

"It's all right," Vic said in a near-whisper. "He's dead. It's all right."

Corbett abruptly turned back, his voice more serious. "What about Zoe, Dad? Who's going to tell her?" The two men exchanged some words in private. Joe couldn't make out what was said, but it sounded from the tone as though the older man was reassuring his son.

A moment later, the flashlight beam fell on Joe again. "He was an old dog," Vic began, "but you never really expect them to die."

Joe nodded, and adjusted his stance once more.

"Fifteen years old," Vic continued, "that's good for a lab."

"Yes."

"But still, it's not easy."

Joe blinked toward the voice. A strand of pale yellow hair dangled over one eye, but he could not brush it away. The dog suddenly felt heavier.

Vic rubbed his beard-stubble and sighed. "My daughter will be heartbroken. She's only seven, you see." He appeared to emerge from a deep thought, and added in a louder, more direct voice, "But these things happen." As he spoke these words, Vic fixed his eyes on Joe's, as if seeking some reassurance from him, some promise.

Joe held the stare for as long as he could, but finally, unsure of how to respond, he turned to the driveway. "I'll just carry him down, then?" he asked.

Together, the three men looked toward the quiet bungalow with its one lightbulb burning above the grassy side yard, but they didn't speak or move.

As quickly as it had come, the fog was leaving, pulling up from the earth like a tarp lifted off a large oil painting. The rich wet colours flooded back, a gash of blue sky, the sodden green of the cherry trees stretching along the road to the river with a shawl of moisture hanging off each branch, the ochre block of the cannery warehouse up on the dyke. Now the white and blue houses of the Greek families appeared across the street, the bright yellow dandelions glimmered on the Mawsons' lawn, and the pink rhododendron and scarlet azalea blazoned the border of the driveway down to the side yard where a child's red Mustang bike leaned against a doghouse of cedar shakes. And nearer, more striking now, the smaller details emerged, the stained scales of the jack spring and its tiny pool of blood, the thin spill of the flashlight, the cracked gumboots, two pairs of eyes fixed sadly on the grizzled fur against the butcher's clean smock and the limp arms of his dark coat hanging down, the few stray hairs higher up on his chest from when he'd first pulled the body to him, and one long white tooth, lightly yellowed as an old piano key, bared in the dog's meaningless grin.

The town had begun to stir. Pickup trucks passed by, tailgates down, fishnets heaped in their boxes, and a clamour of winches, forklifts and shouts rolled off the dyke. Along the street, a few doors were thrown open and children began picking up their bicycles and pedalling off to school. Just like that, the fog swallowed up all the darkness and silence and carried it away.

chapter two

While operating a gillnetter on his own for the first time, Troy Mawson had also been thrust into confusion by the fog. Suddenly his broad hands had become quick blurs in the meshes of his net as he frantically hauled it in, the corks whipping through his chapped fingers in the dull glow of the pick-up light.

Although the tide had been just past slack when he'd set his net near the towhead in one of the many side channels of the river's south arm, it had started to run while he had dozed off in the stern. Like most salmon fishermen, Troy had acquired the necessary skill of falling asleep on his feet, relieving his fatigue while keeping his senses poised at the same time—a state which, when broken suddenly, was conducive only to panic. Once the rushing current had begun to pull great chunks of mud off the near bank, the splashing acted as a nudge to his shoulder. Along with this sound, the chill of the fog had seeped into his skin and joints, so that when he jumped forward, instinctively putting the drum in gear and stepping on its pedal, he felt as though his body was a hundred pounds heavier.

When he'd set near the towhead a few hours after midnight, there had been only a slight mist low over the water, and a half moon bright enough to reveal several fathoms of corkline beyond the circle of his boat lights as he idled from one side of the channel to the other, between two of the many small silt islands clogging the river mouth.

But now, unable to see the low constellation of the ski-run lights on Grouse Mountain to the north, or even the cottonwoods on the near bank, Troy panicked and brought his net in at such high speed that, twice, he was lucky to pull his fingers back before they snagged in the meshes and were snapped off like twigs. The second time, he knew he'd have to slow down. It became a matter of assessing the risks: how long could he leave the net out, how far had he drifted downriver? He knew this part of the Fraser, this particular drift, better than he knew any other. For most of his life, he'd noted the dangers: the spots where sunken stumps snagged and tore at a drifting net, the narrow entrance to the slough that the far end of his net as well as his boat had to slip through, the increasing force of the current as it pulled west along the mainland dyke toward the "dynamite ship," an old metal hulk moored to a rotted pier, and beyond that, to the Pheasant Island swing bridge and eventually the Gulf.

Normally, Troy could locate various markers along the banks, odd-shaped trees or fixed deadheads, to gauge his position and the amount of time he had in relation to the speed of the current. But this morning he was completely lost. For all he knew, his net had already wrapped the point, and he could be picking straight up and down the slough bank. Or he might have somehow slipped inside the slough and was either drifting rapidly toward a collision with the dynamite ship, or, if the pull of the current was different, toward the bridge. Fearing the worst, he tried to calm the pounding in his chest while thinking only of disaster, of ruining the one good net he owned, of losing it, leadline, mesh, and corkline, to the bottom of the river.

Troy was suddenly so intent on the task before him that he could not have remembered his own name. Just as the current tore away pieces of the bank, fear removed him from an awareness of his own actions. He moved only according to the instinct of his upbringing, to orders that had no voice but which were as much a part of him as the blood thumping in his chest.

He quickly lowered the gas to idle and strained to listen. The river sucked and pulled at the bank; it sounded close, a few fathoms from the bow. He stepped nearer the drum, touched the net, and found that he already had a third of it on board. So far, so good. If he hadn't reached the entrance to the slough, he had shortened the net enough to slip inside the far point. If he'd already reached the slough, there was nothing he could do now except turn the drum and hope everything came back.

He gave the boat a little more gas, then stepped on the pedal. The net rolled in, two fathoms, five fathoms. Fortunately, there were no fish or large sticks to pick out—a difficult task, considering the weak light. Troy kept turning his head downriver with the tide even though he couldn't see anything, waiting for the dark bulk of the dynamite ship to loom up in front of him. But there was only the fog, dripping and thick.

Minutes later, with over half of his net in and the sound of the current diminished as his boat pulled away from the near bank, he relaxed slightly, just enough to think about the lack of fish, and how things had better improve if he was going to save enough money to buy his own boat one day soon instead of renting off Reg Tanner for fifty percent of the catch.

But this dream of full ownership, which he'd had since childhood, no longer held the same importance for him. Only a year out of high school, he already felt restless. It no longer seemed enough of a life, sleeping in until noon most days, shooting pool at Dutchie's, playing hockey and ball, getting drunk at house parties, and hoping someday to work only for himself at a job whose prospects offered considerable risk but little security. His mother certainly didn't seem happy with his current behaviour; more and more, Troy had begun to feel uneasy waking up in his room, hungover, bathed in afternoon light, and then stumbling out to find her doing dishes at the sink or sitting quietly in the front room, drinking a cup of tea and watching the songbirds at the feeder, or waiting for Zoe to come home from school. She would make him a cup of tea, offer him something to eat, and sit and talk with him about fishing or his friends until his brother and father got up. Then she would repeat the same motions and offers until the three had been looked after.

But increasingly, Troy noticed, she had seemed uninterested in his friends and his activities, and he felt certain it was because she sensed his own growing dissatisfaction. If I could make a little money, he thought, have a good summer, not blow what I make on pool and booze, maybe in the fall . . .

Suddenly the corkline tensed in his hands, pulled so tight that the drum reversed and he had to move fast to take it out of gear.

"Now what?" he wondered aloud, cursing himself for relaxing, and half afraid that a voice might answer him. But nothing sounded except the wake of his own words. He peered over the rollers. Fog, cold and heavy with moisture, swallowed the taut meshes and the faint light coming from the metal lamp fixed to the stern. He put the drum in gear and stepped on the pedal again, but the drum only whined and kicked back. "Shit!" He paused and listened. Somewhere a freighter blew its horn, but he could not use the sound to gauge his position; it seemed to come from all directions, neither close nor distant. He couldn't wait long. The current pulled him steadily downriver, and judging by the time he'd already been awake, he must have at least entered the bottom slough. But what was this snag? Troy knew he'd have to get off it, put enough pressure on the net until the leadline snapped. He just hoped that the break would be clean, that he wouldn't lose any of the leadline or meshes.

He waited a while before trying again, hoping that the strength of the current would be enough to pull him off the snag. "Come on, come on," he muttered into the river, his body halfway over the rollers, and just the toes of his gumboots touching the stern. "What the hell's holding you?" He cursed again, his face only a few feet above the water.

Violently, the dark bulk of a deadhead lurched up with the swells of the current, and Troy had to jerk back quickly to avoid being struck in the face. Then, as fast as it had risen, the deadhead dropped again with a sloshing sound that Troy had heard in nightmares for as long as he could remember. The sight of huge stumps and logs roiling in dark water, tangled in nets, tearing meshes, had always filled him with dread. The way they bobbed along on a fast tide, like dead things that had come back to life intent on some macabre purpose, and the fact that they hid so much of their bulk below the surface, made them both mysterious and frightening to a child. Even now, jabbing and pulling at this one with his pike pole, desperate to roll it away so he could pick up the rest of his net, Troy could not completely quell his boyhood fears. Sticking the point of the pole into the wood, he briefly imagined a shout of anger bursting from it.

But there was only a dull thunk, and the sickening roll, as Troy's upper body lifted and dropped with the weight of the log.

He couldn't see it well enough to tell if it was clean. If it was, he might be able to roll it away without ripping out a chunk of net. But if it had limbs or a mass of roots, he might have to cut it free. Either way, he prayed the job would be a quick one.

The minutes passed. He strained at the net, yanking at the lead-line with one hand while holding the deadhead away with the pike pole in the other. The log was heavy, but he could raise it just enough into the dim light to see that only a few meshes were wrapped around its smooth top. With a great effort, sweating and cursing, he slowly backed it out of the net, tearing meshes as he worked, fighting the log and his own panic at the same time. Fortunately, the current helped. He used its force as leverage, once he got the meshes free, to manoeuvre the deadhead around the starboard side, and then, with a final heave of the pike pole, he sent the bulk into the fog.

Breathing heavily, he hurried back to the drum and resumed picking up. The deadhead had ripped a large hole in the net, which he'd have to mend back at the wharf. For now, he wanted only to finish the set and call it a night, assess the damage later, in daylight, with his feet on solid ground. At moments like this, he had no taste for the fishing life; its perils, combined with its long, often fruitless hours, seemed a kind of torture. Cold and tired, he could not imagine years of the same struggle, poling deadheads out of nets, fearing a slip into the chill dark current, watching the corkline for the sign of fish that weren't there and perhaps would-n't come until the next tide or opening or season.

But the lure of the river, its islands and marshes, the sheer phys-ical pleasure derived from being outdoors, as well as the lure of money earned under his own management, were intensely pow-erful, especially since Troy had no other plans for the future.

He picked a small red spring out of the net and two pieces of bark before his lantern finally bobbed into the glow of his pick-up light. He reached over the rollers, grabbed the lantern, and hauled it into the stern. Then he listened—nothing, not even the sound of the current pulling at the bank. I must be out of the slough, he thought, I must be past the dynamite ship. Carefully, he felt his way beside the drum up to the cabin and flipped on the inside light. It didn't help. He still could not see three yards beyond the boat in any direction, though it did seem the fog was thinning. Cursing Reg for not having a spotlight on board, Troy stepped back out of the cabin.

"Hey! Over here! Hey!" The repeated shout, deep and panic-edged, seemed to come from downriver and close by, louder each time. Troy grabbed the outside wheel and held one hand poised over the gas in case he needed to make a quick move. He peered into the fog, tensing as the unfamiliar voice grew even louder, echoing around him. One second he could see nothing; the next, he had drifted almost right on top of another boat. He hit the gas and roared back against the current, keeping himself in the same position, but now unable to hear the shouting.

Taking a risk, he fought several fathoms upriver, then idled. Again, the voice broke out of the fog: "I'm not gonna make it! I'm gonna wrap the bridge!" The bridge! Troy had no idea he'd drifted so far toward Pheasant Island. Again, the anxious voice sounded: "Give me a tow!"

Troy hurried into the stern and ran his boat carefully toward the other. "Toss me your bowline!" he shouted. In return, he heard a series of angry curses, followed by what sounded like a smack. Then a small figure scurried along the deck of the other boat. Troy could hear it snuffling and breathing heavily as it approached him and scrambled by into the bow.

A moment later, a boy's face suddenly appeared in front of him, so close that Troy was startled, as though he'd been looking into a blank mirror for days and his reflection had finally appeared. It wasn't that the boy's face resembled his own; it was simply the unexpected appearance of another set of eyes, another mouth, another nose, that broke the prolonged sense of isolation into which Troy had fallen. But more than that, it was the brief yet full stare between them that proved so unnerving. The boy's face was not unfamiliar to Troy. He thought he recognized it from around the wharf, and under calmer circumstances he might even have come up with the name. No, there wasn't anything unusual about the face itself that caught his attention; it was the look of sheer misery that pulsed out from it so powerfully that the features seemed on the verge of breaking apart, as though they had been formed out of the fog and were only waiting for a chance to dissolve. A strange mixture of white and black, like the cratered moon, the face hung briefly in front of Troy.

Then a line dropped into Troy's stern from above, and the face vanished.

Troy secured the line to his cleat and slowly increased the gas until he was holding steady in the current. He had no idea how much net the other fisherman still had to pick up, but if it was more than thirty fathoms, and if the bridge was indeed coming up fast, then the end of the net would definitely wrap the girders. But, for a change, that danger was not Troy's responsibility. He felt almost relaxed standing in the stern, holding the boats in the current, the only tension in his body reserved for the bowline pulled so taut by the pressure that it seemed it could not hold. But if it broke, that was also not his responsibility, as he had secured the other man's gear with the expectation that it wasn't faulty. After such a long and unrewarding twenty-four hours, with few fish around and the last set being so much trouble, Troy found the present situation, in which he could help someone else, to be much more satisfying.

He could hear the terrible squeal of the other drum turning, a sound so wrenched that he was sure the drum gears would slip at any time. The fog had lifted just enough so he could see two shapes moving back and forth in a nimbus of yellow light. Above them, visible as a faint pencil sketch, appeared the span of the bridge, a short wooden structure linking Pheasant Island to the mainland. Its three main girders were spaced just widely enough apart for a boat to be steered through each gap. But on fast currents, the negotiation of that space took considerable caution and skill. And to be drifting down on the bridge with your net still out! That was a jackpot, and usually meant you needed assistance, which in almost every case would be forthcoming from a nearby boat. It wasn't generosity that formed the code of the working river, but an overwhelming sense that everyone needed help from time to time. To withhold it from others was a kind of suicide, a delayed slitting of your own throat. Troy and his brother had learned this from their father at an early age; you try your best to catch as many fish as you can, but you never, never, refuse help to someone else. You can delay it, if the fishing's good and the danger isn't immediate, but in such cases the fisherman who needs help understands. The human and the economic imperatives were balanced in a generally recognized and accepted proportion, though there were those who tipped the balance to one side or the other. Troy's father, for example, sometimes made decisions that were not economically sensible, while younger fishermen increasingly applied their generosity according to a Darwinian rule of competition. Troy and Corbett, however, had remained true to their father's example.

"That's got her!" the voice from the other boat broke through again, barely audible over the engines. Troy lowered the gas, and the line immediately went slack. The boats once more banged together, but this time a scrawny, middle-aged man with a wispy beard emerged from the breaking white. Troy recognized him as Raskin, a newcomer to Chilukthan, who had kept pretty much to himself in the few years he'd been in the town. Other than the fact Raskin had a son and lived in a trailer on the dyke a mile or so downriver of the harbour, Troy knew nothing about him.

Raskin muttered something to himself, then turned his head back with almost a snarl, and said loudly, "Goddamned kid fell asleep! I put my fucking head down for ten minutes, and the next thing I know, tide's running like stink and there's this fucking mess of a fog! Little prick!"

Troy, accustomed to such language but not to such vehemence or to seeing it directed so specifically, could think of no appropriate response. The boy's miserable face, hanging detached in the fog, returned to him, but only vaguely. There were so many kids hanging around the river all the time and none of them exactly lived a genteel existence. Swearing, drinking, and fighting were common activities for "wharf rats," as fishermen called them. Troy couldn't bring the boy's image back, but the man's hardly suppressed violence made him want to, simply out of curiosity. Who could inspire such wrath?

As though on cue, the smaller figure in the other stern scrambled alongside the drum and tried to sneak past toward the cabin. Raskin, hearing his approach, suddenly turned, yelled "Useless shit!" and delivered a kick in the boy's direction that landed heavily. But the boy did not make a sound. Raskin, who had lunged forward from the force of the kick, almost losing his balance, cursed again, his target's silence only angering him further.

"Hey!" Troy finally said. "Take it easy!"

Raskin turned back to him. "What?! What did you say?!"

A little cowed by the man's threatening stance, Troy lowered his tone. "He's just a kid."

"He's a dickhead, that's what he is! And it isn't any of your god-damned business anyway!"

"You shouldn't hit him like that."

"Yeah, and who the fuck are you to tell me what I should be doing?"

Raskin looked ready to swing his gaff hook, but Troy wasn't about to fight on the river, especially in a fog with the tide running hard. One good shove could end in a drowning. Besides, he had learned from his parents to respect his elders, even when that respect was unearned. So he simply turned his back on the man, put his boat in gear, and roared upriver. You're welcome, he said to himself, though he was not really surprised by Raskin's behaviour. The fishing industry, as his father always said, was full of miserable bastards.

The fog had begun to peel away in strips, and though the visibility was still poor, Troy could see the water far enough in front of him to maintain a reasonable speed without having to worry about deadheads or other nets. By the time he'd found the mainland shore, the fog had lifted so much that he could see the innumerable netsheds and wharves along the bank, and the marshes, islands and sloughs on his port side. Only a few boats still drifted downriver, but their shapes were too indistinct to be recognized.

Troy assumed that his father and brother would still be fishing the swing-set, a drift farther upriver. With two of them on board the family gillnetter, one could doze while the other watched the net, and both could then stay fresh through the whole opening. Then again, with the fishing so poor and the fog so thick, his father might have chosen to tie up early. Either way, Troy would find out soon enough, as he was almost at the government wharf and didn't even have enough of a catch to bother stopping to deliver it to the packer.

When Troy drifted in to tie up, the fog had turned to a tangle of thin wisps; it was like entering a room where men were smoking. His father's boat, affectionately named *Old Betsy*, rocked gently in its usual place. Troy moored alongside it. He took the two springs and a jack from under the drum and tossed them on deck, lowered a bucket into the river, and doused the stern and the net to clean off the blood, silt and marsh grass. Then he removed his apron, lifted the fish under the gills, stepped across *Old Betsy* onto the wharf, and walked slowly to the gangway.

Despite the clatter of forklifts and the intermittent shouts coming from the cannery, an otherworldly stillness pervaded the morning, a stillness that always followed a full twenty-four hours of fishing. For Troy, this calm signalled a fresh start. Walking home from the wharf, his muscles sore, his hands scarred, his feet heavy in his boots, he nevertheless felt refreshed. The odd sensation of touching ground after a full day of riding the swells of the river made a clear break between the two worlds. Coming back to the unevenly planked wharf pungent with creosote, the narrow, weed-choked dyke high above the tideline, and the short grey road to the driveway of his parents' house, he always felt his life becoming solid and real again, even as he jerked to sleep over the plate of fried eggs and potatoes his mother always served for breakfast. And as she chided him gently, calling, "Troy, go to bed, Troy," her voice seemed to come from a great distance. Always, he could hear just the faintest echo of it as the darkness washed into him.

He walked down the dyke and turned the corner at the end of Laidlaw Street, thinking only of the cup of hot tea, the concern of his mother, and the long sleep ahead of him. He had forgotten the deadhead, the boy's face, and the confrontation with Raskin, as well as his panic and how he had quelled it. His sore body almost floated toward the house, the squat rock chimney in its angled roof and the faded clapboards always in shadow, giving it the homely appearance of a smudged teakettle.

But when he got there, expecting to find the side yard empty and the kitchen full, he found the opposite to be true. As his boots crunched on the gravel drive, he saw Corbett get up from kneeling beside Zoe and open the gate.

"Shamus is dead," he remarked quietly, nodding back toward the yard.

"What?" Troy sidestepped his brother's lean figure in the gate entrance and looked at his parents and sister huddled in a loose triangle on the wet grass.

"Shamus. He died," Corbett continued. "The butcher brought him home."

"The butcher?" Troy was confused. "What are you talking about?"

Corbett sighed and gestured behind him. "Take a look for yourself if you don't believe me. I'm gonna hit the sack. I'm beat." He trudged up the steps and into the house.

Troy dropped the fish on the grass as he entered the yard. "Mom? What's going on?"

She stood up from where she'd been stroking Zoe's long black hair and when she turned, Troy saw the tears in her eyes. "He's gone, Troy," she said.

Troy was so tired he couldn't take the news in. "What happened? What's this about the butcher?"

"Mr. Meers found him in the fog. He brought him back. You know how Shamus always went to his shop on Mondays, for his bone."

Troy bent awkwardly over his sister, unable to think of something to say that might comfort her. But her heavy sobs had already been exhausted, replaced by a steady breathing punctuated by an occasional sudden intake of breath. Troy looked to his father, who was sitting back on his heels beside Zoe, and waited for him to speak.

After a long pause, his father spoke in a low voice: "We'll cover him up for now. But we'll have to bury him soon, after we get a bit of sleep." He glanced at Zoe, as if to add, "the sooner, the better."

Troy straightened up, allowing his mother to return to soothing the girl. He was too tired to think clearly about Shamus. He felt a kind of wrenching, as though he'd returned to the river and was again drifting toward something dark and unpredictable. In silence, he watched his mother lead Zoe into the house. Then he went with his father into the backyard and helped him drag a tarp from the shed and lay it over the dog.

"Better bring the fish in," Vic said, "the wasps will be at them."

chapter three

A week passed, cloudy and cool. Then April came in with a full week of rain that quickly erased the lingering scent of the dog from the side yard and vacant lot. The heavy skies pressed the black fur deeper into the sandy patch of the harbour where it had been buried, with a child's solemn ceremony of flowers, prayers, and keepsakes for the otherworld (a hair-ribbon, some biscuits, a note of comfort and love for the departed soul). Zoe had cried off and on for days, her grief indistinguishable from the pleasure any imaginative child takes in the high seriousness of death. Yet she would not be consoled. Ultimately, her parents chose to let time heal what their explanations and reassurances could not.

Zoe's brothers missed Shamus's greeting at the gate whenever they came home, but it was a loss supplanted by the more immediate concerns and pastimes of adulthood. Both had net repairs to make, and both, despite Troy's growing indifference to such pursuits, spent many hours shooting pool and drinking. They had shared some memories of Shamus on the day of his death, after their father and sister had buried him, had recollected some scenes of his hunting skills, but their mutual decision to stay sleeping while their father got up to bury Shamus showed clearly that sadness was not an emotion for which either had much time.

Vic was tired, worried by the poor start to the fishing season and by rumours that the canneries were planning to cut prices for sockeye in the summer. He was long past allowing himself to grieve over the loss of a pet, except to the extent that it had distressed his daughter. On the afternoon of the burial, his wife had

tried to stir him from bed three times without success, finally sending Zoe down the hall to the bedroom. Her pleas, not surprisingly,
had worked, but it still took nearly an hour for him to get his
clothes on, eat his supper, and walk out the door into the brisk
wind and approaching twilight. If not for the tears in his daughter's eyes, he'd have dug a hole in the backyard by flashlight a few
hours after dark.

Of the adult family members, only Kathleen regarded the dog's
death as significant, as more than the loss of fifty pounds of fur
and bone that needed to be fed every day. This new absence was
the rung bell of a growing misapprehension, and its peals struck
all she saw or heard or touched, from the rain gushing in the
drainpipes to her daughter's hair to her husband's voice to the
guts of the jack spring she had stripped out after she'd put Zoe
back to bed, served breakfast to the men, and decided that she
needed to do something to keep herself from shaping a noose out
of the bell rope.

When she had looked out the window that March morning,
watching for Vic and the boys to appear through the fog, the sight
of another figure bearing a dark mass in its arms had unnerved
her. It seemed she was seeing the slow descent of her own recent
thoughts in visible form, the black mood that would enter her during the long afternoon of quiet suddenly real enough to be
witnessed at the top of the driveway. But she dismissed such fan-
cies as soon as they came, fought them off, and went about the
business of mothering with a subtle desperation. What was a sorrow that could not be defeated by the needs of others, if not
self-indulgence and failure?

So she turned at her daughter's cry, and went to her with a jacket and shoes, and wept as much out of compassion for herself as
for her child, though she could not identify her sorrow, could not
give it the palpable weight and smell of a dog's carcass in the arms
of a stranger. How much she would have loved to give a physical
shape to her sense of loss. But it was the ripple of the cast stone
and not the stone itself that she felt each day as she pulled herself
out of bed. The inability to know the source of the counterweight
that tried to keep her from her life was the most maddening element of her malaise. She wanted to discount her depression as a
product of the season, as the expected result of the sad anniver-

sary approaching, but that day had never reduced her to such depths before. No, something new had hold of her, and when the butcher walked down the driveway carrying the dog in his arms, she believed she could hear the clap of a strange and foreboding weather in his step.

Now it was almost a week into April and she still could not rid herself of the inexplicable depression that had gripped her. The rain kept falling, softly, heavily, softly again, and then only stopping briefly as though out of sheer fatigue. The days were little more than a black shade of night scrubbed grey, a long dusk that took ten hours to settle. Everything slowed down. The farmers could not get their machines into the fields, songbirds huddled shivering in laurel hedges, and children rode their bicycles as if against a current. Eventually, even the rain no longer poured in a straight, pounding rhythm, but swished back and forth, back and forth, on the Gulf winds.

Yet the vibrant colours of the season—the flash of rhododendron and azalea bushes along the street, the rare slice of blue behind a storm cloud, the scarlet bangles in a blackbird's wings—promised the return of sunlight and with it an end to the general lethargy.

Kathleen made herself a third cup of tea and sipped it while watching the rain through the living-room window. The river had opened again that morning. Vic and the boys had left at seven-thirty, completely covered in oilskins, joking that they might as well have moored their boats to the front gate and saved themselves the walk to the wharf. An hour later, she'd sent Zoe off to school, bundling her up, telling her not to play in puddles and to stay away from the swollen ditches. Three cups of tea, and the first two had gone cold because she was too busy watching the rain and thinking about other things.

The weather had been like this when she arrived on the west coast in October, twenty-six years earlier. Eighteen years old, just married, and away from Toronto and her family for only the second time, and this time permanently, Kathleen had sat in the CPR Station in downtown Vancouver, surrounded by her luggage, waiting for Vic and his father and watching the water stream down the giant windows. All around her, she could hear the strange voices of Chinese and East Indian men, but was too frightened to look toward them. Everything was wet and bleakly exotic, but above all else, heavy; the air, the sky, the unfamiliar sounds: she might have defeated them all with youthful excitement had it not been for the heaviness she still felt at the parting from her parents.

She was her mother's "baby," the last of twelve children, only six of whom had survived the poverty and diseases of the century's first twenty years to live past infancy. How her mother had begged her to stay until Thanksgiving! Just a few more days, that's all. But Vic, her husband (imagine that, her own husband), was waiting for her clear on the other side of the country, in a little town called Chilukthan, by the mountains and the ocean. She remembered saying, "Momma, I have to go sometime, he's waiting for me." And then Albert, her older brother, had taken her aside and whispered, "Katie, just go and don't look back. You're a married woman now, and you're not to come running back because you're homesick or things aren't exactly the way you expected them to be. You're a married woman and you have to act like one." And her mother's tired, gentle face, her bloodshot eyes, looking so long and so deep into her, and through her tears the repetition of the same words, "My baby, my little girl, my baby," while her father, so thin and composed in the dark suit he always wore, sighing, "Let her go, Maggie. We have to leave, she'll miss her train." And the last sight of her mother in the doorway of the porch, and the awful drive down Grove Avenue onto Dundas, out of the neighbourhood where she'd always lived, in several different rented houses through the Depression, where she'd gone to school and learned penmanship and how to sing "God Save the King," and where she had met her husband, a handsome sailor on leave, and from where she was now leaving to start a new life, to be married and to live so far away, where she didn't know a single, solitary soul except Vic and his mother, the one relative who'd travelled east for the wedding. Oh it was too much, she couldn't do it, she'd tell her father to turn the car around and she'd run back up the stairs into her mother's arms. But she could hear her brother's admonishing words all around her, and she could see Vic's smiling face at the far end of the long tracks, and that was just enough to get her off the platform at Union Station and into her seat on the train.

She didn't stop crying until Manitoba, and even after that, the thought of her mother alone in the house with all that new silence kept her tears close to the surface, so that when she finally stepped down in Vancouver to the steady thrum of the rain, she felt as though she'd arrived in a place perfectly attuned to the pangs of heartache.

Then, to make matters worse, Vic and his father were late in picking her up. She sat there, alone, for over an hour, feeling sorry for herself and wondering if she had the courage to get back on the train and go straight home.

But she didn't, and when Vic appeared, hurrying up to her with a big smile, his pale blue eyes apologetic, her doubts evaporated just as if the rain itself had swept across her thoughts to cleanse them. To hear his voice again, so full of tenderness and promise, to look into his handsome face: wasn't this all in the natural order of things, the life she'd been raised for, and which she'd so often been unable to believe would ever be hers? Katie Emmons, the ugly little pogey child, all black curls and saucer-shaped green eyes, with holes in her stockings and second-hand coats and shoes that never quite fit. Katie Emmons, the shy girl at every dance, clinging to her bolder friends like a shadow, afraid to be asked out, ashamed not to be asked, who believed that a man might want to kiss her (because men, especially during the war, were hungrier that way) but would never propose marriage. Was this her, now being driven over the Granville Street Bridge in her father-in-law's truck, with the ocean just there through the rain, just there off to the right, and her husband's warmth beside her? Was this the same Katie Emmons, city-born, the streetcars' rattle her one sure rhythm, swaying now with the windshield wipers and soon to know the softer plunge of fish boats on the tide?

In a matter of moments, she had gone from sadness at what she had lost to wonder at what she had found, and the transition, though she did not define it so consciously, was the result of the love she felt for the young man beside her, the young man who pointed things out to her as they drove by, as though he were a god naming his creation solely for her, bringing the world into existence to give her pleasure. The rain poured down, splattering off the pavement and dimpling the river as they took the little ferry from Lulu Island across to Chilukthan. The sound of the rain, the smell of it, the feel of it on her face as she looked around at this sodden, grey, flat delta, its marshes and sandbars and islands, could not dampen her spirits so long as Vic spoke to her and touched her. The rain fell, and he took its effect away; the rain shook in the wind and whipped across their faces, and he removed the sting from every drop; the rain dripped and soaked and shuddered and hissed, and he made her forget the sound. Between her own tears and a west coast storm, between the rushing of all that water, she held onto her husband as the one buoyant force that could make the world bearable, and more than that, a vital and exciting place.

Kathleen's tea was cold again. With her apron, she wiped her face, then went into the kitchen to put the kettle on for the fourth time. The house was so quiet, and the dripping of the rain so persistent, that she had to struggle to keep herself in the present. There was laundry to do but she lacked the energy to bag it and carry it to the laundromat. Instead, she washed her teacup. As she did so, she noticed a spot of blood on the edge of the sink, the remains of a jack spring she had cleaned the night before. The spot, and her mood, suddenly reminded her of the little jack spring she had cleaned for the butcher the day Shamus died.

Vic had offered it to Mr. Meers but he had left the yard without taking it. So she'd cleaned it and carried it over to his shop the next morning, taking Zoe with her because Vic and the boys were asleep. Kathleen didn't want to bring the girl, fearing that she'd be upset at seeing the man who had found Shamus, but Zoe, surprisingly, did not want to stay out on the street while her mother went into the shop. Instead, she said she wanted to thank Mr. Meers. Kathleen was pleased by her daughter's manners, especially considering that she claimed to be too upset to go to school. Common courtesy was the one lesson Kathleen tried hard to instill in all of her children, a simple respect for other people, especially their elders. Manners were something her own parents had insisted on, saying, "We may not have as much money as some others, but that's no excuse for being rude."

The butcher was slicing meat when they entered the shop, his broad shoulders hunched over the counter, his large, blond head like a boulder set into his body. He looked up a few seconds after the door had opened, blinking rapidly and wiping his hands on his smock, as though he were smoothing down the feathers of a sick bird. Their appearance seemed to startle him, and he coughed, twice, three times, but did not speak. Kathleen admired anew the neatness of the shop, everything so well ordered, the floor clean, the glass counter spotless. Strangely enough, the place had a pleasant smell about it, almost fresh, not what you'd expect from a butcher shop. Everyone said that Joe Meers ran a very respectable business, and was an honest man you didn't have to worry about shortchanging you on a cut or leaving his finger on the scale. Beyond that, and the fact that he was unmarried, had come to Chilukthan from the neighbouring town of Cedar Bay about three years before, and was approximately her husband's age, Kathleen knew nothing about him. She came into his shop only when she didn't have time to walk to Ponick's Freezer Meats a few blocks away, the place she'd been buying meat for years. But she had heard that the new butcher was polite, not prone to gossip or personal confession. Because of this, he was both admired and criticized. In a small town, as Kathleen well knew, a merchant who does not gossip, or at least listen with great interest to his customers' speculations, is deemed trustworthy but somehow unlikeable. People will do business with him because he is fair and honest, but they will also suspect him of superior notions, of setting himself up as a paragon of virtue. "Who does that fellow think he is? I told him about Viola Fenwick letting her hair down at the Fishermen's Hall on Saturday night, and he hardly batted an eye. Just nodded and told me how much I owed him."

Kathleen had heard such talk before, but it was immaterial to her, or to anyone else for that matter. In the past ten years, Chilukthan had grown, not hugely, but to the extent that a merchant could no longer be blackballed out of business for not expressing wild surprise at the hijinks of the Viola Fenwicks of the town. Joe Meers was neither popular nor a pariah, and Kathleen, whose primary requirements of a butcher shop were its affordability and cleanliness, had never really given the quiet man a second thought.

She approached the counter with a smile, lifting the plastic bag chest-high as she did so. "You left without this," she said. "My husband told me he'd meant for you to have it."

The butcher cleared his throat and stared at her as though stricken dumb. Then his wide face broke into an expression of discovery and he tapped the fingers of one hand against his brow. "Oh, yes, the fish, I had forgotten." He glanced at Zoe, and lowered his voice. "There was some confusion . . ."

Kathleen put the bag on the counter. "Yes, well, that gave me a chance to clean it for you."

"But you didn't have to do that. I . . ." He smiled slightly, just enough to reveal a gap between his front teeth. "I could have easily done it myself. I'm used to such work, though not with salmon, it's true."

"Really, it was no trouble. And I . . ." Kathleen had started to say she needed to keep herself busy, to keep herself from dwelling on a sadness she could not even explain, but remembered in time that this was not something she had shared with anyone.

Feeling foolish, Kathleen recovered her composure. "Well, it was really very kind of you to carry Shamus home to us. Not everyone would have done that."

The butcher nodded, pushing a hand through his bluntly cut bangs. "He was a good dog. I was always happy to see him at my door."

"Was he dead when you found him?" Zoe interrupted, her thin voice breaking. She had come up beside her mother, and was staring up directly into the butcher's face. "Where did he die? Where did you find him? Was he barking? How come you put him in your coat if he was dead?"

"Zoe! Manners!" Kathleen whispered quickly, bending slightly down to the girl, then straightening up to address the butcher again. "I'm sorry, she's still very upset. I should have known better than to bring her out today."

The butcher had gone pale as his smock. Kathleen noticed his Adam's apple flutter rapidly, and a look of dismay disturb his placid features. No doubt, he was not used to the outbursts of children.

The shop had gone silent except for the girl's snuffling. The butcher was blinking even more rapidly than before, but just stood motionless otherwise, his arms hanging at his sides. Kathleen noted the blood smears on his smock, and a big blowfly, like a freckle, resting in the hairs of his thick, left forearm. What is wrong with the man, she wondered, feeling uncomfortable yet oddly calm at the same time.

"Well," she finally said, putting a hand on Zoe's shoulder, "thank you again. I hope you enjoy the fish."

When they were halfway to the door, the butcher suddenly spoke, very loudly and evenly, as if he were making a formal announcement. "The dog was alive when I found him."

Kathleen turned back and saw that he had not moved from his spot behind the counter, but that he had put his hands up onto it to support himself. His head was bowed, but he lifted it to speak again.

"I tripped . . . I . . . I found him in the lot at the end of the street. He was lying on the path, too weak to get up. I carried him, I tried to get him home before he . . ." Much to Kathleen's astonishment, the butcher was trembling. He paused several seconds, and finally, in a barely audible voice, while looking directly at Zoe, said, "He died in my arms."

The butcher's speech had no visible effect on the girl. She just kept crying silently, not even raising her tear-filled eyes to look at the speaker. Kathleen stared and stared at the man. She didn't know how to react to his emotion, except to feel that it was generous, even beautiful somehow. How horrible that must have been for him! But . . . why didn't he say this at the time? Did he think it was unimportant? If so, why should the fact be so painful to him in recollection? Strangely, because she knew so little about Joe Meers, Kathleen accepted that he had his own good reasons for acting as he did. Something in the butcher's shy manner, in his deliberateness, suggested that self-expression was painful for him, and Kathleen, because she knew instinctively how shyness and caution could be misinterpreted, had a sudden and startling insight into the man's nature. The moment, brief and fragile, soon evaporated, and left her in the same curious position. Twenty feet from the man, with her hand on her daughter's head, she struggled for a way to break the tension without ignoring his obvious emotion.

"Thank you for telling us," she began. "That must have been hard for you, to find him like that."

The butcher seemed drained. "I would have mentioned it sooner," he sighed, "but I wasn't sure if . . ." Again, he looked at Zoe, who still had her head down.

"Yes, I understand. Please, it's fine. We're all very thankful. Isn't that right, Zoe?" Kathleen stroked the girl's hair, but she did not respond. "Well, we really must be going. We've taken up far too much of your time." Kathleen ushered Zoe out the door and followed, relieved but puzzled by the experience. What would Vic make of this, she wondered, steering her crying child home.

That had happened nearly two weeks ago, almost fourteen full days. Kathleen stared at the blood spot on the sink until its edges blurred and it widened to fill her eyes, and then she knew she was crying again. Oh stop it, stop it, she scolded herself, picking up a dishrag and wiping the blood away. What time was it? Only ten o'clock? How the hours dragged. She plugged the kettle in and walked to the kitchen window. The rain hadn't let up. Small torrents flowed along the street toward the drains, and it was so dark that the streetlamp at the corner had come on. Was that why there were no birds at the feeder? Did they think it was night already? Had they gone to bed? The thought of sleep was so attractive that she almost turned and went down the hall, but instinctively she knew that doing so would be giving in to something that she might never be able to overcome. Besides, Zoe would be home for lunch in a couple of hours, and what sort of mother lies in bed in the middle of the day while her child is hungry?

Just look at that rain! They'll be getting soaked on the river. I hope there's a few more fish this week. Lord knows, we could sure use the money. Kathleen's thoughts rambled on until the kettle started whistling. For the fourth time, she poured boiling water into her cup, and for the fourth time, it went cold before she could drink it all.

chapter four

Moonlight dimpled the black calm of the harbour. From the government wharf to the Pheasant Island Bridge—three miles of docked gillnetters and trollers, ramshackle houseboats, sagging wooden netsheds and rotted wharves, canneries, marine repair shops, warehouses, poplar trees and open dykes—the river was like a smooth fish slowly being scaled. The light from the sky, as well as from various lampposts, windows and a few portholes, mingled into a pattern of subtle brilliance. The night was very still. Occasionally, a muskrat scrolled its wake across the channel, its passage only a sort of sigh, and far off, a dog barked for its supper. But even that sound had a gentle quality to it.

It was mid-April and just warm enough to work in short sleeves after dark. Weeks of rain had finally broken. Chilukthan now soaked in freshness and colour. Buds had popped out on the pussy willows, and the river and the marshes were one big cauldron of spices put on a low simmer. Skunk cabbage or cherry blossom, mud stench or a honeysuckle wind; it was all in the same blend, but somehow only sweetness carried off the water, over the dykes, and down onto the empty streets and just-ploughed potato and cornfields of the delta.

In a netshed on the far side of the harbour channel, Corbett sat alone on a mending bench. A coal-oil lantern at his feet cast a dim amber glow around him and the spring net he was repairing. Just beyond this glow, through the open door of the shed, the tide backed up, carrying the first salt taste of the ocean past Chilukthan toward New Westminster. When Corbett looked up from his work, he saw only the moonlight and a night empty of people. From time to time he would pause, holding the needle of nylon thread loosely in one hand, and with the other take a small piece of smoked salmon from a bundle of wax paper on his knee and toss it into the darkness where a half-dozen stray tomcats would briefly screech and squall over it.

He did not need to be in the netshed. There was no opening scheduled for the river until the following week, and the net was not badly torn. Normally, Corbett left the small repairs for his father, who actually enjoyed the work, but tonight was different. Corbett had made sure his father was busy, and then, after a couple of pints in the Chilukthan Arms, he had made a phone call and driven to the wharf. Once here, he had surveyed the harbour, checking for signs of activity on either bank, almost certain there wouldn't be any, since fishing had closed that morning and no one needed to return so soon. But even if someone did, the netshed was detached from the others along the bank and approachable only by a long gangway or by water.

The only person Corbett expected to meet was Margo Petrovich, whose husband, Dennis, skippered a seiner that had just gone north for the season. Soon afterwards, Margo had made her intentions clear to Corbett, whispering to him in the darkened hallway of the pub one night. Already sleeping with two other women at the time, both younger than him, and single, Corbett was immediately excited by the offer. Sex, like baseball, hockey, and even fishing, was a kind of sport in which you were meant to exhaust your energies, and when an element of danger was put into the mix (bases loaded, overtime, a jackpot on the river, sleeping with another man's wife), well, that only brought a sharpened tang to existence.

Nonetheless, he had hesitated. For a week, he could not bring himself to act, though the thought of a rendezvous was never out of his mind. But with Dennis Petrovich's wife? The man was respected and popular, and not someone to be trifled with. Corbett even liked him, despite the fact he hardly ever smiled or spoke. Ah, but Margo—she was so beautiful . . .

Corbett planned and schemed and imagined the pleasure of having her, but, always on the point of arranging something, he faltered. He told himself that it was wrong to make love to another man's wife, that there were many single women of all ages who would be happy to take him to their beds. He was attractive to women, and they did not normally demand anything of him other than his occasional company. He had an easy way about him, a gentleness. He was a listener, a shoulder to cry on after breakups, an ear for all the petty grievances against parents and teachers and discarded boyfriends; he was fun and cheerful and everybody liked him. Again and again, Corbett told himself he could not make love to Margo because it was wrong, but he had thought of nothing else for a week. The more he thought of it, the less wrong it seemed. What good was being young if no risks were ever taken? He had asked himself this question all week, and then answered it from a pay-phone in nearby Cedar Bay, waiting eagerly for Margo's voice to come out of the receiver.

Now he waited for her in the harbour, mending net and tossing salmon chunks to the cats, his heartbeat quickening as the minutes passed and she did not appear. Maybe she had changed her mind? If so, he was released of all responsibility. He could even tell himself that he would never have gone through with it, no matter how alluring her actual presence proved to be, no matter how inviting the scent of the air and the river and her skin. But if she hadn't changed her mind? Corbett's smile revealed his final opinion: it might be wrong to make love to another man's wife, but in a sense, it was a greater wrong not to.

So he sat in a state of nervous anticipation, half-heartedly working on the net. The night pressed around him, lapping at the coal-oil sheen.

Suddenly, one of the cats mewed and dashed across the open door of the shed. Almost simultaneously, Corbett heard the creak of oarlocks followed by a light plash of oars. Finally, he thought, getting up from the bench and tossing the last chunk of salmon into a dark corner. He stepped out of the shed onto the skinny two-plank wharf running the length of it, and looked downriver.

A small rowboat glided toward him over the patterned light, hurried on by the backing current. A lone figure was at the oars. Corbett kept his silence and waited.

The seconds passed. He heard a loud splash followed by cursing. The figure, closer now but still vague, bent over and disappeared briefly, before the creaking of the oarlocks resumed.

Corbett knew it was Margo by her voice, huskier than most women's, as though she was constantly recovering from a cold. She wore a thin tank top and a pair of cut-off jeans, and her bare shoulders, arms and legs were white as the moon path through which she rowed. But it was her full, loose auburn hair that most caught his attention, shining vividly against the darkness. Corbett's breath came faster as the boat glided in. "Jesus," he murmured as he grabbed the bow, "you look great." Then he paused and added, "I didn't think you were coming."

"I almost didn't," Margo replied, stepping carefully onto the wharf and then glancing around nervously, her large silver earrings swaying with the motion.

Corbett bent over to fix the bowline to the wharf, then straightened up quickly, afraid his guest might vanish like a figure in a dream. But Margo had only moved closer to the open door of the shed, the coal-oil light making a blurred frame around her small figure. "You're sure this is all right?" she whispered.

"The other door's locked," Corbett replied, amused by her girlish hesitation, which contrasted with her usual spirited manner. The change flattered his ego: to make an older, married woman so nervous was a gratifying kind of power. Encouraged, he stepped beside her, and with the back of one hand lightly brushed the upper part of her right arm. "I'm really glad you're here," he grinned.

Margo shivered and closed her eyes. Corbett stared at the flesh of her throat, which was even paler than her arm, then at her breasts rising and falling gently under the thin fabric of her top, as though in rhythm to the lapping current. When he finally lifted his eyes, he saw that Margo was grinning at him. Her mood seemed to have changed. She tugged gently at one of her earrings, and said softly, "Well?"

All Corbett's doubts had vanished. He took Margo's hand and led her into a corner of the shed, toward the pile of burlap net-covers he had laid out for the occasion.

"Very nice," she laughed.

A moment later, they had settled onto the makeshift bed, their bodies moving easily, while the cats scrabbled at the fringes of the light and a musk of smoked salmon scented the air around their breath and hands.

Afterwards, leaning back on one elbow, Corbett smiled at Margo lying naked beside him and felt a strange sense of pride. Sleeping with another man's wife was wrong until you slept with her and found that you were the same person—the moon still shone, the ocean flicked its salt tongue up the river, and the woman herself did not burst into tears or flames.

Meanwhile, Margo, much to Corbett's surprise, began to justify her behaviour. On her back, she stretched out her arms as if to invite the night's darkness into them, and said scornfully, "Don't tell me you don't know what goes on up north. Every crewman has his own Indian girl. Their squaws, they call them. They fall off the trees in Rupert, just looking for some drunken idiot with his pants full of bills and no one to spend them on."

"Dennis told you that?" Corbett asked.

She rolled over on her side to face him. "No, of course not," she scoffed, "but I'm not stupid. I hear things about what the boys get up to when they're away from home. You know Jake Herdson? They say there's blue-eyed Indian kids all up and down the coast because of him. And Dennis is no different than the rest."

"Why did you marry him then? You knew he'd go north to fish, didn't you?"

Margo shrugged and reached for her top. The air had suddenly cooled and a breeze blew in the open doorway, shivering the loose meshes of the net Corbett had left on the rack. "Oh, I don't know. He's solid, makes good money, and he's sweet, he treats me well most of the time, but . . . let's just say I didn't think it through, I was too young."

"So, why don't you leave him?" Corbett, relieved to be back in his familiar position of sympathetic listener, relaxed even further, to the point of drowsiness.

Margo's tone became defensive. "Why should I leave? I've got a good life, no money worries, nice house, Hawaii in the winter. And if I feel like it, I can get my excitement elsewhere, just like he does."

"And do you do this oft—"

She pulled herself into a sitting position and waved her top at Corbett's head, but he ducked away, grinning. "That's real nice, Corb. What do you think, that this is a regular thing for me?" She sighed, and after a brief pause, added, "You're the only one, the first and only, and I'm not planning to make this a habit. Who knows, maybe we'll make it a habit, but I'm not going to offer myself to every guy in the pub who gets up to go to the john."

"Why me?" Corbett could not resist asking.

Margo pushed a sweep of hair from her eyes. "What do you want me to say, that you're amazing, that I've adored you from afar?"

"No, it's just that any number of guys would have been happy . . ."

She smiled, but seemed embarrassed by the compliment. "Do you really want to know? Because I knew you wouldn't ever tell anyone, even if you turned me down. And if you didn't turn me down, I knew you wouldn't get all worked up about it, that it wouldn't be a big deal for you."

Somehow this explanation troubled Corbett; it made his hesitation trivial, his actions a foregone conclusion. While he enjoyed his easygoing reputation, it wounded his pride to think that a woman could so easily dismiss him as a serious possibility. If they felt this way, and he understood that most of them did, he didn't want their feelings expressed in so many words. It was much better to believe that his own carefree attitude showed them the appropriate path to take. He had always felt that when he chose to commit to one particular woman, she would reciprocate as a matter of course. But he rarely thought about such things. Doing so now, if only because of this curious new circumstance, disturbed him slightly.

Distracted, he did not notice Margo's absence until she spoke anxiously from the open door. "What was that? Did you hear that?"

"What?"

"Listen!"

Corbett froze. He didn't hear a sound. Then something brushed him on the leg and he jumped, his heart racing. The cat let out a screech, and Margo, poised in the opening to the river, disappeared.

Corbett started to call her back, but the sound of footsteps on the gangway stopped him.

In a panic, he gathered up their clothes, doused the light, then followed her onto the wharf and joined her in the boat before she could push off.

"Lie down," he whispered. "I'll row." He fixed the oars in their locks as quietly as possible. Voices sounded on the far side of the shed and the lock chain clattered. Corbett pushed the boat from the wharf, but the tide, stronger now, resisted. To go with it, back upriver, would bring them into view from the gangway, so he stroked hard against the current until he began to make progress.

After a few minutes, he felt Margo's hand cool and soft on his calf, her fingers twining his fine, long hairs. Her touch made him row harder.

Soon he had pulled the boat out of the harbour, beyond the section of dyke near the more populated part of town. Now only a huge stand of poplars on one side, and the open river on the other, overlooked the boat's progress.

He rested briefly on the oars, watching the blades drip with moonlight and current. Sweat trickled down his chest and back; a few beads dripped off his long bangs onto his arms. His heart was still pounding. He took in a deep breath of the rich river mud, and, as always, the smell energized every part of his body. If only life could always be like this! Here he was, in a rowboat on the river with a beautiful woman, and all his senses so full that he felt he'd burst if he didn't shout his excitement to the sky.

Instead, he rowed around the point of a small island and joined another channel connecting to the river's main current.

Before long, Corbett reached out and gently cupped Margo's chin, turning her head toward him. Then he lowered his face to kiss her, and slid down into the bottom of the boat. With the oars extended like thin wings and the direction of the boat wholly at the whim of the current, they drifted upriver, gradually borne toward the cutbanks of an island that marked the eastern edge of the Prairie Drift. The island, all bullrushes and sloughs, looked like a field of wheat through which someone had scythed uneven paths. Less than a mile away, Chilukthan could have been on the other side of the earth.

To the boy hunkered down in the rushes on the bank, his hands cold from pulling a submerged net out of the slough, the bodies were unimportant. He could just make out the faces in the dim moonlight as the boat drifted past, and he recognized Corbett because he knew everyone who fished or frequented the harbour. But the scene meant nothing to him. Once he realized that the boat was not occupied by fisheries officers out on patrol, looking for poachers, the boy didn't care who was in it. The activity itself interested him enough that he watched until the current had pulled the boat deeper into the dark, but even that had little novelty for him, as he'd witnessed such scenes before in his own home, as well as in netsheds and on the dykes and marshes around town. He did remember that the man in the boat was the brother of the man who'd stood up to his father that foggy night when they'd almost wrapped the bridge. But again, he didn't care. He was cold, the net was empty, and he knew his father would tear a strip off him if he came home with nothing.

Once the boat had disappeared, the boy flicked on his flashlight again and resumed pulling up the black fathoms.

chapter five

The following Monday morning, with Vic and the boys fishing and Zoe in school, Kathleen stood in the side yard in a pair of gumboots and with a down-filled hunting vest over her tattered housecoat. With her thick hair knotted in a kerchief the same deep green as her tired eyes, she looked as though she'd been weeping ashes.

> Weep not for me, my parents dear,
> I am not dead, but lying here.
> I was not yours, but God's alone;
> He thought it best to take me home.

The verse that hung over her parents' bed in westside Toronto all through the Depression had been echoing in her thoughts for days. Whenever she began to dwell on the past, this sad song for her sister, Bertha, dead of tuberculosis at the age of fourteen, rang mournfully across her mind. Weep not for me, weep not for me. But just as her mother had wept, suddenly, uncontrollably, and for weeks afterwards, until Kathleen, only five at the time, joined in and ran to bury herself in the stiff, flour-smeared skirts, so now, almost forty years later, she also wept despite the quiet voice that bid her not to. In her sorrow, which she knew every April with the same dull pang, lay a wondering sympathy for the hardness of her mother's life. Over the years, their two sorrows had blended, so that they no longer stemmed from separate hearts, but were shunted together like boxcars full of a coal that would never burn. Some days, this past month especially, Kathleen could not even be sure the verse was not for a daughter named Bertha whom she herself had lost. Lately, she'd even wondered if it made any difference what child a woman cries for when she mourns: the loss was all, an ache that shivered in her body like a branch being stripped of leaves.

But now, as she knelt on the damp earth of the side yard and carefully cut and bunched the dripping crocuses, she trembled again with the knowledge that something more than a particular grief had entered her body, a weight that she could not identify but which seemed to mock the heaviness of pregnancy. She was so tired. She slept but never felt rested, and by the end of the day she could hardly keep her head from falling into the plate of cold leftovers she cleaned up after everyone else had done eating. Because she did not understand what was happening to her, she looked for reasons that would be acceptable to any caring person. Who would not allow a woman some tears for the death of her child?

So, for what seemed like the thousandth time in the past month, she took herself back, relentlessly, beginning with the death closest to her, gradually drifting into all the same sad statistics painstakingly recorded in her mother's massive King James Bible over the first twenty years of the century, and finally returning to April 1956.

Kathleen had wanted another child after the boys started school, when she found herself, for the first time, alone as an adult for lengthy periods. Quite simply, she had never developed the inner strength necessary to be alone without feeling the need to serve others. She had lived with Vic only a year before becoming pregnant with Corbett, and even that time was spent at her in-laws' house. Before that, she was herself only a girl, though nevertheless responsible for helping her mother with meals and laundry and other daily chores. So the extra time, rather than being a luxury, turned out to be a source of alienation, as though, without the lives of others to set the temper of her mornings and afternoons, she had become inessential in her own mind, to the point where she almost felt invisible, only coming alive with the sound of the boys' voices.

She and Vic had married so young, and with so little thought for anything but the sheer delight they took in each other's company on his two-week leaves from the navy, that Kathleen did not know how to approach him on terms that would reflect how their lives had changed in the nine years since. During the war, she had written him long, long letters on rolls of accounting paper her brother brought home from his office, endless lists of all the current songs she liked and her predictions for which ones would reach the top of the hit parade—the sort of letters a girl writes when she's in love with a young sailor in wartime, trivial and then suddenly intense with expressions of longing and rapture.

And when he wrote back, one letter to her five, his words only fuelled another outpouring of the same triviality and drama; if he wrote about his routine on the minesweeper, or about Halifax, or German submarines rumoured to be entering the harbour, she incorporated his world so fully into her own that she could not imagine him ever thinking about dying or other women so long as she continued to pick the chart-toppers and espouse her undying love. Even her self-centredness had a serving quality to it, for she could see, despite her insecurities, how much Vic relied on her to dispell his loneliness with her manic enthusiasms for the immediate. They wrote neither about the future nor the past. They restricted their dreams and their histories to his next leave, to her last day at work in the munitions factory. Rarely, if ever, did they touch on their essential attitudes toward living.

But without noses to be wiped or nets to be mended, without lengthy, forced, official separations, with only the empty sound of the last few coins in the house being clinked together and the faint rhythm of all those failed songs humming on the rain-thick winter winds, Kathleen saw her ability to fuse their worlds lessening, and the vision led to fear, the fear to self-recrimination, and the self-recrimination, finally, to the desire for another child.

Vic did not oppose her. In fact, they never discussed the matter openly. It was as if something of their original telepathy still existed despite the absence of a war to heighten their sensitivities. Though Vic saw the aimlessness in his wife's face, and registered her accompanying silence, he did not acknowledge to himself that she needed another baby. He simply didn't withdraw one night, and the nights became months, and the months became two years, and the years became a third pregnancy. That they did not speak of this decision in so many words was entirely consistent with their generation's hard-learned ability for reticence in the face of disaster. Married couples had children: what was there to discuss? They fought a war to make a better world, and who would make a better world only for themselves? For Kathleen, at least, love and sacrifice were twinned stars; if she could not sacrifice every moment of her days, she could not properly love, either the world or her family. It had not been in her mother's store of pithy wisdom to deify self-love, and so Kathleen had no capsule saying to cover the circumstance, except perhaps, "You've made your bed, now you have to lie in it." Compassionate in their practicality, but hardly a gentle hand to stroke the brow, such words were dispensed as much out of despair as wisdom; if you were poor, pregnant continually, and had miscarried so often and lost so many babies (the Bible recorded six) to diseases of one sort or another, and older children as well to illness and accident, you had to accept your situation or go mad from the sorrow of it.

These memories of her mother, which had often brought Kathleen strength, had lately seemed to be an accusation. She could hear her mother's stern but not unkind voice, breaking through the steam of a kettle she always had on to boil: "Lady Jane, don't you be selfish now, this crying isn't doing anyone any good."

But Kathleen cried too from the guilt of not being able to stop. Now she put her hands in the wet dirt, black as her hair, and thought about pushing herself up, but it was as though she could not move unless the earth moved first. The purple crocuses were sweet and fresh on the ground beside her, just like the ones the boys had cut and brought to her in the hospital. Kathleen never knew whether Vic or someone else had told them to do so, or, if they had decided on their own, which of the two had suggested it. Motionless in the spring morning, as though anaesthetized by the scent of the flowers, Kathleen went through the pattern again; first, her mother's pain, and now her own.

In 1956, the nearest hospital was in Vancouver, twenty miles to the north, across the river. At that time, no tunnel linked the south side of the Fraser's mouth to the city, and the nearest bridge lay thirty miles to the east. Normally, Vancouver-bound residents of Chilukthan and Cedar Bay travelled via a small car and passenger ferry that plied the muddy waters between Woodward's Landing and Lulu Island, a much shorter trip than driving to the

New Westminster bridge. But the last ferry ran at nine o'clock, so when Kathleen started having heavy contractions sometime close to midnight, Vic phoned his father, who immediately drove to the house in his beat-up work truck with the words "Chilukthan Plumbing" on the side.

A gruff, stogie-chewing veteran of the Great War who had almost bled to death at Vimy Ridge, John Mawson suffered no fools, and though he liked his son's wife well enough, he generally regarded women as foolish, especially when they didn't have the good sense to time a child's birth to a reasonable hour when the ferries were running. But he was not a man to complain over things he could not control, nor was he without feeling, so when he helped Kathleen into the truck, he did so with as great a degree of gentleness as she imagined he'd used closing the eyes of a trenchmate whose heart had burst from terror in the night.

"The boys, Vic," Kathleen said between gasps, "What about . . ."

"They're all right, they're fine. Mom's on her way over. Everything's going to be all right, don't worry." He spoke as rapidly as she breathed, as though acting out of sympathy. His nervousness was a relief to her, a sign that all was going as it should.

Her father-in-law raced the engine, then slammed the truck into gear and swung it around. Crushed between the two men on the one seat, Kathleen closed her eyes until the circling motion had ceased. When she opened them again, she was startled to catch a glimpse of Vic's mother on the side of the road, strafed by the headlights, waving her hand. The sudden image vanished so quickly that it frightened Kathleen, mostly because she could not see the expression on the woman's face. Was she smiling? Was she worried? She could have been any woman standing on the side of the road in the dark, waving at anyone, at no one, at a fly around her head, at the wet sky pressing down. For the first time during a pregnancy, Kathleen experienced a sense of foreboding about her child, an instinctive feeling that something was wrong.

Sitting between her husband and father-in-law, being propelled down the long, dark highway, flooded potato fields on one side and the thick firs of Burns Bog on the other, with only the truck's headlights and those of an occasional car passing in the opposite direction giving any relief to the black miles, Kathleen trembled at some depth beyond the trembling of her body. She listened for her mother's voice, as she always did at moments of doubt or fear, and expected to be lightly scolded for foolishness. But the scolding did not come, only the sound of weeping mingled with the heavy rain that surrounded the truck and washed against the windshield where the wipers slapped it away. Kathleen kept listening, but there was no "Lady Jane," and the smoke of Vic's cigarette became the steam of a kettle which thickened into flour in her mind, and the night stiffened into a skirt, and she wasn't being driven to a hospital but was running toward tears that she couldn't stop. This unexpected image of her mother's face attached itself to the woman walking by the side of the road, waving and waving, until Kathleen thought that the woman must be waving goodbye to someone, but who? Then the truck was running red lights with her father-in-law grumbling that he'd take his chances with the police and she saw every light as a stilled heart and it terrified her so that she had to look away past the men's faces through the side windows where, finally, she saw the dim lights of the pulp mills on the banks of the river, and the great heaps of sawdust in the gloom, and the logbooms and logs drifting rapidly on the current which flowed crossways to the direction the truck was travelling, and finally she had to close her eyes altogether and concentrate only on the rhythms of her body to stop the unceasing flow of disturbing sounds and images.

They made it to the hospital in time. Kathleen remembered little after she had closed her eyes in the truck, except for hurried voices in the harsh electric light, the numbing of anaesthesia, and finally, hours later, Vic beside her, holding her hand, and the doctor's quiet, "I'm sorry. There was nothing we could do." Something about the baby being strangled by the cord, something about a caesarian section, something about the even paler blue of Vic's eyes, as if they had been rinsed by the rain. And then tears and listlessness, tears and vomiting, and, eventually, visitors, her in-laws, and the boys, six and eight, all dressed up in their little suits, so shy and confused, each holding a small bunch of crocuses, and Corbett sniffling and hugging her and Troy a little standoffish, staring at her open-eyed as though afraid, then saying, "Mommy, are you okay now?" and coming into her arms.

It was so long ago now, nearly thirteen years, before the tunnel was built, before Zoe was born, when Vic's parents and her father were still alive. At that time, Kathleen had been married for twelve years, living in Chilukthan for eleven, as many years as her mother had been dead.

And so the pattern repeated itself, ending again with her mother. Still the earth was heavy under Kathleen's hands and the crocuses fresh beside them. She willed herself to rise, and once she had done so, she willed herself for the day ahead. The river was open for fishing and school was in; she knew that if she did not go now, she would not go at all.

Having changed into her long black coat, Kathleen walked through the near-empty streets of town, her head bent against the light rain, the crocuses like a torch against her dark figure.

In fifteen minutes, she reached the bus stop at the foot of McNeely Drive, the long, twisting road that lay like a sloughed snake skin from Chilukthan to Cedar Bay, and waited. As always, she was early, the bus schedule being no different to her than a doctor's appointment or a parent-teacher meeting: if you need to be some place, her father had advised, you might as well be punctual.

A few gulls screeched from the roof of the Anglican Church, and high in one of the oak trees, a crow cawed in response. The streets were empty. Though the air was intensely fresh, the wind blew damp and cold and the sky was grey with drizzle. It was the sort of day that had made Kathleen deeply homesick during her first year on the coast. She had not imagined it could be so cold when the temperature remained above freezing. The endless weeks of thick, grey overcast broken only by rain, and then by an odd pallid sky like a dead fish's belly, sometimes so depressed her, especially that first Christmas, that she often lay awake at nights listening to the long hoot of the coal trains crossing the flats and dreamed of making the reverse journey, back to the snow and the crisp air. But she had made her bed, and she had promised her brother, and besides, when the loneliness became too intense, she could simply turn to her husband's warmth and shut out the greyness and the rain.

The bus finally arrived, five minutes late. Kathleen got on and took a window seat near the front. She was the only passenger, and as the bus curved along McNeely Drive, out to where the last subdivision gave way to farm fields and barns, pastures for horses and sheep, and the Sacred Heart Church with the massive cedar hedge shrouding the neighbouring monastery grounds, she stared at the blurred colours of the landscape through the rain-smeared windshield. Then she noticed the driver's hands on the wheel, hands like those of any other man, hands for hauling in nets heavy with salmon, for driving a bus, for lifting a baby . . .

She had never seen him. She couldn't even remember if she had asked and been refused, or if, in fatigue and misery and under the weight of drugs, she had seen no point in doing anything but comply with the doctors. When she had recovered a few days later, Vic told her that he had seen the baby, and that the doctor had told him it was fortunate that the child had not lived because he would have been severely retarded. Kathleen could not remember if she had asked Vic to describe the baby, but she could not imagine asking such a question so soon afterwards, and later it was too painful a subject to be broached. Besides, what good would knowing do? Better to imagine a blankness, because how could she ever stop grieving if there were specific details to be forgotten?

In time, she had accepted the death. The demands of her family gave her no choice. The boys needed her, and Vic needed her, and then, there was always her mother's tragic history to act as a balance. One child? And he died before you even held him and looked into his eyes and knew that he could see you and form his need and his love for you in the motion of his tiny mouth? It was not her mother's voice Kathleen heard asking these questions, for her mother would not have made such a cold distinction between one woman's pain and another's; it was her own. No, not her own voice exactly, but her own filtered through the mesh of the world's reasoning and history, the voice she'd learned to modulate while facing a blackboard staring at numbers she couldn't calculate or with her head down over a sewing machine as a teacher called her stupid for not being able to make a straight seam; it was her voice burdened with a thousand other voices that knew better, and in this case, knowing better meant putting her loss in perspective. What if you had held the child and taken him home and loved him and nursed him and he had died a few months later? What then? Well? Count yourself lucky, my girl, think of your poor mother and all she suffered.

And what else could Kathleen do but think of her mother who had gone stone-cold in the night and did not waken when her husband whispered, Maggie, Maggie, and touched her gently on that very shoulder that had borne so much doomed promise? But though she thought of the past, Kathleen could still accept her present in the years following her baby's death, because necessity, as her mother would have said, her face hovering in the steam, is the mother of invention. And there is no way to put a life together again after it's been shattered if you cannot invent it with the labour of your own heart.

So Kathleen believed, instinctively, turning her attention to her family, to the struggle to pay the bills and keep food on the table, and finally, five long years later, to a hoped-for fourth pregnancy.

The bus reached the end of McNeely Drive, then crossed the highway to Cedar Bay, a wealthier and much younger town than Chilukthan, inhabited mostly by professionals who commuted to Vancouver for work and had little connection to farming or fishing except to complain about the smell of cabbages rotting in the fields or the presence of slow-moving farm vehicles on the roads. In the mid-forties, when Kathleen had arrived in Chilukthan, Cedar Bay was mostly bush. A few old families had lived there for years, and the Coast Salish occupied part of the land as a reserve, but most people regarded the place as a summer retreat, somewhere to take the family on a picnic, or to go swimming and digging for clams by the ocean. And, because Cedar Bay sat high on a bluff, whereas Chilukthan, built on marsh and silt and clay, was too soft for graves, the younger town had the area's only cemetery. Kathleen stepped off the bus just outside the iron gates of the Cedar Bay Memorial Grounds, and opened her umbrella. The rain streamed down, and the wind shook cones and needles off the massive trees lining the narrow road to the graves. The air was so sweet that Kathleen could no longer smell the crocuses in her hand. Their scent was overwhelmed by the pungency of the firs and cedars, whose thickness managed to blank out much of the light the day contained. As Kathleen followed the familiar route through the larger tombstones, the neat, more recent rows of clean marble, spotted here and there with a bright wreath, and beyond to the older, more weathered section of smaller stones marked like water-damaged books, the darkness intensified.

Off to one side, just out of the trees, a lone mourner stood without an umbrella in the full rain, head bowed, and Kathleen's heart went out in sympathy. Yet the presence of another person among the graves only widened the hollow she felt, as if it were making room for more than her own loss. She carried this hollowness with her across the wet grass to the far edge of the bluff, where it sloped down toward the bay.

The grave was unmarked except for a small piece of driftwood in which Vic had carved "Mawson 1956," pushed into the earth. They had not named the child, and without a name, it seemed odd to go through all the formality and ceremony of a burial. Besides, in their grief, no one had thought of any kind of ritual. With no official procedures to be met, the parents fell back solely on their own feelings. Kathleen, sick, drugged, and grief-stricken, was in no condition to consider the matter, so Vic, after consulting his parents, decided to bury the child at Cedar Bay.

John Mawson knew the cemetery keeper well, had done plumbing jobs for him and played cards with him. Because regulations were not so strictly enforced then, the man opened the gates one night for Vic, who carried a flashlight, a spade, a small box and the driftwood he had carved at the kitchen table all afternoon, alone in the silent house, with the boys at their grandparents'. In the dark, with no one else around, Vic buried his stillborn son in the moist earth, choosing a spot with a broad view across the flats to the bay.

Kathleen knew nothing of Vic's actions until a few days later, when she'd recovered sufficiently to be curious and concerned. The following week, he took her to the spot and waited patiently as she knelt and wept, laying the crocuses over the disturbed ground. Then, without speaking, they held one another and stared out across the tilled landscape to the white-foamed slice of blue water to the east.

After a while, Vic said, "He's better off here, he'd not have been right if he'd lived," but Kathleen only cried harder, until Vic squeezed her hand and they walked back through the gates and into the plumbing truck and drove down into Chilukthan again.

Now Kathleen knelt and brushed a few twigs from beneath the driftwood. She placed the crocuses loosely over the earth, so as not to make a pattern and draw attention to them. Then she cried softly for a few minutes, while a child's voice that had never lived to be spoken whispered, "Weep not for me, weep not."

For twelve years, Kathleen had made this trip alone. No one knew that she visited the grave. Always, she went when Vic was working, when the boys were in school, and when she was not needed anywhere else, because she did not want anyone to accuse her of dwelling on the past at the expense of the future. Sometimes, when the voice of the carping world rose above her own, she accused herself of this, but always felt duty-bound to honour the child's memory regardless. Each time she did, she felt as if she were trying to find a way to connect with her mother, to make a series of short trips that, when joined, would equal the long black line that cut across the country and severed her from her childhood. Somehow, her mother's suffering became a well into which Kathleen dipped her annual visits to the place of her own loss.

If Vic knew about her visits, he never let on. Up until Zoe's birth, he was noticeably more tender around the time of the anniversary, and sometimes he would pat Kathleen's hand and look at her in a way that meant more to her than if he'd cried and talked about all that might have been. Kathleen was grateful that he left the grieving to her, because she could not separate it from the past she'd lived before him, from the flour on the skirts and the quiet, unexpected tears that had no apparent source and were never explained. She came to view the anniversary, painful as it was, as something she could harbour as her own, something belonging most rightfully to her emotions. That her mother did not prove a threat to that possession revealed just how much she needed her mother's vague presence, needed someone more than they needed her. And the child met that requirement too, for he bid her not to weep, year after year, so that she must have come to the cemetery because she needed to do so for her own sake, and not for his. For that reason, because she feared her own self-indulgence, the satisfaction of some purely private yearning, she kept her visits to the grave a secret. The mocking voice that rose from behind her at the blackboard and above her at the sewing machine, spoke again: "A grown woman with a family who needs her dead mother and dead child is more than stupid and useless; she's crazy as well."

Kathleen wondered if it was true. Until recently, she had always felt in control, or at least capable of facing each day with some strength. But now she felt herself sliding into the well, and the blackness being extended was not of tracks but of rope.

She stood above the grave, her face to the rain. The bay looked so small in the distance. With a deep sigh, she turned to go back. As she did, her left foot twisted awkwardly against a small rock on the wet grass of the slope, and she fell, sliding a few feet before her leg hit a tree.

Her ankle was throbbing when she tried to stand. The pain cut through her every time she put her weight down, so she leaned against the tree, her left foot raised a few inches from the ground, and hoped that she'd be all right to walk in a few moments. When she tried again, she was able to bear her weight, though she grimaced with the effort, and had to pause at the top of the slope before proceeding across the cemetery.

She made it to the edge of the weathered graves before the pain became too much for her. She put the point of her umbrella into the earth and tried to use it as a walking stick when she moved forward again, but it was too flimsy. So, placing it back over her head, she took a deep breath and limped slowly into the newer part of the cemetery.

The lone mourner was still there, in the same spot, like a tall tomb. Kathleen tried to edge past without drawing too much attention to herself. But the pain would not let her alone, and she had no choice but to limp for several yards, almost hop in fact, and then rest against one of the larger monuments. So intense was her concentration on her throbbing ankle and the wet earth just in front of her that a voice almost in her ear brought her up short.

"Can I help you at all?"

The words came from immediately in front of her. Kathleen kept her head bowed and the umbrella tilted over her face. The voice, obviously a man's, sounded familiar, but she could not place it. "No, thank you," she said, "I'm fine. Very nice of you to offer, but no thank you."

Kathleen could hear the man breathing lightly. "It's Mrs. Mawson, isn't it? Are you sure you're all right? I saw you limping."

With her head still bowed, Kathleen could see only the man's lower half, his ill-matched brown shoes and black pants. But her curiosity was less than her desire to be alone. "I'm fine, thank you," she replied, and limped ahead a few feet. But the pain wrenched her ankle with an even greater intensity. To keep herself from collapsing, she plunged the umbrella into the ground and just managed, with that little amount of support, to maintain her balance before the umbrella collapsed. As she did so, she looked straight into the man's face.

It was the butcher. In his dark suit, soaked by the rain, and with his yellow bangs flattened tight against his broad forehead, he looked almost pathetic. Kathleen stared at him briefly, captivated by the absence of his white smock; it was as if he had had a black hole placed in the middle of his body. Then she recovered her manners.

"Oh, Mr. Meers, I'm sorry, I didn't realize it was you." She smiled, forcing herself to be polite, though all she wanted was to get home as fast as possible. "I had a bit of a fall. Must have forgotten to take my clumsy pills this morning. But it's nothing, I just need to take the weight off it every now and then."

The butcher stared at her with an expression of confusion and concern. For some reason, Kathleen felt sorry for him, but she couldn't think of anything else to say. After a while, she cleared her throat, and was about to take her leave when he asked if he could speak with her a moment.

"If you don't mind, it's about your daughter."

"Zoe?" Kathleen was alarmed.

The butcher suddenly looked terrified and put his hands up, as if to ward off a blow. "It's nothing," he explained hurriedly. "At least, it's not important. I just thought, since I happened to meet you here, that I would mention it." He paused to catch his breath. "You haven't been to the shop lately, not since . . ."

Kathleen suddenly remembered when she'd last heard his voice, and she remembered that Zoe had been with her then. The knowledge calmed her a little. "Not since Shamus died."

"Yes." He wiped his brow with his sleeve, but that only pushed all his bangs to one side; the rain still ran down his heavy face. "There's a bench just under the trees there." He pointed to the near side of the cemetery.

"All right," Kathleen said as pleasantly as possible, "but I can't sit long, I have an appointment in town." With a supreme effort, she walked to the bench, her eyes watering from the strain.

Joe did not know how to begin. He wasn't even sure if the situation was worth mentioning, but the sight of Mrs. Mawson in this unlikely place seemed like a sign, another tear in the pattern to which he might as well attend, just as he'd attended to the dog's death. In the weeks since that disturbing event, he'd found it impossible to return calmly to his routine. He still did all the same things the same way, but gradually he had made some alterations to the design of his life. Because he found it increasingly difficult to sleep, he tried to relax by going for long walks late at night, down along the dyke past the government wharf and out toward Pheasant Island. Also, he had decided, as a result of the troubling and almost embarrassing sadness he felt at the dog's absence, to visit his parents' graves on a weekly instead of a monthly basis, if only to give his grief a more appropriate outlet.

And then there was the girl. From the moment he had seen her in his shop on the day after the dog's death, Joe had felt as though she were blaming him for something that he didn't even know he was guilty of. So he had admitted the truth about Shamus dying in his arms. With the little girl's eyes on him, he could not keep that knowledge to himself. Yet the telling did not ease the strange sense of guilt. Instead, it grew with each day, until Joe, either from the guilt or from just thinking about it, began to feel haunted.

"Your daughter," he began. "Would you say . . . please pardon me for asking . . . that she is happy now, that she is over the dog's death?"

If not for the butcher's soothing and kind voice, Kathleen would have been offended by the question. As it was, she frowned when she replied. "Yes, very happy. Why do you ask?"

Joe felt sick. This is wrong, he said to himself, I must be losing my mind. The woman's eyes flashed with emotion, and Joe suddenly realized that he was involving himself for the first time in one of his customers' private lives. He hurried on, condensing what he had to say into a few sentences when he had wanted to be methodical and calm. Now having crossed a line, he immediately wanted to step back, erase everything he'd said, follow his wet footsteps back to his solitary spot beside his parents' graves, and from there back to Chilukthan and his shop and his old life.

But since he could not go back, he went forward: "I only ask because your daughter is at my window every day, sometimes twice a day, just staring at me. And she runs away whenever I go to the door."

Joe took a deep breath, and wiped his brow again, though it was sweat and not rain that his sleeve smeared this time. He looked at the woman seated beside him, her eyes so wide that her whole face seemed a reflection of the trees beyond, and he was ashamed. Why did he have to worry her with his own imagined terrors? For he believed them to be such, heard the idiocy of his words for the first time. Who could understand why a girl's face would disturb him so if he could not understand it himself? Suddenly weighted with self-awareness, Joe understood that a little girl outside a window could be only a trivial amusement to a healthy mind. With dread and embarrassment, he waited for a response.

At first panicked by the mention of her daughter, Kathleen soon realized that there was nothing to be concerned about. In wonderment, she stared at the butcher, his wide, flushed face, almost like a child's if it were not for something in the eyes, a kind of painful consciousness that so obviously belonged to adulthood. For the first time, Kathleen noted that this man had been the lone mourner standing still beside a grave, and her look softened. Clearly, like herself, he had his own losses to contend with.

She smiled thinly and sighed: "Zoe has always been a funny child, what my mother would have called a deep one. Really, Vic and I are always amazed at the things she comes out with." Kathleen felt herself losing track of the conversation, and tried to remember an example. "Once, when we were carving a pumpkin for Halloween, she held some of the pulp in her hand and asked why the pumpkin's blood wasn't as dark as the salmon's. Well, we didn't know how to answer that, because we'd never thought of the pulp that way before, even though it did make a kind of sense. And Zoe, she just looked at us, you know, the way a child does, waiting and thinking, until Vic said that fish just had darker blood, that was all. Yes," Kathleen looked away across the graves, her voice trailing off, "she's a deep one."

Joe blinked as some sweat trickled into his eye. Then he noticed that the woman was crying, very softly, and he was stricken with pain at the thought that he had been the source of her tears. Twice, he opened his mouth to speak, but somehow, he sensed a strange and fragile aura around her that made him keep his silence.

Kathleen took a Kleenex from her bag and blew her nose. She had felt the tears coming, as they did so often lately, tears without a specific origin, that travelled in her, and escaped from her, naturally as breath. She managed to keep the panic from her voice when she remembered the butcher, and turned back to him apologetically. "I'll have a talk with Zoe," she said, "I'll ask her not to look in your window."

Joe had no response. He was mesmerized by the nakedness of the woman's emotion. It made him feel ridiculous and small; he could feel himself shrinking in her eyes. The longer she looked at him, the more he wanted to turn away, but he couldn't bring himself to do it. The rain, increasing, shuddered in the branches above them, and a few drops splattered on Joe's hands, which he held splayed on his knees. In the storm, the tombstones resembled a flock of grey gulls huddled deep into themselves for protection. Joe looked at his hands until the whiteness of them, so like marble, became troubling. Then he lifted and shook them, as though trying to start his blood flowing again.

"Goodbye," Kathleen said, her voice sounding distant even to herself. She stood, winced at the pain, and started for the gates.

Too surprised to move right away, Joe finally followed. "Are you going back to Chilukthan? Let me give you a ride. I have my van." He pointed vaguely toward the parking lot.

Kathleen wanted nothing more than to sink into the wet earth and sleep. She didn't want the butcher's company or anyone else's. She just wanted to lie down, only for an hour or so, before Zoe came home from school.

She turned around. "No, thank you," she said, with such firmness that Joe did not insist. He simply nodded, and stood motionless, blinking away raindrops as he watched her limp slowly through the gates and disappear.

chapter six

Asleep on the living-room couch, Vic did not hear Kathleen arrive home from the cemetery. He had left his wet gumboots and dripping oilskins in a pile by the kitchen door and was snoring with his head resting loosely in the palm of one hand. Above his weathered face, a few strands of white hair stuck up in a cowlick, the result of being released from the tight constraints of a skullcap, while below, a bright smear of blood hung like a scimitar across the chest of his plaid workshirt. A heavy smell of gasoline, mud and cigarette smoke rose off his body. Occasionally, his left leg twitched, a scowl clouded his features, and his even breathing thickened to a choke quickly shaken off and replaced by the same smooth breaths as before: it was the sleep of a fisherman still on the river, deep, stolen and guarded, attuned to currents and night noises.

But now he was firmly in the grip of a haunting and surreal dream. He saw himself pulling in a net filled with dirt and the jawbones of mudsharks, and then he was pushing a wheelbarrow down a long, sloping street, in starlight, with what looked like birchbark shavings falling over the sides. Suddenly, the shavings lifted and became curls of long blond hair hanging over the blue and bloated face of a young man, at which point Vic jerked awake and almost slipped off the couch. Seconds later, he drifted off again, back to the same sloping street that seemed to run forever down to a body of black water gleaming always in the starlit distance.

Kathleen did not wake him. She stepped over the pile of clothes and went into the bathroom with her ankle throbbing. She ran some hot water in the tub, filled it with epsom salts, and soaked her feet to the calves. She could hear Vic's snores coming faintly from the living room. The sound distracted her from the day's heavier preoccupations, but not in a positive way. If Vic came home early during an opening, she knew it could only mean bad news. For Kathleen, a shortage of money was inseparable from grief. She had learned this too from her parents, who had struggled all their lives to pay the bills and to rise out of the humiliation of poverty.

Early in her childhood, Kathleen had learned to dread the knock at the door, or the midday sight of her father seated at the kitchen table reading the newspaper classifieds. As a result, ever since her marriage, she had been determined to honour her debts. No matter what the cost, she made sure the Mawson name was financially respectable. Often, the price for that good name was an even more intense form of self-sacrifice, an even greater doggedness about "putting a little aside for a rainy day." In this, she was not unlike other fishermen's wives, who knew the cyclical nature of their husbands' earnings, but Kathleen did nothing without the sense that some critical authority was watching her and just waiting to bring the sharp pointer down on her unprotected hand.

After soaking her ankle for ten minutes, she wrapped it in a tensor bandage and returned to the kitchen. Then she plugged the kettle in and returned to the living room.

Vic was still sleeping, and she watched him with both tenderness and sadness. Despite his hair, he did not look much different than the young sailor she'd fallen in love with twenty-five years before, but the twitching and scowling were certainly signs that he had lost the carefree nature of those days. As always, she wished that she could ease his worries. Her love was such that she would spare him every unpleasantry if she could in any way carry the extra burden herself. So her love, as well as her memory, became at times a burning anvil that she had to hold until the weight and heat were so much that she needed to rest. And Kathleen believed that all she really wanted was for someone to notice the scars and the smouldering in her hands for them to heal and soften overnight.

But if Vic did notice, she was not aware of any significant

change in him, nor did she see any perception in the eyes of her sons, who surely were old enough now at least to approach an understanding of the worlds of work and worry.

The kettle whistled and Kathleen left the living room. When she returned, Vic was sitting up, rubbing his temples and yawning. "I've just made you a cup of tea. Do you want something to eat?"

He shook his head. "I've got to get back to the wharf. I left Corbett down there to wait for George. Just thought I'd come up and relax for a bit, get away from the waterfront."

"George?" Kathleen sat at the end of the couch and stared anxiously at Vic.

He shrugged. "Yep, broke down again. The old girl's having a rough start to the year."

"Again? We just paid to have the boat fixed." Kathleen had already begun to calculate the last bill. What was it? Forty dollars for a new battery? In her worry, she stood, forgetting about her ankle, and gasped as she shifted her weight back onto her strong leg.

Vic looked at her sideways, then scowled. "What's that bandage for?" Immediately, he suspected her again of doing too much, of pushing her body beyond its limits. The suspicion, as always, resulted in a response part concern and part irritation. He knew how much Kathleen did for him, and knowing it, he felt as much guilt as gratitude, so that when she took on an even greater burden, he sometimes reacted with impatience.

Kathleen dismissed his concern. "Oh, nothing, I had a little fall. What's wrong with the boat? Is it serious? Are you missing out on lots of fish?"

"What do you mean nothing? I saw the way you moved just now."

"Just a little sprain, I'll be fine." She kept talking as she went for the tea. "Will you miss the rest of the opening?"

"Don't know. Won't know what the problem is until George takes a look at it. Maybe it's just the plugs. But we're not missing anything. Skunked the last set. Had a half-dozen on the first."

Kathleen came back into the room and handed him a cup of tea. "That's worse than last week."

"I know. It's a bad year for springs."

They were silent for a while, drinking their tea. Then Vic asked how she'd fallen.

For Kathleen, remembering the incident was like repeating the fall, only this time it was something more than her ankle that felt the effect. Despite her fierce determination to overcome the sorrow that weighed her down, she began to sink. She tried to compose herself by mentioning the conversation she'd had at the cemetery, though she was careful to hide its context. "I bumped into Joe Meers today. He was asking about Zoe."

Vic looked up. As Kathleen suspected, this mention of their daughter attracted his full attention. "Oh," he said with gravity, "and what in the world does he have to do with Zoe?"

Kathleen, smiling, related the butcher's concerns. "I told him that she was a deep one."

Vic nodded, then put his cup down. "Still, I don't like the sound of it. What's she doing hanging around the butcher shop like that?"

"Oh, it's nothing to worry about. She probably just wants to ask him about Shamus. I don't think she's gotten over that yet. I should never have taken her with me when I brought him that little jack. Maybe you should have a talk with her, tell her not to go near the shop for a while."

They were silent again. Rain fell against the window and into the chimney grate. Wind gusted through the maple tree in the front yard. Vic dozed off, his mind returning to the sloping street and the body of black water in which a line of fire now blazed. The blond hair lifted, the bloated face smiled, the mouth opened, and Vic was pulling a net out of it. Soon there were salmon in the net and stumps and he could hear voices shouting desperately in the distance.

He woke with a snap to find himself alone. Kathleen's cup was on the table. Vic got up and went into the kitchen. She was not there. He paused, listening. Before long, he could hear, at a slightly different rhythm to the rain, the sound of weeping. He walked down the hallway to their bedroom.

Kathleen looked up at him, panic-eyed, from the bed. She was on top of the covers, fully dressed, her arms crossed and her legs bent at the knees. "I don't know what it is, something's, oh I don't know," she said as he approached, the fear in her voice different from any he'd heard before. "Vic, I don't know what's happening!" She looked at him with such desperation that he froze, unable to say anything or even to touch her. Finally he knelt beside the bed and put his hand on her forehead, as though he could think of nothing else to do but check for a fever. She was cold, clammy, and her eyes shivered like tadpoles under his hand. "What is it? What do you want me to do?"

"I don't know, I don't know. I feel so cold." She rubbed her arms and looked at him for the first time without sympathy for his confusion. Stunned, he reached down to the foot of the bed and pulled the bunched quilt up over her. "Just have a little rest," he said, "you'll feel better. I'll wait for Zoe to come home before I head back to the wharf."

"So cold, so cold," Kathleen whispered, and her voice was at once the voice of her mother and her child. She could not hear herself, or step out from behind a darkness that was hers alone. There were too many voices and too many depths. Her mind raced to distinguish them, but it could not pry them apart: 1907, 1907, 1908, 1911, 1912, 1912, 1913, 1917, 1928, 1945, 1956. Who died, whose child, what year, who left, who stayed, who grieved? Each question belonged to a time, and each time belonged to someone, and someone could not be her, could not possibly be her, because she did not have the answers, she did not know how to tell the time properly.

Vic held her hand until she fell asleep because he did not know what else to do. Then, shaken from the sudden absence of her voice and stare, he stood, as if waiting for instructions. But the person whose love had told him for so long what needed to be done, the person whose love he sometimes heeded and sometimes didn't, was not telling him now.

Eventually, once the silence had become too much, he walked back to the couch in the living room and waited for Zoe to come home from school.

chapter seven

*L*ike most families, the Mawsons had little knowledge of their town's origins. They weren't uninterested, but neither were they scholars, and to discover anything about the distant past would have involved considerable research. History was European, American, and to a small degree, Central Canadian, but the huge salmon runs and the Cariboo gold rush and all the other forces that had built their town were never mentioned in the schools or discussed on the wharves and in the shops.

And yet something in the landscape of Chilukthan, its winding sloughs and broad marshes, and the long roll of the Fraser toward the ocean, suggests a glorious antiquity. An emperor on a high dyke, watching mesmerized as an African princess floats toward him on a barge sculpted of ivory and onyx, seems as believable as the truth, which is much younger and only incidentally romantic: the picnics and the apple-picking after the pioneer backbreak born of private empire building.

In the middle of the nineteenth century, two English brothers followed the scent of fortune north from California to the Cariboo goldfields. With a Victorian talent for recognizing opportunity, they quickly assessed the potential of the wet sprawl of marsh and silt on the lower Fraser, and pre-empted several hundred acres from the Salish Nation (as well as the one strange but somehow pleasing word of their language). Yorkshiremen, practical and bull-strong, they sensed the black gold in the undyked and unturned earth, and threw all the energy of an unsetting sun into the task of making farms from mud and clay. Once the stumps had been dragged out, and the land drained, and the first wharves and houses built, the two bachelors, visages dark as Bibles, eyes like ink splotches in a prayer book, stood one night overlooking the Fraser's still tide, and thought of marriage and fatherhood.

And so Chilukthan grew, out of a world of particles. The gold dust gave way to a bonanza of silt, the richness and promise of the silt stirred the seed in the bachelor loins, and that same night, right under the wondering stares of the brothers, pieces of finger-long silver drifted by the millions out to sea, salmon fry banking themselves for a huge return to their mountain creeks of birth.

That wealth would come soon. The brothers had listened close-ly to rivers long enough to hear such an obvious clink of money. If they failed to strike it rich finding gold in a flat pan, they'd do so by putting silver in a round tin. They weren't alone. A wander-ing assortment of Scots and Americans also settled along the river mouth to build their fortunes on the backs of the salmon. The runs were huge, untouched except by the Natives, who harvested a small amount for food and ceremonial purposes. A man had to be blind if he couldn't see the king's crown stamped in the sock-eye's gape.

Canneries sprang up all over the lower Fraser, several dozen of them by the turn of the century. Chilukthan grew on pilings out into the current. Wharves, netsheds, small floating villages in the sloughs for the cannery workers and fishermen to be closer to the kill: suddenly human footsteps had almost outnumbered the salmon below them. But the fish were so plentiful that lowering a net into them was like waving a handkerchief over your head to touch the air. Gaff hooks rained down into silver flesh and tossed it high onto scows, and the scows, sunk to the waterline, were tugged into docks where Chinese and Native cannery workers chopped and gutted and shoved the red meat into tins. Meanwhile, the Yorkshire brothers and their Scottish and American counterparts added up the profits and listened grate-fully to the gush of blood and entrails sliding down chutes and back into the muddy current.

Farmland spread as the dyking improved. The lost gold of youth reappeared in the cornfields of Chilukthan, and the unfound nuggets were ploughed out of its potato acres. When the cornstalks reached their highest point, the salmon runs peaked, and the fat cobs and sleek fish rivalled each other for the promise they contained. Horses and boats went out into the harvest, and coming back together, made a small fortune for the town's pioneers. Now the pianos could be barged in for the parlours, now the daughters could sit down to play, now the Sunday afternoon visits to far-off neighbours could be undertaken. And if the Yorkshiremen had to replace a piano key with a tooth yanked from a horse, they could; if they lost a daughter to disease and had to father another, they could; if they needed more pilings, more workers, more elm trees, they could find them. Resourceful, proud, successful, they laid their broad hands on a happy ledger and loved the sound and the smell and the look of the always-falling rain outside their windows; it was fast and rich and myriad as the salmon fry, and it made the crops grow, and they thought of the rain as a partner with whom they didn't have to share the profits. Not like men, not like the damned Scots and Americans (even a Negro now!) always muscling in on their drifts on the river, not like the fishermen grumbling that they weren't paid enough. But who paid the Yorkshiremen for their sweat and toil? Who? They did, by the labour of their own backs. And if now they could afford to hire labour, well, what of it? Here's the world: we own this much of it, and if you own less, that's a fact, but we're hardly responsible for it. At least the China Boss keeps his crew in line. And the Indians, the women, they know enough to show up when the fish are running and disappear again. But these damned fishermen! We'll have to talk with the other canners, see what can be done.

And so, by the turn of the century, the canneries had formed a tight monopoly of interests. There was labour unrest, and by then too, several salmon runs, exploited for decades, had trickled to almost nothing even in some peak years. Canneries shut down, jobs were lost, profits lessened, but the cannery owners survived and even flourished. They cut back enough, limited competition enough that they managed to retain their economic and political power. Besides, there were other businesses now. Vancouver was becoming a large city, and there was money in construction. Pilings rotted along the river, netsheds housed only muskrats and spiders, and skiffs like open graves filled up with rain.

But Chilukthan remained a fishing and farming town. It grew, despite the changes, but as slowly as the silt islands built up in the mouth, by a gradual accumulation of particles, one child, two children, a stranger trying his luck, a Chinaman run out of the city for gambling debts. The rain fell, the crops grew, the salmon returned: people lived. Electricity, telephones, cars: all came in their turn and changed the town. But always the silver ran down one side, and the coal trains brought a second darkness down the other side, and the same spinning wheel, the same plough in the stars, raised the seasons up and buried them back under.

The Yorkshire brothers died, as they had lived, vigorously and with a fierce ambition, their hearts exploding in their eardrums as they counted up their profits in the Lord. Their sons inherited and went on, less fiercely, but they went on, proud pioneers who'd write memoirs of the tough but love-filled and romantic past, all danger and adventurous childbirth and lazy afternoons picking blackberries. The Great War took some local boys. They fell in the Belgian mud and breathed the distant Fraser as they gasped and died. Prohibition made a millionnaire of a local entrepreneur who ran rum into Washington State and later became a recluse in a giant mansion on the far shore of Pheasant Island.

Naturally, the Depression hit the town hard, but Chilukthan was small and rich in natural resources, so the residents managed to pull together to see that everyone came through. A few set fires, a suspicious death or two, a proud family taken down a notch: all common events in rural communities across the country.

But the river afforded much compensation, its wide current sweeping majestically past with its cargo of moonlight and salmon, its massive weight like a reel of history and time, its depth at once an invitation to exotic shores and a looming graveyard of sodden ghosts. To step away from lamplight and human solace to find this unending flow of black before your eyes was to be raised from insignificance and frailty to a state of divine detachment: that you could co-exist with such power and splendour and not be overwhelmed meant that you belonged to more than a family, a town, a race; you belonged to something you couldn't even name except you knew it was immense and outside all contemplation. A star would melt in the west, and it was the end of your cigar burning down, or a seal in the channel would cry to break the long, deep silence and it was the cry you had raised from the cradle and lost forever. Hearing it put a delicious fear in your heart, so that you could not move for minutes afterwards, terrified at the fragility of the universe and the blank scroll of your shadow in it. Then the wind would pick up, and back among the houses a door would slam, turning your mind to its mundane entrances and departures, fleshing out and bloodening your spirit so it could open the general store, nurse a child, shoe a horse, or gut a fish. And then you'd sigh and snuff out the light in your fingers and walk back down the dyke into the world of voices.

Vic's father, John Mawson, had almost bled to death in that world, filling his boots to the brim in a foxhole at Vimy Ridge until some other soldier jumped on him, saw the pool, and hoisted the wounded man to an aid station. Twenty years later, when John moved his family, a wife and three teenaged sons, to Chilukthan from the rain-drenched and creek-burbling mountainside of North Vancouver, he often sought relief from the world by walking on the dyke and staring into the river until all the echoing noises of the century stilled and only the wind in the rushes and the lapping of the current were left. Some nights, he stayed out so long that the first light of daybreak eating the stars seemed like an erosion done by the current and his own eyes. At such times, he hated to turn back to the wrenches and pipes of his trade, back to cards and booze and the trivial details of running a business, even back to caring about how he portioned out the residue of his affection.

But he always turned, as the river and the sky did, slowly but inevitably, and for the sake of continuance. When war came again, he watched from the open doorway of his shop as the boys drilled on the street. And he chewed down on his cigar a little harder, and said nothing when his own sons signed up. He just shook their hands firmly and nodded and watched them go, harbouring but not articulating his hope for their safe return.

Vic, the youngest and most like him, enlisted for adventure more than patriotism, and because it was the right thing to do. And though John knew well what fate awaited his laughing, blue-eyed son, he could think of no way to protect him. So he chewed down even harder, retreated to moody silences and long walks on the dyke, during which his son's existence, as well as his own, became meaningless and therefore ennobled.

For three years, Vic was stationed on a minesweeper in Halifax.

John knew only that he worked as a telegrapher, and listened for SOSs while the ship patrolled the North Atlantic, searching for survivors and bodies after U-boat attacks. One month, the boy wrote to say he'd met someone, and six months later, that he was getting married in Toronto.

When the war ended, all of John's sons returned home safely. And a few months afterwards, Vic's young bride also arrived in Chilukthan. Ah, but she was a pretty thing, so shy and polite. John liked her; she was neither loud nor pushy, and though she looked frail, she wasn't afraid of hard work. And that was fortunate, since Vic, as John expected, returned with no ambition except to keep out from under any other man's thumb. John never asked his son about his experiences, nor did he discuss his own, but he suspected the Forces still whipped you for acting like a man when they wanted you to be a boy. And, as John muttered grimly to himself, a whipped man is no good for a world built on hierarchies and injustices; he can only survive if he sets his own terms.

So when his son found his way into salmon fishing, an insecure but independent livelihood, John was neither surprised nor pleased. He knew enough fishermen to realize that the life was dangerous and difficult, and that only the most ambitious ever achieved economic success. But so what? His son might as well be on the river, which was that much closer than the dyke to the thrum of the ineffable.

John lit another cigar, and another, and another. The ash heaped up into nights, years, the birth of grandchildren, the death of his wife, the failure of his business due to backstabbing, undercutting competition that did shoddy work with cheap supplies because that was the new way, get in and get out and take the money. The years mounted to nearly two decades, and he heard the revellers behind him ring in another new year, 1962, 1963, it made little difference as far as he was concerned what number they chiselled into his headstone because he could just as easily have been hacked into history on the war memorial in downtown Vancouver and had his young ghost annually bugled into a passing glory, it made no difference. He would have liked his ashes to be scattered over the river on a high tide runoff, but he never shared that wish with anyone, and he left no will because he didn't think there was anything to leave. He died in hospital after a brief illness, whispering to Kathleen who was holding the hand of his pretty little granddaughter, "I'm not coming out this time."

So Chilukthan lost another citizen. The local paper eulogized him as a master plumber and veteran of the Great War, and then the town properly returned to its television sets and its economic optimism and its councils' plans for urban renewal and an increased tax base now that they had the tunnel and were no longer cut off from the city with its vast range of opportunities. But mostly, the town returned to bowling leagues and skating at the rink and childbirth, to drive-ins and dinner parties and grief, to sockeye runs, May Day Parades, and broken parts on the combine, to laughter, remorse and cunning. And for some it returned to Kennedy and Pearson, the Cold War, the shrill voices of newspaper editorials. Subdivisions spread over fertile farmland, more people began commuting to work in Vancouver and knew so little of their own surroundings that they would buy an old salmon in a supermarket for five times what they'd be charged for a fresh one down at the wharf. The harvests of Chilukthan's pioneer days no longer reflected the town's self-image. Barns sagged, wharves broke; there were no more Harvest Balls or Fishermen's Dances. Occasionally at first, and then with increasing frequency, long-time residents began to speak wistfully of "Old Chilukthan," of community togetherness, of knowing your neighbours.

Even the river had changed. Silt islands and dredging diverted the main current away from the town, creating a calmer channel and harbour, so that you had to walk farther westward down the dyke to feel the river's true force. But few people took that walk, only the local "characters," the drunken fishermen who lived alone on their boats, the old Chinaman who collected bottles and talked to himself, those who gave Chilukthan its "rural charm," as long as you didn't have to pass them on the street or sit beside them on the bus. Eventually, the original townsite would deteriorate to such a point that a new one centred around a huge shopping mall would be built farther to the east, nearer the highway and the spreading subdivisions, far from the waterfront and netsheds and boats, far from the Mawsons' small bungalow.

That shift was still ten years in the future when Vic, standing in the stern of his gillnetter, removed a cigarette from the pack in his jacket pocket and stared downriver toward the sleeping town. A small moon afforded the only light, casting a few buildings on the dyke into dim relief. They looked like charcoal rubbings, or craters the moon had lowered to rid itself of the weight.

It was after midnight and very still; even the river was slack. The match trembled in Vic's cupped hands and briefly revealed his unshaven face as he lowered it to meet the flame. Two hundred fathoms away, the night light marking the end of his net was just as small as the burning tip of the cigarette held loosely between his lips. Every five or ten minutes, a salmon hit on the corkline with the sound of a champagne bottle being uncorked, one loud noise and then a sort of fizzle as the fish struggled to get free of the web.

Behind the drum, Corbett was stretched out on the deck asleep, and a hundred fathoms upriver, at the head of the drift, Troy had just finished setting his net.

The night was cool but pleasant, and Vic sighed deeply with satisfaction and relief. The tide would not turn for hours, and so he had little to do but smoke and reflect. He flicked some ash into the blackness, then took a long drag and stared back toward Chilukthan.

It had been a hard month. The fishing was a disappointment, and the rumours about poor prices for sockeye seemed well grounded. Shamus had died. And, worst of all, Kathleen was still in the grip of some sickness. For a week now she had remained in bed, weeping and complaining about being cold (no matter how high he put the thermostat, or how many blankets he put over her); she wouldn't eat anything except a bit of dry toast, and couldn't even manage a smile for Zoe. At Kathleen's request, Vic kept the children away. But they knew the situation was unusual and were beginning to show signs of frustration and worry. Troy and Corbett were old enough to fend for themselves, but Zoe had to be looked after, and Vic found himself taking the bulk of the responsibility. Asking for help would have involved explaining the situation to someone outside the family, and since the deaths of his parents, he had no one he felt he could confide in except Kathleen. So he had no choice but to leave Zoe on her own at night when he was fishing, though he did come into harbour if the fishing was poor and the tide unpromising. But mostly he

TIM BOWLING

retained his faith that Kathleen, despite her condition, could be relied on if Zoe needed her.

He took another long drag on his cigarette and looked at the stars. How beautiful it was to be on the river at night, with the net out and only the splash of salmon to break the silence. Everything was so calm; it was as though he had no life except what was immediately in front of him, as though he were nameless and perfectly alone. If only a man could keep his thoughts clear.

Vic flicked the burning nub of his cigarette into the water and watched it sink. Then he took another from the pack, lit it, and aimed for a moment's reflection pure and still as the tide.

chapter eight

*I*t was approaching daybreak. Joe had been walking along the dyke for hours, all the way from town, past the bridge to where the river broadened toward the ocean, and back again. Only the stars were out, faint as dust, though earlier he had thought he'd heard laughter rising up out of the marshes. But the sound came from far away and might have been his imagination or a heron announcing its workday in the tidal flats.

Joe chose his imagination as the likelier cause. It was the reason, after all, that he had begun to go for long early-morning and late-evening walks. Ever since the dog's death, he had not been able to keep his thoughts settled; it was as though the strange fog of that day had been a kind of low-grade anxiety seeping into his bones. And then, the next day's disturbing meeting with Mrs. Mawson and her daughter, followed by the girl's unnerving appearances outside his shop, had only compounded his growing sense that life was spinning out of his control. Finally, the rainy day at the cemetery had made matters much worse; he had accomplished nothing by speaking to Mrs. Mawson, except that he now saw the dark faces of her and her daughter as part of the same general darkness that had crept in with the fog to unsettle his calm.

So he walked to unburden himself of the tension in his muscles. He stared blankly at the stars. He tried to specify the source of his unease, but the more he tried, the worse he felt. He told himself repeatedly that he was a good man, and this belief compensated for what he regarded as his failures and insufficiencies, his lack of a more intense reality. But ever since he'd stepped out of his shop into the fog, the idea of virtue as an excuse for inaction no longer seemed acceptable. On that morning he had encountered, in the shared emotions of the Mawson family, a yawning absence in himself. He now saw nothing in the girl's face or her mother's but an accusation, as if they were screaming, "You are a coward!" But even if they did, Joe realized that he would have no defence against the charge. "I'm a good man, don't you see," he might say, "I have hurt no one. No one can blame me for their suffering." And he might believe it, as he did now, because he suspected that to look straight at the truth was more terrifying than to search endlessly for it.

He walked upriver past the bridge, the marine repair shops and boatworks, to the point where the dyke turned eastward again, back toward the town centre. On his left, the river flowed; on his right, puddles of rainwater gleamed dully between the furrows of a potato field; and straight ahead about a half mile off, like the ruins of some ancient village, were the netsheds and wharves of fishermen who did not moor in the harbour. Joe slowed his pace, unwilling to end his walk with the same sleepless stare at the ceiling and that cold hour over a breakfast he had to force himself to eat.

As he approached the sheds, low and black as beached whales, the sky began to brighten in the east. A grey pall rose off the silt islands and the sloughs, and the mountains beyond Vancouver deepened their outlines, became the dull blue of a heron's wing, just as wide and brittle-looking, as though made up of the same thin bones. The silence was broken only by bird noises in the marsh, a chorus of low hoots and cries and the occasional piercing trill that, dying away, deepened the silence it had disturbed.

Some gulls hovered over the first wharf, screaming greedily, then suddenly dropping out of sight; they looked like pale hands slapping down on the wharf. But they did not stay down, nor did they fly away. Their indecisive motion piqued Joe's curiosity.

He moved closer. The gulls were sleek and greyish, but big as hawks. Their fierce screams intensified as they clashed over the wharf, one dropping just long enough to be followed and chased by another.

Soon Joe reached the netshed from which a gangway lowered

down to the wharf at the level of the river. A small electric bulb hung from a wire over the entrance to the gangway, and in its wan circle of light he could make out a net-rack and what looked like a fishnet stretched across it. At least that's what he thought the dark shape was.

Normally, he would have walked on, but the awfulness of the birds' cries, the fact that the shape didn't seem bulky enough to be a net, made him hurry down the gangway for a closer look. Immediately, the large birds flew off to perches on the netshed roof, from where their sudden silence seemed worse than their screams. The hard-running tide knocked the pilings together; even their creaks, and the creaks of the nearby gillnetters pulling at their ropes, sounded as if they came from the open beaks of the gulls.

With a sick feeling in his stomach, Joe stared at the dark shape on the rack. It was a boy, maybe eleven, twelve years old. He was fully stretched out, his sharp-boned face to the sky, his wrists and ankles knotted with thick rope. Clothed only in a T-shirt and jeans, he had a mass of fishguts wound around his torso with nylon twine. One long intestine snaked down his left leg, the result of the gulls' constant pulling. A mingled stench of guts and alcohol rose from the body as Joe forced himself to lean over it. The boy was unconscious, his face wet with dew, one cheek and his forehead bruised. There were also bruises on his bare arms, and bits of blood where the rope had chafed his wrists and ankles. Joe touched one wrist. The blood was dry. "God help us," he murmured, looking wildly about for assistance. But he was alone. The dyke was bare, the morning quiet but for the ripping of the current through the pilings.

He felt the penetrating, narrow gazes of the gulls on his face as he bent to the wharf. It was covered in bottles and broken glass. He carefully picked up a piece of the glass and thought of sawing at the thick rope, but then realized it would be easier to untie the looser knots at the rack first, let the boy down, and untie the knots against his skin when there was more daylight.

The sky brightened further and dawn touched the boy's face gently, reddened the wounds at his wrists and ankles. Joe worked cautiously, half-expecting the boy's eyes to open any second, but they remained closed. Confused, his heart thumping, Joe kept looking up at the dyke for help, though he knew it was too early for most people to be out, especially this far from the centre of town, where only a few farmhouses were scattered over the wet fields.

But ten minutes later, after he had worked loose two of the knots, swinging the boy to one side like a hinge, Joe saw a thickset man wearing a dirty plaid shirt and suspenders appear at the top of the gangway.

"What the hell's going on!" the man shouted, stomping down the steep planks. Joe assumed from the man's manner and dress that he was the fisherman who owned the wharf.

When he arrived at the net-rack, glowering and panting, he looked ready for a fight. As calmly as his strained nerves would allow, Joe quickly explained how he'd come upon the boy, how the gulls had been pulling at the guts still tied around his waist.

"Damned lucky they didn't hang the guts off his face," the fisherman said. "Could've poked his eyes out."

"Who?" Joe asked, amazed at the man's indifference.

"Oh, that crowd of good-for-nothing wharf-rats always hanging around. He's one of them. I seen him on the river lots of times. Belongs to that fellow Raskin, I think. Yeah, that's right. That's him."

Joe squatted beside the boy, almost wanting to protect him from the man's harsh words. "What should we do with him?" he said.

"Oh hell, I don't know. I suppose we can cut the ropes off and throw a couple of sacks over him. He'll come around sooner or later."

Joe shook his head. "I think we should take him home."

The fisherman laughed, revealing a mouthful of rotten teeth. "Go ahead, but believe me, you won't get thanked for it. Raskin doesn't give a rat's ass for the kid." The man fell silent before Joe's concern, then changed his mind. "Okay, listen, let's put him in the truck and take him up to the house if it'll make you feel better. The wife'll look after him, clean him up a bit." He paused again, and stared down at the wharf. "Just look at this mess! I tell you, if he was my kid, I'd kick his ass from here to kingdom-come and back again!"

Joe recoiled from the words, wanting to argue, "But he's only a boy. Look, can't you see that he's hurt?" And suddenly a chill of memory passed through him, of times in his own childhood when he had been helpless before the taunts of others, or when he had been left by himself, cut off from what seemed like all the laughter and warmth in the world. Again, he felt a sudden urge to criticize the fisherman's attitude, but he knew it would be pointless to do so.

Instead, he remained quiet, cradling the boy's head in one arm while the fisherman untied the last two knots. The head was bristled, and in a few spots almost bare. Joe couldn't believe how light and fragile it was; there was nothing between his arm and the pulse that throbbed against it. He looked at the boy's eyes, still shut, and wondered at all the energy contained in such a tiny skull.

The fisherman finished his task, and said impatiently, "Well, let's get a move on."

Joe looked up, startled. He had almost thought he was alone with the boy.

Then, with the rope trailing from the body like seaweed, he helped carry it up the gangway and over the dyke, while the gulls dove screeching at the twined guts sinking in the current.

chapter nine

A mile inland from the river, the three o'clock bell abruptly ceased its shrill ringing, and for thirty seconds the L-shaped two-storey school building was surrounded by such a pregnant silence that its walls seemed to tremble from the pressure. Two dozen gulls and crows perched on the swings and teeter-totters, drawn there by the chance of finding some child's unwanted sandwich. But even these noisy scavengers fell quiet and fidgeted nervously, lifting and putting down their scrawny legs, one after the other, and turning their beady, blinking eyes toward the three red doors facing the playground.

Only the rain made noise, falling steadily on the soccer and baseball fields, which were, as always at this time of year, flooded, and in some low places under two feet of water. A small, black sea lapped the goalposts and backstops, but broke into streams and creeks around the playground itself, the tetherball-pole and jungle-gym, the swings, teeter-totters, and various climbing apparatus. The rain touched everything, leaving heavy drops beading on the monkey-bars and rims of the basketball hoops, shivering the flat surface of the flooded fields, running down the uncurtained windows of the classrooms, and bouncing off the cement just outside the red doors, which trembled now like oven doors burning at high temperature. Twenty-five, twenty; the pock-pock-pock of the rain counted down the seconds as the birds fidgeted and the echo of the bell's harsh cry vibrated strangely around them.

Finally, almost in unison, the doors jumped forward, the gulls and crows scattered with a mass shriek, and three bright streams poured out of the building as though it were a hive filled with coloured bees. The streams immediately swarmed together, and then broke apart again, the yellows, greens and blues flying off in all directions, some toward the black sea, some around the other side of the building to the bicycle racks, and some to where the school bus waited. The rain, as if angered by this challenge to its energy, fell even harder, darkening the sky to coal, but the children did not care. They stood in it laughing, their faces upturned, their tongues out, or just ignored it altogether, shouting at one another, scattering paper from their hands, striking out with lunchboxes and arms and legs.

From inside the school, Miss Gallagher looked out on the rain and children. The sight always made her smile, partly because it meant her workday was over, but mostly because she was grateful for the children's theft of gloom, how they swelled up into it and beat it down so easily while the coffee-soaked voices in the staff room struggled to survive these prolonged absences of the sun. A young teacher, newly hired, Miss Gallagher had no time for the gripes and complaints of her colleagues. Do we not, as teachers, have a responsibility to surround the children in our care with only positive energy? Some children, she continued thinking, have a hard enough time at home; can't we at least guarantee them light and happiness for part of each day? Reluctant to speak her thoughts aloud for fear of alienating her older and more dour colleagues, Miss Gallagher instead focussed her beliefs directly on the seven- and eight-year-olds in her care, convinced that if she did not keep them all smiling and laughing she was a failure as a teacher.

She looked back from the window to the Mawson girl fidgeting beside her desk. "Now, Zoe," she smiled, "I don't want you to worry, you're not in trouble. I just wanted to talk with you alone for a minute."

The girl, dark-eyed and dark-haired, with a pretty oval face, simply stared in response, then glanced quickly back and forth from the window to the door. She held her purple Betty and Veronica lunchbox to her chest, as though for protection, and rolled backward slightly on her heels. In her left hand she held a piece of foolscap paper on which she'd crayoned a picture of her house beside the river. In it, she'd drawn all of her family, including herself. Her father and brothers were on their boats, her mother was in bed, and she was standing across the river beside what looked like a grave (there was a cross with the word "Shamus" printed on it).

Miss Gallagher leaned closer, almost whispering. "Sweetie, is everything okay at home? You can tell me, I just want to help if there's something wrong, if you're upset about anything."

The girl shook her head and looked to the door again. Miss Gallagher frowned. She had known Zoe for almost a whole school year, yet she felt the child was still a stranger to her in a way she couldn't describe. Zoe Mawson was bright. She laughed and smiled a lot, and she took part in playground games and had friends. But there was something odd about her too. It was in her stare, Miss Gallagher had decided; the girl sometimes wore the expression of someone much older, someone who knew something but wasn't sure what to do with the information. Her assignments were always highly imaginative, if not always strictly keeping to the subject, and her questions were often downright peculiar. Once, when the crayfish had escaped from their tank in the night and were found by the janitor in the hallway the next morning, Zoe had wanted to know if crayfish could feel the stars through their shells the same way she could feel the sun through her clothes. Well, how could you answer such a question? Miss Gallagher had said that it wasn't very likely, since crayfish don't feel the way we do, to which the child responded with that disconcerting stare.

Certainly Mrs. Mawson seemed normal enough. In fact, Miss Gallagher had found her very pleasant and sweet-natured at parent-teacher interviews. A bit tired, perhaps, but many of the mothers, even those who were much younger, looked tired.

"Are you sure everything's okay at home? I hope you know, sweetie, that you can talk to me if you have a problem."

The girl nodded.

"I see that you've got your painting from today. Are you taking it home to show your parents?"

"Yes."

"I wanted to ask you, Zoe, why you drew your mother in bed. Is she not feeling well?"

"Daddy says she's tired. I'm helping with the cooking. Troy likes lots of relish and mustard on his hamburgers, and pickles, but Corbett just likes mustard. And Daddy likes his patties burnt."

Miss Gallagher smiled again, relieved to hear the child speaking like a seven-year-old. But when she looked down at Zoe's writing assignment from three weeks before, the young teacher's smile disappeared. The assignment had been to write about the fog, which Zoe had done, but she had written about it in such a peculiar way. Obviously, the family dog had died, but what was all this about a butcher carrying the animal into the yard, and about the dog being warm and the butcher's eyes being wet and the black furs on his white body and where did the heartbeats go, did they go into the man's arms or did the fog swallow them? And now, weeks later, she had drawn a picture with a grave in it and her mother asleep in bed. Surely a child should be over the death of a dog by now. And every mother gets sick from time to time, but the picture made it look as though the mother's usual place was in the bed, just as the father's was on his boat. And why was the girl shown in three different places—across the river, in the house, and beside what looked like a small store—but not one of them was the school?

"Zoe," Miss Gallagher said as gently as possible, "are you still sad about Shamus?"

The girl shook her head.

"Are you sure? You can tell me if you are, it's okay."

Zoe could see the bright jackets of the children blurred through the window, and in her desire to be outside she could not think of a way to give Miss Gallagher the answers she wanted. She liked Miss Gallagher. She was pretty and nice. But she sometimes didn't give very good answers, not like Zoe's family, who always listened to her and didn't get a funny look in their eyes when she was talking. Now she wanted to know about Shamus, but Zoe didn't want to talk about that because Miss Gallagher would get that funny look in her eyes and then she'd make her stay even longer. So Zoe shook her head again.

I'll phone her parents, the teacher resolved, I'll have them come in for an interview, just to make sure everything's fine. "All right, then, run along," she sighed, but not without some satisfaction. She felt responsible and proud whenever she tried to help one of her children, even if the results were sometimes less than what she'd hoped for. "Be careful not to get your picture wet," she added, but the child was already out the door and down the hall.

Five minutes later, Zoe was squatting at the edge of the playground's black sea, pushing into its furred depths with a stick and humming softly to herself. A younger boy joined her and said that he could skip a stone five times, did she want to see? He threw it as hard as he could but it didn't skip at all, so Zoe found a stone and threw it but hers didn't skip either, and they both laughed.

After a while, the boy wandered away, splashing through the water, and Zoe picked up her painting, soft as pulp from the rain, and reluctantly made her way homeward. Now that her mother was sick, the house was always dark and quiet, and Zoe dreaded entering it, afraid that she would find everything worse. Dawdling, she now moved from black puddle to black puddle as though they were piano keys and she was learning Chopsticks. Into each puddle she stared deeply, sometimes finding pink worms on the surface, or oily spots where someone had dropped an orange peel, but mostly she stared at her own reflection and made faces. Once, while she was bent beside the water, a boy raced through on his bicycle, splashing her, and she yelled at him and dropped her picture, which became so wet that the colours smeared. She broke it into wet pieces as she walked along toward town.

Eventually, she reached the butcher shop and peered through the rainy window. The butcher was behind the counter wrapping something for a customer. Zoe stared at him and heard, as always, his voice repeat "The dog was alive when I found him." The words thrilled her; it was as though an adult had really spoken directly to her for the first time, as though he had spoken only to her. Zoe watched his arms moving slowly through the blurred glass, and imagined them lifting Shamus up out of the fog as he whimpered and they looked at each other with sad eyes.

Whenever she pictured the man bending down to pick up her dog, she always smiled and felt comforted. And sometimes she even wondered how the man felt, if finding Shamus really meant anything to him, or if he had forgotten all about it.

One day, when she was looking through the window, the butcher stared back at her and moved toward the door. But Zoe was too shy to talk with him, so she had run off, excitedly, believing in her heart that the man knew how she was feeling. That was why he'd spoken those words, "The dog was alive when I found him," because he understood without even asking that Zoe was curious about that. Almost always, adults—except for her parents (and they only sometimes)—did not seem to understand what Zoe was thinking, or at least they pretended not to care. But the butcher was different. For Zoe, he was part of a larger, all-encompassing interest in the meanderings of her own imagination, in the wonderful, unanswerable questions that lay in the guts of salmon and in the depths of puddles. She studied the man's movements as though he were a piece of chalk scribbling a new language on a blackboard; if she watched him long enough, maybe she could learn the words to answer her own thoughts.

After a while, she continued on her way, taking the familiar shortcut through the vacant lot of tall grass and blackberry bushes and then along the bottom of the dyke near the government wharf. She remembered that the river was open and decided to climb the big cherry tree at the end of the street to look for her father's and brother's boats on the Prairie Drift. But the rain was too heavy and the sky too dark to see beyond the harbour, so she climbed back down and walked the remaining half-block home.

She took the key from under the garbage can at the side of the house and unlocked the door into the kitchen. It was dark and quiet. Zoe hoped every day that her mother would be feeling better, but now, after so long, she had adapted a little to her mother's absence and even enjoyed doing more things around the house; it made her feel bigger. But on those days when fishing was open and the house was dark and empty, Zoe still felt very small and frightened, so she always went down the hall to check on her mother.

The bedroom was close and even darker than the kitchen. A bowl of tomato soup, untouched, and a piece of toast, were on the TV table beside the bed.

"Mommy, are you awake?" Zoe moved closer to the motionless form under the covers. She waited.

The form stirred, rolled over, and her mother's large eyes opened up to her. In a weak voice, Kathleen whispered, "Hi, sweetheart," and unclenched her fist at the same time.

Zoe put her hand in her mother's, and sat on the edge of the bed. Her mother's hand was hot and moist. "Are you feeling better yet?"

"Zoe, precious Zoe," her mother said, closing her eyes. When she opened them again, they were brimming with tears.

"What's the matter, Mommy? Are you going to be sick? Do you want the bucket?" Zoe looked frantically around the room, but her mother just squeezed her hand, then whispered, "I'm fine, just tired. Why don't you go watch cartoons, honey, okay? Mommy wants to sleep. That's a good girl."

Zoe leaned forward and kissed her mother's forehead, which, unlike her hand, was cold and dry. Her mother smiled weakly and rolled over. Zoe left the room, quietly pulling the door behind her.

Soon, with a bag of potato chips and a glass of milk beside her on the hardwood floor, she was sitting cross-legged in front of the TV set, its blue glow the only light showing in the house as twilight deepened and became darkness.

Hours later, when her father came in for a bite of supper and to check to see if she was all right, Zoe was fast asleep, the milk spilled out in a curved line from her body, and shining in the gloom like a rib.

chapter ten

D ays later, Chilukthan was still soaked with puddles and prey to steady, black rains. But when the sun finally broke through early one afternoon, it seemed the dawn had just been delayed for several hours. Everything appeared fresh and new, and the sudden warmth turned the waterfront into a steam bath. Quickly, the moisture burned off, the haze of drizzle lifted, and fishermen left their net-sheds to work and converse on the wharf and on the decks of their moored gillnetters.

The government wharf, on the mainland side of Chilukthan Harbour, was no more than a lily-pad collection of small, planked surfaces floated on thick logs. There were a dozen surfaces in all, starting with the large one on pilings at the level of the dyke (it never moved, being built above the high-tide line, and was connected to a sizable netshed). From there, a rickety gangway, hinged to allow movement with the tide, led down to the smaller patchwork-quilt of tiny wharves to which various fishermen tied their boats. These wharves, jumbled together and covered with nets, net-racks, engine parts, stained buoys and bright red life-jackets, and a wide assortment of junk, stretched two hundred fathoms farther up the harbour. Directly across from this long, linked float, only a stone's throw away on the opposite bank, was an equally makeshift collection of netsheds and wharves. When fishing was closed and the fleet tied up, boats, often moored three or four to a spot, so crammed the channel that you could almost walk across the harbour by jumping from deck to deck.

The Mawsons shared a netshed on the far bank, but when the

weather was fair they worked on the government wharf at the end farthest from the gangway. Here, they could be out in the open air among other fishermen, soaking up the sun and listening to the talk.

This particular afternoon, Vic stood in the stern of *Old Betsy*, rolling the drum, while Troy and Corbett, facing each other across a net-rack, pulled on the corkline and leadline respectively, keeping up with their father's pace. By separating the net in this fashion, they hung it on the rack so that the torn meshes could be seen and more easily mended.

The harbour was quiet except for the sound of the drum being turned and the two lines slapping against the rack. Down by the gangway, two fishermen were sitting on crates, exchanging views on the poor fishing, but their voices carried away on the breeze. Periodically, a gull cried from the cannery roof and wheeled away oceanward, or a blue heron squawked as it rose from the rushes on the far bank and flew clumsily over the river.

Troy suddenly felt the heat of the sun heavy on his neck and shoulders. "Wait a sec, Dad," he said, and dropped the corkline. With a quick motion, he removed his T-shirt and flung it on the wharf. The other two paused, Vic with the heel of one hand against the drum, and Corbett loosely holding the leadline like a rein. The silence deepened for a few seconds, then the work resumed.

But the blur of white shirt seemed to have changed the mood. For twenty minutes, each had dwelled on the same thought but either didn't want, or know how, to broach the subject. Now Troy, sensing that he had put a crack in the silence, turned again to his father. "How's Mom today?"

Vic looked up. Two or three starlings darted through the sky high above the dyke. He slowly turned to watch them land in the cottonwoods across the channel. Then he took a drag on the cigarette dangling from his lips, and exhaled with a sigh. "The same," he said evenly.

Troy nodded and glanced across the rack at his brother. Corbett showed little expression beyond mild interest. The two had not spoken of their mother's health except to ask each other how she was feeling from time to time, especially when either of them had been away from the house for an extended period. For the first few days, they had simply assumed she had the flu, but when a week had passed and she still ventured out of the bedroom only to use the bathroom, the brothers began to feel her absence as something unusual. By not talking about it, they hoped the situation would resolve itself. So they avoided the house as much as possible, ate out often, and concentrated on what they felt they could control—their own lives.

Troy, whose worrying nature brought him closer to his mother on some emotional level, felt her prolonged absence more keenly. Yet only in the past few days had he realized that neither his father nor his older brother planned to take any steps to remedy the situation. Their inaction irritated him enough that he finally decided to address the problem.

"Shouldn't we get the doctor in? There could be something really wrong."

Vic watched another starling speed above his son's head and settle in the cottonwoods. He had expected the subject of Kathleen to come up at some point, but he did not relish speaking about something so clearly beyond his understanding. And he especially did not want to talk about it with his sons, neither of whom was old enough to understand the first thing about life, and certainly not about living with a woman.

"She doesn't want a doctor," he finally responded, flicking his cigarette into the river. "She just wants to sleep."

Troy, tapping one of the corks with a closed fist, nodded respectfully before speaking again. "But she's been sleeping for almost two weeks. How much sleep does she need?"

"Whatever sleep she needs is what she needs," Corbett said, annoyed. He too was concerned about his mother, but he couldn't believe she was seriously ill. Even if she were, he believed in his father's ability to do the right thing at the right time.

Troy opened his fist and smacked the cork. "What does that mean?" he said with scorn. "Whatever she needs? I don't think it's normal for anybody to need two straight weeks of sleep." He glared at Corbett; lately, Troy had lost patience with his brother's laid-back attitude, believing it masked a basic laziness.

Corbett leaned forward over the wooden rack, his hair brushing the bunched meshes of the net. "And I guess you're the expert on sleep, eh? Studied it in school, did you?"

Troy was about to respond when his father interrupted.

"She's just really tired. She just needs a good rest." Vic scowled and put his hand back on the drum.

"That's right," Corbett agreed. "She's just tired."

Troy hesitated, then looked straight at his brother and forgot about his father for a moment. "Oh come off it, she's more than just tired. Haven't you noticed anything different lately? She doesn't pay attention half the time you're talking to her."

Corbett tugged at the leadline and shrugged. "I don't blame her if you're the one doing the talking."

"Yeah, very funny, but you know what I mean. There's something more than tired going on."

"Like what?" Corbett snapped. He looked at his father, hoping for support, but he was staring tight-lipped at Troy.

Troy didn't notice. He was still glaring at Corbett. "How should I know? I'm not a doctor. But we should at least get someone in to look at her. Maybe she's really sick."

"Are you deaf?" Corbett yelled. "Dad says she doesn't want a doctor!"

"Okay, and if someone was drowning and didn't want help, would you just stand there and let her sink?"

"Nobody's sinking. And where do you get off telling Dad what he should do?"

"I'm not telling him," Troy argued, growing red in the face. "I'm just saying that we ought to make sure there's not something really wrong."

"As if you know anything about women," Corbett sneered. "Come on, smart guy, tell us everything you know about women and sickness."

Troy shook his head in disgust. "Oh, I forgot, you're God's gift to women. I guess making out with sixteen-year-olds makes you an expert, eh? Well, I hate to be the one to break it to you, but Mom's not sixteen."

"Shut up, the both of you!" Vic cut in, tired of their squabbling, which only heightened his sense of his sons as boys rather than young men. "You don't know what you're talking about," he said more quietly, looking first at Troy, then Corbett. Finally, he began turning the drum again. Another fathom of net landed with a thump in the stern.

Corbett and Troy took the hint. Soon only the faint creak of the drum and the slapping of leadline and corkline sounded underneath the intermittent noise of the starlings still flocking darkly into the cottonwoods.

After a while, Vic squinted up at the birds. The unusual number of them made him even more anxious than the argument about Kathleen. What was going on lately, he wondered. Nothing seemed as it should.

He lowered his gaze just in time to see Ed Leary stride across the gap between two tiny wharves and stand towering over Troy. Ed was a broad, powerfully built fisherman, perhaps a half-dozen years older than Vic, with a bushy, salt-and-pepper beard which, along with his stare, was the most striking feature of his weathered, round face. His eyes, two perfect dark circles between his tight skullcap and beard, seemed to move forward when he spoke, like camera lenses. The effect was caused simply by his tendency to lean forward as a way to punctuate his words, but listeners often felt they were being studied, judged, and found wanting. Although Vic had known and respected the man for over twenty years, he experienced the same discomfort around him. Even without the stare, and the reputation for speaking his mind no matter how unpopular his views, Ed Leary was an intimidating person.

He stepped past Troy toward the boat, and nodded. "Afternoon, Victor. See you hooked a few snags this week." He stared at the drum with an almost affectionate regard. "Not too much damage, I hope."

"No, nothing more than usual. Just enough to keep these characters out of trouble." Vic instinctively leaned away from the penetrating eyes. Ed was the only person who called him Victor, which wasn't his full name, but Vic had never bothered to correct him, and it was far too late and unimportant to do so now.

"The good old Prairie Drift, eh? Jesus Christ, what a rat's nest that is!" He laughed, deep and long, then stopped abruptly; the effect was like a gun going off. He motioned toward Troy and Corbett with his head. "These young fellas joined up?"

Vic nodded, falling easily into the joking patter most fishermen used with each other. "Sure, their mother wouldn't let them in the house otherwise."

"Good, good," Ed smiled, but seemed distracted. High above him, another, larger flock of starlings, thick as a five o'clock shadow, stubbled the sky. "Looks like we're in for a fight this year on prices," he finally said.

"So I hear," Vic replied, his suspicion confirmed that Ed's visit wasn't merely social, but part of his job as the local union rep.

Ed continued, frowning: "The companies want to cut sockeye by a cent, and pinks by three. Can't make a decent living off that. Most of the boys are pretty unhappy about it, ready to take a stand if they have to."

He reached out and fingered the loose web while the silence built up around him. Then he adjusted his body to face all of the Mawsons at once. So much energy flowed out of him that it seemed as if his large shadow was wrestling the ground. "How about you fellas? You prepared to walk if it comes to that?"

Vic had known the question was coming, though he suspected it was aimed more at Corbett and Troy. But he answered for all of them. "Don't you know me well enough by now not to have to ask that question?"

Ed looked genuinely apologetic, and immediately softened his voice. "Sorry, Victor, it's just that these days, well, it's not like it was ten years ago. We're always hearing talk of guys breaking away, saying they'd cross lines to fish. We just want to make sure you fellas are on side, that you're getting the whole story."

Vic scowled. He was damned if Ed Leary or any man was going to stand there and teach him anything about being a good union member. "You're wasting your time here, Ed. My boys aren't scabs."

"Come on, Victor, I'm not saying that."

"Sure sounds like it."

Ed seemed embarrassed, but stubborn. "Listen, I could hear the arguing all the way up by the shed. Things were sounding pretty heated."

Vic's voice also grew quieter. "That was something else. Nothing to do with fishing."

"Oh?"

"You wouldn't be calling me a liar, Ed, would you?"

"No, no, no," Ed hurried on, "if you say it was something else, it was something else. Christ, Victor, I'm sorry, it's just that this

goddamned industry is so full of selfish bastards now that I sometimes forget who I'm talking to. Some of these young guys
especially think they don't need a union, think they can just go it
on their own, every man for himself. It gets tiring having to
explain the world to them. It's like they're little babies, for chrissakes, and you gotta wipe their asses and spoonfeed them. Ah, if
we could just spend our time fighting the companies and the
politicians instead of ourselves . . ." His voice trailed off sadly.
Then he turned and glanced at the sky. A steady stream of starlings was pouring across the harbour.

"More birds than fish," he grinned, then looked back at Vic.
"There's a meeting called for next week. Just thought you should
know about it, it's important. We'll be putting the posters up with
the time and place."

"All right," Vic said. "Thanks."

Simultaneously, the four men became aware of the increased
noise around them, an incessant high-pitched chatter flooding
down from the cottonwoods. It was as though the afternoon had
gone mad with its own silence.

"Goddamn," Ed said, his eyes training in on the trees, "would
you look at that!"

Thousands of starlings had swarmed the trees, turning them
into tall pillars of shivering ash. And still more flocks poured over
the dyke to settle in the branches.

"Must be too much water in the fields," Vic mused, again
uneasy at the sight. The sheer number of birds provided a noisy,
dark swirl that seemed like something a person could drown in.
"Greedy things," he said, irritated. "Real nest-robbers."

The men stood silently watching the black wake ripple the
trees, which had now almost disappeared under the massing
flocks. Several people had gathered on the dyke, drawn by the
noise and the streaming darkness in the sky.

A skiff containing three wharf-rats puttered slowly down from
farther up the harbour. One of the rats was Raskin's boy. As the
skiff passed the wharf where the Mawsons and Ed Leary stood, the
boy turned blankly to look at Troy and Corbett, his eyes like bruises below his pale brow, his mouth like the slice in a fish's belly.
Then he quickly looked away.

Troy recognized him vaguely from the day of the fog, but he

had more important things on his mind now. A strike! That would ruin everything. Over the past month, Troy had decided that he'd fish by himself, earn as much as he could in the summer, and then take his time in the fall and winter to look around for another job. With a nice nest-egg built up, he felt he could be choosy, not have to rush into something he didn't like because he was desperate for money. But a strike! No, that would be a disaster. Of course, he also thought, if it was short and we made the companies keep the prices up, I'd have an even bigger nest-egg. But that was a real gamble. Damn!

The starlings' screeches increased in volume and drew more people from town to the dyke, including a couple of girls Corbett knew. He pointed at them, made a chattering motion with his hands, and laughed when they took his meaning. A teaser and a joker, that was his reputation, and he tried to live up to it whenever possible. As for the argument and the imminent strike, his father knew what was best for the family, and the union knew what was best for its members. Simple. Meanwhile, baseball season had started, the weather would soon be warmer, he had a chance of getting his own boat for the sockeye runs, and he was having a great time with Margo Petrovich. Except for his mother being sick, life couldn't be better.

The two older men were less able to overlook the strange presence of the starlings. Both understood the gravity of labour action, as both had been through it many times before. The unending noise and the shivering black in the sky helped to dampen their spirits. It was as though all the possible violence and tension of the weeks to come were being played out in a condensed version directly in front of their eyes.

Suddenly, one of the boys in the skiff raised a shotgun, shouted "Fucking birds!" and blasted into the trees. The starlings, screeching even louder, exploded into flight, choking the sky and flooding over the river.

chapter eleven

*E*arlier that day, Vic had wakened at first light, using the same internal alarm clock he used on the river, not trusting the mechanical variety. Zoe had no need to be readied for school for a couple of hours, so he'd stared at the ceiling, trying again to figure out what he should be doing for his wife. Kathleen, fitfully asleep beside him, showed no signs of coming out of the depression she'd been in for nearly two weeks, but whenever Vic suggested that the doctor be called, she insisted that she'd be fine, that she was just tired. Then she'd turn away to hide her tears, and he was left to wonder if he should call the doctor against her wishes.

But if she said she was fine, wasn't that enough? In all their married years, through the deaths of their child and parents, through the births and child-rearing, the poor fishing seasons and shortage of money, Vic had come to rely on Kathleen's uncomplaining strength. Seeing her now in such a vulnerable state was a mystery he had never before had to confront. Each morning, he expected to hear her moving around in the kitchen, and each night he expected to be greeted with a kiss at the door and a series of questions about his day—who he'd talked with, what the fishing had been like, whether he'd heard any rumours about the season ahead.

But as the days passed and Kathleen remained in bed, Vic began to imagine his life without her steadying presence, and the thought filled him with a sadness so deep it was hardly distinguishable from fear. More and more, he fell back on his faith in her ability to endure hardship. To do otherwise meant to lose faith in his entire world, in the cycle of the salmon that kept his family fed, in the tides and winds.

Yet as he lay in bed, Vic could not quell the fear entirely; it forced him to look at his wife in a new way, to try to imagine what it meant, emotionally, to be this woman sleeping at his side. Because he could not find a more obvious reason for what ailed her, he settled on the loss of their child. Vic knew well the anniversary of that death, and since it coincided with the beginning of Kathleen's illness, he accepted it as the cause of the latter, overlooking the fact that she had faced the loss with her customary strength every other year, relieving him of the burden of her pain so he could concentrate on his own, which was brief, and cold, and disturbingly resonant with the squelch of a spade into the wet earth.

He thought of it again now, the lonely drive to the cemetery, the trickle of his flashlight beam through the tombs to the bluff, the smell of the earth and the sound of his digging. It had been a strange and unnerving experience, reminiscent only of a certain patrol he'd been on in the North Atlantic during the war.

His ship, HMCS *Comox*, regularly patrolled the rough waters off Nova Scotia, usually to clear mines from the area around Halifax Harbour, but sometimes to chaperone a convoy or to pick up survivors and bodies after U-boat attacks. One twilight, in the middle of winter, with ice on the decks and a thin mist rising off the sea, the *Comox* was called out to look for survivors from a number of merchant marine ships that had been sunk while on their way into Halifax.

The thick stench of burning oil filled the air, making it hard to breathe, but that was easier to cope with than the sound of drowning men. Their cries punctuated the eerie calm as the ship drifted slowly through the darkness, its spotlights raking the low mist. Vic, who had been relieved by another telegrapher on that particular patrol, stood on deck, peering into the gloom, every cry freezing his blood. Afraid for himself, and pitying the men in the water, he felt the same desire to scream out, to issue the same urgent plea to be raised from his terrifying situation as if by the hands of a god.

But there were no hands except those trembling on the rail in front of him, and no eyes except his own lighting on the body floating in the sea, face-down with long blond hair billowing out around it, as though the death already involved a departure of the soul, the ethereal leaking out from the skull and shoulders. Vic watched the body rise up on the swells, and the white nimbus shimmering around it. The screams in the mist took on a scavenging sound, as though great birds had gathered around the ring of flaming oil to feed off any unrecovered bodies. And even when the body had been brought on board, and the face revealed, young as Vic's own, the hair would not quite release it, but clung to the brow and cheeks like the arms of a starfish to a rock. What an awful sound that heavy, waterlogged body made when it was dragged across the metal deck, the same sloshing, Vic would realize years later, that a deadhead makes when it rolls around in a net, the sound of water taking its own back.

Burning oil, wet graves, tangled shapes: sometimes he could not keep the dramatic moments of his life separate. Was it the salmon that had the life strangled out of them as they thrashed, or was it children? Were those simply gulls crying above the coal-oil lantern burning at the end of his net? When he sank his gaff into the head of a spring, why did it sound as though the earth instead of bone was being split open? In nightmares that came most often when his sleep was already troubled by the anxieties of his waking life, Vic saw these images conflated into grotesque scenarios: he digs a grave on a bluff only to find salmon swimming in it, a doctor hands him the bloodsoaked head of a man in a blanket, he drifts into the North Atlantic in his gillnetter, picking bodies from his net, he pushes a wheelbarrow full of blond hair through the streets of Halifax. Waking with the sweats, and even sometimes crying out, Vic nevertheless managed to dismiss these troubling images completely from his mind. Because there was no guilt or remorse associated with them, they did not torment him at a conscious level. If he had let a man drown, if he had willed his child to die, if he had poached fish from the river, then these images might have filtered into his waking life and forced him to confront his past and therefore his present and future. But drama had simply happened to him; he had not sought it out. Now, he wanted only to avoid it, to make a set on the river free of snags, to enjoy his daughter while she was still a child, to have a quiet and undemanding home life.

But of these desires, only one was currently in reach, and so Vic concentrated on looking after his daughter.

He did so now, getting out of bed, getting dressed, and stepping quietly into Zoe's room. She was asleep on her back in a pile of stuffed animals, her face so calm that he stood over her for several seconds, trying to imagine what dreams she might be having, this little girl whose imagination always struck him as miraculous. A deep one, Kathleen called her, and he had to agree. But it was a pure joy to watch Zoe's face go still with only her eyes wild and open, so like her mother's, and to hear such strange questions come out of her mouth, questions that forced him almost every day to look at his world again, and then once more. How come the blossoms on the cherry trees and the apple trees are different colours, but the cherries and the apples are both red? That had been the latest puzzler, and he couldn't answer it, could only smile at her and shrug and say that he'd give it some serious thought and let her know if he came up with the answer. This had seemed to satisfy her. Zoe moved so quickly from one subject to the next that she appeared to be less interested in answers than in finding new questions.

Vic looked around the room. The morning light angling in through the window brought a number of gnarled objects into view, various pieces of driftwood that he had brought home for Zoe over the past three years. Any unusual shape carved and polished by the tide and tangled in his net always wound up on top of the cabin, so that when he came home the next morning, there would always be a little gift for her. Vic loved to hear what she'd say each piece of driftwood resembled, especially when he'd imagined the same, because that proved to him in some small but significant way that they shared an intellectual as well as an emotional bond. Yes, she was a deep one, but she was their daughter, she lived in their world, and that knowledge was a great comfort to her parents, who sometimes feared Zoe was growing away from them too quickly.

But she was just a seven-year-old child when Vic finally woke her. She hugged him, and he helped her to choose what clothes to wear. Then he went into the kitchen to make her breakfast and to pack her lunch for school. All of these domestic details were new to him, and consequently he did not do them well, nor did he

have any interest in doing them better. Zoe had the same breakfast and the same lunch every day, just as the family had a limited
menu for supper each night. Sandwiches and canned soup, hamburgers and canned soup, grilled cheese and canned soup; there
were few variations. And Vic's care of Kathleen was equally limited, built on toast, canned soup, cups of sweet, milky tea, and
aspirin, most of which she didn't touch anyway, except for the
aspirin. He had a bachelor's slack habits and a bachelor's indifference to changing them, though what he missed during
Kathleen's absence was so much more than her domestic management; he missed the immense feeling of emotional shelter that
she provided. But just as he was content to be no better and no
worse than most fishermen in terms of how much money he
made, his acceptance of himself with regard to his marriage was
equally uncomplicated. He worked, and Kathleen worked, and
together they got by, plain and simple. But if Kathleen couldn't
work, how long would it be before the getting-by became impossible? Ten more days? A month?

Vic tried not to think about it. He saw Zoe off to school, then
went back to bed and slept until half past twelve, when the phone
woke him. As always, he let it ring, six times, seven times, eight
times until it stopped. Answering the phone was something else
Kathleen had always done; Vic had no interest in talking with people when he couldn't see their faces.

But the ringing reminded him of the one exception he had
made, a phone call he had never told anyone about, not even
Kathleen.

A few days after they had lost the child, Vic brought Kathleen
home. As she was still very weak and grief-stricken, he answered
the phone one morning so that it wouldn't wake her. It was someone from the hospital, telling him that he had to dispose of the
body of his son.

"I beg your pardon?" he said, not understanding. He had
assumed that because the child was stillborn the hospital would be
responsible for the body.

"We need you to claim your child's body," the voice repeated,
clinical and cold.

"Yes, all right," Vic finally managed to respond. "I'll be there
this afternoon."

He asked his mother to come over to the house, and then borrowed his father's truck and took the ferry across the river to the city. Everything afterwards was a blur of forms and signatures and long hallways and official expressions and nurses' uniforms, until finally he was driving across the Granville Street Bridge again with a black metal container on the seat beside him and the sound of the windshield wipers like a wet heartbeat filling the cab.

Waiting for the ferry on Lulu Island, Vic decided he would not share this experience with anyone. What good would it do if more than one person had the image of their dead child lying cold in a metal box in a hospital room, unnamed, waiting for a dignified end to its sad journey? Kathleen certainly did not need to know. It would be best to keep this private, to act as though he had known all along what the hospital procedure was, to say that he had requested a few days of quiet reflection before he picked up the body. And even then, Vic decided he would only tell his father, who could help with the burial arrangements. He would tell him that the body had been kept in a private room, in a small coffin with the name Mawson inscribed on it.

Never in his life had Vic known such a strange and intense half hour as that drive from the hospital back to Chilukthan with his son's wasting body beside him. Yet somehow, those moments had calmed rather than deepened his grief. He realized slowly that he had been given a rare opportunity to complete the cycle of his child's brief life, that he had been placed behind the wheel to share this last part of the journey, which would end with the soft hole on the bluff and the lowering for the last time of the small weight in his hands. A kind of gratitude mingled with his sadness. He could almost hear the child breathing contentedly beside him. On that drive, Vic believed he understood something that he'd never known before, that death was not as final as the world maintained and that any heart could go on beating so long as it was added to another, so long as it formed an underpulse to the rhythm of memory.

Yet the drive had been so extraordinary that Vic could not bring himself to answer the phone again, for fear that it would tarnish the private and cherished memory of his diminishing grief.

Now, once the ringing had stopped, he leaned over and kissed

Kathleen on the neck. She didn't stir. So he got up, dressed, and went into the bathroom. Five minutes later, he went into the kitchen, where Troy was making himself a sandwich. Corbett was still asleep in the boys' bedroom.

Vic plugged the kettle in for tea, told Troy to make it for him, and stretched out on the couch in the living room to stare out the window and worry about the lack of fish. He smoked cigarette after cigarette while rubbing his temples, until it seemed that the smoke came from the friction of his fingers against his skull.

Finally, after worrying for nearly an hour, he went back down the hall, rousted Corbett from his bed, and told him to come down to the wharf. Then he looked in on Kathleen again.

She lay awake, curled in the foetal position. Vic watched her for a while, feeling sympathy and helplessness in equal portions. He could not help thinking of other times he had walked in on her in bed, such as that February of their first year of marriage. Again, his memory touched on graves, the sloping cemetery in Dartmouth nearby where they'd rented a cheap room. Newlyweds unable to stay apart after Vic's official leave, they had decided that Kathleen would move to Nova Scotia to be near the *Comox*. The arrangement hadn't lasted long, since he twice failed to report back to his ship, and was threatened with disciplinary action unless, in the words of the captain, he sent his wife home immediately. But while it did last, how wonderful it was to climb up through the weathered tombs of Portuguese fishermen, eighteenth-century stones deep with snow and white and sparkling as his navy uniform, how wonderful in the crisp air to be following the urgency of his breath and his pulse through the meandering rows, how wonderful to take the key from his pocket and unlock the door behind which his young bride was sleeping and quickly undress and slide into the warmth beside her.

How many years ago now? Vic looked down at his wife's dark form, and a chill went through him. Why couldn't this still be a cheap room in Dartmouth? Why couldn't the woman lying in the bed turn to him with so much light in her face that he'd be blinded again and again into amazement at his good fortune? And how had the meaningless, shining graves of youth so rapidly become personal and black as char? Nothing had changed but time. Vic felt that if only he could stand in one spot long enough, then maybe time would work the same effects in reverse. But he knew he couldn't do that.

"I'm going down to rack the net," he said softly. "Do you want anything before I go? A cup of tea, some toast?"

Kathleen managed a weak smile, but her face was heavy, puffed and dark around the eyes. In a listless voice, she asked for another blanket to be put over her, then rolled onto her back and blinked until tears fell from her lashes. Vic could not see them in the faint light, but he knew nothing had changed; it was as though the depression was so much her own business that he became a trespasser whenever he took hesitant and futile steps toward understanding it. Gently, he laid the blanket over her and then left the house.

An hour later, with the wharf-rats' shotgun blasts still echoing over the river, and the starlings thick and noisy in the sky, Vic turned toward the gangway to see Zoe hurrying down it, her bright red sweater under the mass of birds like an ember burning through a heap of ash.

Meanwhile, the boys in the skiff had finally stopped shooting, and the crowd on the dyke had dispersed. Ed Leary followed Vic's look, saw the girl rushing toward them, and suddenly felt a deep misgiving about the future. Children. What kind of world were they going to inherit, after all? The impending strike already depressed him, but he knew it was necessary, though knowing that didn't make the situation any easier. He thought of all the struggles he'd faced over the years to organize the fishermen so they could protect themselves, so they could receive a fair share of the profits of the industry. And what good had it done if the same basic battles had to be fought again, over and over, with always a new crop of young fellows so brainwashed by capitalist rhetoric that they believed they'd do just fine on their own, that they fancied themselves as entrepreneurs who could weather all the storms of market forces? Ah, it was a losing battle. When he was younger, Ed believed the fighting was sufficient, but now he was tired of the lack of progress, tired of having to convince the very people who should have shared his outrage of the necessity for mistrusting authority, for keeping a wary eye on the politicians and the big money that bankrolled them. It was bad enough fighting the courts and the media, but to have to fight the workers too?

Ed watched the girl rush toward them, and he resolved, as always, to give the bastards hell one more time. Bring on the Red slurs, bring on the letters to the editor, bring on the court injunctions: he'd been through it all before, and what was one more fight with a world thick with chattering, nest-robbing, greedy starlings compared to the alternative of just giving in? Sure, it might be futile, but when had it ever been anything else? Around and around we go, he thought, as the girl swept past him and into her father's arms. Unconvinced by his own pep talk, Ed nevertheless chuckled deeply, winked at the girl who was staring at him, then turned to go.

"Who's that?" Zoe whispered, struck by the man's girth and thick beard.

"That's Mr. Leary," Vic told her. "He's the man who helps us get lots of money for our fish."

"How?"

Corbett suddenly reached in and began to tickle her. "He snaps his fingers and turns them into dollar bills, that's how."

Zoe squirmed and giggled, but she kept her eyes on the man as he walked up the gangway and disappeared over the dyke. Then Vic put her down on the wharf, and told her to stay close by while they finished racking the net.

When the job was done, Vic and Zoe headed home. Troy and Corbett, sullen and quiet, got into their cars at the foot of the dyke and drove off in different directions.

The bright, warm afternoon grew dull again toward twilight just as Vic had decided to do some work in the backyard. He had to get rid of the caterpillar nests in the cherry and apple trees, a process which involved wrapping a gasoline-soaked rag on the end of a long stick, lighting the rag on fire, and then burning the nests, all the while being careful to snuff out the flames before they spread to the rest of the tree. As Vic raised the stick into the branches, Zoe asked him why the caterpillars had nests and the bees had hives.

"Birds have nests," she said, "but caterpillars don't fly, so how come they have nests and bees don't? Bees fly so they should have nests like the birds."

Vic nodded, lowered the stick for a moment, then responded: "Well, caterpillars grow into butterflies, and butterflies fly like birds, so that's why they have nests." He was satisfied with this answer; it seemed logical in some way.

But Zoe frowned as she squinted up at the burning branch.

"Will they still be butterflies after we burn them?"

"No, honey."

"Why not?"

Vic hesitated, then decided against telling the full truth. "Maybe they will be, maybe somewhere else."

The white gauze of the nest sizzled over them, and a few caterpillars rained down on the grass. It was darkening quickly, and the small flame burned brighter and brighter, ash peeling away like thicker pieces of twilight. Vic torched several more nests and now the night itself seemed to be burning and crackling. Bits of white smoke, thin and fuzzy-looking as the caterpillars, drifted out of sight high over the branches.

Finally, the nests began to fall to the earth, as the fire ate through the thin branch ends. One after another, like shooting stars, the nests crashed down and hissed in the wet grass. Vic walked slowly to the first dull light and stamped on it. Zoe, seeing this, moved farther away to inspect one of the still-burning piles. Inside the flames, caterpillars squirmed, little black shapes, dozens and dozens of them, just like tadpoles netted from a ditch.

Vic finally reached her, and waited while she finished her inspection. He did not mind killing things in her presence. It was foolish to try to hide death from a fisherman's daughter who had seen the blood and guts of salmon almost all of her life, but sometimes he worried that he didn't know enough about this great mystery to answer her questions. It also struck him how rarely he'd ever pondered death on his own, despite the intimate, almost daily experience he'd had of it. How many fish had he killed in the last twenty-five years? Thousands, tens of thousands, but that had been barely enough to eke out a living. What would prosperity be, he wondered, all of the starlings and the caterpillars and the salmon killed and added together? He watched his daughter poke a stick into the dying flame and felt an overwhelming desire to protect her from the smoke and the surrounding night and the hard facts of killing. What was the difference, oil burning on the sea, gasoline burning at the end of a stick, salmon blood burning under your boots as you leaned over to gaff another one?

Vic turned toward the back of the house. No light shone in the bedroom window. The house itself might have fallen from a branch and sizzled out in the grass.

"Come on, Princess," he said gently, "it's too dark." He stamped on the final burning nest, over which Zoe hovered, watching the brightness close like a red mouth under his boot.

chapter twelve

Kathleen believed she had no more reason to be depressed in her forty-fourth year than she had in any of the previous ten. She had long ago lost her parents and a baby, she had always been concerned about money, and she had carried memories of grief and poverty around with her since childhood. The rains fell hard each year, the long months of twilight and drizzle came and went, the salmon and pheasants and mallards were gutted in the sink beside the counter where the pears and cherries and tomatoes were canned. She faced her world with common sense, energy, and a sort of nonchalant satisfaction on the best days, and with stoic resignation on the worst. What could one expect from life after all? You worked hard and you made the best of things. Kathleen repeatedly drew on her mother's store of simple expressions: "The Lord helps those who help themselves," "Idle hands are the devil's workshop," "What's done is done; there's no use crying over spilt milk."

Besides, her life, as she well knew, was not without stretches of almost unimaginable joy and contentment. Some days she felt such an intense love for her family that she actually paused in the middle of whatever she was doing simply to marvel at her good fortune. Over the years, she had come to feel the same way about Chilukthan, its sodden maze of fields and sloughs and gravel roads, the intoxicating freshness that its heavy rains brought out of the earth, even in winter, and the mild temperatures and the long crimson sunsets over the delta, the gulls and the bald eagles circling, drifting high on the wind currents. To think that she had been born and raised in the middle of Toronto and had wound up married to a salmon fisherman on the coast of British Columbia! Looking back, she could not imagine how it had happened. The sheer unlikeliness of the change still amazed her; where had she found the courage, and how had she managed to make it all happen? On the good days, these questions made her feel like someone out of the ordinary, someone other than herself, a woman capable of disappearing from one world and reappearing in a completely different one thousands of miles away.

But this sense of power did not keep the bad days from eventually exerting a stronger pull. For so long, she had built her life over an old and sinking foundation of grief, inadequacy, and loss. Suddenly, when she returned to the distant past for the little emotional comfort it had once given her, the whole structure of her world, crossbeamed with a long history of inherited pain, rotted, sagged, and collapsed.

Three weeks had passed since she'd taken the crocuses to the cemetery. Now, by a sheer effort of the will, she began to fight her way back. As inexplicably as the depression had set in, it diminished. Kathleen had found just enough energy to keep the darkness from washing her away completely. Zoe's daily visits, the feel of her hand and sound of her voice, the warmth of Vic's body against her each night, the smell of rain and wind in his hair, the ringing of the telephone, the heavy footsteps of Troy and Corbett, their bedroom light switching off and on, the scent of meat cooking, the sunlight drying the raindrops on the window and throwing shadows across the bed, birdsong at daybreak, the whistle of the coal train, Vic's even, measured breaths, the beating of her own heart: all of these were strands in a small net that lifted her, very slowly, out of what she remembered and into what she could still experience.

One still morning in early May, with Vic breathing gently beside her, Kathleen re-entered the world. She got out of bed, put on her housecoat and slippers, and left the bedroom with no intention of immediately returning.

She looked in on Zoe, but her bed was empty. Corbett and Troy, however, were sound asleep in their own room, which, when Kathleen opened the door, emitted the rank smell of sweat, cigarette smoke and stale beer. A pile of change and keys glistened on the hardwood floor between the two beds, and clothes were scattered everywhere. The boys themselves, one on his stomach and the other on his back, snored loudly, with the full indulgence of bull sea lions stretched out on the rocks at the mouth of the river. An alarm clock on a small oak table read 10:30.

Kathleen gently closed the door and walked into the kitchen. With the blinds drawn, the room was only twilit, but even so, the signs of haphazard housekeeping were everywhere: dirty dishes were piled in the sink and on the counter, half-filled pots rested on the stove, and boots and jackets covered the mat in front of the door. Kathleen moved slowly through the wreckage, like a diver who had discovered a sunken ship, and pulled up the blind on the window facing the street. Daylight streamed into the gloom, washing over the chairs and table and, to Kathleen's amazement, her hands. She had not looked at them for so long that they were as strange to her as the house through which she moved. Placing them on the windowsill as if to bathe them in light, she could feel energy flowing back through them and down into the rest of her body. They were pale and slightly shaking, like seeds that had survived a deep frost, and from them a new life did indeed seem to be taking root, or rather, her old life was being invigorated.

She stood for several minutes in silence, watching the chickadees and goldfinches light on the branches of the maple tree and on the laurel hedge along the driveway. Then she opened the window to breathe in the rich spring air, heavy with riversmell. Mud, pollen, fish, earth, flower blossom, marsh grass: just like the river, the air carried so many scents on its current that they were impossible to distinguish.

By the time Kathleen heard a red-winged blackbird's lilting cry, so soft and playful, drift down from the telephone wire across the empty street, she felt she had turned so far away from the past three weeks that she could not have found them again. They were powerful, but only like a night sky recalled at mid-afternoon; twenty-one days as significant and meaningless as twenty-one stars. Already, she could not imagine them, nor did she even realize how long she'd remained in bed.

She walked to the bathroom and drew a bath. While the water was running, she began to put the kitchen in order. A cereal bowl and a half-filled glass of orange juice on the table suggested that

Zoe was indeed at school, since she always had the same breakfast during the week, changing it on Saturdays and Sundays for some strange reason of her own—she liked to eat scrambled eggs while watching cartoons, Kathleen remembered with a smile. And the date on the paper, which Kathleen brought in from the mailbox at the side of the house, also showed that it was a weekday.

The routine chores that only recently had contributed to her immense fatigue now brought a feeling of accomplishment. Kathleen worked quickly and efficiently, stopped long enough to take her bath, and then finished what she'd started, stacking the dishes away, picking up clothes, dusting the coffee table and end tables in the living room, all the while opening windows and doors to let in the fresh air.

Finally, after checking the fridge and cupboards to see what food was in the house, she accepted the blackbird's invitation and dressed to go into town to do some grocery shopping.

Still wet from the recent rainstorms, Chilukthan was like a resting fish moving only to the rhythm of its gills. A moist wind blew off the river just hard enough to shake raindrops from the trees and telephone wires, and to ripple the puddles on the streets, while a faint trickle of running water sounded everywhere, going down drainpipes and into gutters. Though the sky was heavy and darkened even more by large, scudding clouds, the day seemed underlit with a promise of sunshine: any minute, and the slumbering town would kick and burst into light.

Kathleen felt this energy within herself too, and hummed quietly as she walked. Even a mild, lingering soreness in her ankle did not slow her pace as she moved down the main street, waving in response to a honk from a passing car or smiling at the occasional person she passed. The town centre was not busy (it rarely was), but Kathleen welcomed every sign of the external world with almost a thrill of pleasure.

Just short of Meers Butcher Shop, she chatted for ten minutes to Mrs. Soulos, whose husband was also a fisherman. Apparently, the openings had been poor for everyone, and now the possibility of a strike hung over the industry. Ah well, the women shrugged, sheltering each other from the difficulties such an event would foster, we'll manage somehow. And with mutual respect and sympathy of the kind that only exists between people whose lives are governed by the same immediate and arbitrary forces, the women parted.

Warmed by the camaraderie of the exchange, though still troubled by its content, Kathleen decided to go into Meers' shop to buy some pork chops. Normally she would have walked to Ponick's store, but with so much to do at home, she thought it best to hurry back.

Kathleen entered the shop and immediately sniffed a strong, unpleasant odour of meat. Looking around, she saw streaks of mud and crumpled pieces of brown wrapping paper on the floor. More paper, bloodsoaked and torn, lay scattered on the countertop, amongst knives, sausage casings and bits of hamburger.

The butcher, bent over behind the counter rummaging in the displayed meats, straightened up when Kathleen cleared her throat. His appearance startled her. He looked ghost-white, his face paler than the dingy, blood-caked smock he wore. His temples, which he was now rubbing, also showed traces of blood, as though he'd worn the skin away. Even his bright shock of hair, which Kathleen remembered as being combed smooth, had been disturbed; strands of it poked out from the rest at odd angles, heightening his boyish appearance.

For a while, he stared slack-jawed at Kathleen, then suddenly glanced toward the window, seeming confused.

Kathleen couldn't help but notice his distress, and for some reason it saddened rather than alarmed her. Vaguely, distantly, she saw him again, hair plastered flat in the pouring rain, his black suit among the tombs. But that particular memory had turned back on itself and was sinking into space or earth or wherever it had come from. She remembered the butcher's kindness but not his words, his courtesy but not his concern. Oddly, she remembered only snapshot images, the clash of his brown shoes against his dark pants, the rapid blinking of his eyes, the violet spread of the crocuses and the glimpse of ocean. But even these pictures were fleeting and inconsequential, and she went through them rapidly, as though instinctively protecting herself from the blackness in which they had grown. She approached the counter, smiling, aware of the butcher's strange demeanour, but mystified as to how to deal with it.

Slowly, he turned away from the window to face her. His eyes were twitching, and the muscles in his temples flinched. Kathleen saw him swallow hard and clutch the counter. Moisture formed on his brow, and he wiped at it swiftly with the palm of one hand, leaving behind a small smear of blood from one of the pieces of meat he'd been touching. Now his face looked even more like his smock.

"Is everything all right?" Kathleen ventured. "You don't look well. Perhaps you should sit down?"

"No," he said hoarsely, shaking his head. "No, thank you." He looked toward the window yet again, but this time his mouth opened wide and he froze.

"My goodness, what is it? Are you sick? Are you having . . ." Kathleen followed the butcher's gaze to where it fell on her daughter. "Zoe? What's she doing here?" The girl was peering through the glass, her face an inch from it, her hands cupped like petals around her eyes.

Just then, in a small voice that carried more weight than if he had shouted, the butcher gasped "Oh, dear," and clutched the counter again, his head swinging around like a mallet.

"You're really not well, are you?" Kathleen said. "You'd better sit down." As she moved around the counter, she motioned at Zoe to stay outside, then immediately turned her full attention to the butcher. He looked awful. Kathleen hurriedly brought a chair out from the back room and helped him into it.

"I don't know what it is," he said, trying to catch his breath, "but I'm sure it will pass, I just need a few minutes." He leaned back and stared at the ceiling, one thick hand flat against his bloodied smock.

Once again, looking at him, a vague memory from the cemetery grounds began to stir in Kathleen. Something the butcher had said, something about . . . wasn't it about Zoe? Kathleen looked to the window where her daughter still stood, peering in, her eyes saucer-wide, her breath making a tiny smudge on the glass. What was it? The sight of her daughter at the butcher's shop unsettled her, but she could not relate it to the man's distress. Still, there seemed to be an uneasy alliance between the two events. But right now, she had more pressing concerns.

She leaned over the white face again. There was such confusion in it, such helplessness, that before she was even aware of what she was doing, she had taken a handkerchief from her purse and had begun to mop the butcher's wet brow. "Are you going to be all right? Should I call for an ambulance?"

Joe could see a shadow above him, and he could feel something brushing his skin, warm as a kiss. But he knew it could not be a kiss. What was it? From a distance, through the pounding in his ears, he could just make out a soft voice speaking to him. "I'll be all right," he said calmly, turning toward the sound. "Just a bit dizzy, but I'm fine, thank you." He closed his eyes and breathed deeply as the warmth settled deeper and deeper into his skin.

chapter thirteen

D riving away from the wharf on the afternoon of Ed Leary's visit, Corbett sped west along the narrow farm roads toward the Gulf. Though he didn't want a strike, he accepted the necessity for it as easily as he accepted the necessity for repairing the holes in a net; these were the realities of fishing, and Corbett would do what the union and his peers required of him, plain and simple. He'd made that decision as soon as Ed Leary had opened his mouth. For that reason, as he drove into the dying light, humming along with the radio and slapping the side of the steering wheel, he had something quite different on his mind, the one thing that had consumed his thoughts for weeks now.

To his surprise, Corbett found himself thinking about Margo constantly. Standing at home plate with the bases loaded and the count full, he thought about her; trying to gaff a big spring before it slipped out of the meshes, he thought about her; walking into the house to find it dark and only a pot of cold soup on the stove for his supper, he thought about her; and even flirting with other women, he thought about her. It was a new experience for him, and he was exhilarated by it. The fact that she was married did not interfere with his present happiness. Corbett no more thought about the distant future than he did about the past: strike out, lose the spring, eat the soup, miss the other women's hints—what difference did it make? He'd see Margo again soon enough, they'd rendezvous according to plan, they'd talk, laugh, make love, and he'd leave feeling as though he'd never been aware of his senses before.

Gradually, with the reckless disregard of someone who had gone too far ever to go back, Corbett was forgetting the moral considerations that had kept him from blindly pursuing Margo in the first place. He became lax about hiding the affair, unable to keep his eyes off her at the ballpark or in the pub, and lately he had even found the sneaking around less exciting than before. Yet he retained enough of an instinct of self-preservation, and enough respect for Margo's feelings, to keep the relationship a secret. Only when Troy had made that insult about sixteen-year-olds had Corbett come close to threatening the secrecy. Now, grinning broadly, he pushed down on the gas, driving to kill the long minutes before nightfall, waiting for the dark that would hide his approach to Margo's house.

Miles away, in the Chilukthan Arms, Troy raised a glass of beer to his lips, took a long swallow, and tried to calm himself so he could focus on what had just happened. It seemed definite now that the strike was going ahead, and he hated to think of losing his summer income. Then again, why would Ed Leary be making special visits to ask good union members how they'd vote if a strike was guaranteed? Maybe there wouldn't be enough support for a strike? But if there wasn't, would the canneries really offer less money than last year? Troy took another long swallow of beer and tried to imagine what would happen if the fleet tied up while the sockeye were running. He remembered other strikes from childhood, when his father had gone on strike just when the big summer runs started, how he'd lost much of his year's income and how tense and out of sorts he'd been. And then the canneries generally raised their offer anyway, which meant that thousands of dollars had been lost for no good reason. At least that's how it had seemed to Troy as he listened to his father discuss the strike with other fishermen on the wharf. The canneries could afford to hold out for a couple of weeks, even if they eventually gave in to the union's demands. But for an individual fisherman, those two weeks could mean the difference between a decent year's income and chicken feed, between making boat and house payments or sinking in debt to the bank. And if you sank deep enough, you might not surface again.

Troy remembered the tension of previous strikes, the last one coming when he was fourteen or fifteen. His father never seemed to sleep; he just sat on the living-room couch in the dark, chain-smoking and rubbing his temples. Troy had stolen down the hallway on several nights, sometimes seeing the end of his father's cigarette burning a red hole in the darkness, and sometimes eavesdropping on his parents' edgy conversations, his mother's voice questioning and nervous, his father's replies monosyllabic and heavy. The strain had been immense, especially once the sockeye entered the river and you could walk along the dyke and see them jumping, or lie awake at night and imagine thousands and thousands of them speeding silently past the moored boats and racked nets; it was like throwing down your pan and taking an axe to your sluices once you'd found some gold dust in a stream. Troy had hated it, hated the powerless feeling that went along with the anxiety, but he had known enough about the canneries even then to direct his hatred at their greed rather than at the union, which, after all, was only fighting to get a fair price for the catch. But hatred is rarely a calm or enjoyable emotion, and Troy remembered the stomach-churning anxiety more than any victory on prices.

"Hey, Moss, you awake?"

Deep in thought, Troy heard the voice from very far away, but forced himself to look up toward it.

A familiar face grinned back at him, obviously amused by Troy's intense concentration. "I thought you were asleep. I called you three times."

"Oh, hi Ross. Sorry about that, I didn't hear you."

"I figured that. Thought I was going to have to cuff you on the back of the head." Ross sat down heavily, banging his glass of beer on the tabletop. "I probably could have taken the beer right out of your hand, could have saved me buying one."

Troy smiled. He liked Ross, a classmate from high school, a guy he played hockey and baseball with. There was something comforting about his chubby, red-cheeked face; it was like looking at a ripe apple before you pick it. "Yeah," Troy said. "I've got a lot of stuff on my mind. Just thought I'd have a beer and think things through."

"What sort of stuff?"

Troy ordered another beer, and then related what had been troubling him.

His friend listened closely, nodded, drank his beer, occasionally emitted a "No shit?" or "Is that right, eh?"

When Troy finished, Ross leaned forward conspiratorially and said, "I tell you what you should do. You want to do like me and get in at the post office."

"The post office?"

"Oh yeah, it's great, no pressure at all. Up with the sun, sort the mail, walk your route, and you're done by lunchtime." Ross lowered his voice. "And the benefits. I'm telling you, it's plum. Great pay, full pension, and you can retire in twenty-five years. Think about it. I can quit when I'm forty-five."

Troy sipped his beer. He'd still be outdoors doing something active, and there wouldn't be the pressure of drifting down onto a snag or of setting in the wrong place and missing the fish. And the paycheque would be regular, money you could count on.

"We have strikes too," Ross shrugged, "but nothing like what you're talking about. Hell, I can't imagine having to sit there while your whole year's income is swimming by. When we go on strike, at least the mail doesn't keep delivering itself; we don't have to watch the letters fly down the street." He laughed, then paused when he noticed Troy's expression. "No, seriously, it's a great job, you should think about it."

"Are they hiring?"

"Sure, off and on, full-time, part-time. You should apply. You never know. Maybe I can sniff around a bit, see what the chances are."

"Hey, that'd be great, I'd sure appreciate it."

"No sweat. You ready for another?"

Troy nodded, suddenly buoyed by optimism. The post office! Why not? Maybe it wasn't the most exciting job in the world, but he could do it for a while until he found something else. Or maybe he'd really take to it? Maybe he couldn't make as much money in such a short time as he could fishing, but the idea of a regular paycheque was definitely appealing, especially with another strike looming in the fishery. Mom would be happy, Troy concluded, pleased as always by the idea of pleasing her. He took another swallow of beer, then he and Ross began to discuss the baseball season.

At the same time, Corbett decided it was dark enough, and

turned his car up onto the dyke, just far enough from Margo's house to be unnoticed. She lived in one of the old farmhouses off the road to the bridge, a nineteenth-century gabled and verandahed building at the end of a long driveway bordered by weeping willows and poplars. The house had been a wedding gift to Dennis and Margo from his parents, a fact that had at first made Corbett uneasy, but one that he no longer considered. He hurried down the dyke, across the road, and into the shelter of the tall trees.

Darkness fell quickly, flowing thick through the branches and spreading across the ground. Back toward the town, over the potato fields, Corbett saw headlights nosing along the curve of the river, someone driving home perhaps, and the sight inspired him to move even faster. This was the first time he'd tried to see Margo without her knowledge, but, feeling the way he did, he had no doubt that she'd meet his arrival with equal passion.

Light spilled out from the windows on the ground floor, its brightness merging with the night and then pushing it back the way the river pushes the ocean back on a run-out tide. Much to his disappointment, Corbett noticed a car he didn't recognize parked by the front verandah, and as he got closer, he noticed figures moving across the windows. Cautiously, he approached the house, trying to get a good look at its occupants. From behind a shrub on the front lawn, just outside the circle of light, he saw Margo. She moved back and forth from the kitchen to the dining room where the other figures had settled, their backs to the window. Corbett's hopes that the visitors would not be staying long were dashed: Margo was serving dinner. But to whom? He decided to take a chance, go around to the back porch, and attract Margo's attention while she was in the kitchen.

He waited on the porch for five minutes, trying to quiet the tail-slapping and friendly barking of Margo's springer spaniel. She must have joined them at the table, he realized, about to give up and return to his car. But just then she appeared, lovely in an emerald blouse with her full auburn hair done up in a bun, the white of her skin even more noticeable on her throat and around her lipsticked mouth. Corbett stared at her in a kind of wonder, as unprepared as always by how her beauty transformed itself, becoming deeper and more intense with each change of clothes or expression. For a moment, he simply stared at her, watching her breasts sway as she leaned over a pot on the stove, the curve of her thigh clear against her skirt. He became so entranced by her presence, and so impressed with his own good fortune, that he almost forgot to get her attention.

He rapped lightly on the window, not wanting to frighten her. When she didn't turn away from the stove, he rapped again, a little louder. This time, she looked around, and Corbett pressed both hands against the glass, so that they looked like giant leaves around his expression, which was broad-grinned and deliberately comic. But Margo didn't laugh or even smile. At first, she seemed stunned, and then she scowled, and motioned at him to go away, but he didn't want to leave. Instead, he rapped again on the glass, and pointed toward the kitchen door.

Still scowling, Margo hastily crossed the kitchen, opened the door, and stuck her head out into the darkness. "What are you doing here?" she said in a hoarse whisper. "Are you crazy?"

Corbett laughed and leaned forward to kiss her, but she pulled away. "Stop fooling around!" she said, panicking. "You're not supposed to be here. I didn't say you could come tonight. Go. And don't let anyone see you, whatever you do!"

"Who's the company?" Corbett asked, the hurt beginning to grow in him.

"Dennis's parents, for chrissakes!" Margo suddenly stepped toward him and clutched his arm. "Where's your car? You didn't come down the drive, did you?"

"No, I'm not stupid."

She released her grip, and sighed. "I don't know about that. I told you right from the start, nobody can know. Do you hear me? Nobody." She glanced nervously over her shoulder.

"This is new," Corbett said. "I didn't think it really mattered to you all that much."

A stern look darkened her brow. "Listen. I'm not just talking about me. Do you know what Dennis would do to you if he ever found out about us?"

"Aw, I'm not worried about . . ."

She jerked forward, as if about to strike him. Her eyes flashed as bright as her dress. "Don't be an idiot. You don't know him like I do." She paused, listening for sounds behind her, then continued. "You have to stop staring at me all the time, do you hear me? And you can't come here unless I say so, understand?"

Annoyed by her bossy manner, but cowed by his feelings for her, Corbett had no response. He simply stood there, patting the dog out of reflex. Was she mostly concerned for his safety, or the safety of her marriage? For the first time, and all at once, the awareness of his feelings and the reality of the situation came together, and he experienced a sense of hopelessness as deep as it was sudden.

Margo noticed his downcast look, and, in a softer tone, said: "Tomorrow night. At the usual place, okay? Ten o'clock." The door shut behind her.

Corbett walked around the side of the house and up the long driveway, not even bothering to hide himself or to look back. The dog trailed him, jumping happily at his side. Their two shadows in the dim moonlight, the one still and straight, the other jigging around it, seemed cast by a man carrying a sack of kittens to be drowned.

Several hours later, Corbett drove home from the Sundance Pub on the east side of town. He'd spent the night drinking and shooting pool, mostly drinking. As always, it had cheered him up for a while, the beer and the loud company of others, but gradually the effects had worn off, and he had become depressed and morose. Now he just wanted to fall into bed and sleep.

He parked in the driveway, stopping just in time to keep from hitting Troy's rear bumper. Then he climbed out of the car, shut the door quietly, and stood staring at the house. It was completely black. He opened the gate and stepped into the side yard.

A noise came from out of the darkness, a sort of tearing and hard breathing. Corbett walked toward it until he saw a dark outline on the grass just beyond Zoe's bedroom window, near the apple tree. The sound was even louder now, and he recognized it, but didn't feel much like making a comment, as he would have done on other occasions. Instead, he listened for a few seconds with a sort of vague sympathy, then turned and went into the house, fumbling to put the key in the lock even though the door was open.

Troy didn't even hear his brother drive up. On his hands and knees in the wet grass, he hadn't heard anything over the sound of his retches and the thrumming in his head. "Oh Jesus," he moaned, his throat raw, the stench of his own vomit causing him to retch even harder. He felt as though he were bringing up his insides. "Oh Jesus," he moaned again, stretching out and pressing his face to the cool grass. What had begun in optimism and celebration was ending in misery and stench. Never again, he kept repeating to the damp earth, never, never, never again.

All around him in the darkness, the cold char of the caterpillar nests waited to be plundered by daybreak and the first birds.

chapter fourteen

*T*he afternoon was brisk and grey. A cool wind riffled the surface of the river and bent the heavy seed-ends of the bullrushes half over until they looked like tightened catapults. In the sky above the harbour, some gulls circled silently, their flight slow and then rapid, depending on whether they buffeted or caught a wind current. Fishing had been closed for over a week, so the gulls, missing their favourite diet of fishheads and guts, circled in a kind of desperate prowling.

The four boys on the dyke huddled close together as pilings. The oldest, a teenager nicknamed Ling Cod because of his bulging eyes and thick lips, held a match to the end of a cigarette, then drew it in slowly and exhaled. Red-haired and thin, he looked much like a lit cigarette himself, smouldering away just a few feet from the cold ash of the tide. He handed the cigarette off to one of the others, then pulled something wrapped in newspaper from his dirty mack jacket and knelt on the ground.

After working busily for a few seconds, Ling Cod snatched a fishing rod off the gravel. "You do it," he smirked, straightening up and handing the rod to Raskin's boy. The other two boys chuckled, nudging each other. Raskin's boy silently accepted the rod, then hesitated. He held it in front of him, knowing what they wanted him to do, and wanting to do it because if he didn't he knew they'd scorn him and come up with some other trial more dangerous or painful. Yet he still possessed a child's sense of justice, and did not share the others' belief that the planned act was justified. So he stood with the rod dangling in front of him, its tip slightly weighted, and tried to decide before they made up his mind for him.

He couldn't. Ling Cod punched him hard on the shoulder, snatched the rod away in disgust, and said, "I'll do it." The other two copied his scornful look, though they did not hit the boy. He had shrunk back into himself anyway, like a spider bunching up in its web, and was prepared to move quickly before another punch or kick could land on him. He withdrew a little from the group, aware that he'd be punished somehow, yet finding again in the punishment a kind of attention preferable to complete abandonment. These were his friends in the one respect that mattered: they included him in what they did. And though the inclusion was rough and humiliating, it was also consistent and had its calmer moments. Who else would take the time or make the effort to include him in their activities? Who else would smoke and drink with him, even if he supplied the cigarettes and alcohol?

Ling Cod cast the line far into the harbour, where it landed with a loud smack. "Here, birdie, birdie," he half-whistled, while the other two followed his eyes skyward. The gulls dropped quickly, angling straight toward the spot where the line had landed. They settled on the river and began pecking at something and flapping their wings. Ling Cod waited patiently. "Got to get it just right," he said, "got to wait til one of them swallows it and takes off. Now!" He relaxed the tension on the reel and the line zinged out as a gull rose higher and higher, a bit of fishgut trailing from its beak. Ling Cod turned to the boy. "You should be doing this, you chickenshit. You could get even."

The boy took another step back, as though he too were being jerked at the end of a line. Ling Cod let the gull climb just high enough to be back in the wind before he started to reel in the line. A few seconds passed before the slackness tightened. Then the gull screeched madly and dipped down with the sudden pressure.

For a few minutes, it seemed as though nothing moved but the gull careening wildly in the sky and the skinny boy gleefully jerking the rod back and forth. The gull screeched so harshly it sounded as if the sky was being ripped in half. Raskin's boy cringed under the screech, and tried to shrink into the ground. Neither he nor the other boys noticed the two men approaching from the direction of the cannery.

Deep in conversation, Vic and Ed walked along the dyke, the larger man shaking his head and holding his thick arms out in front of him, as though trying to push the wind back to the Gulf.

"I went down to Pheasant Island yesterday," he said with a deep sigh, "and it was like I was the enemy. I'm telling you, Victor, these youngsters are going to ruin the whole industry for the rest of us, especially for guys like you and me who don't want to be chasing goddamned fish all up and down the coast. That's the way things are going, you just watch. Highliners, all of them, who don't give a good goddamn where they fish or who they fish for or how they go about it. I'd laugh if it wasn't so serious."

Vic took the dangling cigarette from his mouth, and, pushing back his skullcap, angled his eyes upward at Ed's broad face. "They won't support a strike?" he asked.

Ed rubbed his bushy beard with the palm of his hand, as if it were a pelt he was assessing for quality. He spoke almost indifferently. "Oh, I suppose they'd go out with the rest of the boys at first, but as soon as they hear the test-sets, they'll be so itchy you'll be able to hear them scratching all the way up to the Mission Bridge."

Ed stopped walking, and turned toward the river. "The bugger of it is, they'll probably do just fine for themselves. Let's face it, nowadays if you're hungry enough and greedy enough and don't give a damn for anybody else, you can make out all right. But what the hell kind of industry is that?"

He shook his head again. "You work hard to build something up, you think it's important, you make gains, and then . . . ah, what's the use? You know what they said to me down at Brunovs' float? They said the union's got nothing to do with prices, they actually said this, Victor, for chrissakes, they said it was all about supply and demand, the open market. They as much as told me I was an old fart who had lost touch with reality. Reality! Jesus, they're so soft, they don't know what reality is, they didn't grow up in the hard times like we did, they didn't put their lives on the line like we did. And now they're telling me, me! about the fishing industry!"

His dark eyes widened until they seemed to swallow the rest of his face. He punctuated his words by thumping a fist into his open palm. "Where were they when we were fighting for UI and Workers Comp? Where were they when the runs were so depleted we were lucky if we saw ten sockeye an opening? I'll tell you where they were; they were sucking the hind teat, that's where! And damned if they're not still wet behind the ears! The open market? What open market? The one that the companies and the banks use, the one the politicians think about when they send the cops out to bust up a picket line? Open market, oh yeah, it's open all right, as long as they like the look and the smell of you at the door. But if they don't, you'd better watch your fingers before they snap them off. I can't . . ."

Ed paused again, almost out of breath. Then he noticed Vic's raised arm pointing toward the sky over the river.

"What's got into that gull?" Vic asked, cupping a hand over one eye. "Listen to it!"

Ed followed the other man's gaze, relieved to have the subject changed. He had to be careful what he said around the waterfront; the last thing he wanted to do was scare union members off with his personal politics. He knew from long experience that there was a big difference between a fisherman who'll belong to a union and a fisherman who'll agree that the whole capitalist system is rotten to the core. There weren't too many of those around, in the fishery or anywhere else. But what about Victor Mawson? He knew a thing or two about power, and who had it, and why you needed to get some to survive, but that was all. Maybe he'd go as far as voting NDP. Hell, might as well not bother for all the difference that would make. What is that gull screaming for?

The two men noticed the line, the rod, and the boys simultaneously.

"Hey!" Vic shouted, throwing down his cigarette and plunging into the wind. "What are you doing?"

Raskin's boy immediately sprinted off the dyke toward the field at the foot of the street. The others froze, but two of them ran downriver as the men hurriedly approached. Only Ling Cod remained. He looked at the men, looked behind him, then down at the reel. He backed away a few steps, but forgot to release the reel, and the tension pulled the rod out of his hands. He made as if to retrieve it, then cursed loudly and sprinted along the dyke after the other two boys.

Meanwhile, the gull flapped wildly over the river, its pain and panic dragging the rod slowly across the gravel. For such a big man, Ed Leary was surprisingly quick, and he raced up to put his foot down hard on the rod. The gull screeched even louder, locked again in the surrounding grey.

"No sense letting him drag this around," Ed said, sickened by the sight. He picked up the rod and held it, small as a ruler in his hands. He could feel the pressure in his wrists, but wasn't sure how best to relieve it.

With a gesture of despair, he appealed to Vic, who was looking at the sky, the furrows in his face even deeper than usual. "Can't just cut the line, Victor."

"No," he responded, turning. "No, I guess not."

The gull yanked again and raised its fractured siren another pitch.

"That's almost enough to make me let some more line out." Ed considered, but quickly decided against that option. It might ease their discomfort, but not the gull's suffering.

"Only one thing to do," Vic muttered, an imploring expression in his eyes. "Have to reel it in."

Ed cursed at the ground. "I don't understand it. How can . . ." He stopped himself, realizing that he'd been asking the same question all his life in so many different situations and so many different forms and that there'd never been an answer. How can . . . what? How can someone torture a bird for kicks? How can someone vote for those who hate his guts and laugh at him behind his back?

Ed spun the reel and watched as the gull, its beak wide apart, blood dripping from it and spattering its feathers, came closer, drawn down by a power even its frenzied terror couldn't outlast. Ed watched it come; he couldn't look away, despite his desire to do so. What would be the use? Looking away wouldn't remove the blood or the hook from the gullet. So he kept his eyes trained on the gull until it finally landed on the dyke, hopping back from the two men, every hop bringing another cry and more blood from its beak.

Vic spotted a chunk of driftwood in the rushes near the top of the bank. He walked over and picked it up, all the while grateful that he hadn't reeled the bird in. It was bad enough to see it and hear it, let alone feel such panic in your own hands. The idea of a bird swallowing a hook seemed an immense act of cruelty, as though it was the element itself and not the death that disturbed. For twenty-five years, Vic had heard and seen salmon thrashing with the same frenzy in his net, and he had lifted them just as surely out of the river as this gull had been dragged down from the sky. But it was the difference between many deaths and a single death, between the impersonal and the personal. The salmon's frenzy did not increase the moment they hit the net; it was merely interrupted, held back from its natural conclusion by a matter of weeks. But this gull? Even it knew what an abomination its death would be. To be jerked out of the sky by a hook in the gut was unnatural. Vic felt the wood rough against his palm as he moved forward, at once pitying the gull and hating it for the stupid, indiscriminate hunger that caused its pain.

"I'll move to one side," Ed spoke up, realizing that the gull would just hop around in circles, away from anyone who approached. "If I tighten the line real short as I go," he added, "you should be able to get a good whack at it."

Sick to the stomach, Vic moved in, the shrieks of the bird ringing in his ears so loudly that he felt he'd lose his balance. With every step he took, the gull lurched back, but the line held so that the hook yanked the bird forward, forcing its beak open. Blood dripped heavily on the gravel. Vic waited for the best opportunity. He didn't want to botch the job by delivering wild blows, but he also wanted the deed done as quickly as possible. He tensed the muscles in his arm. Then, grimacing, he smashed the driftwood onto the gull's back, closing his eyes at the second of impact. When he opened them, the bird was moving but feebly, much of its strength already gone in the struggle with the rod.

"Once more oughta do it," Ed encouraged. The two men exchanged a glance of mutual sympathy, as if to say "We should not be brought to such acts, we don't deserve this."

The gull wheezed hoarsely now, one wing dangled like a loose oar, the other spread across the gravel. Vic cracked the bird over the head and its wings collapsed. Ed took a knife from his pocket, cut the line from the beak, then kicked the gull over the bank; it landed with a slap on the current, and the noise brought a few other gulls low over the river, where they hovered screeching.

"Sorry about that," Ed muttered. "I just didn't want to look at the damned thing anymore."

Vic had become so accustomed to the gullcry that at first he didn't hear Zoe calling to him from the end of the street. He shrugged in response to Ed's apology, and only turned slowly, as though coming out of a daydream, at the sound of his daughter's voice. When he saw her standing right behind him, her hair flickering like dark flames around her oval face, he blanched, the idea that she might have seen him hit the bird filling him with dread. But there was no pain in her expression, only the familiar deep curiosity. Vic recognized it but only with slight relief. Not until she ran up to him and asked what had been happening did he relax.

"Oh, some boys were throwing rocks at the seagulls. We made them stop."

Zoe looked at Ed, who was still holding the rod.

Anticipating her question, he smiled down out of his thick beard. "They were fishing too. I guess they didn't have any luck with the fish, so they thought they'd try the birds."

Vic positioned himself in front of the bloodied gravel, his body blocking Zoe's view of it as he took her hand and turned toward the street. Ed, unsure what to do with the rod, rested it against his shoulder and went with them. They descended from the dyke, skirted the edge of the field, and walked around the corner into a wall of fluttering blossoms, which the gusting wind shook from the street-side cherry boughs.

"Do you know what this is?" Ed winked at Zoe. "It's warm snow." She showed him her curious look, but remained silent. Ed leaned down and forward so that his dark eyes seemed to reach out, and tried to lose himself in the child's innocence, as if it was a world separate from the one he had to live in. But he knew only too well that it was not separate; it was only a glass bubble being tapped relentlessly by power because power always needed something fresh to corrupt.

"What's the matter? Cat got your tongue?" Vic said, pulling gently on Zoe's arm. She laughed and broke away from him, her hair swirling with blossoms as she skipped up the street.

The two men watched her go, at once pleased and anxious at the sight, the pleasure lying in her vitality, the anxiety lying in the only direction a child can go—into time, the next day, month, year. For Vic, the anxiety was particular, mingled with the thought of how many ways a child can leave her parents, while for Ed, the anxiety was not bounded by the lives he could see and lose, but widened into the image of generations skipping out of blossoms into poverty, drudgery, helplessness. They watched her go, feeling themselves a mile behind already, their legs dragging like anchors over the sidewalk.

From the tall grass at the end of the street, Raskin's boy looked after them. He had nowhere to go, nowhere that he wanted to go. He crouched under the memory of gullcry, watching the rod wave and sink into the swirling blossoms, and feeling the warm blood jerk in his wrists.

chapter fifteen

Once Kathleen had adopted tiredness as an explanation for her breakdown, she had a foundation on which to rebuild her emotional structure. It was as though, having been pushed by unseen hands over an embankment into dark water, she had resurfaced with the idea that her body, of its own free will, had sought the water as a form of baptism. Nothing, therefore, had made her sick but her own desire to be well: this paradoxical explanation made perfect sense to her on an emotional level, for though it put the responsibility for the depression solely on her shoulders, it also validated the breakdown. How could the world accuse her of selfishness when she had merely rested in order to become an even better wife and mother?

So time was given back to her. She had lost its linear progression even in the week preceding the breakdown. Voices had spoken but they had not fallen on the air she breathed; she'd seen her hands moving but they hadn't felt the shape of the object in front of her. Now she had regained control of the hierarchy of past, present, and future, even if the three weeks in bed remained only a blur of images. Time was given back, and she took it just as she'd taken most things in her life, not with a justified sense of ownership, but with a surprised and humble gratitude. "What's the matter with you, lying around in bed?" the blackboard voices would have sneered, but they had been quieted by her own interior command, gentler, framed in her mother's affectionate manner, "Lady Jane, you've had a good rest, now it's time you settled in to work again."

On the day of the butcher's collapse, when Kathleen and Zoe returned home, the rest of the family were still in bed. But as Kathleen made Zoe a sandwich, footsteps sounded in the hall and Corbett appeared. "Hey! You're up," he grinned, giving her a big hug and lifting her slightly off the ground until she cried, "That's enough, put me down, put me down."

Corbett quickly apologized and backed away with a look of concern. "Are you okay? Are you feeling all right? You're not sore or anything?"

Kathleen was still a little uneasy. The scene at the butcher shop had been so sudden and dramatic that she had not yet assessed its full import. Her world, though familiar, had to be confronted anew, and she walked in it cautiously for fear of going too fast and disturbing the balance she had recovered.

"I'm fine," she replied with a smile, "a little tired, but fine." She offered to make Corbett a sandwich.

Minutes later, Troy entered the kitchen, blinking sleep from his eyes. He stopped short on seeing his mother. "Oh, you're up," he stated more to himself than to her, then fell silent.

"Yes," Kathleen said, "I'm feeling better. Would you like a sandwich? I'm making one for your brother."

"Sure. I mean, yes, please." Troy struggled to find the proper response to the situation but finally gave up and went into the living room. .

Ten minutes later, Kathleen went down the hall with a cup of tea. Vic brightened at the sight of her, and quickly adjusted his position to make room for her to sit. Finally, he thought, smiling and touching her thigh, something good has happened. But Vic knew Kathleen well enough to understand that she'd want no fuss made about the past three weeks. They were spilt milk, water under the bridge. If she wanted to talk about her illness, she'd do so when she was ready.

So he took the cup of tea, and listened while Kathleen told him about the butcher's collapse. A nice man, they agreed; he'd been very good about Shamus. "But he seemed very upset about something," Kathleen said reflectively, and once more a vague echo of Joe Meers' conversation at the cemetery stirred in her memory. Had he mentioned Zoe, she asked herself. Yes, but why? Something about the dog, that must be it. Yes, that had been kind of him, the way he carried Shamus home. "Oh well," she spoke up again, "he seemed better when we left the shop. I hope he'll be all right." Then Vic dressed, and the family had lunch together in the living room.

That had happened three days ago. Since then, Kathleen had reacquainted herself with the present to such an extent that the distant past might as well have been acted out on another planet. It didn't take her long to transmute her depression, which had been unfathomable and terrifying, into worry, which derived from its usual source. There was little money coming in, not enough to cover the bills. Kathleen read Vic's tally book with increasing anxiety; opening after opening showed such a poor catch of springs that she knew the expenses for the gas were barely being covered. On top of that, there was a large service bill to be paid at the garage, a new sockeye net for which the cannery deducted payments each opening, mortgage payments on the house, property taxes coming due, the phone bill, the power bill and more. During her illness, Vic, who left all the money matters to her, took what he needed for groceries out of her rainy-day fund in the bureau drawer. There hadn't been much in the fund to begin with, and little of it remained now. At least our credit will still be good at the stores, Kathleen reasoned, trying to dispell her concern but not succeeding. As always, their economic future depended on the unpredictable largesse of the river and its salmon, on the two or three weeks in summer when the sockeye left the salt of the ocean behind to swim frantically up the Fraser, seeking the creeks and streams of their birth. To trust your whole year's income to such a brief period when so many things could go wrong had always seemed perilous and fate-tempting to Kathleen, but she understood how important it was for Vic to retain his independence. What other job, suitable to his skills and temperament, would allow him to be his own boss?

On those few occasions when there had been no choice, when they just had to have some extra money, Vic had done what he could, hiring out as a construction worker or farmhand. But Kathleen had hated to see him so dispirited. And then her own pride had rebelled, her own sense of justice: we work hard, she often told herself, flaring up, and we're honest. Why should it be so hard to live without always having to toe someone else's line?

Musing in this way, she calculated how much they owed, what she could pay immediately, what would have to wait for the next opening on the river. She added and subtracted, added again, subtracted again, tried to estimate how many springs at so many cents a pound would pay off how many bills. The figures darkened the page. But it was supposed to be a banner year for sockeye, the real money fish. Early predictions had the returns at their highest levels in a decade. There was a good early run of sockeye heading back to the Stuart River, then an even better run of Adams River sockeye in August. And was it a dog year too? Kathleen thought so. How nice it was when the dog salmon were running and there would be cheques to cash, albeit smaller ones, right through November.

But more than figures darkened the page in front of her. She imagined newspaper headlines there as well, early warnings about labour troubles in the fishery: the canneries could not afford to pay last year's prices for fish, the world market was flooded with salmon, the Alaskans had had two good seasons in a row, the wages of the onshore workers were too high, canneries would have to be shut down, the fleet was inefficient, there were too many boats, and so on. Always the same stories, year after year, yet the canneries usually ended up paying a good price at the end of the season, and their profits increased regardless. Sometimes, the gill-net fishermen had sacrificed part of their precious, brief fishing time, losing thousands of dollars each in the process, only to have the canneries actually pay more after the strike than the price the union had sought. It was victory, but at a high and sometimes disastrous cost. Kathleen knew about the repossessed gillnetters, the independent fisherman forced out of the industry while doctors and lawyers were busily buying shares in seine-boat licences. It was enough to make her spit! Some rich doctor in the British Properties feathering his nest when he already had more than enough to live on.

And what about her boys? Kathleen wondered if they'd ever be able to make an honest living catching salmon. Troy was the more serious, not so trusting of others, more ambitious; maybe he'd manage all right. But Corbett? She shook her head. He didn't even worry about not having his own boat to fish. He was just naive enough, she knew, to expect to survive on the good nature of others. In this respect, he was certainly his father's son.

She thought of Vic again as she stood in the kitchen window staring at the deep-blue range of the Coast Mountains beyond Vancouver. It was a beautiful, clear afternoon, and the mountains looked close enough to walk to. But Kathleen brought her eyes back over the river's long tide to the immediate foreground, the end of Laidlaw Street and the government wharf tucked around the corner. Vic had gone there two hours before, after lunch, to mend net in preparation for the next opening. Kathleen had watched him go, the lightness out of his step, the cigarette shrouding him in wisps, the russet-fringed cherry blossoms turning the street into a mockery of a church aisle. She knew the worry-spots he'd gouged into his temples, the restlessness of his sleep, the empty Players packs left out in the living room and backyard. Already, he was feeling himself a servant to someone else's command. As always, Kathleen longed to keep the ember of independence burning in his eyes so that she could join him at the end of the day in the belief that they had control over their lives, that honesty ought to mean at least some freedom from the pangs of inferiority. She had watched Vic disappear around the corner, blossoms flecking his gumboots like salt spray, and her desire to protect the sweet, funny sailor of her youth once again became a promise. Strike or no strike, she concluded, I'll see to it that he suffers no humiliation for our keep.

Zoe suddenly sprinted past the house, headed for the field or the dyke. Kathleen opened the kitchen door and whistled for her. The girl, eager to claim her perch in the cherry tree, did not want to stop, but she agreed to accompany her mother into town to do some shopping. That wasn't as much fun as the tree or the wharf, but Zoe liked to be with her mother, especially after her long absence.

Kathleen took the girl's lunchkit and her artwork, put them on the kitchen table, and walked outside into the warm, spring air. Blackbirds whistled over the yard, their sleek, black bodies speeding by, and sparrows twittered on the power line stretching from across the street to the neighbour's house, the shadows of their wings like Chinese brushstrokes on the pavement. Closer, a sun-drugged queen bee lolled on a rhododendron flower, and the smell of freshly cut grass wafted on the breeze.

As Zoe skipped ahead, humming to herself, Kathleen planned

the menu for the evening meal. I'll use what's left of my own canned things, she decided, the last of the summer beets and beans. But I'll pick up some hamburger too. I'd like to see how Mr. Meers is doing as well. Then I have to go to the bank. Kathleen's thoughts continued like this all the way to the butcher shop. Such a nice man, she reflected, opening the door, I do hope he's all right.

Joe was in the cutting room muscle-boning a round of beef. He had just trimmed the udder fat away and cut the hanging tenderloin off by sliding his knife between two vertebrae along the hindquarter. Now he was carefully severing the tendon along the shank and slicing a seam along the hind shank bone and shank muscles. Slowly, he freed the meat from the bone, making a slight tearing sound, and then cut through various joints, removing muscles and popping out bones he could identify in his sleep: aitchbone, tailbone, rump knuckle bone. Only the soft knee cartilage and connective tissue around the knuckle were left to trim away.

Never more relaxed than when he was butchering, Joe loved the logical patterns of the cuts, the way his sharp knife seamed the meat from the bones and severed the tendons and muscles. The rhythm of his handsaw through the backbone of a lamb carcass was soothingly repetitive. And every time he split the fat around a kidney, and the dark organ suddenly appeared, he felt like he'd unwrapped a present. For Joe, the pleasure of butchering was simple: to take a carcass full of bones and cartilage and fat, and transform it into smooth, plastic-wrapped portions of meat for the customer to carry home; there was real satisfaction in such artistry.

Joe, who had learned butchering from his father, was considered somewhat eccentric by others in the trade. He chose to bypass the usual distribution channels, purchasing his meat directly from a slaughterhouse, mostly so he could do the breaking, boning, and cutting himself, but also because his father had taught him to be wary of purveyors and purchasing agents. Few industries, he had been warned, are more plagued by kickbacks and other forms of commercial bribery than the meat industry. From a very early age, Joe had been raised to believe that a small businessman had a better chance of success if he oversaw every aspect of his operation. "Learn to do things yourself, Joseph," his father had advised, "and you'll have less chance of being swindled. It only takes one crook to ruin you. Remember that." In the ten years that he'd been running his own business, Joe had heeded this advice. For seven years in Cedar Bay, after inheriting his father's shop, he had done everything himself, until a mall development forced him to relocate. Embittered, he decided to move to Chilukthan, where he continued to work alone, not even employing a boy to deliver meat or sweep up. Though he had sound financial reasons for not hiring help, Joe could not deny that his recent collapse had been precipitated by extreme exhaustion. How else to explain his puzzling behaviour around Mrs. Mawson and her little girl?

He had just put the tip of his knife in the seam between the knuckle and the top round when the bell rang over his door. He wiped his hands on his smock and walked out of the cutting room to serve the customer. When he saw who it was, he experienced no shock, though he did find it unnerving how often the mother and daughter appeared whenever he thought of them. But was this really the little girl for whom he'd developed such feelings of guilt and panic? Joe smiled at her. She was a pretty child, dark like her mother, and not bratty and loud like so many of his customers' children. Ah, what a foolish man I am, he concluded, moving up to the counter.

"Good afternoon," he said, "a lovely day."

Kathleen was pleased that he seemed to have recovered from his attack. "Yes it is, very lovely," she responded, "the mountains are clear as a bell."

An awkward silence descended, which Kathleen filled quickly by asking him how he felt.

Unaccustomed to any concern for his own welfare, Joe blushed and stammered that he'd only been overtired.

"That must be going around," Kathleen smiled, "I haven't been quite myself either these past few weeks. All that rain we've been getting; it was enough to make anyone exhausted. If only we could bottle the sunshine."

"Yes." Joe could think of little to say, but for some reason he did not feel awkward in this woman's presence. There was such an openness about her, as though she didn't look on him as a merchant poised to sell her an inferior cut of meat. That was it, he realized with a start, she doesn't treat me the way other customers do.

Then he did something he had never done before. With the little girl looking up at him again (she had been reading the names of the displayed meats to herself in a kind of singsong chant), he offered her a treat. "Do you like bologna? Would you like to try a slice; it has garlic in it."

To Zoe, the man offering the bologna was no longer of particular interest, now that Shamus's death had faded from her thoughts. "Yes please," she said, holding out her hand.

"That's very nice of you," Kathleen said, worried that she might have to pay for the bologna.

"Thank you," Zoe mumbled, chewing the edge of the slice in quick little bites.

Joe was suddenly very happy. He couldn't ever remember being so happy serving customers before. But this was special; he didn't even feel like a butcher. What was happening to him? Did he have to be terrified by people before he could feel comfortable around them? It was a disturbing question, but he was too relaxed to take much notice. The child's pleasure at the taste of the meat shone in her eyes. Joe was about to give her another slice when her mother intervened.

"That's a nice treat, Zoe, but I don't want you to spoil your supper." She looked back at Joe, just to assure him that she did appreciate his kindness, and then added, "And supper is why we've come." She paused, eyeing the display case. "I'd like a pound of ground round, please."

"Lean? Extra lean?" Joe inquired, revelling in the unexpected joy he had discovered in their company.

Kathleen knew she'd have to sacrifice quality in the name of economy. "Just regular, please. It's going in a chili." This was not true, but she felt some explanation was necessary, particularly since the butcher was watching her so intently with his big, wet eyes. He really is an odd man, she thought.

Joe disliked selling fat hamburger, but he knew that many of his customers wanted the cheaper meat. The idea of giving it to Mrs. Mawson to feed to her daughter seemed an outrage, but Joe wrapped up what she asked for.

"Well," Kathleen said, snapping her purse shut, "I have to get to the bank before it closes. I'm glad to know that you're feeling better. You want to make sure you get some rest." She paused, then added confidently, thinking of herself, "There's nothing like a good rest to give you your energy back. Come along, Zoe." She directed the girl toward the door.

"Thank you," Joe blurted out when they were halfway there. He couldn't think of anything else to say, but he wished more than anything that he could keep them in the shop just a while longer.

Kathleen looked back, gave a little wave, and ushered Zoe out of the shop.

Another customer entered at the same time, an older woman who always watched Joe carefully when he weighed her purchases. So the business day proceeded, coin in the register, and new cuts to be packaged. Strangely elated, Joe went about his work with a secret smile hovering on his lips and the scent of garlic never quite fading from his fingers. Already, he was looking forward to their next visit, and began to assess the state of his shop as though it was a parlour. The grinder will have to be polished, he decided, and I should have another clean smock to put on; this one is a mess. He placed his hands over the still-wet blood much as a woman tries to hide a blush.

Later that evening, Kathleen took a cup of tea into the backyard where Vic was sitting by a driftwood fire. As she approached the end of the house, she saw his face shining in the firelight. He was leaning forward on his knees, staring into the flames, occasionally poking the wood with a stick. Whenever he did so, his face brightened for a second, large ashes pawed the light, then the surrounding darkness crept back to the edges of his skin. Kathleen knew at a glance that the worry he had carried with him to the wharf that afternoon had only become heavier as the day progressed. He'd been silent and distracted through dinner, hardly even responding to Zoe's conversation.

Struck by the vulnerability of his posture in the gloom, Kathleen blamed herself in part for the burden that he carried. If only she had been stronger, he would not have known the grief of a dead child, nor would he have struggled alone for the past three weeks, worrying himself sick about money.

She cleared her throat to signal her presence, then sat in a chair beside him. "Don't leave your tea too long," she said, handing it over, "I poured it a few minutes ago."

Vic nodded, but did not turn from the fire. "Where's Zoe?" he asked after a pause. "Is she coming out?"

"In a little while. She's reading one of her books."

"Oh." He paused again. "She'd like it tonight. The bats are out."

"Are they?" Kathleen scanned the darkness overhead for a flit of motion.

Vic fell silent again. He poked the fire and a rush of warmth touched Kathleen's legs. She bunched her collar up around her throat, for the air still had a chill in it, more obvious now that the fire had warmed the bottom half of her body.

After a few minutes, Vic mentioned the strike. Unless something surprising happened, like a change of heart on the part of the canneries, the union was going to hold a strike vote. "Some time in the next couple of weeks," he added, "down at the wharf here."

"Well, that doesn't necessarily mean there'll be a strike, does it? The vote might be no."

Vic poked the fire again, and pulled his face back from the heat. "Not with the prices they're offering. If we agree to fish on those terms, we might as well not bother. I'd make more money saving the wear and tear on the boat and nets."

Kathleen tried to come up with something encouraging to offset his resignation, but the idea that the same fish he had caught last year were suddenly less valuable confounded her. She leaned back and looked at the sky. It was rich with stars, blossoming with them, whole boughs of constellations and galaxies. The sight made her giddy with a sense of weakness, as though she half-expected to hear a loud crack and the whole dazzling vastness would crash into the sea. How long ago was it that this same vastness only meant brilliance, each star as particular in its promise as the ring Vic had placed on her finger? Was it only getting older that wrought such change, or a failure to age with enough strength? Kathleen brought her eyes back to the brighter flames and to Vic's still profile.

"Have you heard anything from the union?" she asked, anxious to offer some kind of hope. "You know you can't trust all the talk on the wharf."

Vic took a pack of cigarettes from the pocket of his plaid work-shirt and shook a cigarette free. Then he leaned forward and lit it in the fire. "Ed Leary's been down a couple of times. He's nervous about not getting enough support for a strike if they call one. Some of the young highliners are saying they don't need a union at all. Of course, if you want to run all up and down the coast, corking everybody in sight . . ." Vic's voice trailed off in weary disgust. He dragged on the cigarette, then exhaled. The smoke shrouded his unshaven face. "Oh, and there's an information meeting tomorrow night. Eight o'clock. I have to remember to mention it to Troy and Corbett."

"I'll tell them," Kathleen said, getting up. "Have your tea before it's cold." Then, only half-believing it herself, she added, "We'll manage. We always do." When he didn't respond, she mentioned the one thing almost guaranteed to raise his spirits. "I'll send Zoe out. She'll want to see the bats."

Vic watched Kathleen fade into the darkness. Then he took a sip of his lukewarm tea and returned to tending the fire. He poked the heavy driftwood, and the heavy, resistant contact only brought the recent killing of the seagull back to him. The terror and pain the poor creature had been in! Those little buggers! And how much the bird wanted to be in the air; you could almost hear it pleading in a human voice.

He shivered despite the heat, suddenly recalling a time when he had encountered a similar case of cruelty for its own sake.

It had happened during his naval training in Dartmouth. Along with several other trainees, Vic had been ordered to jump into a swimming pool in his canvas uniform to practise treading water under possible combat conditions. The exercise itself was logical, but not the perverse delight the two officers in charge took in carrying it out. As soon as a trainee, beginning to tire, grabbed the edge of the pool, one of the officers would step on his hands and push him back into the depths with a long pole, all the while grinning and saying "You won't last long in the Atlantic if you can't do better than that."

This had happened to Vic twice before he'd gone under and was finally dragged out, barely conscious. All he could remember later was the sharp pain in his fingers, the awful sensation of swallowing and coughing up water through his mouth and nose, and the grin on the wavering face of the officer who yelled "No you don't, Mawson!" almost gleefully.

As long as the war had lasted, he hated the rules that made him salute and say "Yes sir," that told him when to get up and when to go to sleep, and that made him send his wife away from Halifax or face a court-martial for repeated dereliction of duty (he smiled suddenly, remembering how he'd twice missed the ship's departure from port, running down the sloped streets as his comrades waved and laughed from the deck). He had vowed that when the war ended he'd find some way to avoid such powerlessness in the future, some means of living that would allow for independence but not at the expense of all else he valued, time with his wife being the most precious item.

And he had succeeded, for the most part, as much by his own labours as by Kathleen's managerial skills and her willingness to accept his limitations. Together, they wanted to raise a family, and togetherness meant time, and time meant not working at something that would force them to be apart most of their waking lives. For Vic, it meant fishing the Fraser River instead of going north. What good was a few extra thousand dollars if he had to spend three months away from his family?

So they had scraped by, year after year. At times, Vic had broken his vow and worked for someone else, but it had always felt like failure to do so, a weakening of his youthful resolve. Those times had been few, as the salmon fishery provided just enough income in the good years for the family to ride out the lean ones, but lately it had been getting more difficult to save. And now? The canneries were cutting prices again, forcing a strike, and Vic knew he could not afford to miss out on the summer's big sockeye runs. If he didn't have a good catch this summer, he might not be back to fish the next one. But what else could he do? He was nearly fifty years old, and he'd fished virtually all of his working life.

He poked the wood and the flames spat out into the darkness again. "No you don't, Mawson," the voice laughed down from the upper fringes of the light.

But soon a sweeter voice woke him from his anxious reverie. He turned and saw Zoe approaching across the grass, and the sight put his worries on hold for a while. He lifted his face from the heat and began to watch for the bats, their flight over the rooftops and treetops swift enough to be the ash trails of dying stars.

chapter sixteen

*I*n June the freshet swelled the Fraser's currents. The snowmelt poured into the upper reaches of the river, howled through the canyon, and finally rushed the murky tides over the broad flats and marshes, shooting a huge plume of silt from the mouth all the way to the shores of the Gulf Islands. It was as though a million underwater cannons filled with silt were fired on every runoff, and the sound of the banks being torn away was the continual explosion. A whole world tumbled unseen to the coast, a world of mud and trees, drowned livestock, industrial chemicals, sacked kittens, used condoms, runaway log-booms, dead fish, bottles and assorted trash, untreated effluent and wrecked cars. But the surface of the river showed little more than an excess of driftwood and thicker smears of moonlight; it even seemed calm and unchanged. Only the gillnet fishermen understood the difference, as they freed bloated cattle and stumps from their nets and felt the river thundering below them as though it not only reflected the sun and the stars but had swallowed their energy and was burning with it.

At freshet-time more than any other, the river became its own country, unmapped, unbordered, unnamed, a stretch of infinity howling between points of light that warm nothing and no one. What did it care for the names of towns and men? Chilukthan? Fraser? It didn't even care enough to make a distinction between human flesh and excrement; it just rid itself of everything in a revolving blur, gnawing the height of the mountains so it could build a new island in the mouth. Most Vancouverites, stunned by the blue-black beauty of the surrounding range, did not understand how that grandeur and their own was being devoured bit by bit and thrown back past their upturned gazes, just as they did not see the myriad shadows ferociously climb the tides under the neon flickers each summer, or did not honour the poured silver of each spring.

But if they could understand or see, the freshet was the time to do so. Now the river burned like a scythe in hot oil and cleaved the banks; now the tide seemed mad to share its knowledge with the same blank infinity that stretches between the lit heart and the fired hands.

The netshed door on the government wharf had been slid open and a yellowish light churning from three coal-oil lanterns gathered thickly around the boots of three dozen fishermen standing outside. They spoke together in small groups, their voices subdued, and flicked the burnt ends of cigarettes into the river, black and heavy as diesel. A single electric bulb swayed over them on a thin wire attached to a pole, as though a bubble had risen from the coal-oil and got stuck there. The night was calm, but the tide rattled against the pilings and knocked the moored boats together. This restlessness was transmitted through the wharf into the bodies of the men. They fidgeted as they talked, picking their legs up slowly from the heavy light, like flies on flypaper. Behind them, the netshed glowed like a kiln, while dimly, through black clouds, the moon, small and nearly full, made its silent shout through the darkness.

Ed Leary surveyed the crowd. A good turnout, he thought, most of the local membership, even the young buggers from Pheasant Island. From the doorway of the netshed, he glanced around him at the familiar faces and assessed the situation. Ossie Reddick, the toothless old Wobbly: cynical, crotchety as hell, but probably on side. The Samsons and Larches, long-time river gill-netters and good union men. Same with Buck Hidachi and Johnny Toukalos. Fellows who'd been around the wharf a while. Not like some of these part-timers. Who's that one? Ah, so many berry-pickers nowadays I can't tell one from another. Barney Google? Jesus, what's he doing here, the crazy coot? Probably thinks there's a free drink in it for him. The Brunovs. Well, at least they showed up, the selfish bastards. Look at them, standing there like goddamned roosters ready to crow. Can't even tell them apart, the pug-nosed sons of . . . Victor Mawson and his . . . no, just one of them, can't see the other. Mcalvaney, Smith, Kesseridge. No problem with the last two anyway. But the rest, the younger ones? I'd better keep things simple. Politics is just wasted on some of them.

So Ed scanned the crowd, his twenty-five years of union experience allowing him to measure the mood of any group of fishermen as quickly as some of them take the measure of a tide. He figured the majority would support the union's position on a strike, but there were just enough grumblers to raise doubts in the minds of the membership, most of whom, as he well knew, dreaded the thought of tying up even for one opening. He looked around again at the unshaven, anxious faces, and briefly felt an exhilaration sweep through him, a sense of his own power to persuade and organize. It wasn't necessary to win every man over; even one, if it's the right one, could be enough. Ed had known the force of peer pressure to cause law-abiding citizens to spit in the faces of the RCMP, and he had known it to scatter picket lines as well; it was a matter of spelling out the facts and trusting to the good sense of the members to recognize what lay in their own best interests. But was that really all?

He rubbed his thick beard and tried to convince himself that this was true, but he knew it was partly false, for the power of his own rhetoric had been responsible for swaying men when the cold facts couldn't do it. He knew that, and sometimes the knowledge troubled him, especially now, when he no longer felt the energy and the zeal of his long-held convictions. Lately, he had begun to doubt the effects of all his labour, seeing the tendency toward greed and selfishness among the new generation as the sign of something he still didn't want to accept. But what if it was true, what if it was human nature for a man to fend only for himself? What if selflessness instead of greed was the real aberration?

He stared at the dangling lightbulb until he had almost hypnotized himself, and then he shook off his doubt again, as he had been doing every day for months, and headed for a fish crate on one side of the wharf.

From where he was standing, Vic saw a huge shadow cross the light in front of him. He looked up to see Ed pass by in his rolling gait, and thought immediately of the man's nickname, "The

Russian Bear." It suited him, Vic thought, or at least the bear part did. As for the Russian part, Vic wasn't too sure about that. He knew that Ed had been a communist at a time when that was a dangerous thing to be, when it meant the police had a file on you and you were likely to be tossed in jail for union organizing. When Ed had done time for refusing a court order to bust up a picket line, some people had thought it served him right for being a lousy Red. But most fishermen, Vic included, had respected the man for having the courage of his convictions, even if those convictions were suspect. That had happened in the early fifties. Christ, was it really that long ago? Nearly twenty years?

Vic watched Ed climb up on the fish crate, and his mind went back to other meetings, other speeches. Ed could talk, no question about that. And mostly he knew what he was talking about. But he had been a bit silly at times, Vic had to admit. All that stuff about brotherhood and the, what was it, the bourgeoisie? That sort of talk got him his nickname. Vic smiled, thinking of how the boys would yell at him sometimes, good-natured mostly: "Headed for the salt mines yet, Ed?! Hey comrade, I could sure use a slug of vodka!" And he'd take the barbs good-natured too. But when the insults were serious, when a strike was on and some people shouted at him, that was a different story. Once, Vic remembered, Ed had got so angered by the insults that he'd lifted Willard Benson over his head and told him that if he couldn't tell the difference between a Soviet and a Marxist, then he'd better shut his trap before he tossed him in the goddamned chuck.

Vic smiled at the recollection, his fondness for the man at a peak since the incident with the gull a week before. Communist or not, Ed's a decent sort, always has been. Vic looked around. Not many of the boys would go to prison for their beliefs. His eyes fell on Troy leaning against the net-rack, but Corbett was nowhere in sight. For a moment, Vic wondered about the strength of his sons' convictions. He did not doubt what they were, but he could not measure their strength. Would they go to prison for what they believed in? For that matter, would he? Just then, Ed began to speak, and Vic let the questions drop, realizing that he had no idea of the answers.

Ed stated the union's position clearly, emphasizing the severity of the price cuts given the current rate of inflation. "You fellows know that's a ridiculous offer," he said, "and I'm not going to insult your intelligence by telling you why. What other worker allows his income to be lowered like that from one year to the next? Not the owners of the canneries, not the minister of fisheries."

He hesitated, to give his last words more weight, then raised his voice. "If the market's so bad, why are we the only ones who have to make up the difference? No, we can't afford those prices. And what's more, they know we can't afford them, and that's why they're pressing us, just to see how strong we are, to see if we're organized enough to fight them. And I know we are. Hell, what's the alternative? We've got to show them that we won't fish for those prices. And if that means a strike, well, we'll have to show them we've got the guts to strike. We've done it before and we can do it again."

A dissenting voice came out of the crowd: "Yeah, we'll tie up, we'll lose our season on sockeye, and the seine boys will get their price on pinks. Why should we lose out for them?"

Ed looked toward the voice; it belonged to one of the Brunovs. He wouldn't be saying that, Ed scowled, if the seine crews were here instead of up north. Still, he's got the others thinking. I'd better hit the pocketbook again. "What do you suggest we do then? Just take the offer, fish for next to nothing, all because we don't want to see other fishermen get a good deal? That's not going to accomplish anything. Besides, no one's saying you're going to lose the season on sockeye. It won't come to that. The canneries can't afford it. All this talk about a glut is just bluffing. When they see we're serious, they'll table a decent offer long before the Stuarts hit the sandheads."

After a pause, during which the crowd murmured positively to Ed's words, the same dissenting voice sounded again: "If there isn't a glut, then the canneries will give us a decent price after we've delivered the fish. Everybody knows there'll be an adjustment, there always is. Better to catch the fish and worry about the prices after than not catch them and have piss-all to show for the season."

Another heavy silence fell over the crowd. Ed sensed he was losing ground, so against his better judgement he played the card of past experience. "That doesn't work," he started. "It's been tried and it's exactly what the canneries would love to see. If you honestly believe that the canneries will pay you a fair price just out of the goodness of their hearts, just because their profits are so high that they'd feel guilty not to share them, then you must still believe in Santa Claus and the tooth fairy."

Scattered laughter burst out among the fishermen, and Ed immediately regretted his words; it was never wise to ridicule anyone. To compensate, he lowered his voice and stared straight at the Brunovs.

"Listen. You can fish for what the canneries are offering, but if you deliver at that price, that's the price they'll give you. Adjustments only happen because the union's in there fighting for them. That's the plain truth."

The dissenter, scornful but somewhat cowed, responded with a sort of schoolyard brag. "Then maybe we should just sell our fish ourselves, to hell with the canneries."

"That's great," Ed nodded, "but do you know how many fish that could be? Do you know how much work it is to sell tens, even hundreds of thousands of sockeye?"

"Oh, I don't figure I'll get that many."

The voice was almost sneering now. Ed began to lose his patience. "So you're talking about yourself. I'm all right and to hell with everybody else, is that it?"

The dissenter backed down, perhaps sensing the unpopularity of his position. In a quieter voice, almost petulant, he remarked, "I don't see any point in letting good fish go by when I can catch them."

"The point," Ed said coldly, "is that if you let some go by, you can make a decent income off the ones that haven't even hit the Straits yet."

The fishermen murmured their approval, and Ed felt it was a good time to conclude. "Look, we're still negotiating in good faith with the canneries. We've got some time. There's a chance we'll get another offer. If we do, we'll vote on it. If we don't, we'll take it from there. But just like always, the decision to strike is up to you. I'm just here to tell you what most of you already know." He paused one last time for effect. "If you don't stick up for yourselves, nobody else is going to." Then he stepped down from the fish crate into the thick yellow light.

Troy watched his father's face for a reaction, but the features looked unchanged from before the speech began. Troy half-hoped that his father would speak out against the strike, say something so sensible in favour of fishing right through the summer, despite the poor prices, that everyone would have to accept his argument. Troy didn't disagree with Ed Leary; he suspected the man was right, and the suspicion so depressed him that he hoped someone would come up with an argument that sounded better. But maybe Ed wasn't right? Maybe Todd Brunov had a point after all. It did seem a shame to let the fish go by. Once gone, they were gone. For some reason, Ed's guarantee that the canneries were bluffing didn't sound too convincing. What if they weren't bluffing, Troy had wanted to ask. What then? We can't catch fish that aren't there. Even two bucks a pound would be worthless if you only caught fifty fish for the season. Shit! We can't tie up! I need the money. Shit! He spat into the boiling current and passed between the other fishermen on his way to the dyke.

Light spilled creamily from the moon and splashed off the hood of his car. Troy climbed in, gunned the engine, and drove off in the direction of the pub.

His father watched him go. For perhaps the first time, he recognized his son as a fisherman rather than as a boy, someone who had a vote and the same right to exercise it as he had. But as he watched Troy walk through the crowd and pass by him, Vic doubted that the rights were the same between the generations. They don't know, he thought, they don't know how bad things can be. He watched Troy disappear around the netshed, not imagining that a strike could mean anything but an inconvenience to someone so young. For Vic, a strike involved a threat to his entire way of life, but he knew it could not mean that for someone with so much time in his favour. At least Troy had shown up, he acknowledged, thinking suddenly of Corbett's absence. Vic was not accustomed to seeing his sons as separate individuals; he knew they were different on the surface, Troy quieter and more serious, but he believed them to be, at heart, honest and respectful young men who still lived the irresponsible life of boys—drinking, playing sports, and racing their car engines. What could a strike mean to them except less money in their pockets and more time to hang out with their friends? Yet Troy had shown up, and Corbett was

God knows where. Vic passed over the thought quickly and joined the men milling around Ed Leary by the open netshed.

Five miles away, in the northwest corner of Pheasant Island, past green-dotted potato and strawberry fields, alongside a willow-shrouded slough bordering the saltmarsh, a single car was parked, half-concealed in hanging fronds. Its two passengers were not inside, but lay naked on an opened sleeping bag laid out on the grassy slough-bank, their flushed faces to the sky. A moment earlier, the darkness and silence had been almost total; the night seemed to curl in on itself like a wing and to breathe so calmly that the moon had become a stilled heartbeat swaddled in down. But now the same moonlight that had splashed off Troy's hood crashed silently through the leaves of the willow, so suddenly and with such life that it was as though a flock of doves had descended on the calm waters of the slough.

Margo suddenly sat up, clutching her blouse to her breasts.

"It's nothing," Corbett assured her, "just the moon coming out."

"I thought . . ." she started. "I thought I heard someone."

"Who'd be out here at night?" Corbett still lay on his back, his arms behind his head.

"We are." Margo spoke these two words so quietly that they might have been a confession.

Corbett did not notice the tone. He was too full of the moment, too caught up in his own senses. His life had been condensed into the particular touch of one woman, into touching her and being touched in return; all else seemed important only to the extent that it deepened his appreciation of her. She made the disappointment of a bad opening on the river easier to take, just as she intensified his pleasure in the smell of the freshly cut outfield grass.

"Corb," Margo said, touching his thigh. "We have to talk."

"What about?"

"About this." She made a sweeping gesture with one arm.

Corbett grinned up at her. "What? The slough?"

"I'm serious."

"Okay, you're serious. But I don't know what you mean."

Margo had pulled her blouse on and was buttoning it up, not looking at Corbett. "I'm tired of sneaking around, doing it on sleeping bags and old fishnets and in the backseat of your car. For chrissakes, I'm not a teenager." She snapped off the last sentence and turned her back on him.

Corbett sat up now. "You're the one who doesn't want to go to your place."

She spun around quickly. "I know, but . . ." She hesitated, then continued very gently. "I don't want to sound cruel or anything, Corb, but you're what, twenty-two?"

"Almost. So?"

Margo inhaled deeply. Corbett noticed that she had misbuttoned her blouse; it hung partly open and revealed a glimpse of white skin. "Well, you're still living with your parents. I just . . . it's . . . you don't even have a place for us to go. And you don't even seem to care."

Corbett didn't care; he never gave much thought to that part of his life. Staying at home was convenient; he could come and go whenever he wanted, and chip in some rent and food money from time to time. His parents certainly didn't object—they seemed to enjoy having him around.

"Well," he said after letting her words sink in, "I thought we were having a good time."

"We are. At least, we were." Margo frowned, and hugged her knees to her chest, remaining silent.

Corbett felt helpless. What could he do? Rent a motel room? No, she wouldn't go for that. Move into his own place? With what? Even if there had been a bigger return of springs, his share of the catch wouldn't amount to much, certainly not enough to live on his own. He thought about getting another job, but he loved to fish, and the sockeye season promised to be a good one. "There's a good chance I'll be getting my own boat this summer," he blurted out, "and then I can move."

"Oh shit," Margo cursed lightly, leaning toward him, her hair falling in her eyes. "Corbett, we can't . . . I can't . . ." But his offer seemed to touch her. She kissed him again and they fell back on the sleeping bag.

The moon yawed into a bank of cloud and the doves vanished, folded back into the night's smooth cape. A swirl of doused cigarettes rushed under the Pheasant Island Bridge to the sea, while back in the quiet streets of Chilukthan, the shadows of worried men collapsed into each other like dominoes.

chapter seventeen

Weeks passed. The heavy spring rains let up and the river levels dropped again as the freshet eased off. Increased sunshine dried the fields; potatoes, peas, corn, and strawberries flourished in the heat as the light stayed longer on the earth. At twilight, children marvelled at the gigantic shadows cast on the grass and sidewalks, and ran laughing at the kites of their trailing selves. Meanwhile, the blackberries fattened along the dyke, and in nearly every yard and vacant lot, plums and cherries swelled in the heat, daubing the leafy branches with colour, juices poised to burst the smooth skins.

A general air of expectancy flowed across Chilukthan like the Gulf breezes bristling the surface of the river, its whole length an empty sleeve about to be filled.

Somewhere in the Pacific, hundreds of thousands of Stuart River sockeye had heard the inexplicable call of home and were rushing south for the Fraser estuary, bound for the mountain creeks and streams they had left behind four years earlier. Two years at sea, feeding off plankton and squid, had fattened them up, made them strong and fast, prepared them for the last burst of energy they would need to fight their way upriver to spawn in the gravel and die. Behind them, millions more Adams River sockeye still drifted, listening for the same call. And so the mouth of the Fraser hung open, like the night sky in the hour before the stars appear, a vastness without definition.

Chilukthan trembled at the desire of its surrounding forces. The wharves and streets and houses seemed connected to a seismic register separate from the rest of the world, as though an earthquake had started in a million tiny tremors that only a fishing town could feel.

Everyone felt it. Vic Mawson and his sons, fishing the Prairie Drift and barely catching enough springs to pay their expenses, felt a shiver in their forearms as the empty fathoms slid through their hands. Kathleen, looking out her kitchen window as she washed a sinkful of dishes, felt a fleet shadow cross the left side of her face, while Joe Meers, getting ready to close his shop, thought he heard a splash when he lifted his bloodied smock over his head. Raskin's boy, smoking in the stern of his father's boat, felt the heat of the sun thrash in his hands and fall away, again and again, while Ed Leary, tuning his shortwave radio, heard the crackle as a long lit fuse that had begun to burn down, three weeks, two weeks, one week. Only a child, dreaming in the cherry boughs, could rise on the silver excitement of the salmon's approach and meet it without need or fear. Only a child, whistled home, could feel the thrill of her own return in every step.

Starlight filtered down into the salmon's brain, the familiar lilt reached the child's ears, and the bones of a dog still pinned its white map to the inside of the earth.

It was one of the last seasons for porches and vacant lots, for children whistled home from solitary games, and for the river's dominance. All the old ghosts had begun to fade, their figures vanished from the skiff and plough, their lust and romance unread, their drifts and furrows erased. It was one of the last seasons for people to work where they slept, for a dog to walk a known path through the town, and for anyone to study the map of its absence. Independent shops would be replaced by franchises and mega-stores, the harbour would shrink between condominiums, and farm fields would be turned into subdivisions, giant greenhouse operations, and golf courses. On the river, chemicals would spill and shut down fishing, and great sturgeon would die mysteriously, their prehistoric bodies rotting on the banks. No one would fish any longer for springs or early sockeye at the river mouth; the season would be condensed to the summer months. The salmon runs would increase in number, but the genetic diversity would be lost; fish would be farmed in pens and fed on chemicals, and would escape to mix with and weaken the wild species; logging would destroy streams and creeks until the salmon had few places to return to, and the fish would increasingly become playthings for wealthy tourists. Crabs would be too poisonous to catch, the ling cod and rock cod and oolichan would all but vanish, and the beautiful steelhead and coho would become so rare that local poets would invoke them as ghosts.

It was one of the last seasons for silence, for walking out under stars with only your heartbeat and your breath, for picking fruit in wild orchards and for befriending stray animals. The traffic on the highway would never again fall quiet, exhaust would obscure the mountains in a brown haze, and eagles would die in the fields from pesticides leached out in the rain. It was one of the last seasons for coal-oil light and linen nets, for stores closed on Sundays, and for corner groceries with glass-bottled soda kept on ice in huge coolers. The local paper would be owned by a chain, teenagers would eat their lunch at McDonald's, and American filmmakers would turn Chilukthan into small American towns. It was one of the last seasons for reading sports on the sports page, for train trips, and for churchbells. It was one of the last seasons for citizenship, for paperboys, for schools that teach music and drama, for living where you grew up, for the heron's stillness and for dogs barking to each other across the quiet miles, for catching tadpoles and spying on muskrats, for the beautiful light of the sun.

It is always one of the last seasons for some kind of beauty, and this was it for Chilukthan, though no one knew it at the time, but simply went about their lives, conscious of beauty and its absence, as people always are, the heart and its pain forever in season, the pinned map open under the whispering grass.

For weeks, Joe had felt the excitement of a latent hope surfacing through his routine, a hope centred on something as small as an innocent affection for the smiles of others. He had come to view the random visits of Mrs. Mawson and her daughter as invitations into a world he had never known.

With his nervousness abated and his guilt absolved, he allowed himself the strange luxury of connection. He spoke to the woman and her little girl with an ease and friendliness that were the better part of his character but which he had lost under self-consciousness and a fear of intruding on anyone else's privacy. And once he had opened up to them, lowered his awkward defences, he found it easier to extend his friendliness to others, though with more caution.

The change effected in him by his odd relationship to the Mawsons began to take hold in the rest of his world, so that for the first time in decades his fear of life as an arbitrary force had turned into a quiet excitement at the inexplicable nature of experience. Some days, Joe almost reeled with the knowledge that the man he was and the man he presented to the world were suddenly closer than flesh and shadow. Could it be that a dog's death forged the first solid link in the chain that bound him to this new reality? He humbly believed this to be the case, overlooking his decision to look for the animal and then carry it home, overlooking all the Mondays he had put aside a juicy bone and listened with kindness to the scratching at his door. As far as he was concerned, once he laid the dog in the side yard, he started a process of renewal which made his old routine fresh and vital.

In practical terms, Joe did not change much. He merely rediscovered the pleasure in simple tasks, and in doing so, found that pleasure cannot be insular, but that it flows outward, the swept floor changing the overcast sky, the clean smock encouraging the purchase of a new dress shirt, the pleasantries with customers inviting the possibility at least of a more engaged emotional world.

But always, behind this newfound confidence, appeared the image of Mrs. Mawson and her daughter, the two dark and pretty faces, the same polite manners and quiet voices. And the long, black eyelashes of the woman, like strands of fine silk covering her jade-green eyes, so that when she looked up from her purse and smiled, it was as though she had made a gift to Joe of everything her look had held and reflected. He felt a new warmth flush his face, and the feeling made him both excited and ashamed. A married woman, for goodness sakes! Embarrassed, as though the whole town behind him could read his thoughts, he fumbled briefly with his key as he locked up, then strolled home from his shop.

It was a beautiful late afternoon. A breeze sighed in the roadside maples and swallows snapped out their butler's tails on the telephone wires. As he walked, Joe added up the days since he'd seen Mrs. Mawson and Zoe. Could it be a whole week already? They had been in last Monday afternoon. He remembered hearing that her husband and sons were out fishing. Yes, that was a week ago and he hadn't seen them since. That's strange, he thought, they had started to come in to buy hamburger a couple of times a week. He had taken to wrapping up a higher grade of meat and labelling it regular, just because he hated to think of the Mawsons eating an inferior product. Had they always bought cheap hamburger? Joe knew this wasn't the case. He was aware the fishing had been poor so far this year, but had it been so poor that the Mawsons could not afford to eat well? What if they stopped buying meat altogether? They'd have no reason to come into his shop.

He stopped outside his house to consider the possibility. Swallows sliced the air around him, which was rich with the smell of freshly cut grass, but he took no notice. What if they didn't come into the shop? Would his new self bear up under the absence? He considered these questions for a while, then fell back on the hope that Mrs. Mawson would return the next day. But even this hope seemed inappropriate, and Joe entered his house a little dispirited, though with the same resolve to change clothes and go out for supper, something he had begun to do on a regular basis.

Kathleen waited on the doorstep for Zoe to emerge from the vacant lot. She whistled again, then stepped back to check the pots boiling on the stove. She turned one of the elements down and returned to the doorstep. Zoe called out to her from the sidewalk as she ran toward the house, waving a long morning-glory vine in the air. As always, Kathleen felt an overwhelming urge to shelter her daughter from the privations she herself had known as a child.

Kathleen shuddered at those memories, but the past only worried her now to the extent that it explained or reflected the present. The anguish of the month before had gone completely, only to be replaced by the more straightforward anguish caused by a shortage of money. The possibility of a strike had almost become a certainty. How to make ends meet? The same old question, the one she seemed to have been both asking and hearing all her life. To never ask it or hear it, to be divorced from the subject of money: what would that be like?

Kathleen poured Zoe a glass of milk, and took the morning

glory from her hand, the white gape of its flower like an opened mouth. Maybe they're having a good day, she thought, maybe there'll be enough fish to pay for some pork chops or a small roast. I hope they at least bring home a little jack. With that thought, Kathleen returned to the doorway to watch the sun settling crimson over the river mouth in ever-widening streaks. Red sky at night, sailor's delight, she murmured, and closed the door.

The sun dripped heat on the hands of the fishermen as they drifted slowly downriver, their nets a hundred fathoms apart, their corklines quiet. Corbett stood in the stern of his father's gillnetter, cracking the dried fishblood in his palm, picturing the tiny bunch of freckles at the base of Margo's throat, just in the middle of her collarbone. Near the bridge, Ed washed his hands in the vivid light, thinking dully of the one taunt every unionist hears, especially when a strike is on, and knowing that he'd soon be hearing it again. Three boats upriver, Raskin's boy stared transfixed at the deepening sky, his attention like gasoline poured over the light and flaring it straight across the horizon, as though the sun was a fish being gutted. Up the slough at the bottom of the Prairie Drift, Troy watched the light splash into a bucket of water that he used to clean his stern, and wondered if he'd see that much blood when the sockeye entered the river. His father, two boats behind and tucked in close to Wilkies Island, lit another cigarette and only saw the sun reflected off the calm channel and Corbett's bare shoulders. Beyond the reflection lay the harbour and the listing, brine-soaked town, its banks and shops. Vic squinted through his breath of smoke, and turned his eyes upriver, following the glittering flow of the red surface tide. He was the first to see the whale.

Its large dorsal fin wavered in the light along the far bank and moved downriver slowly as a plough. Black as a winter night between stars, the fin quivered like the handle of a knife whose blade meets resistance while it cuts. After a few seconds, the fin stopped dead, then angled across the channel, headed for the sandbar between Wilkies Island and the old pilings of the wingdam just above it. A wake of thick red sunlight spilled away from the fin so that the river itself seemed to be splitting open.

At first, Vic was too shocked by the sight to speak. In over twenty-five years of fishing, he had never known a killer whale to enter this part of the river. On rare occasions they had been spotted up in the main channel where the water was much deeper, even going as far as New Westminster in their pursuit of a seal, but it was unimaginable to see one in the narrow shallows of the Prairie Drift. Vic stared open-mouthed as the fin came closer, following the corkline of the boat just behind his, and then, very quietly, he said, "Corbett."

Corbett turned and noticed the expression of wonder on his father's face. It was the only look that could match the soft but imperative tone of his voice when he spoke the single word. Corbett had never heard his name spoken in such a way, and so he followed his father's eyes upriver, already in a state of wonder and expectation. At the sight of the whale, he too was stricken into a momentary silence.

When the whale reached the sandbar, it suddenly reared out of the red tide, water crashing around its marbled black bulk as the force of its progress hit the shallows. A violent thrashing ensued. Massive and strange, the whale moved like a shadow eclipsing its own radiance; the elements of air, water, and flesh did not join easily, but clashed together in a catastrophe of noise and struggle. Vic and Corbett stared, dumbstruck, unable to predict the sequence of events. They simply kept a loaded silence as the whale heaved its bulk over the sandbar. Everything was mud and crimson splatters of sunlight and a sleek and glistening wall of blubber. For one terrible second, the whale opened its huge jaw, exposing tiny, sharp teeth and a tongue wide as a ploughed furrow. Then the vision passed, the water calmed, and only the fin remained, a dark kite blown along the bank straight toward the Mawsons' boat.

"Should we pick up?" Corbett asked, never taking his eyes off the whale.

"Too late now," Vic answered, nervously dragging on his cigarette. In truth, he didn't know what he should do, but he remembered hearing on the wharf that killer whales never got tangled in nets because of their incredible sonar. But did they smash into boats? He wasn't sure about that, so he watched with trepidation as the fin approached. Above him, Johnny Toukalos was taking no chances. He was picking up at high speed and already had half his net in. The same was true of Dick Robertson just below. Vic kept his eyes on the fin. Just as it looked as if it was going to slice his boat in two, it stopped and veered to the east, following the curve of his net across the river.

"Where's he going?" Corbett said. "The water's no deeper on that side."

"It's deeper than crossing over the sandbar. Maybe he'll thrash his way through again. But I don't see how he's going to make it all the way out to the Gulf."

"Maybe we should pick up. What if he decides to tear through the net? Did you see the size of him? I'll bet he could pull us right under."

"He won't touch the net," Vic said with more confidence than he felt.

In silence again, they watched the whale reach their scotchman and pass around it very slowly. Then the fin drifted downriver for a hundred fathoms and cut back toward the near bank. The water on either side of it fell away like the red flesh of sockeye.

Near the slough mouth, Troy panicked and wheeled his net in as fast as he could. He'd heard the noise upriver, like a long, rolling clap of thunder, but hadn't seen what was happening beyond the sandbar because the boats behind him were blocking his view. But he sensed that something wasn't right. Dick Robertson was picking up at high speed for no apparent reason, and the mystery of the noise itself was unsettling. By the time Troy saw the fin round the end of his father's net, he had started his engine and put his apron on, ready to bring his net in. Once he realized that a whale was on the Prairie Drift, once he'd blinked away the mirage of it and saw the fin growing larger as it sped toward his boat, he pressed his full weight down on the drum pedal, not even taking the time to be wonderstruck. Only afterwards, when the whale had passed right by his bow and disappeared down the slough, did he look around him as if he'd been hit, his blood like an extension of the sunlit river, energized by the force that had gone through it.

With difficulty, the whale manoeuvred slowly westward through the silt-laden waters of the river mouth. It emerged from the slough, rubbed along the shallows of the marsh opposite the dynamite ship, and headed for the fork in the river where the current branches west to the bridge and north to the main channel.

Gillnetters lay everywhere in its path; boats and buoys marked a series of floating portals through which the whale would not go, so it simply criss-crossed the river, its high fin like a decoy in a midway game. Some fishermen panicked and began to pick up, while others cursed and whistled their bewilderment to one another over the radio, hoping that the "blackfish" would scare a few springs into their nets.

But the whale caused a greater problem for Raskin's boy. From the stern of his father's boat, he watched the fin approaching, quivering in the sunlight, and had to decide quickly whether or not to wake his father in the cabin. Which decision would result in a more severe beating? If the whale damaged the net, the boy knew he'd be blamed. But if he disturbed his father's sleep for something trivial, the punishment would be even worse, containing an element of scorn and mockery. The whale raced toward him, its fin the black hand of a clock heavily counting down the seconds. Expressionless, the boy watched the whale's deep weight brush past the boat, a roiling mass slick with crimson. He could almost reach out and touch the black fin, which looked both rubbery and hard as sinew. He inhaled and held the breath, hoping the thing would just go away, knowing that his father would not hear about it from other fishermen, since he associated with them only if he needed their help. The whale passed and its wake gently rocked the boat, slaps of red water smacking the sides. The boy exhaled and watched the fin until it had shrunk to the size of a burnt match.

Three boats downriver, Ed couldn't keep summer off his mind. He didn't have the heart for it. Battling powerful forces for thirty years had worn him down to the point where he lacked the usual relish for a good fight that a strike involved. Yes, there had been small victories, but it seemed to him now that the war was unending and might never be won. The courts, the media, the canneries, and worst of all, the brainwashed mind and greedy hand of the individual: all these forces now seemed to form a union greater than the one he represented. And what of his union? Were its leaders any different? Lately, Ed had begun to believe that the executive was equally insensitive to the workers in the industry, especially the Fraser River gillnet fishermen. Was it really worthwhile to risk a season's fishing for the principle of a penny? The executive and the canners were grappling in a deathlock of ideology, a power struggle that existed above the daily concerns of fishermen. Yet Ed knew from long experience the necessity of the struggle. If you gave up a penny or a half-penny, how long would it be before you gave up much more than that? Intellectually, he understood and accepted the union's position, but emotionally he found himself increasingly on the side of the gillnetters and their families, and not for his own sake. Look at the Mawsons, for example. Ed thought back to the beating of the seagull and the terrible sadness in Victor Mawson's eyes, the tender way he blocked his daughter's view of the blood. Goodness is a dying art, he concluded, then heard the excited voices on the radio. A blackfish? Here?

He stepped out of the cabin just as the whale exploded over another sandbar about fifty fathoms from his boat. Holy shit, Ed mouthed, a smile suddenly brightening his features. Here was the real power! Just look at that! He stared transfixed at the whale as it heaved itself over the bar with a mighty lunge and loud smack, only its fin still in the sunlight, shaking like the shaft of a harpoon around gobs of blood. Ed watched the fin sink into the haemorrhaging western sky as the whale desperately sought a path out of the maze of shallow sloughs and channels. Near the bridge, it veered north, instinctively choosing the deeper course to the sea, and finally the thin black line disappeared on the horizon, leaving only the one-coloured aurora of the sky, its richness more of an ill augury to Ed than a promise of delight. He was not a religious man, but once the whale had gone and he could reflect calmly on its strange visit to the river, he could only see the power and the red wake and the long vanishing as a portent. But of what? Of something natural, a bad spell of storms or an earthquake? Or of something man-made, a clenched fist striking bone or a shotgun raised across a deck? Ed rested against the side of his stern and looked at his thousand white corks as if they were worry beads taken from the neck of a beaten and bloodied man. How am I going to do this again, he asked himself, staring into the red tangle of light on his thick forearms.

Two hundred miles away, the Stuarts shivered like filings in the salt depths, poised to move. And much closer, in a small restaurant cutting steak, Joe raised his eyes to watch the sunlight lift off the sidewalk like flame. If he knew that the warmth in his chest belonged forever to the summer weeks ahead, that the March fog and July sun poured from the same source, he did not question the logic of the connection. He hummed a little to himself, and moved the blade through the tender flesh.

chapter eighteen

*B*y late June, the evenings grew lazier and soft-hued, and people began to stroll happily through the lukewarm streets. The heat and light of the afternoons seemed another season altogether, and only when the round sun broadened out and dropped to meet the level gaze did the special feel of approaching summer really come alive in Chilukthan. At least that was how Troy and Corbett felt, cleaning up the last of the food from their supper plates and grabbing their supple, oil-softened gloves as they headed out the kitchen door, bound for another game at the ballpark.

Despite everything else going on in their lives, the brothers smiled to themselves as they walked up the driveway to their cars. They were still at an age when playing baseball retained a direct link to the more carefree summers of childhood. The wetted-down infield dirt, the bright, fresh outfield grass, the huge chestnut trees behind the backstop and dugouts, the pear orchard just beyond right field, the bleachers filled with kids and seniors, wives and girlfriends, or potential girlfriends: everything about the park thrilled them at a level that wasn't even conscious. They didn't put on their uniforms, they simply arrived at the games the way you arrive at places in dreams.

Troy and Corbett starred for different teams, and it was an unspoken tension between the brothers that Corbett played with the Brunovs. Troy hated the Brunovs' tactics. They bent the rules when it suited them, bringing in ringers for important games and laughing and high-fiving whenever the game was going their way, while grumbling and complaining when it wasn't. Most of the time, Troy ignored them, but at least once a summer he let his temper get the better of him. Corbett did not interfere, embarrassed that his younger brother took things so seriously. More and more each year, the two were spending their time apart, choosing different friends. Even when they worked on nets or shot pool at Dutchie's, there was tension between them, a slight distaste for being in one another's company. Now they only saw each other incidentally in the course of their lives, at the house, the ballpark, the wharf, the pub, through the flames at bonfire parties. They were as dimly aware of each other as they were of their own shadows.

So they drove in separate cars to the park, joined their opposing teams, and prepared for seven innings of competition, during which they'd try their hardest to beat each other while at some level still half-hoping that the other would not make an error or strike out at a critical time. Their private criticisms stopped at the point of public failure.

The Pheasant Islanders won the game 12-6. As always, the Brunovs crowed about the victory, but Troy was in too good a mood to be much bothered by their antics. He had heard some promising rumours from his friend Ross about possible hirings at Canada Post, which alleviated much of his concern over the upcoming strike in the fishery. Besides that, it was a beautiful night. He loved how the sun angled its thick light through the leaves of the pear orchard and chased shadows across the uncut grass, how the air seemed to be made up of a million fragrances, from the rich, wet dirt of the infield to the cherry bubblegum snapped in a child's mouth to the musk of leather rising from his own glove. Troy glided through the innings, going four for four at the plate, crushing one pitch so deep into centre field that the ball rolled right past the stone cenotaph commemorating Chilukthan's war dead and out of the park. If fishing sometimes disturbed him because of the feelings of powerlessness it often created, baseball worked the opposite way; he never felt more in control than when he had a glove or bat in his hand.

When the game ended, the players shook hands near the pitcher's mound, then retired to their respective dugouts to drink beer. Children materialized out of the dusk, chasing each other around the infield and sliding into home plate, while some of the wives and girlfriends slowly gravitated toward the dugouts. Others preferred to wait in the cars, hoping to speed up the post-game socializing.

As the dusk thickened and the moon hung round and small as an old pop fly in the darkness, players from both teams gathered around the pickup trucks and muscle cars angled randomly behind the backstop. Radio music floated out of an open window to challenge the laughing voices.

Corbett was in his glory. He had removed the dirty top of his uniform and now, a cold beer in hand, he leaned over a truck hood chatting to a trio of women. From time to time, he turned to contribute a friendly gibe to the general proceedings just beyond him. He knew that in a short while he'd get into his car, drive home, have a quick shower, and steal away with Margo again down the empty farm roads to the long causeway by the coal port where only the sound of the ocean and their breathing would disturb the silence. How much he had come to rely on their meetings! The disappointment he'd experienced at her house had been largely forgotten in the wake of more memorable nights. Once again, he no longer thought of the limitations to the affair, because that would have involved looking too far beyond the next day, the next touch. And in his heart, Corbett believed that everything would work out fine in the end. The world, as his mother liked to say, is what you make it, and Corbett accepted the truth of that line as naturally as he accepted the rightness of his desires. Now, caught up in the vigour and promise of the evening, he did not notice that the tenor of the conversation around him had changed. Only when he heard Troy's mocking laugh did he step away from the women with an apologetic grin and join the uniformed bodies behind him.

"You can laugh all you want, Mawson," Todd Brunov was saying, "but that doesn't change the facts. Just wait and see. We're not going to tie up because a bunch of old farts get their balls in a knot over a penny or two."

"You're going to scab?" Troy responded, nodding as if he wasn't really surprised by the statement, but doubted the action would follow to back it up.

"Scab," Mark Brunov scoffingly repeated, absently bouncing a softball against his bared bicep. "What the hell does that mean anyway?" He was short and stocky as his brothers, though a little older, almost thirty. But like the others, he wore a sneer on his lips as a kind of membership in an exclusive society. "If a scab is someone who wants to work instead of sitting on his ass, then I guess that's what I am."

"A scab," Troy said slowly, "is what covers over pus." Several of Troy's teammates laughed loudly. The Brunovs, reacting, resembled squat bulldogs straining at their leashes.

Corbett tried to lighten the tension. "Ah, there's not going to be a strike anyway. These things always get worked out."

"What are you talking about!" Troy snapped at him. "Always worked out? Where have you been? We're striking, no doubt about it."

"Maybe you are," Todd cut in. "But while you're home counting your pennies, we'll be loadin' up."

"I'd like to see you try it," Troy grinned, "I'd like to see you show your faces around town after."

Todd made a dumb show of terror, widening his eyes, raising his hands defensively, and shaking his upper body. "Oh, yeah, we're scared all right. A bunch of old-timers too fucking stupid to know when they're being ripped off. Oooh, we'd better stay home, eh Curt?"

Curt Brunov nodded slowly, as if he was falling asleep. Then he stopped and stared straight at Troy. "If you can't see what a joke the union is, that's your business. We'll look after ourselves."

Troy ignored him. "Who are you calling stupid exactly?" he said, stepping toward Todd, who instinctively moved back.

"Figure it out," he said, edging slightly toward his older brothers.

Troy looked at Corbett. Their eyes met briefly, then Corbett turned to his teammate. "Come on, Todd, let's have another beer."

"Don't worry about it, Moss," Mark said without looking at him.

Corbett didn't respond right away. He only wanted to keep the peace. Finally, he grinned and said, "You guys should be the ones to worry. If you keep blabbing, I'll drink all the beer."

But his attempt at diplomacy failed. The insults escalated; Troy spat the word "scab" at the Brunovs, while they sneered and called his father stupid for wasting his time on the Prairie Drift.

During this whole exchange, players from both teams had moved to their respective sides. The women too had gathered around. Music still poured out of the car window, and the intermittent cries of children came from the moonlit diamond.

Troy didn't like to fight, but he was prepared to when it was necessary. And he had long felt that the Brunovs had it coming to them. To calm himself and to clarify the situation, he repeated the word "stupid," then paused before asking Curt if he was prepared to back up his latest insult.

"Your brother thinks he's pretty tough," the latter smirked at Corbett, then stepped forward, gesturing to a large teammate in the same motion.

But just as a fight seemed inevitable, a young girl pushed her way through the members of the Brunovs' team, and started tugging at her father's shirt. "Daddy, Daddy," she whined, "Danny threw dirt at me! Look!" She turned her tear-stained and dirty face up into the moonlight. Her presence immediately made the men uncomfortable. Abashed, the older players began to disperse. The younger ones, Troy and Corbett included, followed. What had seemed to be an intensely significant argument quickly became no more serious than a debate over a called third strike.

But Todd sent one last comment out into the cooling air as darkness enveloped the departing bodies. "Next time, Mawson!" he shouted. Even his own teammates cringed at the hollow words.

Two by two, headlights winked on, casting vivid strips of green on the ground. Engines revved and the headlight beams swung around wildly as the cars and trucks reversed away from the diamond, their low moonlight whitewashing the long picket fence of chestnut trunks.

Corbett sat quietly behind the wheel of his car. We all just want to make a living, he mused, we all want to fish. What's the point of arguing over the details? And Troy! Jesus, he's a hothead!

He put the car in reverse and raked his own headlights through the trees. Somehow the motion of the light reminded him of Margo, her pale hands warm on his chest. He shifted gears as all other subjects faded away at this first thought of her touch.

Pulling out behind his brother, Troy could still feel his heart pounding. How he wanted a crack at Todd Brunov! It would have been worth taking a few punches just to get in one good shot at that little chickenshit! He sped up behind his brother's car and wondered what he was thinking. He's probably pissed off at me, Troy scowled, he's probably worried that he'll be kicked off their team. At least he could have said something when they called Dad stupid.

Still angry, Troy tailed Corbett across town, unable to put the incident out of his mind. He replayed every word that the Brunovs had spoken, and what really gnawed at him was that he could not deny the truth of some of their comments. He also doubted the logic of striking over a penny when so many fish were returning to the river. As well, he had long wondered why his father and others fished the Prairie Drift when other drifts nearby were more productive. Troy had even been toying with the idea of trying his luck off Steveston, up in the main river. The catches were higher there, but he wasn't sure he had the necessary experience to survive among so many boats on a part of the Fraser that he did not know well. But didn't you have to go where the fish were? Wasn't that the whole idea? It irritated him that he could find no acceptable defence for his father's position. Sure, his father worked hard and was honest, and the Brunovs were bastards, but did you have to be a bastard to make a good living? Ah, the whole thing's a mess. I'd be better off out of it. Maybe the strike will be short, and I can still sock some money away before the fall. And maybe by then I'll be in at the post office.

Twenty minutes later, once he had calmed down, Troy parked in the driveway behind Corbett's car and went into the house.

His mother stood over the ironing board, pressing a shirt. She was pale and drawn and her hair hung limp over her eyes. Troy wished he had some good news to give her, or wished he could find some way to ease her concerns about money. He knew how much she suffered through a bad season or a strike, but he could not bring himself to share his pain with her. His love was welled up by the fear that any tenderness shown his mother would be immediately interpreted as a condemnation of his father. He feared this because he believed his father was partly accountable for the tiredness in his mother's posture. If he had fished harder, if he had tried his luck up north or off the west coast of Vancouver Island, if he had gone into herring or crabbing, anything might have alleviated the hand-to-mouth grind. Because his mother's situation was not likely a foreshadowing of his own middle years, Troy could allow himself a gentleness toward her, whereas his father mostly represented a path that he did not want to follow.

"Where's Dad?" he asked now, hanging his ball cap on the back of a chair.

"In the yard. He's got a fire going. Didn't you see it?"

"No. I guess I didn't look."

Kathleen lifted the shirt up by the sleeves, then flipped it over onto the board and started pressing again. Her movements were automatic and fluid. Without looking up, she said, "You should go and sit with him a while, tell him about the game, take his mind off things."

Troy did not relish the idea. He was fed up with fishing and all the worry that it brought. "Maybe in a bit," he finally said, and sat in the chair. "I want to have a shower first."

"Your brother's in there right now. I'm pressing him a shirt." Kathleen put the shirt on a hanger and hung it in the doorway to the hall. "I think he's got a date."

"Probably."

"Any idea who with?"

"Nope."

Kathleen stared at her youngest son with a resigned sadness. Just a few short years ago, he and Corbett had been inseparable, and she would often hear them talking in their bedroom long into the night. But now they hardly spoke at all to one another. As always, Kathleen began to wonder if she had done something wrong, if the lack of closeness between her sons was a result of her ardent hopes that they would be friends as well as brothers. Maybe I pushed them together too much, she wondered occasionally, maybe I should have encouraged them to have different interests.

Barechested and with his hair dripping water, Corbett stepped into the kitchen and kissed Kathleen on the cheek. "Thanks, Ma," he said, lifting the hanger down. Then he noticed Troy across the room, paused, and went back down the hall.

Kathleen noticed his hesitation, and the scowl on Troy's face. "What's the matter? Have you two been fighting?"

Troy said no and then changed the subject. "I talked with Ross today. He says there's a good chance I'll get in at the post office before the end of the summer."

Kathleen's expression darkened. "Didn't you agree to fish Reg Tanner's boat?"

"Yeah, but there might not—" Troy stopped, embarrassed. He didn't want to mention the possibility of a long strike. "If I get offered a job at the post office, I'd be crazy to turn it down."

"But you made a deal, didn't you?" Kathleen said. "You promised to fish the whole season."

Troy had thought his mother would be delighted to hear about him getting a chance for a more secure job. "Well, sure, but it wasn't written down or anything like that."

Kathleen frowned again. "But you gave your word?"

"I guess so."

"Did you or didn't you?"

"Yeah, I did. But Reg can find somebody else."

"That's not the point and you know it," Kathleen said adamantly, her eyes fixed on Troy. "If you agreed to fish the whole season, you should fish it and then start looking around for other work."

The recent tension built up at the ballpark caused Troy to lose his patience. "Fishing!" he snapped. "Why do you want me to stay in fishing! I'm sick of it. It's a lousy job. You never know if there's going to be any fish, and when there are fish, your boat breaks down or there's a strike or something else happens. I don't want to be poor all my life. I want to make something of myself. I don't want to be just another guy scraping along on the river."

Corbett entered the kitchen again. When he saw his mother's hurt look, he glared at Troy. "You know, you're a real jerk."

Troy immediately regretted what he had said, but, hating the self-righteous tone in Corbett's voice, he only glared back.

"Do you ever think before you speak?" Corbett persisted. "Do you ever think at all?" He pushed his hair out of his eyes and stood in the middle of the room with his arms crossed. "What's wrong with you anyway! Where do you get off thinking you're so high and mighty? Dad's outside. Why don't you go tell him he hasn't made anything of himself, huh? Go on, bigmouth, go out and tell him."

Again, Troy could find no way to explain himself. As always, his words had been misinterpreted. Of course he respected his father. But Troy wanted a different life for himself. Why was that so hard to explain? Why did he always end up as the villain?

Corbett's smug expression taunted him. All he could think to do was respond in the same manner. "You're a big talker now, aren't you? But you sure didn't have much to say for Dad at the park." He mimicked Corbett's words. "Come on, Todd, let's have another beer."

"Stop it! That's enough!" Kathleen flared, her green eyes flashing. "I don't want to hear another word!"

The kitchen door pushed open and Vic stepped in. "What's all the shouting?" he asked sternly. "They can hear you halfway down the block." He was unshaven and smelled strongly of woodsmoke. Smudged spots of charcoal blackened his temples.

"Go on, big shot, tell him."

"Corbett! Be quiet!" Kathleen cast him a warning look. It was bad enough that her sons were fighting, but she would not let Vic be hurt by what they had said.

"Tell me what?" Vic looked at Troy, who was staring with such rage at Corbett that even his father was taken aback. "What's been going on in here?"

Noticing the look on his mother's face, Corbett decided not to push the matter any further. "Nothing," he said, crossing the room. "I'm going to be late, I'd better go."

Troy reached the door before him. "I've got to move my car out of the way." He edged around his father and stepped out into the cool air.

Once Corbett heard Troy's car start up, he followed, saying he'd be out late and they shouldn't worry.

Vic waited for Kathleen to explain what had happened. And as she had been doing for so long, she found a way to shield him.

"Corbett's team won again. I guess he was rubbing it in too much. You know how he likes to tease. He can always get Troy's goat."

"What was Troy supposed to tell me?"

"Oh, I don't know. Something about the game, I suspect. It wasn't important."

"Your eyes were flashing." Vic smiled a little to himself. He often teased Kathleen about her Irish temper; it was a small joke between them, since Kathleen's Irish roots were distant.

"Oh, I could just throttle them sometimes. Why can't they just get along? They never used to fight."

"It's the strike," Vic sighed, "it's probably getting to them too, just like everybody else." In truth, he wasn't very interested in his sons' arguments, dismissing them as trivial. He had more important things to worry about, which was what he'd been doing in the yard, staring into the flames, smoking, rubbing his temples. The talk of a strike was heating up. Next week, there'd be a union information meeting, a discussion of the companies' latest offer. How much was enough? Would he vote to strike over a few pennies per pound? Vic had been going over all of the arguments, trying to determine the right thing to do. He could not afford to miss out on the sockeye, but he knew the importance of supporting the union. After all, it was the only force that could guarantee a fisherman would be treated fairly and with some respect by the companies and the government. Without the union, how long would it be before the prices started to drop so low that fishing would be no different than striking, a losing proposition all the way? Vic had been thinking recently about his father, his fierce sense of justice and integrity. And he'd been thinking about Ed Leary too, who'd gone to prison for his principles. But finally, he'd thought of his wife's recent illness, and he hated the thought of putting her through all the stress brought on by a strike. Vic knew that Kathleen shared his worries, but he also knew that she was every bit as principled as his father or Ed Leary. He had come in to discuss the situation with her, but now, sensing that she'd been upset by the boys' fight, he decided to wait.

"I just thought I'd have a cup of tea," he said, then disappeared back into the fragrant darkness of the yard, where the dying embers glowed vivid orange, packed tight as the roe in the bellies of the salmon still swimming far at sea, poised to move at the magnetic hint of the earth and the ancient, indelible scent of home.

chapter nineteen

Normally, Ed Leary enjoyed the drive from Vancouver south to Chilukthan. He loved the sense of dropping from the mountains to the tidal flats, a gentle amusement-park ride that nature had gifted the south coast of the province. As his truck descended, eventually crossing the Oak Street Bridge, he revelled in the clear view of the river, a silent, soiled ghost fluttering seaward, the power of time and mystery coiled in its currents. He would drive over it, looking down, knowing that in a matter of minutes he would also be going under it, his truck vanishing into the mouth of the Deas Island Tunnel.

Each time he left the city, he anticipated this slow descent into the sudden dark, feeling almost a childish excitement, as though the tunnel represented a gate to another world. Coming out on the Chilukthan side, he always experienced a profound sense of renewal: the air was richer, the trees fuller, the fishermen not born like other people, but gathered up out of river mud and kerosene and old moonlight, their bodies as haunted by the particular qualities of blood as those of the returning salmon. Delight and reverence best described Ed's feelings whenever his truck climbed out of the tunnel, its headlights mining the all-day black: delight to be home among the sights and smells and sounds of the river mouth, and reverence for the mystery of the salmon's return, its intensity and faithfulness.

But tonight, he found no pleasure in the familiar drive. He stared straight ahead, tight-lipped, while Crowthers, the vice-president of the union, lectured him on the need for a quick and firm response to troublemakers in the membership.

"You've got to stamp it out right away. A few sparks and before you know it, whoosh, you've got a raging inferno on your hands. I'm telling you, once you lose control, even a little, you've lost it for good."

Ed took a deep breath and turned slightly to his passenger. Crowthers was a thin man in his early forties with buck teeth and a yellowish moustache so sparse that it resembled the hairs of a very old toothbrush. His eyes were tiny, restless, and as close together as the dots on a pair of dice. He had a high-pitched voice that became extremely grating when raised, which he used to his advantage at meetings to drown others out. Many years ago, Crowthers had crewed on a halibut seiner for a few seasons, and somehow he'd exploited that limited experience to climb to a high position in the union. Once there, he revelled in power like a drunken Caesar.

The sun was just setting, its light angling gold over the delta. Ed and Crowthers were headed for a vote meeting of the Chilukthan local. The companies had tabled a final offer, which the union was advising its membership to reject, and Crowthers had been chosen by the executive to accompany Ed, just to make sure that everything went smoothly. Ed had been outraged at first by the obvious insult of being chaperoned, and then by the choice of Crowthers for the job.

"I can handle the situation," Ed had argued, "and besides, the boys don't take kindly to outsiders coming in to tell them their business."

But the executive had remained firm. "Just an observer, Ed," they had assured him. "No need to take it personally."

"Christ, it's not personal," Ed had flared up, "I know these men. If you send someone in there to lecture them, you might as well tell them to accept the offer."

"Lecture," they had smiled, as though to a child. "Who said anything about lecturing?"

Ed could tell that rumours were beginning to circulate about him. He could just imagine the talk: Leary, the guy out in Chilukthan? Didn't he leave the party after Czechoslovakia? Yes, not quite committed. A bit of a loose cannon. We'd better keep an eye on him.

Ed listened to the nasal voice droning on in his truck and sud-

TIM BOWLING

denly realized that he was being purged. He looked at his passenger again, and chuckled quietly. It was funny, wasn't it? This little loudmouth with the soft hands lecturing me about solidarity, this weasel hiding behind his union title, playing big shot across the table with the canners when he's more like them than the men he represents. With regret, Ed thought about the year he'd spent in the BC Pen, the awful days and nights he'd suffered in the hole just because he was a communist, the long absence from his wife and kids. Back then, he'd had no doubt the sacrifice was worthwhile. What use is a life without principles, without serving others in the cause of justice? But now, he was no longer sure what justice was, or how to achieve it, or even worse, if any but a scattered few really cared about it. Somehow, the canneries' offer seemed beside the point. Ed felt strongly that it had to be rejected. The canners were making such gross profits at the expense of the fishermen that a strike was the only logical response. Yet he had no illusions about the union and its lackey mouthpieces. Ah Christ, just listen to him!

Crowthers was so animated that saliva had formed at the sides of his mouth. "I know about these breakaway types. Stupid as bricks. They read the newspaper and watch the TV and their mouths hang open at the logic of all the propaganda. Free market this, free market that. Who are these troublemakers again? Brunovs, was it? You'll have to point them out to me when we get there. I'll take care of them. These types usually curl up and blow away when you shout them down. You have to stand up to them, throw their faulty logic back in their faces, and just like that they run off home with their tails between their legs."

Ed was amused. "I'll remember that," he said, "when I make my speech." He wanted to embarrass Crowthers, pretend that he didn't know that Crowthers had been told to address the gathering.

But his passenger wasn't in the least bit embarrassed. "Weren't you told? You won't be making a speech tonight. I'll be doing that." He almost burst his buttons at the thought. "This is no time for compromises. The union wants things laid on the line, no fooling around."

"Is that what I've been doing?"

Finally, Crowthers seemed to catch something in his driver's

176

tone. He stared at him briefly, then changed the subject. "I hear you haven't come back to the party yet. Is that right?"

The insufferable, self-righteous little bastard! Temper, temper, Ed cautioned himself, don't make it easy for them. "That's right."

"Any particular reason?"

Yeah, Ed thought quickly, because it's got too many little shits like you in it. "I no longer share the party's support of the Soviet concept of Marxism," he said, already tired of the discussion.

"Really? And what concept do you support?"

Ed didn't even turn his head. The tunnel was fast approaching, and he accelerated in the hope that when he reached the other side, Crowthers would have vanished. Finally, he responded in a way that even Crowthers understood to be the last word. "My own," he said.

By the time they reached Chilukthan Harbour, the sun had set and the sky had turned blue-black. A few barn swallows swooped over the dyke, snapping termites out of the air. At such an hour, just before dark, it was almost impossible to distinguish the termites from the nightfall itself. Only the sharp instincts of a swallow could distinguish a late meal from a mote of dusk.

Ed parked among the other vehicles, then waited while Crowthers gathered up the ballot box and composed himself. His passenger seemed to go into a trance. He bowed his head, muttered briefly into his chest, all the while keeping his pale hands on the dashboard. Ed resisted the desire to ask him what exactly a communist prays to.

After a half-minute, Crowthers snapped to attention, said "Okay, let's get going," and jumped out of the truck.

Ed led the way up the dyke to the wharf with Crowthers right at his heels. Like a pup, Ed concluded, a goddamned wolf-pup.

It was low tide and the rich smell of the river flowed in the air like a second current. Mud, brine, fish-stink, leaf-mulch, oil: all his life, Ed had tried to pick out the individual smells of the Fraser, but they were close as the finely braided strands of a thick rope. If you tried to untangle them, you'd wind up with only a meaningless snarl, whereas together, the smells formed a noose around every sense, drugging you into a kind of pleasant oblivion.

The men on the wharf fell quiet when Ed and Crowthers turned the corner of the netshed. The voices had been low to begin with, a bee-like drone that communicated more than any words the high degree of tension in the crowd. When the voices stopped, it was as though everything else stopped to listen, the tide, the breeze, the falling night. Crowthers cleared his throat but didn't speak. The eyes of forty men were trained on him, and he seemed surprised by the intensity of the collective stare.

Dozens of tiny red glows hung from mouths or shivered slightly at hip level, and the smoke from them made faint pillars against the darker, northern sky. A loose chain clanked against a mast. And still no one spoke. The chain clanked again.

The tide was so low that the gangway was almost vertical, giving the impression that the upper wharf was even more enclosed than usual. A group of latecomers had taken up a position by the narrow passage along the netshed, so that the gathering seemed to have been constricted into a much smaller space, shut off from both the land and the river. The red glows shifted, some dropping, others rising, like embers in a dying fire when a charred log breaks.

Vic and Corbett leaned against the netshed. Corbett was stunned by the gravity of the situation. The serious faces had been surprising enough, but he had never known such a heavy and prolonged silence to fall over a crowd. It made him nervous. What was it Mom always said? The calm before the storm.

Troy stood alone on the other side of the wharf, near the gangway. In the growing darkness, he tried to read Ed Leary's expression. Was it pleased? Worried? He couldn't tell. Let it be a good offer, he prayed, let's just get all this over with.

When the chain clanked a third time, Crowthers nudged Ed in the back, and in a low voice said, "Can't we throw some light on things, for chrissakes?" Ed wanted to laugh out loud at the man's obvious unease, but instead he addressed the crowd. "Somebody want to open the shed and switch the lights on?"

The familiar sound of his voice eased the tension a little, and once the shed door slid back and the light fell forward over the wharf, cutting the men in two at the knees, even Crowthers had recovered from the long silence. He hurried to the brightest spot, casting furtive glances at the faces around him as he moved, and then motioned Ed toward him. "Introduce me, " he instructed.

"What?"

Crowthers scowled so that the hairs of his moustache wriggled like a caterpillar. "Introduce me, I said."

Ed was amazed at the man's gall. "What do you want me to say?"

"Just tell them who I am. I'll handle the rest. Oh, and . . ." He paused and leaned closer. "Which ones are the troublemakers?"

Annoyed, Ed considered pointing out the wrong men, just to see what would happen, but he decided against it, figuring things would be interesting enough as it was. He nodded slightly toward the Brunovs, fifteen feet away, perched side by side between the bars of the net-rack. In their black sweaters and oil-stained jeans, they stood motionless, arms crossed, looking like pistons about to fire. Cocky buggers, Ed thought, then stepped onto the fish crate.

He hesitated. Everyone present thought of him whenever they thought of the union. Whether they respected him or not, they knew who he was and they expected to hear the news from his mouth. Instead, they were getting Crowthers, a stranger, and worse, one they'd sense right away was a desk boy, a paper shuffler, no more connected to the real world of fishermen than whatever eastern idiot was currently the minister of fisheries. Ed made a mental shrug, as if to wash his hands of the whole business, then addressed the crowd.

"We've got a lot of things to discuss tonight, so there's no sense wasting anybody's time. As you know, this is a serious situation." Ed felt the words heavy as stones in his mouth. What was Crowthers, after all, except a huge waste of time? He sighed and went on. "This is Cal Crowthers, from the union office. He was directly involved in the negotiations with the companies, so he'd like to say a few things about their latest offer."

Crowthers glared at Ed as they passed. Then he mounted the crate. "Actually," he began in his high-pitched nasal voice, "as most of you probably know, I'm the vice-president of the union." He paused for effect before resuming. "And I'm here to tell you that there's never been a better opportunity for the labour movement than we have right at this present time, in our industry, in our province, and worldwide. Brothers, let me tell you, we are making great strides everywhere against the greed and monopolies of the capitalist elites, we are on the edge of a new day, when the working man will at last hold the balance of power, when he won't have to crawl, cap in hand, to fat-cat bosses for a fair wage and safe working conditions, when he can fully expect to earn the rewards that he has reaped by the sweat of his own brow."

To punctuate his point, Crowthers touched his forehead with one pale, clean hand. Then, in a conspiratorial tone, he continued: "But brothers, this day can't happen unless we are prepared to band together and to do what's necessary to resist the cabals of the politicians and the capitalists, unless we put aside our differences for the sake of the common good, whether that's here on the Fraser or in Vietnam or Chile or wherever working people are struggling to overcome the oppression of the moneyed classes. We can't let up for a minute." He stopped briefly, adjusted his tie, then hurried on. "Complacency is death to our struggle for fairness and we can't buy into the propaganda of the bought press, we can't be fooled into thinking that the capitalist system can allow for progressive social change, we must present a unified opposition to those who would benefit from the fruits of our labour, who would live on our backs to fatten themselves at the trough of their own greed, without any thought to the millions of workers who only ask for a just deal, reasonable compensation for their skill and their time."

The fishermen shuffled their feet. One or two grumbled to themselves, and someone cleared his throat and spat on the wharf close to where Crowthers stood on the crate. But he took no notice, suddenly thrusting his fist into the air.

"Brothers, now is not the time to weaken, now is the time to clench our fists and shake them in the faces of those who would deprive us of what is rightfully ours, here, on the Fraser, everywhere on the coast, and everywhere that our brothers and sisters are sharing the struggle. Solidarity! That's what I'm talking about, and it's never been more important than it is right now!"

He paused again, wiping the spittle from his lips, and was about to resume when a clear voice shouted, "What the fuck's the offer!"

At this, the men raised their impatient, scowling faces almost in unison. A few burning cigarettes were tossed down and stomped on. Ed couldn't help grinning. But Crowthers only gained strength from the interruption, as though he needed opposition to clarify his own views.

He glared in the direction of the Brunovs, even though the question had been shouted by Ossie Reddick, the old-timer who had no patience for what he called "patronizing bullshit." Crowthers' voice strained at its gears as he continued his assault on the breakaway members. Ignoring the question, he launched into a lecture on the way unions operate, how the members had to trust their executive to do the job for which they'd been elected.

"We're the front-line fighters," he explained shrilly, "we're the ones getting dirty in the trenches for your sake, we're the ones who have to sit across from those company bastards and wade through all their legal horseshit to make sure you're not getting a raw deal! How do you think you'd fare on your own? I'll tell you how. You'd be pissed on!"

From his position on the crate, Crowthers looked as if he was ready to do just that to the Brunovs lined up below him, their sneers hanging like tiny bats in the dim light. "Don't think for a minute that you can survive in this industry without the union in there fighting for decent prices and working conditions. Wise up! Read a little history, find out what it was like when the canneries had a dozen splinter groups of fishermen to play against one another. They were laughing, let me tell you, all the way to the friggin' bank, and they're just itching to laugh at us again."

Crowthers kept his eyes on the Brunovs. He'd come to the meeting with one agenda, to browbeat the dissident members into obedience. But the Brunovs only sneered back at him, scornful of his strong-arm tactics, which carried no weight because Crowthers had no reputation among the local membership.

Ed could feel the men losing patience. They had come for concrete information and if they didn't get it soon, Ed knew they'd be in no mood to consider the union's advice. Obviously, Crowthers had lost sight of the big picture. In his desire to force the Brunovs into submission, he was alienating everyone else. Ed could see it happening, and part of him was satisfied by the expected turn of events. In all his years of union work, he'd never lost sight of the big picture, the simple need for fishermen to get a just deal from the companies. Still, he remained silent, unable to mount the enthusiasm to get involved.

"We're not your fucking brothers!" Curt Brunov shouted, his thick lips pulled back in a snarl, the finger of one hand stabbing at the darkness between him and the union vice-president. "And we don't give a shit about Chile! Just tell us the offer and let us vote on it!"

Crowthers' eyes rolled wildly in his reddening face, and spittle flew from his mouth. His voice rose like gullcry over the murmurs of the crowd. "Are you deaf or just stupid? BC, Chile, the whole goddamned world, it's one and the same thing! Can't you understand that? The companies that are screwing you are screwing people all over the world! Do you know who owns BC Packers? Huh? Weston Food, that's who. And Weston Food is a British outfit. How about Canadian Fish? Eh, come on. The New England Fish Company. That's right, the fuckin' Americans, the same Americans exploiting the whole of Central and South America! And you don't give a shit!"

Somebody shouted, "Hey, Ed, who asked you to bring your commie friends around here anyway!"

All right, Ed decided, enough is enough. He tapped Crowthers on the leg, and motioned him to step down. Impolitic as he was, the vice-president at least recognized the futility of further shouting. With a snort of derision, and a thrust of his arms to show that he'd done all he could to make the members see sense, Crowthers jumped off the crate, picked up the ballot box, and melted into the darkness along the netshed. No one paid him much attention.

"Thirty-nine for sockeye," Ed began, "and no guarantee of sticking to that through the Adams. Thirteen for pinks, 18 for dogs."

A collective groan followed this announcement. The offer was several cents below last season's prices, only a penny more than the previous offer.

Corbett glanced at his father, whose stern expression provided a depressing commentary on the situation.

Vic knew that he had no choice but to reject the offer. He'd been prepared for disappointing news, but this was worse than expected. Obviously, the companies were already laughing at the union, testing it, as though they'd heard rumours about dissension in the ranks. Again, Vic's sense of justice conflicted with his longing for peace. He only wanted to be left alone to earn enough money to get by. Was that too much to expect? Thirty-nine cents! We can't fish for that price.

Troy couldn't see his father in the shadows, so he watched the reaction of the Brunovs instead. What are the big talkers going to do, he wondered. Like everyone else, they looked annoyed, and Todd was chirping quietly to the other two, who hardly moved their large heads in response.

"Obviously," Ed continued, once the reaction had died down, "the union position is that we reject the offer. It's an insult. They're not taking us seriously. We don't have any other choice."

"Like hell we don't," Mark Brunov interrupted, jumping out from beside his brothers; it looked as though one plank in a dark fence had been kicked in. "They're bluffing. Besides, there's a lot of fish coming back. Even at a couple of cents a pound less, we'll still make more than we did last year. If we don't fish, and we miss out on a couple hundred, who cares if we get a few more cents afterwards? We'll be losing more if we strike."

Ed felt some of his old fire return, fuelled by the Brunovs' unrelenting opposition, but even more by the atmosphere surrounding him. He was standing on a fish crate on a wharf at the mouth of the Fraser River, fighting the greed of the monopolies. It might have been 1901, or 1938, or 1955. The prices had changed, but the argument seemed as old as the river. He could have been speaking through the mouths of any impassioned, mud-splattered, scale-fingered ghosts. He could have been speaking Greek or Japanese or Coast Salish. Standing there in the wash of light, under the thickening stars, with the river pointing its drenched, pungent arm westward to remind him of the salmon massing in the far depths, Ed could not turn away from what he'd always believed to be an inherited responsibility. If he had lost his faith in the ability of men to meet their potential, he had not quite forsaken that part of himself that had first given rise to the faith. It lay dormant, buried under a slide of empty rhetoric and bald propaganda, all the jostling for power among various hierarchies, the competition that bruised and bled both the gullible and the informed, that made people stand on fish crates in the half-darkness explaining again and again the realities of the world. He felt it again now, the burning in his veins that made time meaningless, and his own bones merely the hardened smoke of a million cigarettes dropping ash in millions of anxious vigils.

"You just don't get it, do you?" He pointed at the Brunovs. "You just won't get your noses out of your own asses long enough to smell what's really going on. I'll say it one more time. If you don't stand up to the companies, if you let them set the agenda, they'll walk all over you and not even care if your bodies rot right there on the ground to make mulch for their goddamned roses!"

"Exactly," Crowthers began, "that's just what I . . ."

"Shut up!" Ed roared, turning. "You've done enough talking for one night!"

Crowthers, glancing around indignantly, shrunk back into the shadows.

Ed continued: "You boys fish herring. Probably figure you've been doing pretty good, eh? Had a good season this past one, did you? What did you get, thirty bucks a ton? What do you think? Is that fair market value? The value set by the marketplace, supply and demand. You boys are big on that. I sure hear you crowing about it, how you're going to go it alone, be little entrepreneurs selling to the highest bidder. That's smart, that's what the big shots do, that's what the newspapers preach and the politicians, that's the ABCs of the system. Okay, fine, put your faith in them instead of the people you work beside, that's your goddamned business, I guess." He waved his hand in their direction, as if to erase their presence. "I'm sick of talking to you, I've got grandkids I could be toilet-training instead. Go on and scab, do what you want. But let me share one little piece of information with you before you enter into your beautiful partnership with the fine folks at Weston Food Incorporated and the New England Fish Company, which is probably, even as we speak, being bought out by Weston too, just like all the little canneries we used to have all up and down the coast."

Even in the dim light, Ed's eyes seemed to project, drawing all the other eyes on the wharf into them. His shadow swayed across the planks like a small tide pulled by its own invisible moon.

"For two years," he resumed in a quieter voice, "the companies have been selling herring roe to the Japanese . . ." His voice rose to a kind of deep snarl. "For six hundred bucks a ton!"

The words echoed strangely through the air, as the fishermen, dazed into silence, blinked at the black wastes above the netshed.

"We haven't released that to the media yet," Crowthers whispered in a panic. "You weren't supposed to mention that."

Ed ignored him. "That's right. Six hundred bucks a ton. Quite a tidy little profit."

"You're full of it," Curt Brunov scoffed. "You're just desperate."

"I don't care what you think. This is my last word on the subject. Put your faith in a system that's no more free than a gaffed sockeye and you're putting your faith in people who don't give a rat's ass for what happens to you or your families."

Ed stepped down, grabbed the ballot box from Crowthers, set it on the crate, removed the pencils and the little slips of paper, and waited. "Your call," he said.

The men began to come forward, still in a state of shock, to take the pencils and paper. Some, like Vic and Ossie Reddick, were visibly impressed by Ed's rhetorical skills, while others couldn't get beyond the content of his speech. Six hundred bucks! They couldn't conceive of that kind of deceit, though they did not doubt it, most of them having long experience of company tactics. As Ed had expected, the members of his local could not wait to make their small protest against their own vulnerability once they'd heard the news about the latest company plunder. After muttering among themselves for a moment, they took the pencils and the paper, and one by one, went into the netshed to vote, returning to put their ballots in the box.

In the silence of the voting, a muffled sound drifted across the narrow harbour, then a cracking and splintering. Almost as one, the men looked up and saw the burning netshed on the opposite bank of the channel. By now, night had settled so thickly over the river that the bright flames seemed to be flowing through a gash in the air, as though the darkness had been cut and was bleeding. But the wound was still being made. A terrible sound, as of flesh being pulled back, rose over the harbour, a harsh tearing followed by more and more flame spitting and sizzling out across the dark channel. The wood of the old netshed erupted like dry straw. Grey smoke lifted from the brightness and dissolved somewhere above the treetops, while a shivering, animated reflection spread over the water, lapping slowly toward the lower wharf. Soon the windshields of the moored gillnetters caught the fireglow and held it, as though they were moving rapidly through a rough, red sea, tossing wet sparks and embers off the glass.

On the upper wharf, the fishermen began shouting orders and scattering down the gangway. Corbett ran around the corner to the house to call the fire department, while Vic and Troy, like the others, hurried to soak their boats in case of any drifting sparks. Two fishermen whose vessels had powerful hoses drifted into the channel and directed ineffective sprays at the flames, hoping to contain the blaze to the one spot. Fortunately, there was a considerable gap between the burning building and its neighbours, and the breeze was blowing from the north, which kept the flames from spreading to the nearby sheds.

Ed stood on the lower wharf, directly across from the fire, his face flushed with heat even at that distance. Somebody's losing nets, he thought, somebody's season is in a hole already, strike or no strike. Who works in that shed? He looked down the wharf. A silent group stood nearby, their faces red-bathed and motionless, though the light flickered wildly on their skin. Ed joined them, asked some questions, and learned that the Samsons, in a stroke of good fortune, had just removed their new sockeye nets the day before. "Let's hope we get a chance to use the damned things," one of them replied without enthusiasm.

Meanwhile, a siren had begun to cry in the distance, growing louder until the flashing lights of the fire truck could be seen upriver, crossing the little harbour bridge that joined the island to the mainland. Ten seconds later, the lights reappeared, spinning wildly against the dense backdrop of the poplars, as firemen rushed down the narrow gangway with their more powerful hose.

Eventually, they extinguished the blaze, but the shed was only a charred ruin, its roof and walls collapsed into an ashen heap. As the fire died, the fishermen faded back into the darkness, their faces still hung in silence, only their eyes red. No one spoke. The fire had stirred their superstitious instincts; it was a bad sign, perhaps a warning. But of what? Of the troubles to come? Or maybe it was aimed at those who voted to accept the offer, if any did. The shed was no more than a crusted scab on the bank, covering over the wounded darkness. The fishermen, hands in pockets or fumbling for cigarettes, did not move for several minutes after the fire had been put out. Each seemed to be reading some greater significance into this event. Few could remember the last time there'd been a fire in the harbour. Why now? Most of the fishermen, conditioned to read the portents of tide and wind, could not accept a coincidence wherever elemental forces were concerned. Most felt, uneasily, that the weeks ahead would bring unpleasant answers. Even the Brunovs, fresh from marking to accept the offer, stared gloomily across the channel.

"Dad," Troy said, "what do you figure? About the strike, I mean."

But Vic didn't hear the question. He was still staring at the black channel where, up until a few moments before, the fire had been reflected. The image was as near to the battle scene in the Atlantic as anything he'd experienced since: the night, the shouts, the flickering light across the dark water, and the overwhelming sense of helplessness. The only real difference was the absence of bodies in the channel, but Vic saw one there anyway, the same blond hair flowing out, rising and falling from around the skull. Like the other men on the wharf, the sense of control he'd felt rejecting the companies' offer had dissipated in the sudden burst of flame. Now he only felt a hollow in the pit of his stomach, and a dryness in his mouth. This is not right, he repeated to himself, this is bad, something's not right about this. But he couldn't pin it down.

"Dad?" Troy said again.

Finally, Vic turned to his son, who asked his question once more. "I think we'll strike," Vic responded, the worry plain in his voice.

As if on cue, Crowthers, puffing out his skinny chest, shouted from the upper wharf, "Any of you guys that didn't vote yet better get up here! We're leaving!"

A few fishermen mounted the gangway, their knees slowly entering the netshed light. Ed followed, depressed at the prospect of driving Crowthers back to the city, but hoping that he'd be less talkative after the way the meeting had gone. I'll bet he can't wait to report me to the executive, Ed thought, for conduct unbecoming a mere local rep. To hell with it. If I know the fleet, and the canneries, we'll be tied up for a while, that's the cold fact. Crowthers can go piss up a rope. Ed set his jaw firmly and left the darkness behind.

The stars thickened in frozen schools over Chilukthan, making the sky one-half of the same pregnant reality below the surface of the river. The breeze picked up, clanking the chain and furring the channel. As the tide came up, the breeze gathered strength, and by the middle of the night, it would be howling over the flats, repeating the same command, each word older than language, each word like moss over blood: now, now, now, now.

chapter twenty

The door to the shop swung open again, shivering the little bell, and Joe looked up with the familiar flutter in his chest and wrists. But it was never her. The door kept opening and closing, and the air around the flesh of those who entered seemed a howling absence.

Joe sighed. Where was the full, dark hair tied back in a patterned kerchief, the dark-lashed green eyes so wide they seemed to reflect the entire world, and the light, almost hesitant steps toward the counter? Why did she not return?

Another week had gone by. Neither Mrs. Mawson nor her daughter had appeared in well over two weeks. At first, Joe pretended that his new involvement in his own small world relied on nothing but the force of his own conviction. He smiled and chatted to his customers, ate out in a local Greek restaurant, went for strolls in the lovely late evenings, and generally delighted in all the sensations and experiences he'd taken for granted, dulled by his long familiarity with them.

But gradually, he had become nervously aware of the limitations to his changed self. As the days passed, his new activities and responses evolved into just another pattern. He smiled at customers and waitresses, purchased the most modern equipment for his immaculate shop, and took a greater interest in the blossoming Chilukthan landscape. But all the while, he recognized a forced quality to his efforts, as though he was performing for an audience that never clapped or even showed up to watch. Eventually, he had begun to face the hard truth that whatever strength he had discovered in himself was founded on a particular source: he depended on the quiet grace afforded him by a woman, a wife and mother.

And so the days passed, the door swung in, and the little bell shook. Joe looked up half-hoping and half-afraid, and the equanimity of the weeks before slowly began to unravel.

He'd heard about the strike, and it worried him. He sensed that Mrs. Mawson (he would think of her briefly as Kathleen, and then, feeling a rush of shame, bow his head) would not patronize his shop if that meant buying on credit. The unspoken sympathy that he believed existed between them told Joe that her absence was due to economic hardship and not embarrassment or fear rising out of any complicated feelings she had for him. But the realization made no substantial difference to his need. He wanted to see her because she cast back that reflection of himself he so desperately wanted to believe in. In her eyes, he might not have been an object of romantic love, but at least he existed as a man independent of the smock he wore and the cleaver he raised. When she spoke to him, it was neither mere gossip nor the slightly condescending dialogue most customers conducted with tradesmen; she always looked at him in a caring way. Joe liked to believe this look was a small gift to him, and not just a general act of her nature. With this belief, so minor and harmless in his view, he had supported the idea that his life had not exhausted all its possibilities for change.

After weeks of sunshine, the weather had turned. Now Joe sat behind his counter, staring at the midday darkness crowding against the glass, until finally the rain started, long trembles of it blurring his view of the street, drops tapping the window. He kept looking up, the tapping a prod to his memory, but he did not know what he should be remembering, if it wasn't simply this dull, drear metronome of solitude.

The phone rang, and he got up heavily to answer it. "Yes," he said. "Yes, Grade A, the best quality." He paused. "Until five, that's right." Another pause. "You're welcome."

The storm mimicked his conversation, rising and falling. He felt a huge weight settle into his muscles. The receiver in his hand looked like a charred bone. He put it down and walked to the door. Why wouldn't it open? Why did the rain mock the sound of the bell? He stared out the window at the low sky. A group of boys scurried past on the other side of the street. One of them lagged a little behind, and Joe thought he looked familiar. Yes, it was the boy he had untied from the net-rack; the same dirty T-shirt, torn jeans, and sharp-boned face. Joe felt a brief pang of guilt. But there was nothing more he could have done; the fisherman and his wife had said as much. Still, the boy's appearance only made the day gloomier. Joe sighed and looked to the sky again.

Two large black clouds shunted together like boxcars. He watched them for a while, feeling that his loneliness, which had become the only real consideration in his life, was shabby and outcast, the sort of thing that dies in the fireweed and thistles alongside a railroad track, dies there because it will not make the leap onto the passing train. I am a coward, he told himself for what seemed like the millionth time, I am not even brave enough to be foolish.

But when he turned away from the window, and the clouds shuddered on without his attention, he realized that there could never be a final turning away from himself. It was an old truth, but it came to him clothed in a strange radiance. Suddenly, he realized that he was poised between the leap and the slow sink into the ground. His muscles weren't tired, they were tensed. Something had been set in motion, and one way or another, he was meant to see it through to the final stop.

The realization flooded him in a sort of calm. Whatever happened now, whatever he did or didn't do, would involve coming to terms with his feelings for a married woman. Those feelings shuddered through him again, disturbing the calm: he imagined loosening her kerchief and watching her hair cascade over her shoulders; he saw his fingertips tracing her soft lips. Disgusted with himself, Joe snapped out of his reverie and turned his heavy-lidded eyes back to the door.

A half mile away, Kathleen sat at her kitchen table, ignoring the weather. Vic was on strike. She didn't even think of her sons being in the same position. They were young enough to take this in their stride, young enough to do something else, but she knew Vic's anxieties were well grounded. If he had to change to get by in a changed economic reality, was she making it more difficult for him by supporting his idealism?

And then there were the practical considerations on top of the emotional ones: what were they going to do for money? Already, she'd had to cut back on groceries, making an early use of the canned goods stored up for the winter. What if the strike lasted more than one or two openings? The Stuarts were here and moving. At night, Vic lay awake as though he were counting them as they went by. Even when he slept, he was restless, a current of the river trembling on the sheets beside her.

From a great distance, Kathleen heard her father's calm voice as he leaned down and gave her a silver dollar just before she boarded the train to come west. "Never spend it," he had said, "no matter how much you might want to. Then you'll never be controlled by money, you'll control it." It was advice she had often had to remember. In the early days of her marriage, she believed that coin was all that stood between her and utter despair. But it wasn't the logic of her father's words that gave her strength; it was the kindness that accompanied them. He didn't make any warning comments about her choice in love, nor did he paint a gloomy picture based on the hardships that he had encountered most of his days, from unemployment to the deaths of so many children. He simply gave her one small bit of silver that meant more to her somehow than the loaded nets of a thousand sockeye runs. That coin, and Vic's ring, were invested with more significance than any bank account or fish book, but she could not barter her father's kindness or her husband's proposal. For that, she needed money divested of kindness, the silver dollars imbedded in the salmon's flesh.

Kathleen held the coin in her open palm. She missed her parents, their capacity for endurance, their uncomplaining acceptance of fate. What must it have been like to outlive so many children? They never spoke of their many losses, just as she and Vic never spoke of their own. But maybe, she thought, her parents did speak of it when they were alone, maybe that was the only way they could not talk about it every waking moment of their lives. There was so much that she had never asked them, their deaths preceding the longing for knowledge she had really only possessed for the last few years. What was the difference, what had kept her mother going when Kathleen had succumbed to that very darkness which was never spoken of, though it buffeted the mind so often? Ah, this is not doing me any good, she finally decided, putting the coin back into its little box of tissue paper. Then she noticed the rain on the window. I'll make a fresh thermos of tea for Vic, she thought, plugging in the kettle, and Zoe can take it to him.

At that moment, Vic, Corbett, and Troy stood among a large group of fishermen on the upper wharf, listening to Ed Leary's instructions. "We'll have one picket line here, outside the cannery, and we'll patrol the river as well, to make sure no one has snuck out during the night and anchored. Just a half-dozen boats ought to do it. Any volunteers? Okay, good. Should just be routine stuff. We're not expecting any trouble. The vote, as I've said, was pretty near unanimous. Otherwise, the rest of you fellows might as well show up here a little before eight. Any questions? All right, then, I guess that's all. See you in the morning."

Troy had been one of the fishermen to volunteer for river patrol. Just the thought of standing around all day made him restless. He'd rather be doing something, even if that meant having to watch the sockeye jumping around his boat. Like his father, he had not slept well since the night of the last meeting a week before. He could not reconcile the union's position with his growing sense that the gillnet fishermen were just pawns in a power struggle. And despite himself, he could not shake the fact that the Brunovs might very well have a point. The fish were here, now. Why not catch them and bargain later? Troy remembered the awful tension of the last strike, and he saw it again in the slump of his father's shoulders, the shroud of smoke that rarely left his face, the creases in his brow and the bruises on his temples whenever it did. And the palpable worry in his mother's eyes was even worse. Troy could not stand to be around the house. He got up earlier, and stayed out all day, at the pool hall, the wharf, the ballpark.

Corbett kept away from the house a great deal too, but he also avoided the pool hall and the beach parties. More and more, he was spending time with Margo, trying to demystify his feelings for her by saturating himself in her presence. Each time they made love, he tried afterwards to deny the truth, that he could not walk away from her. He laughed, he played the cavalier role of his local reputation, but he did not believe in it any longer. Margo only became more desirable. He'd never been with a woman who had such a good sense of humour, or whose willingness to laugh equalled his own. He'd never been with a woman who was genuinely interested in sports and fishing, even to the point of telling him things about those subjects he hadn't known. Margo seemed so confident; she even acted as though she could get along just fine by herself if necessary. Corbett couldn't stop thinking about her. The situation was both terrifying and wonderful. He existed in a perpetual state of bewilderment that would not allow him to focus on any other part of his life. At the ballpark, he played so poorly that the Brunovs thought he was doing it on purpose because they had insulted his family. But Corbett wasn't interested in that old argument. His only interest in the strike was personal; when would it be over so he could make some money and get his own place? Margo was still bothered by what she called the "sordidness" of their affair, and Corbett was too much in love to risk losing her over something as trivial as money and his domestic situation. Yet his thinking on the subject was so confused that he vehemently defended the strike even while he wanted it to end. If his father believed in the strike, that was enough for Corbett. Loyalty to himself, to Margo, and to his father's ideals did not conflict in his imagination. He believed that the strike would be short because he wanted it to be. How could the world conspire against him for long? He was young, handsome, in love. Let a few fish go by; we'll load up on the first day back. Corbett smiled in anticipation, then noticed his brother's dour expression across the wharf. What's he got to worry about, he wondered, it's only a few bucks to him.

The rain fell heavier, driving the men off the wharf. Soon, it fringed the telephone lines in black shawls and dropped an early dusk out of the clouds. Vic headed home, slowly, despite the water streaming down his cheeks. He met Zoe just as he rounded the corner of Laidlaw Street. She was running with the thermos warm as a live bird in her hands. He forced himself to smile broadly at her. Then he tossed his cigarette on the pavement. It blinked a few times and went out. He picked his daughter up and held her warmth against the fear and the images that wouldn't let him sleep: the burning water and the steep hill, the blank face on the little body he would hold only to lower in the earth, and the terror in the eyes of the gull as he bashed its head in. Vic held his daughter even closer. How can I protect you, he breathed softly into her neck.

chapter twenty-one

When Corbett heard that Dennis Petrovich had come home because of the industry-wide strike, he could not easily absorb the information. He had overlooked Margo's marriage for so long that he no longer even thought of it as an obstacle. Quoting another of his mother's sayings, he would tell himself to cross that bridge when he came to it.

But now he did not know how to proceed. He'd been living exactly as though life was nothing more complicated than a base-ball game: step up to the plate, and as long as you keep hitting, the inning never ends. Corbett believed in the idea of three chances, three outs, and so far he'd not even used one. But the appearance of Margo's husband seemed to change the rules. Suddenly, Corbett realized that he was going to get only one chance. Worse yet, he wasn't sure he was going to be able to con-trol the situation. For the first time, the awful thought hit him that Margo might actually choose to stay with Dennis. She had made no promises to leave. Have we even talked about it, he wondered. Now Corbett understood the danger he was in. He did not fear Dennis Petrovich; he feared his wife. The thought of not being with Margo was so painful, and so sudden, precipitated by the strike, that he almost drove straight to her house the moment he heard that Dennis had come back.

Instead, he waited. Maybe the strike would end quickly. If so, Dennis would go north again, and without him around, Corbett could work on persuading Margo to leave the marriage.

But the days passed, the companies made no new offers, and

Corbett's worry mounted. What if the strike lasted another week? How was he going to see Margo with Dennis in town? He wondered if he should just confront Dennis with the truth, tell him there were no hard feelings, but that his wife wasn't in love with him anymore? No, Margo wouldn't like that, and if she was deciding between them, such a rash act might jeopardize his chances. Dennis was older than Margo, and she was nearly ten years older than Corbett, so he knew he'd have to avoid looking like a kid in any meetings with them.

But he could not restrain himself from driving by Margo's house several times a day, trying to catch a glimpse of her. Once, he phoned, but had to hang up when Dennis answered.

After four days, Corbett could stand it no longer. He decided to park on the dyke at night and watch the house, waiting for Dennis to leave. The first night he chose, he waited for three hours without success. The second night, he had just shut off his engine when a dark figure burst from the house. A minute later, a truck shot out of the drive, accelerated on the road with a violent squeal of its tires, and sped wildly toward town.

Corbett sprinted down the dyke and across the road into the protection of the poplars. A strong wind off the river yearned in the high branches and sprayed moonlight against the front of the house. He approached cautiously, his heartbeat increasing with every step despite his repeated self-instructions to relax. He moved along the side of the house to the kitchen. Through the back window, he saw that the kitchen was dark but that a light shone in the hallway. The spaniel barked once, but stopped immediately at the sound of Corbett's voice. The house seemed empty. Maybe Margo had gone out? But her car was in the driveway. Had she gone to bed already? If so, Corbett knew he'd have to wake her somehow. He'd break in if necessary.

He moved around to the front of the house. Finally, peering through the living-room window, he saw Margo lying on the couch. He rapped lightly on the glass, but she didn't move. He knocked louder. She sat up, alarmed. In the dim light, Corbett could see that her hair was loose and hanging over her face the way it sometimes did after they'd made love. She looked so vulnerable that he wanted nothing more than to lie down beside her and whisper that everything was going to be fine. But once he realized that his knocking had frightened her, he hurried to the door, which was, oddly, ajar, and called out, "It's me, Corb." His voice sounded strange and harsh in the emptiness. He tried again. "I'm coming in, okay?"

"Yes," Margo answered dully, "all right."

She was sitting with her head in her hands when he entered the room. He could tell that something was wrong, but he didn't know how to begin. Just four days apart from her, and he felt awkward somehow, as though they had never touched at all. The feeling came mostly from the ominous silence she was keeping. He had planned on rushing to her and taking her into his arms, but such an act seemed brutal in this atmosphere. Corbett waited for her to look at him.

When she did, he was not prepared for the listlessness in her manner. "Well?" she asked, peering out from under her hair.

"Well?" he repeated. "Is that it? I haven't seen you for four days."

She leaned back against the couch and closed her eyes. "I know," she said wearily. "I almost called you at your parents' place, to tell you not to try and see me while Dennis is here."

"I saw him leave," Corbett suddenly recalled. "He was driving a bit out of control. Did you two fight or something?"

Margo laughed hollowly, then grimaced and gently touched the back of her head. "Fight? What could we possibly have to fight about?"

"Does he know?" Corbett said, both alarmed and excited. "Did you tell him about us?"

Finally, Margo turned toward him and opened her eyes; they were as dull as her manner. "Of course not," she sighed. "He figured it out that I've been with someone, but he doesn't know who. I wouldn't tell him."

"Why not? He's going to have to know sooner or later."

Her voice became edgy. "Then it had better be later. He was drunk and looking to kill someone. I've told you before, whatever happens, I don't want you to be hurt." She rested her hand on his knee before falling back on the couch again. "Let's just be patient, wait for the strike to be over. When he's gone, we'll straighten things out."

What did she mean, straighten things out? Corbett could

detect no promise in her tone and he was afraid to push the matter any further. He moved closer to her on the couch. "I've missed you," he said, and ran a finger down her cheek and across her lips.

"Corbett, please," Margo pleaded. "I've missed you too, but you have to go. Please. Just be patient. When the strike's over . . ."

"That could be weeks. I can't—"

Margo gripped his caressing hand. "Don't be stupid, I'm trying to protect you!"

Corbett almost said that he wasn't afraid of anything, but the boast sounded childish even to him. He held back, but couldn't bring himself to leave. So he just sat there until Margo told him again.

"At least let me kiss you," he said.

Margo relented, but as soon as his lips touched hers, she pulled away. "Corb, please, you have to go."

He wondered if this was one of those times when he should disregard the difference in their ages and act toward her the way he would with a woman younger than him. But he sensed an unyielding resolution in her, and for one of the few times in his life, he decided to be prudent.

"Will you be all right?" he said, rising from the couch.

She nodded. "Just don't do anything, okay? Just wait until he leaves town."

Corbett looked at her pale, upturned face in the semi-darkness, hesitated again, and finally turned away. He stepped softly through the ribs of moonlight on the hardwood floor and out of the room. Then he shut the front door with a click, and walked slowly up the driveway under the murmur of the wind gusting in the poplars.

He climbed the dyke but did not go straight to his car. He walked to the edge of the river and breathed in the rich, familiar smell of mud and brine, thinking seriously for the first time that the strike was the most important obstacle in his life. The wind furrowed the moonlight in the Pass and pushed white ripples up the near bank. The bullrushes soaked in the oily light, their full heads dripping like torches guiding the salmon home. Corbett waited until he heard a jumper splash beneath the sound of the wind, its bright, hard body dazzling in the darkness. One cent, he thought suddenly, a lousy cent. Another splash. Another. He turned back to his car, while everywhere behind him, from the salted mouth to New Westminster, the Fraser continued racking the silver on its abacus.

chapter twenty-two

All night, Raskin had felt the word "now" thrumming in his chest and veins, injected into him like poison, giving his blood the same feverish quality as that of the salmon jumping and flipping and streaming past his trailer in the long darkness. At one point, when the moon slid behind a bank of cloud, he considered slipping out onto the river and poaching, the risk of being caught by a fisheries patrol boat less than that of being hassled by strikers during the day. But he suspected that the government, anticipating such a move by fishermen who didn't plan to strike, would increase their patrols. And if he was caught poaching in that situation, Raskin knew his boat and nets would be confiscated. For that reason, he didn't even send the boy out in the skiff. What if the government traced the little bastard back to him and decided to confiscate his gear as well, just because he was the father? Raskin knew enough about the government to know that he didn't trust them farther than he could spit. They were always on his case as it was, sending goddamned social workers around because of the boy—stupid, nosy bitches usually, asking all sorts of questions and looking at him with disgust. How many times would he have liked to smack one of them, just to wipe that snotty look off her face?

Instead, he'd just kept moving along the river, from Port Coquitlam to New Westminster to Annieville to Finn Slough and now to Chilukthan, always keeping a step or two ahead of the government agencies. If he had never before feared that one branch of the government might use another branch against him, that social services might contact the fisheries, it was only because he'd never felt such a gut wrenching as he felt now, awake all night with the salmon running, an opening scheduled, and a strike set to keep him from fishing.

Raskin had never scabbed during previous strikes. The stakes had never been high enough for him to risk the repercussions of the other gillnetters, and like many scabs, he harboured a secret desire to be respected by the very people whose throats he was cutting.

But this summer was different. The spring catch had been terrible, and now the Stuarts were coming back in numbers that could turn his season around in just a couple of openings. It wasn't fair that he had to tie up. As always, the world was doing everything it could to bugger up his life. If it wasn't his woman dying and leaving him with a kid that the law said he had to look after, then it was a bunch of bastards forcing him to miss out on one of the biggest sockeye runs in years. It wasn't fair. He never got a fucking break.

At dawn, he paced on his little wharf, watching to see if anyone else had decided to risk going out. But the river was calm until almost eight o'clock, when six gillnetters drifted out of Chilukthan Harbour. Raskin hid in his boat as they passed, cursing them. He recognized Ed Leary, that fat bastard, and the Jap, and that mouthy young shit who towed him away from the bridge in the fog. What was his name? Wilson? Something like that. His old man also fished the Prairie. Telling me I shouldn't hit the little prick when he fucks up. Bad as a social worker. He probably thinks I've forgotten about that, the mouthy little shit.

The word pounded in Raskin's body all morning, so that by the early afternoon, he'd started drinking to stop the sound. He went into his trailer, grabbed a few bottles, and returned to his boat. He tried to drown the word, but it kept leaping up to his lips, fierce as the salmon he wasn't allowed to catch. Now, now, now, now!

After a while, he fell asleep, but woke when the patrolling strikers returned to harbour. It was late afternoon; the sunlight had softened and begun to drip like egg yolk over the marshes. Raskin started drinking again. He knew he couldn't hold out much longer, and that if he was going to follow through with his plan, he'd have to down enough booze to give him the courage.

By nightfall, the word came to him from far away, more like an urgent whisper than a shout, but it was even more powerful that way; it had a kind of sexual force in it now, a climactic momentum. Raskin felt a trembling in his limbs that was only partly the result of the alcohol he'd consumed. No less than other fishermen, he wound the frenzied pulse of the salmon into his own so that his wrists and throat and chest leapt against the air, beating and beating against it until he'd made a space for his desire to thrash in and die.

Eventually, he stumbled up the gangway into his trailer and yelled for the boy, who seemed to materialize out of the close air.

"We're going out!" Raskin roared. "Fuck them!"

The boy swallowed hard. He knew that his father would not be able to stay tied up, but had hoped he would be overlooked. The idea of scabbing was meaningless to him, except that he knew it was dangerous and unpopular. He had wanted to stay away from home all day to avoid just such a situation, but as always, he feared the repercussions: scabbing might be dangerous, but angering his father was even worse.

He followed him now and untied the boat while his father started the engine. In the silence, the sound was thunderous, and the boy feared that everyone in Chilukthan must be rushing down to the dyke to watch them pull away from the wharf.

But only darkness flowed over the dyke. Soon, the engine was idling and the rush of the current rose above it, the river running out rapidly as though pouring off a cliff.

The boy could tell the tide was too low and fast to make a decent set, but he also knew that it made no difference what he thought. Even sober, his father never listened to him, so there was no point talking to him when he was drunk. The boy glanced at the tide line on the islands as they sped past, hoping that it was high enough to keep their leadline from catching all the snags on the bottom of the Prairie.

The boy's knowledge of the river equalled that of any other creature born and raised to breathe its mud and read its currents. He was as comfortable in the sloughs and marshes as a muskrat, and he even moved the same way, quickly through the light, dipping and swerving into the shadows to avoid observation. Sharp-boned, with small eyes the colour of silt, and sleek, close-cropped hair stretched over his skull tight as a hide, the boy looked nocturnal, as though he spent his days on earth as a ruse to conceal the nature of his subaquatic origins. There was a swiftness in his look and reaction, and an overpowering sense of solitude that added to his oddly unhuman appearance.

At the top of the drift, Raskin flung his scotchman almost into the reeds opposite Wilkies Island, then raced across the channel, the net reeling off the drum and slapping into the water boiling behind the stern. He kept the boat lights off. Who needed lights if there were no other boats on the river?

Fortunately, the net did not backlash on the drum, so when Raskin reached the bank of Wilkies again, almost running into it, his corkline lay invisible across the narrow drift.

He jammed the boat into neutral, then stepped on deck, breathing heavily. The boy, crouched near the fish box, hoped that his father had forgotten about him, which at first seemed likely. Raskin clambered into the stern and listened for kickers, intermittently snarling "Come on, come on." The boy listened too. A few muffled splashes sounded in the distance, on the far bank which the sockeye often favoured because the current was weaker there. Raskin grabbed the corkline in one hand, feeling for tugs. Once, he swayed and almost fell over, cursing and kicking his drum pedal.

A minute passed. The boat had almost reached the first slough already, so Raskin began to pick up, still in darkness. After only a few corks had wound onto the drum, a sockeye came over the rollers and landed with a thud in the stern. Raskin tried to pick it by feel, but the meshes were too tight around its head and he couldn't snap them off. Cursing and staggering, he suddenly remembered the boy. "Get a flashlight!" he ordered, as if speaking to the sky "And get your ass down here!"

The boy did as he was told, but the sockeye were so plentiful, and Raskin so drunk, that it was obvious even to him that he could not work at a fast enough speed. "Give me that light!" he finally snapped. "You pick!"

Ten minutes later, the current hauled them past the dynamite ship, and the boy sloshed around calf-deep in sockeye, most of which he just snapped from the meshes, knowing that he could not afford to pick them out carefully. As he worked, he tried to kick some of the fish back under the drum so that he wouldn't keep snagging them every time he tried to work a new one out of the meshes. Meanwhile, his father cackled gleefully and sprayed the thin beam of the flashlight indiscriminately over the catch. "We're knockin' the shit out of 'em! What did I say? Huh? Look at 'em all!"

Eventually, the boy hauled the scotchman over the rollers. He was standing in complete darkness, catching his breath, when the boat lunged forward and swung around back upriver. He fell heavily into the stern, his impact softened by the heap of slippery flesh rolling like mercury from one side of the boat to the other. When he tried to get up, putting pressure on one hand, he felt a sharp stinging pain from where a bullhead had stuck its barbs into the flesh of his palm. He touched the spot with one finger and smeared the warm blood across the area.

He was wet, cold, and sore already, but he knew the night was only beginning. His father, still drinking, was racing up the river to make another set, so fast that the dim stars above blurred into a series of long comet tails; they filled the sky thick as the salmon the boy had just wheeled out of the current. And his blood moved with the same swiftness, foraging for release, his whole body raked with nerve ends, his heart swaddled in heat so that his insides felt charred.

The panic did not lessen for two sets, until the tide had run down and gone slack. By then, the boy was dripping sweat and his father, sobering up, stayed in the cabin to start on another bottle.

Stunned, and grateful to the river for putting an end to the dizzying events, the boy leaned back against the drum and closed his eyes. In the channel, the sockeye still came on, relentless, driving forward with the whole weight of the stars on their backs, crashing into the net. The boy listened to the sound, amazed at the flurried repetition after all the quiet weeks of dragging for a few springs a day. He had no real financial stake in the sound; his excitement and satisfaction were tied only to his current escape from his father's anger and to an innate attachment to the world of the river. The fish soundlessly moving their jaws under him, and the stars deepening above: the thrill of the season's energy charged all his senses to such an extent that he could not sleep. With his eyes closed, he absently picked the scales off his cold hands.

The noise stirred him first, then the lights. He jumped forward and down in one motion, his eyes dragging the faint gleam of Chilukthan with them as he moved. In the slime and blood of the catch, he knelt, peering over the side of the boat at the half-dozen mastlights swinging near the bottom of the drift. As he watched, each light grew larger, and soon the boats threw even broader swathes of light from their bows.

Terrified, the boy crawled under the drum and hoisted himself on deck. He almost tripped as he entered the cabin, but caught the edge of the door to balance himself.

At the sound of the boy's entrance, Raskin staggered to his feet, eyes bloodshot and widening. Despite the alcohol, he retained a sixth sense that warned him whenever he was threatened, and now he acted as though he had just been waiting for the night's good fortune to turn sour. In his hurry to look outside, he knocked the bottle off his bunk; it fell with a clatter but he paid no attention, his eyes focussed on the lights moving upriver. "Shit!" he half-moaned, then turned and stared at the boy, as if seeking his instructions. Five seconds passed. Finally, he fumbled for the key and started the engine, kicking out at the boy as he did so. "What the fuck are you waiting for! Pick up! Pick up!"

The boy did as he was told, but this time he brought the net in at a much higher speed and didn't bother to pick the fish out at all. He simply wrapped them on the drum, all the while staring downriver as the mastlights and spotlights blended into one burning white mass. He had only picked up about twenty fathoms when a spotlight hit the corkline and veered rapidly toward him. Then another closed in on him from a different direction, and another, and another. The radiance seemed to tear his eyes open. His hands on the net writhed like they had been dipped in boiling water, and he lifted them halfway to his face, holding them out as if they weren't even attached to his arms. His heart beat against the swirling lights so rapidly that he wanted to catch it and quiet it in his hands, but he was afraid to touch his hands to his body. He stood, his eyes fixed on the boats, his forearms extended.

"Pick up!" Raskin roared from the door of the cabin. "Jesus-fuckingsonofabitch! Pick up!"

But even his father's curses could not break the spell. The boy was stricken with terror at the revolving beams. They fluttered around him like huge wings, blood-heavy and hunger-driven. He stood motionless while the sound of the boat engines increased, becoming the steady, high thrum under the scavenger's attack, the heart that drove the wings against his shivering body.

At his deck wheel, Troy watched with growing fascination as the spotlights of the other boats narrowed the night into one tiny image of fear. Where had he seen that look before? Yes, in the fog at the start of the season. It was the same kid! It must be Raskin out scabbing. Troy wasn't surprised, though he had hoped that Todd Brunov had put his money where his mouth was for once. It would be much more satisfying to confront Todd on the river than this poor kid who was probably only doing what his old man told him to do. Troy followed the lights in, worried for the boy's sake, but as angry as the other fishermen that someone was catching salmon during a strike.

"Nothing stupid, boys," Ed's deep voice cautioned over the radio. "There's no sense in anybody getting hurt. Just let me talk to him." Ed turned toward the scab's boat, hoping he could make the man pick up and go home without too much trouble. If not, he wasn't sure he could keep the other fishermen from acting with violence. The smell of sockeye was on the river, and Ed knew from long experience what that rich, moneyed musk could do to men's emotions. Let the man be reasonable, he prayed, stepping on deck as he pulled alongside the darkened gillnetter.

The spotlights had lifted from the boy to fall on his father with the same intensity. Before Ed could even open his mouth, Raskin cursed loudly and scrambled into the cabin.

"Watch it, Ed!" somebody shouted.

But he didn't have to be told. He'd spent enough time on picket lines to recognize the signs of possible violence. He positioned his boat so that the cabin and fish box were protecting most of his body, but he was still able to see the splash of light on the scab's empty deck.

As expected, Raskin re-emerged, cursing at the top of his voice and waving a shotgun in all directions, as though his body were on a swivel.

"Pick up, you fuckin' scab, or we'll cut your net!" a voice yelled from behind one of the beams of light.

Raskin swivelled around again. "Just try it!" he shouted back, "and I'll shoot your balls off!"

Ed knew he had to intervene, but sensed that he wouldn't have much success. Still, it was his responsibility to prevent anything from happening that would give the media and the courts ammunition against the strikers. So he spoke in a loud but calm voice: "This isn't doing anybody any good. Just put the gun away. We're not cutting your net. We just want you to know it's in your own best interest not to be fishing now."

"I fish when I want!" Raskin responded. "It's nobody's goddamned business!" He pointed the gun at Ed's boat.

Meanwhile, one of the spotlights had peeled away from the others to trace the corkline again. Several corks were bobbing and pulling, and a few fish tails and heads showed above the water. The fisherman behind the spotlight drifted his boat into the net and began pulling at the corkline with a pike pole.

At the same time, some of the other fishermen were taunting Raskin, threatening all sorts of repercussions if he didn't pick up immediately. Raskin, now caught in the crossfire of voices as well as lights, kept swivelling around, pointing his gun in all directions.

Ed went into his cabin and tried to calm things down over the radio, pleading for his fellow strikers not to do anything rash.

"Think of the companies and the papers," he said. "This is just what they want us to do."

Where's the kid, Troy wondered, staring at the stern. Once the spotlights had shifted, the darkness had swallowed the boy and his terror, but Troy knew he was still there, motionless. The drum was not turning, even though Raskin kept shouting at the boy to pick up. Troy strained to see the small figure at the outer edges of the spotlights' glare, but the contrast between the light and the dark was too great.

The voices shouted on, the radio crackled, and the lights sprayed over the cabin and deck. Troy drifted in closer to the stern to look for the boy. Just then, one of the spotlights strafed along the drum and out over the net, hitting the boat along the corkline. The light seemed to snap as it brought the lifted meshes and the pike pole into focus. Raskin howled and pointed his gun in the direction of the light.

"Look out!" Troy cried, ramming his boat into gear and hitting the gas.

The shot and the crunch of wood hitting wood exploded at the same time. The boy collapsed across the hammock of loose net and then vanished as the spotlight veered briefly skyward.

Troy hurried onto the bow, breaking the strange silence that followed with demands for light. He jumped into the stern of the other boat just as the light dropped again, so that it looked as though he had pulled it down with his arms.

Ed shouted over the water, "Get the fuck away from that net!" then ordered the other boats away.

Raskin looked more impressed by the fact that he'd actually fired than concerned by the effects of his shot. The collision had knocked him onto the deck. He got up slowly, still cursing the fisherman raiding his net.

Disgusted, Ed yelled at him. "You stupid bastard, you've just shot your kid!"

Raskin ignored him. He just kept swearing until he realized that no one was paying any attention. Then the reality began to sink in, and fear took over. He stared open-mouthed at the scene in the stern, panicked by the thought that the law would really come after him if he'd killed someone.

Troy reached out to the figure sprawled over the meshes and corks, afraid of what he'd discover. Oh god, he whispered, oh god, oh god.

But the boy sprang up at Troy's touch as though he'd been burned. His gape was feverish, and his jaw muscles worked ceaselessly, gulping at the air under lidless and unblinking eyes. He slipped as he backed away, but never took his gaze off Troy.

Sure that the boy had been killed, Troy was so stunned by the sudden motion that he didn't know how to react. "Take it easy," he said after a long pause, stricken by the boy's terror. "I'm not going to do anything."

But the boy only pushed himself farther back against the side of the boat, so far back that Troy thought he was going to turn at any second and jump into the river.

"It's okay," Troy said again, unable to look away from the boy's tensed form; it was like staring at a muscle stripped of flesh, a piece of the night throbbing with sinew.

"Get the fuck off my boat!" Raskin snarled from the deck, his gun pointed straight at Troy.

"Do as he says," Ed counselled from somewhere in the darkness. "That's enough stupidity for one night."

Troy, suddenly conscious of the fish piled around his legs, the heavy, snapped mint scent of their skin, the sloshing sound of their last futile efforts to complete the cycle, looked down into the swimming black. The same tension thrummed below him as hung in the air around the boy's face and shoulders, the same pulsing desire to be somewhere distant. For a few seconds, Troy was overwhelmed by a feeling of detachment he'd never known before. He felt his heart beating and his blood moving, but they did not seem to be part of his body; they seemed to go out of him and into the strange force flexing its wild hunger in the stern.

But as strangely and suddenly as it had come, the feeling passed, and Troy returned to the situation at hand. "I'm going," he said evenly, then pulled himself up onto his bow.

In a moment, he had swung his boat around and joined the others, their spotlights rippling toward Chilukthan.

At the head of the patrol, Ed couldn't wait to get home. These confrontations seemed more and more senseless, the sad dancing of Christians and lions in which power delighted, eyeing the entertainment from their imperial boxes. Year after year, decade after decade, it was always the same depressing struggle to undo the propaganda that set workers against workers. Ed was tired of the struggle, but he did not have it in him to give up. He kept seeing that boy in the stern, the gun going off in his direction, the light veering away, and the darkness. Was this to be the image he would remember from all his years of hard work? Was that it, a poisoned mind yelling "fuck off" at a shivering boy?

One last victory, Ed told himself, one last decent contract and they can find somebody else to keep the blood off men's faces. But even as he thought the words, he doubted he had enough control of the membership to prevent acts of retribution against Raskin and anyone else who scabbed. Ed had seen the fish in the net and in the stern. And he knew that the other fishermen had also seen them and that they'd be spreading the word. A settlement to the strike was not imminent. As each day passed, the summer was going to heat up even more. Ed hunched his broad form over the wheel and tried in vain to shake the resonant image of defeat from his mind.

All night, the Stuarts pushed on to their own sudden defeats or last mortal victories in the distant streams, and all night the boy touched his cold skin to theirs, his blood sparking and spitting for the same bold escape. When day broke at last above Vancouver, he was still in the stern, his fingers tangled in meshes, and his heart pounding at his ribs as though they were bars of loose gravel. Now, even the light of the sun was dangerous, like the light of the boats, the fixed dull light in human eyes, all the light he could not keep from his body. Naked in such brilliance, he held the salmon like armour to his chest.

chapter twenty-three

*F*ive days passed. Now the nights crackled under their trellised galaxies and the air tarnished the bright silver bodies of the rushing salmon. Now the corncobs had fattened in their husks and threatened to burst them like boys' shoulders in outgrown suits. Now the river and its catacombing sloughs remembered the glacial touch and the paddles and the armstrokes and the cries of the coast's human dead. And now darkness fell over the bloodfat evening light like an executioner's hood. Everything became night and pregnant silence. The heart copied the sun and went down in the body, and the body became driftwood on the same charged current.

Fishermen unable to sleep floated through the streets and along the riverbanks, their necks harnessed to the current. Some carried vials of battery acid to pour on the nets of scabs, while others paced the wharf beside their own boats, resisting the urge to throw their reputations away just to have that cold silver weight their palms. And every night, sirens rent the stillness, as something else, a netshed, a pile of fish boxes beside a cannery, a boathouse, went up in flames. Always now, somewhere in the kerosene black of the first hours after midnight, a fire would build silently until it finally raged to life and screamed awake the mute bedrooms of the town.

The river had opened again two days after Raskin had first gone out. And this time he was not the only fisherman to break the strike. The word had spread not only about his scabbing, but also about how many fish he'd hauled in. As a result, when the canneries held firm to their last offer, some non-union fishermen decided the risk of being blackballed was worth taking. As each day passed without a settlement, and the Stuart run peaked, fishermen eyed each other suspiciously, with a half-concealed hope in their bloodshot eyes, as if waiting for someone to say, "Ah, what the hell, might as well make a set before they're all gone."

But no one would say it. Most just muttered into their fidgeting hands and tried to convince themselves that the strike would be settled any minute and that they wouldn't be forced into making a decision that would cost them their self-respect. Meanwhile, the scabs were harassed, on the river and in the town. The government, at the request of the canners, sent police patrols onto the river to protect the men who were fishing, but after a while the protection wasn't necessary. Few of the strikers could stomach being on the river while others were hauling in fish, and fewer still believed so firmly in the union's position that they were prepared to face arrest. Slowly, hour by hour, the solidarity of the strike was dissolving under the magnetic pull of the salmon and the growing sense that the gillnetters were being sacrificed for the sake of the seiners. Only the older fishermen and a few of their sons held out with any conviction.

The town no longer moved in rhythm with the events of the fishery. The local newspaper decried the violence of the strikers, accused them of setting the fires, and called for the police to start making arrests. Much of the citizenry either agreed or was indifferent, the world of the river already fading into the clamour and rush of the daily commute to Vancouver. And for those who wanted a fresh salmon, one could always be bought on the black market the Natives conducted through their ceremonial-food fishery.

The Mawsons remained tied up. Vic hardly slept. He sat most of each night beside a fire in the backyard, chain-smoking and poking at the embers with a branch snapped off the apple tree. Nothing had changed for him. He needed to fish for the money, but his self-respect prevented him from breaking the strike. He attended the daily union meetings on the wharf, tried hard to believe that he was doing the right thing, and caught a few hours of restless sleep during the afternoons. More and more, the strike was throwing him back into all those moments in his life when he had had no control over events. The longer the strike lasted, the more Vic mulled over his vulnerability and the more he sank into feelings of guilt and self-loathing. Yet he understood that the strike, hard as it was, offered him some control in a world where he had rarely known it. Despite his doubts, he still believed that a man's power often lay only in his willingness to recognize what he shared with other men. But what happened to this logic when fewer and fewer men accepted it? Vic pondered the question long into the embered and smoke-filled nights.

Corbett also had a hard time sleeping. He spent most of his time drinking and playing ball. Sometimes, he simply drove for hours down the farm roads of Chilukthan, often passing Margo's house fifteen or twenty times. For lack of anything better to do, he attended the union meetings, but only to hear if the strike was over. He didn't care about the terms. He'd fish for a quarter per pound if it meant that Dennis Petrovich would return north. Once, when he was very drunk, Corbett almost turned down Margo's driveway, convinced that he could talk with Dennis and come to some reasonable arrangement. But he restrained himself. Never in his life had he felt so powerless. The feeling made him irritable, restless, and so obviously unhappy that everyone believed he was struggling under the pressure of the strike.

That's what Troy believed, but only because he could not understand any other reaction to the way the summer was unfolding. Jesus, how could any fisherman not be upset by the strike when all those sockeye were swimming past by the hour? Troy could not be inactive. He hung around the wharf day and night. He went out on river patrols, despite the fact that it tortured him to watch fish hitting other men's nets when his was still on his drum. Each day, he ate himself up, angered by his father's and Corbett's passive acceptance of the strike. What the hell's the matter with you, he wanted to shout at them, but held back for his mother's sake. Couldn't they see what was happening? If we're not going to fish, we have to keep the pressure on the scabs, we have to do everything we can to make a better deal! But Troy only seethed with these unspoken thoughts; he could not openly criticize his father, and since that day at the ballpark, he and Corbett had not been on speaking terms. Finally, once the Brunovs had broken the strike, Troy's anger became so intense that he could not even be around the house. The worry and the sense of weakness were so palpable that he wanted to shout the walls down.

Instead, he started staying at a friend's place and only came home for supper.

Kathleen, too, felt the tension in the house, and though it saddened her that a split seemed to have formed between her sons, she had little time for whatever their dispute was. Like Vic, she felt that nothing had changed for her. Money was still her main concern. Vic's strike pay was insignificant, certainly not enough to put away for the winter. Kathleen also had her doubts about the strike, especially when she heard rumours about what the scabs and the Indians were catching. The Stuarts had returned in large numbers, and it was cruel that her family could not share in the riches. But Kathleen would not show her doubts to Vic. It was hard enough for him without her questioning worries. No, they had been through it before and they would survive, even if it meant that she would have to find a part-time job. So she lay awake at night, the dim glow of Vic's fire on the bedroom window, and the distant whine of a siren increasing to a harsh scream.

On the sixth day, there was a change. The union circulated word of a meeting to be held in Chilukthan Harbour that evening at nine o'clock. The Mawsons and all the remaining strikers could hardly contain their hopes. Vic and Corbett went out into the yard after supper and sat by the fire. All through the meal, they had speculated on whether the companies had made another offer or whether the union was just trying to keep its membership behind the strike. Despite the scabbing and the big catches, the majority of fishermen had remained tied up, so the canneries, feeling the pinch, might very well be wanting to settle.

"Hard to say," Vic mused now. "The companies might think we're weakening. They might be making the same offer as before."

Corbett couldn't even remember what that offer had been, nor did he care. "We'll accept it, won't we? What with all the fish around and guys breaking away?"

Vic studied his son carefully, surprised by his seeming anxiety to have the strike end. Since when did Corbett care so much about missing out on fish? "No reason to," Vic answered, "not if we'd be settling for the same price we rejected a week ago. No point in that."

Corbett stared into the flames. He wished he could tell his

father about Margo, but the last thing he wanted was his parents' disapproval. He had already decided that, no matter what the offer was, he would vote to accept it, even if such a move worked against his father.

Meanwhile, Troy's situation had suddenly become more complicated. He had not been home for supper because he'd heard that Reg Tanner was looking for him. Now he stood in the older man's backyard, listening to his opinions on the strike.

"This is it for me," Reg said, crossing his long, bony arms over his sunken chest. "Whatever happens tonight, I'm going out for the next opening. And if you're fishing my other boat, I expect you to be out there too. Or I'm going to have to get someone else."

Troy coughed nervously. "What if the offer's no good? My dad says the companies might just be making the same offer to test how strong we are."

Reg scratched his sharp chin with a finger thin as a twig. "Could be. But I don't much care. I stand to lose more money this way than if I go out for whatever it is they offer." He paused, as if offended. "Listen, we tried, but a strike's no good if guys start scabbing without paying for it. I'm not gonna sit back while the scabs are catching my fish."

But you'll just be another scab, Troy thought, you'll be one of the reasons the strike will fail. He didn't say the words aloud, but the older man read them on his face.

Reg yanked his grubby skullcap off his head and crumpled it in his hand. "If you're not gonna fish my boat, just say so! There's other guys, you know, who are itching to get out there and make some money!"

"No, I'll fish," Troy countered, panicked at the thought of losing his boat in the middle of a big sockeye season. Also, he remembered what his mother had said about honouring his word. But she couldn't have foreseen this, Troy thought, she wouldn't want me to keep my word by scabbing. "See you later," he said, and walked back to his car through the lengthening shadows.

By quarter to nine, most of the fishermen had started to arrive at the harbour. Vic and Corbett walked over from the house, neither one speaking. There was nothing more to say until the union made its position clear.

When they reached the foot of the dyke below the wharf, they passed two fishermen standing beside a pickup truck. One of them was Dennis Petrovich, a well-built man with a short neck and a body almost the same width from the shoulders to the ground. His dark, sharply sculpted face was grim as he yanked the collar of his dog who had stood on the wheel well to growl at the other man. "Get down!" Dennis ordered, then acknowledged the newcomers with a slight nod.

"Quite the guard dog you've got there," Vic said.

Dennis grabbed the dog's muzzle and held it shut. "Oh, he's just nervous around people, that's all."

Corbett felt his blood pounding in his neck. He hadn't expected to see Dennis, though of course he should have known he'd attend the union meeting. The presence of Margo's husband made him nervous, as though it was a foreboding of ill fortune or a kind of unintentional taunt. As always, Corbett responded to his nerves with humour.

"Ah, Skip just doesn't like pitchers," he grinned at the man who was the target of the growls. Then he reached forward and patted the dog on the head. "Eh, boy, you prefer catchers, isn't that right?" The dog wagged its tail and the other man laughed. Dennis shifted heavily and stared at Corbett as if he'd never really noticed him before.

"Better see what all the fuss is about," Vic said, and he and Corbett started up the dyke.

The upper wharf was once more packed with fishermen. The only difference from the weeks before lay in their faces, which were more serious and drawn, decidedly older in the faint hues of the setting sun, like charcoal sketches discovered beneath oil canvases. Also, the men smoked more cigarettes and smoked them faster, the butts sizzling into the river in a steady stream. Few of the men spoke, and those who did hardly raised their voices above a murmur. No one had to say anything. The river would open again in two days, the Stuarts were still coming, and this was the last chance for an easy resolution to all their difficulties. As one, they waited for Ed Leary to arrive.

Ed scowled as he climbed the dyke to the wharf. Ten minutes late, and he still hadn't decided how to say what the union executive had told him to say. He had been walking the dyke most of the evening, rubbing his thick beard so hard it was as though he was trying to tear it off. The companies, sensing dissension in the union ranks, had come back with the same offer as before. And this time the union executive had recommended acceptance. Accept, Ed repeated incredulously, accept? What the hell was he supposed to say to these men who had given up huge catches for absolutely nothing? Bastards, goddamned bastards! Ed couldn't believe that his union, the one he'd believed in and even gone to prison for, could be so gutless and irresponsible.

When Ed had been told the news, he could hardly believe it. The executive had essentially caved in to the companies right at the critical moment, without so much as a whimper of resistance. Jesus, what was he supposed to say to the men? Sorry, fellas, about those thousand sockeye you've each missed out on for nothing, better luck next year?

Only when he stepped up on the fish crate did he make his decision, only then did the term "swan song" enter his mind. This is it, he said, surprising himself a little, this is the last speech I'm ever going to make.

It was a beautiful night. There'd be a full moon and a perfect high slack, and the same would be true on the night of the next opening. If the boys fished, they'd probably load up. Ed turned his black, probing eyes to the worried faces in the crowd, cleared his throat, and put his hands out as if he was weighing each word as it left his mouth.

"I've fished on the river for almost forty years," he began, "ever since I was a boy and Newt McCullough first took me out in the Pass in his old one-lunger. I grew up in this industry back when a fisherman had nothing to fall back on but himself, and I saw a lot of strong men break down when everything they had worked for disappeared because of bad luck, an injury, a fire, two bad seasons in a row, and I saw the families of dead fishermen, men who'd drowned or had heart attacks or whatever, get bugger all for compensation, not even something to help them bury their dead."

He felt a sudden knot in the pit of his stomach as he spoke the last word; it seemed to clunk to the wharf and then echo across the channel. Uneasily, Ed sensed that he was delivering a eulogy and that the subject of it was standing in front of him, gazing up in a hundred disbelieving faces. He rallied, and shook the image away. Now his voice rumbled out of his mouth.

"And I know what happened when we fought for decent wages and working conditions, I know the scare tactics the companies used to try to break us when we organized all up and down the coast, and I know what it's like to have every goddamned authority in the land tell you that you're a troublemaker and a threat to the Canadian way of life just because you want fair treatment for the work you do."

He dropped his hands and filled his broad chest with the sweet summer air. The men on the wharf hardly breathed or moved at all.

"I've always been a union man," Ed thundered on, "I've always believed that the only way to protect myself against greed and power was to put my faith in other men who knew what I was fighting against. And we made gains!" He raised his voice even higher as if declaring this truth to the last of the sun. "Compensation, better prices, more say in how the resource was handled. Gains, real gains. And we made them because we stood together, because we knew that the system was in place to benefit those who invented it. This wasn't a mystery. We all knew it, we all accepted it, and the union always fought to represent our common interests as fishermen, plain and simple. Well, something's changed, and I'm asking you to be patient and listen to what I have to say before you put the latest offer to a vote."

The men still did not move, yet they appeared to press forward in a dark tide. Their heavy, eager faces, bunched so close together, made Ed think of salmon pulled up in a net. The smell of the river mud seemed to flow from their parted mouths.

"You all think you know what a scab is," Ed continued, pressing his bulk forward against the tide. "You think he's something evil, that he's out to cut your throat just because he's a greedy bastard. Well, that's not what a scab is. A scab is just a man like any other who believes he doesn't need anybody but himself to get by in this world. And he believes this because that's what the whole power base of society is telling him to believe, every day, over and over, you don't need anyone, you can make it on your own. And eventually he learns to believe what he's hearing, despite all the evidence in his own life that it isn't true, despite the fact that someone birthed him and raised him and wiped his snotty nose. Or maybe he wasn't so lucky, but if he wasn't, he knew it, knew in his heart that he was missing out, that it wasn't natural to have no one and think that it was fine. Who can live that way? The canners don't, the politicians don't, the judges don't, even the goddamned journalists don't. But they're busy telling you all the time that the only proper way to live is to be a scab, to turn your back on everyone who's in a position to help you, to trust them and some magical market system to look after you. But they don't know anything about how you live, except that they don't give a shit about it."

Ed curled his lip and pounded a fist into his open palm. "If I've learned anything in my life it's that you've got to live it with your eyes wide open, but it doesn't do any damned good if you don't take in what you're seeing. Jesus Christ! The salmon have their eyes open when they're dying, but what good does it do them when they're lying in your stern gasping, what the hell does it mean to see the world if you're useless to act on what you see?"

Ed paused again, and it seemed that his own shadow stood up from the wharf to listen. He lowered his voice. "The world is changing. More scabs every day, more talk about the free market. You all laugh when someone stands up here and talks about South America. Hell, sometimes I even laugh with you. Who gives a shit about grape-pickers in Chile? Nothing to do with us. But if you're blind to the rest of the world, then you're not going to see what's going on right under your goddamned noses."

Now his tone filled with disgust. He tried to pick out the Brunovs in the crowd, but all the fishermen suddenly looked the same to him, unblinking, slack-mouthed innocents.

"Oh, you'll look right at it, you'll watch the springs disappear, you'll watch the river fill up with shit until you have to wear gloves to keep from being poisoned, you'll watch whole streams and runs die because some company cuts down trees in a watershed, but you won't see anything because you don't know how to look! Is this commie talk? Is this what you've been warned about since you were laid in the cradle?"

Ed shook his head and laughed so deeply that his whole body seemed to come at the crowd in waves. Then, scowling, he stared straight into the motionless faces. "The salmon are blind, but at least they see enough to know where they're going, at least they have to be ripped out of the water before they stop trying to live."

With these words, he seemed to go into a brief sleep. The heavy, mingled smells of the tide wafted into his nostrils, and he gulped it down as though he'd never have another chance to do so. In a few seconds, he recovered, and turned to the matter at hand.

"The companies have repeated their offer of a week ago. Thirty-nine cents for sockeye, 13 for pinks, 18 for dogs." Now Ed hesitated, still unsure whether he should announce the union's recommendation. He felt betrayed by it, but he knew that the membership had a right to hear the whole truth. "I hate like hell to say this, but the union's position is that you accept the offer."

The crowd reacted as Ed had expected, with a combination of disbelief and anger. Somebody shouted, "What the hell have we been striking for!" and that sentiment was written on all the faces darkening in the settling dusk.

Ed drew himself up to his full height and made his last appeal. "This is the hardest thing I've ever had to say. In fact, it makes me sick to say it. But if you do what the union wants, and end the strike, then you're all scabs, every single one of you, and you'll always be scabs. If you can live your life that way, fine. But remember, sooner or later a scab gets picked, and when that happens, you'll be on your own to stop the bleeding." He stepped down from the crate and held the ballots out on his open palm.

Underneath the wharf, pressed tight against a piling, the boy finally came out from under the spell cast by the booming voice. He didn't understand the words, but he sensed somehow that he was being directly addressed, as though the eyes the voice had talked about were trained right on him. But their gaze wasn't critical or cold; it was accepting, forgiving. When the voice stopped, and the murmur of other voices began again, the boy felt himself hurled back against his solitude. He hurried across the muck of the low tide toward the neighbouring cannery. From a burlap sack stashed high against the bank, he removed a jerry can and some newspapers and rags. Then, hunched over and moving swiftly, he made his way to the river's edge where he'd roped a skiff to a piling. He climbed in and drifted soundlessly back toward the government wharf. Once there, he chose one of the moored gill-

TIM BOWLING

netters at random, placed the papers and rags in the stern, poured gasoline over them, then tossed a struck match into the pile.

Breathing heavily, he jumped back into the skiff, returned to the underside of the cannery, and crouched there in the mud, waiting once more for the circle of light to widen and bring the world into his small orbit, if only for a while. The shouts, the siren, the brilliance that he alone had started, controlling it as if from his very fingertips: all of this made his heart thump so violently that he'd had to force himself not to set more than one fire a night.

But now the excitement came again, as it always did, this time the panicked shouts followed by a swirl of bodies as the fishermen exploded down the gangway to untie the other boats from the one on fire. On his knees, peering out into the frayed edges of the light, the boy watched, mesmerized by how easily he could put the cold world into motion.

But the fire did not last. The fishermen managed to douse it with buckets of water pulled from the river. When the boy saw this, and saw that the men remained on the wharf, he panicked, fearing that they would soon search the area. He had miscalculated, figuring that he could escape by skiff once the fire had been put out, but the men did not leave. Terrified, his heart thudding in his ears, he scurried to the bank and crawled up through the rushes to the top of the dyke. After a quick look around, he jumped up and sprinted across to the vacant lot.

He did not see the girl until he had almost run past her. She was standing at the end of the sidewalk, watching him.

Zoe's first thought was simple curiosity. Why was he running so fast? But then she realized that if he saw her, he might tell on her. She was supposed to be in bed, not out checking on the bird's nest she'd discovered in the cherry tree.

Now she knew that it was too late, that she had been seen and might get into trouble. So she dropped the stick she was holding and ran as fast as she could back along the sidewalk.

The boy plunged into the tall grass as though trying to pounce on his own heartbeat. She saw me, he whispered to himself, she's going to tell. And the fear of being caught was so great that he had to stop running. He threw himself face down on the earth and tried to convince himself that she hadn't seen him, or that if she

222

had, it had been too dark for her to recognize him. His blood snaked through the whole length of his body. What was he going to do? Maybe she hadn't seen him? But what if she had? The boy lay there until darkness gnawed the trees away and subdued voices passed by on the street. He was cold, and not even the image of fire could warm him, though he thought about it over and over, wanting to burn the mistakes he'd just made. He lay there, shivering, until the moon picked him out, and he fled again from its harsh, accusing light.

chapter twenty-four

*B*y early afternoon of the following day, dark rain-clouds scudded over Chilukthan and a cool, briny wind ruffled the feathers of the sulking gulls. The sky was dull and bleached thin under clouds that rolled like orcas over an ocean of burnished pearl. Everyone waited for the rain. Even the seconds ticking on a wristwatch sounded like a soft shower.

Kathleen went to the kitchen window to check the sky. The boy was still there, in the crook of the huge fir in the field across the street. That's odd, she thought, he's been there a long time, I wonder what he's doing. She'd first noticed him at least an hour before, when he'd walked slowly past the house, staring down the driveway. One of those boys from the waterfront, she had guessed, a skinny, sad-looking boy in a dirty-white T-shirt and torn jeans. Had she seen him around before? She couldn't remember; he didn't look familiar, and she couldn't put a name to him. But then, new families were always arriving in town; she couldn't keep up anymore. Besides, she had more important things on her mind.

Vic had gone to the wharf that morning hoping that the union would have the vote results, but they hadn't been counted yet. Lots of locals to hear from, Ed Leary had told the anxious men milling around the waterfront, should have the results sometime tonight. Vic didn't have high hopes for the outcome. He figured that the membership would accept the offer, which, as far as he was concerned, meant that the fishermen had lost. Kathleen had approved of Vic's voting to continue the strike, but she could not deny that a settlement, even on poor terms, would come as a relief. Thirty-nine cents a pound was better than nothing, and there was always a chance that the price would be adjusted at the end of the season. Then again, even if Vic returned to work, there was no guarantee that the season's catch would carry them through the winter. Either way, the vote would not necessarily alleviate the family's problems. So Kathleen understood why there was little joy in Vic's manner when he returned from the wharf to say that the results had not come in. She realized along with him that acceptance meant defeat, and that rejection only meant more anxiety with no promise of a better settlement.

Still, she knew she should have felt more optimistic. That had always been her response to Vic's worrying; she achieved a balance by countering his concerns, at least outwardly. And she had done this so often that she had developed a basic faith in her optimism, regardless of how forced it was. No sense looking on the dark side, she would tell herself over and over until it seemed that there was no dark side as long as she chose to ignore it.

But lately, despite herself, Kathleen had experienced a significant dampening of her spirit, as though whatever had been lost through the spring and first half of the summer might be lost forever. And she did feel a definite sense of loss. Her breakdown, frightening as it had been, had put her into direct contact with the pain that is more than just individual, that speaks from some common source to the wonder and fragility out of which all life is fashioned. As a result, Kathleen sensed that her relationship to her own history had altered. She somehow seemed to stand outside herself and look back on some other woman who had married, lost her parents, lost one child, and raised three others. In itself, this sensation did not disturb her; she accepted it as a product of moving from one part of life to another. But Kathleen, like anyone, had grown attached to the immediacy of her familiar emotions, and experienced a sadness at their passing.

Her dead child: she still thought about him occasionally, at night or when the rain seemed to invite her old tears back to the surface. But the relationship seemed more distant; he was with her parents in that cold inaccessibility of the fading past. Yet how could she ever expect or want to leave any of her love completely behind? Before, at sudden rare moments, her lost son had spoken

TIM BOWLING

to her more directly than her surviving children. How would he
speak to her now that she had changed, if only slightly, how could
she go on translating his strange and oddly soothing words?

She stood in the window watching the boy. He had not moved.
Even from such a distance, she could feel his eyes looking straight
back at her. What did he want? Kathleen had never noticed him
hanging around their neighbourhood before.

"Can I go outside now? I'm all finished. See." Zoe turned at the
table and held up her empty soup bowl.

"It's going to rain," Kathleen sighed.

"That's okay. I like the rain."

Kathleen smiled at her daughter's enthusiasm. She just loved to
be outdoors. Takes after her father and brothers, Kathleen
thought. "All right, but stay by the yard where I can see you. I
don't want you going near the river today."

"How come?" Zoe pouted.

"Because I say so, that's how come," Kathleen responded. Zoe
did not need to hear about the real threat of violence that accompanied the strike. If boats had been set on fire, and people were
shooting, there was no telling what else might happen before a
settlement was reached.

Still pouting, Zoe moved to the mat by the door and pulled her
boots on. Then she grabbed her coat and reached for the doorknob.

"Do your coat up," Kathleen ordered, "and put a hat on."

Zoe did as she was told and then scampered out the door, a
gust of heavy, wet air blowing through the kitchen in her wake.

The boy tensed when she appeared, and immediately tightened his grip on the jackknife in his pocket. He had been waiting
for this moment for hours, going over and over it again, trying to
steel himself to do what he believed was necessary. The knife felt
slick and cold in his palm. He gripped it even tighter, his eyes
frozen on the girl, who squatted at the edge of the driveway, poking at the wet gravel with a stick. Was she going to tell on him?
Maybe she already had? Trembling and confused, he cast all of his
emotions toward her small body, seeing it as something he could
burn just like anything else, a skiff, a shed, a piece of wood, some
grass. He stared intensely, as if at once willing her to burst into
flame at the touch of his gaze and willing himself to move across
the street while flicking open the knife.

Just then, Kathleen turned back to the window. The boy had jumped down from the tree, but was still looking toward the house. Out of the corner of her eye, she saw two black figures turn the corner at the end of the street, and somehow that small distraction sharpened her focus on the boy. His posture had changed. Kathleen could feel her own muscles tense as she watched him. He stepped out of the field onto the pavement and then stopped, as though unsure about his next move. Kathleen saw that he held one arm rigidly to his side, and that his hand was closed in a fist. Suddenly, he began to move with purpose, crouched over, almost leaping across the road.

With shock, Kathleen realized that the boy was looking at Zoe. But looking was too passive a word; he was studying her, and with such intensity that a shiver went down Kathleen's neck. She turned her head as the boy turned his, as though they were connected by a mutual interest in the little girl.

Panicking, Kathleen yanked open the window and shouted Zoe's name. The shout hit the boy like a slap. He reached the sidewalk and stopped abruptly. Kathleen ran to the door, flung it open, and raced outside in her slippers, all the while shouting Zoe's name.

She reached the front lawn just as Vic and Troy arrived from the wharf. They had also been watching the boy, but with casual surprise rather than fear.

"What the hell's going on?" Vic said, stunned by the panic in his wife's voice and manner. "Zoe's right here. She's fine."

The boy had already turned and fled up the street.

Troy watched him go, and tried to puzzle out why the sight was suddenly so disturbing. "What did he want?" he finally asked, the image of the boy's crouched and terrified figure on the Prairie Drift flashing back to him.

Kathleen took Zoe in her arms and stroked her brow. "I don't know. He was watching . . . he seemed to be watching . . ." Kathleen hesitated. Had she imagined the look in the boy's eyes?

"Watching what?" Vic asked, annoyed.

Kathleen took a deep breath and let her daughter go. "Who is that boy? Do you know him?"

Troy nodded. "Sure. That's the kid Raskin almost shot. His own kid."

"Raskin? Isn't he the one who . . ." Kathleen chewed her lip. "Troy, did you say anything to him that night? Did you swear at him or . . ."

With a sinking feeling, Troy understood the point of his mother's questions. Jesus, would he send his kid around to get even with me for jumping on his boat? "No," he answered. "No, I didn't say a word to him."

Vic lifted Zoe into his arms. Looking out from around her hair, he scowled at the other two. "Oh for chrissakes, let's not get carried away about this. He's just a kid."

Kathleen was neither convinced nor comforted, but she decided not to press the issue. I'll keep a closer eye on Zoe until the strike ends, she vowed, then changed the subject. "Any news yet?"

Vic waved a hand dismissively. "Might not hear until tomorrow. Must be a closer vote than I thought if it's taking them this long." Suddenly, he whirled Zoe around until, laughing, she cried at him to stop. "How's about we look at that bird's nest?" He set her on the ground and, hand in hand, the two walked off down the street.

Kathleen could not get the boy out of her mind. Something about the weight of his expression, the way he held his body, asked a question that she felt she should be able to answer. But it was more than a question; it was a soundless plea.

"How old is he?" she asked Troy, a shudder beginning at the base of her skull.

"I don't know, eleven, twelve, somewhere in there. Why?"

Kathleen had not risen from the grass where she'd knelt to hold Zoe. Now she gazed up at the massing black shapes and prayed that the rain would hold off. Not now, she breathed, not now, but already the rich aroma of the soaked earth filled her nostrils.

"Don't worry about me for supper," Troy said, not noticing the strange expression on his mother's face. "I'll pick up a burger or something."

When she only nodded in response, Troy turned to his car in the driveway, climbed in, and drove into town.

All day, he had chastized himself for voting to reject the offer. It seemed stupid now to throw away the whole Stuart run because of what Ed Leary had said. Sure, his speech made sense at the time, but if the world really was changing, what good did it do to

resist the change? If we don't move with the times, Troy concluded, we're screwed. And what'll I do if the offer is rejected? I can't
scab. But if I don't, I'm not even going to have a boat to fish when
the strike gets settled.

He pulled into the parking lot of the Chilukthan Arms and
noticed Corbett's car. Troy wondered how his brother had voted.
Then he laughed at himself. It was ridiculous to think that Corbett
would ever do anything other than what their father did. And Troy
knew without even asking how his father had voted. Hell, everyone on the wharf knew that. Maybe Ross is here, Troy speculated,
maybe the post office job will come through and I can chuck the
fishing, no matter what Mom says. The thought cheered him
immensely so that he even managed a slight smile as he entered
the crowded pub.

Corbett, sitting in a dark corner, didn't notice his brother come
in. "Fifty-fifty," he grinned at a drinking friend across the table.
"And he supplies all the nets and gear and pays for any repairs that
the boat might need. Can't beat that, eh? Once this strike is over
. . . Yeah, I figure we'll all be out there next opening. Too many
scabs. A strike won't work unless everybody's out. Shit, even if the
vote is no, there'll still be a hundred boats on the river."

"You gonna fish anyway? If the strike's still on?"

"Won't need to find out," Corbett said, downing a last mouthful of beer. "Take it from me, it's over." He got up from his chair,
clapping his friend on the shoulder, and motioned in the direction of the river. "I've already got a net racked at the shed.
Thought I'd better get it ready. Still lots of Stuarts out there.
Probably some other fellas too. Money, money." He chuckled and
headed for the exit, stopping three times on the way to talk with
other friends.

Nearly an hour later, when he finally got outside, the sky was
even darker, but the rain still held off. The clouds had locked into
place and lowered, so that the day seemed to be nothing but a
thin strip between two fields of black earth.

Corbett moved through the heaviness as though the sky was a
vivid blue. He even whistled lightly and jingled his car keys in his
pocket. Everything was finally going his way again. The strike
would soon be over, Dennis would go north, and Corbett would be
able to talk Margo into leaving him. Now that he had his own boat

to fish and would be making some real money, he could move out of the house, get an apartment, and ask Margo to live with him. It was perfect. For the first time in almost two weeks, he felt like his old self, confident, happy, wanting to share his good fortune with everyone he passed on the street. Hell, even the scabs, what did he care about them?

Corbett had not really listened to Ed Leary's speech. He knew Ed was a good guy, and funnier than you'd expect for a communist, but Corbett had known how he'd vote long before the union leader had opened his mouth. What was there to decide? The sooner Dennis was gone, the better.

Corbett sped through town, east along the river road, and finally crossed the harbour bridge heading for the netsheds. He parked under the ashen poplars and almost floated down the gangway. It took him a while to fit the key into the lock on the shed door, but he was in such a good mood that he could have fiddled with the lock for an hour without becoming frustrated. But only a few minutes passed before he opened the door and stepped into the shed.

A sockeye net was stretched out in the dim light angling through the chinks in the roof and walls. The corks hung in a bunch on one side of the rack, like onions, and the torn meshes draped down old and forgotten as cobwebs. Corbett manoeuvred around the net and unlocked the river door. He slid it back and stepped outside onto the little wharf.

The harbour was deserted. After all that had happened, the main wharf across the channel seemed to be recovering from the heavy tread and the harsh shouts of the fishermen, most of whom had readied their nets long ago and had no reason to be near the river until the meeting later that night. One or two, more cautious than most, had been watching their boats and nets all week, but since no acts of property damage had occurred during daylight hours, even these men had decided to risk taking a break. The harbour seemed as quiet as it was during the winter months.

Drawn into the silence, Corbett stood on the wharf for several minutes, remembering the sight of Margo clumsily rowing toward him, remembering the sound of her voice and the smell of her skin. He blinked and the images disappeared. Now only a lone muskrat moved on the water, its black nose just above the surface, its long V-wake fanning lightly against both banks.

He took a piece of wax paper from his jacket pocket as he stepped back into the shed. "Here kitty, kitty," he whispered to the dark corners. At his bench, he picked up a hanging needle and began to mend a hole in the web. When one of the toms finally appeared, Corbett took some ham from the paper and tossed it on the ground. He watched the cat sniff at it, and laughed as it pawed the food suspiciously and meowed, shrinking back into a corner. "Hey, silly, what's the matter? Not good enough for you? Hey?"

Then Corbett heard a thump by the gangway door and looked up just as Dennis filled the entrance and blocked the grey daylight trickling in.

"Hey," Corbett said, rising, a slight catch in his voice. He felt his body go limp, but he smiled and tried to appear casual. "How are things?"

"Cut the bullshit, Mawson. You know why I'm here." Dennis stepped into the shed, slamming the door shut behind him. A two-by-four extended from his right arm as if it had been strapped on.

"Do I?" Corbett swallowed hard and glanced over his shoulder at the river. If he had to, he could go for a swim.

"Just shut the fuck up!" Dennis took another step forward.

Corbett had the rack between him and the river. Unless he moved soon, Dennis would continue along the far wall and cut off his escape. But Dennis had stopped moving. He just stared at Corbett and sneered. "I can't fucking believe it. She decides to screw around and she can't even pick a man to do it with. Jesus fucking Christ."

And then, as though he'd been spoken to by some presence outside himself, Corbett realized he wasn't going to move either. He didn't even want to lie or joke his way out of the situation. For the first time in his life, he believed that he owed it to himself to be serious no matter how dire the consequences. More than that, he owed it to Margo. If he couldn't be serious about this, then why would a woman like her ever choose to be with him?

He cleared his throat nervously. "You can do what you want, but it won't do you any good. I won't stop seeing her."

Dennis laughed coldly. "Oh, I think you will, you little shit." He stepped forward and this time kept coming. Corbett put his arms up, but the alcohol had affected his perspective and his balance. The first blow caught him on the neck and knocked him back. Gasping, he flung his arms wildly over his face, but the second blow landed on his right leg. Corbett heard a sharp crack and collapsed sideways. The third blow followed so quickly that his nose spurted blood before he even hit the ground. Writhing, a stabbing pain in his leg, he gagged and tried in vain to fend off the kicks hitting his midsection. It became so hard to breathe that all he could taste was blood, thick and warm in his mouth. Soon after, he lost consciousness.

Troy drove slowly down the gravel road to the netsheds. He wanted to tell Corbett about Raskin's kid, tell him to keep his eyes on their boats across the channel. He had no particular desire to speak with his brother, but thought it would be a good idea to tell him of the possible threat to the family property.

Troy nervously eyed the black horizon. It was one of those strange afternoons when the rain had not yet started but the phantom sound of every old storm was cradled in the branches. The air's hushed quality only made him more anxious as he parked beneath the poplars and started down the gangway.

He had noticed the truck beside Corbett's car but thought nothing of it until Dennis Petrovich stormed past him, ignoring his greeting and almost knocking him over.

What the fuck's his problem, Troy wondered, and then, as he approached the shed, a sickening recollection of bar-room gossip suddenly brought him up short. Dennis Petrovich? Didn't somebody say that . . . no, not Corb, Corb wouldn't mess with . . .

Troy's heart beat faster as he entered the shed. "Corb?" he said quietly. It had been a long time since he'd spoken his brother's name with anything but dismissal and scorn. "Hey, Corb, where are you?"

Then he saw him lying against the far wall, the lower half of his body in daylight and the upper half in shadow. A big tomcat was sniffing around his midsection and meowing brokenly. "Oh shit," Troy whispered, jumping over the hung meshes.

When he reached Corbett and saw the blood on his face, and the two-by-four lying across his blood-matted hair, Troy felt sick. Bile began to rise in his throat. He couldn't even tell if his brother was alive. At first, Troy just knelt beside him, shouting his name and shaking him by the shoulder. Then Troy started to cry, and the feel of the tears on his cheeks made him respond: he grabbed a bucket by the river door, dipped it in the muddy tide, and splashed a handful of the water on Corbett's face. "You dumb fucker," Troy choked out, "you dumb, dumb fucker! Wake up, come on, come on." In desperation, he threw more and more water on Corbett's face until he finally stirred. His eyes flickered open and he groaned.

"How bad is it?" Troy said. "Can you move?"

But Corbett's eyes closed again and he did not respond.

Still trembling, Troy felt his fear give way to anger, anger with Corbett for his stupidity, anger with Dennis Petrovich for what he'd done, anger with the whole fishery, and, finally, anger with himself for not somehow preventing the situation. He looked at Corbett's bloodied face again and wondered what to do. The folks can't find out, he decided, I have to take care of it myself. Besides, Corbett wouldn't want anyone else to know either.

He gathered his brother in his arms, holding him under the neck and knees, and tried to stand. But Corbett's lean body was surprisingly heavy, and Troy had to put him back down. After a few seconds, he tried again, heaving, forcing himself to shut out the groans which seemed to come from his own lips. He staggered out of the shed and up the gangway, praying that his unseen steps would keep landing on the planks.

Overhead, the clouds were thick gauze soaked in diesel oil, but they would not spatter drops on the earth. The sky pressed so low and heavy on his neck and shoulders, Troy felt he was carrying the weight of the whole season in his arms.

He finally reached his car and with difficulty managed to place Corbett across the backseat. Then, behind the wheel, Troy wiped at his eyes until his blurred vision cleared enough that he could see where he was driving. If he drove very quickly, he could be through the tunnel and to Richmond General in fifteen minutes.

"Jesus, Corb," he winced again at his brother's pain as the car hit a bump in the road. "What the hell did you think you were doing?"

chapter twenty-five

The afternoon deepened and the clouds ushered in a premature night. Most of the citizens of Chilukthan, depressed by the streetlamps pinging on and by the general slablike weight of the air, retreated indoors. By five o'clock, the streets were all but deserted. Occasionally, someone appeared at the edge of a sagging verandah or in a narrow shop doorway, leaned forward and looked up, and then sprinted for a car, its headlight beams soon afterwards smearing light over the blackened roads.

The winds remained steady off the river, but they were light and did not move the clouds. In the harbour, the gulls on the peak of the sloping cannery roof had stiffened to gargoyles, their unblinking gazes medievally unimpressed with earthly concerns. Below them, the tide, sludged as boiled coffee, filtered its grounds slowly seaward, while the gillnetters and other boats looked abandoned, their planks gone back to nature, their bow and stern lines holding fast to the roots of cottonwoods.

Electricity in the town might as well have been torchlight, for no one felt a comforting modern distance from the weather massing outside. Even the voices on the radios and televisions were suddenly ancestral and grave, speaking from a strange world whose relevance was somehow vague and disquieting. Some people pulled curtains and dropped blinds, others spiked their hot drinks with a little rye or rum, while a few remembered the quilts they used to sleep under as children. In the dingy pubs, sitting sullenly around the chipped and glass-ringed tables, several older fishermen had lowered their voices, half-listening for the first drops of rain, as though they were already standing in their sterns or cabins, bloody fingers turning the pages of tide books. Yet none of them, despite the urgency of the season, wanted to be on the river at that moment. Soon enough, each mused, his breath fogging another beer glass, soon enough. Finally, one muttered aloud "Not fit for man or beast," and the others nodded like rain-weighted petals.

Only Joe Meers, alone in his shop, longed to be outside, away from the smooth, pale-yellow walls, bare except for the large posters showing the sectioned body parts of cows, away from the red-checked tablecloth draped over the top of his glass display case, away from the bulky black cash register on the counter beside him and the doorway just beyond his slumped shoulders, a gap so narrow that he almost had to squeeze through it to reach the back room.

He rested his large head on one fist, pressing heavily on his supporting elbow. The numbness in his arm almost pleased him; it was a sensation, at least, something physical. It seemed he'd been living in his imagination so long that he'd forgotten that his body could feel. Work didn't give him the touch he wanted, nor did the daydreams that even his sense of propriety couldn't stop him from indulging in.

He had stood patiently behind his counter for another whole day, smiling at customers while barely hearing their voices, weighing meat, wrapping it up, and staring at the little bell over the door that never shook at the touch of her hand. How long had it been now? Three more days, four? His life had been distilled to one haunting question: what will you do if she never returns? He understood that there was only one answer: he would forever live with the image of himself as a man who could not commit even the slightest act of will, not even when his own life was at stake. He had no illusions about his future happiness. Mrs. Mawson, he would repeat a hundred times a day, annoyed with himself, but the annoyance could not restrict his desire. Happiness? What was it, if not simply this feeling that even her imagined self brought into his life?

All day, the approaching storm seemed to push at his back, urging him to do something, to phone her and say he had a sale on ground round, to walk by the house at lunchtime with the chance of seeing her and saying hello, anything other than this unending anxiety of tiny raised hopes whenever the door opened, and disappointments when she was not behind it. Hour after hour, he stared out the window, wondering how he had come to rely on the gentleness in this one woman's face. What did he know of her, after all, except that he had no business thinking of her as anything but another customer, despite the unspoken emotional bond that he believed existed between them?

Finally, at closing time, Joe removed his smock and hung it on the peg. Then he shut off the lights and walked out the door, shivering as he felt the glowering sky fall unflinching on his scalp. The key almost bounced in his palm as he held it in front of him. He touched it with the fingers of his other hand and moved it toward the lock. Still shivering, he pushed the key against the lock and almost dropped it. On the third try, very slowly, he placed the key in and turned it until the lock snapped shut. Then, without looking at the sky, he pocketed the key and strode quickly down the street toward the dyke.

At the same time, a mile downriver, Raskin's boy crept into the trailer after spending most of the afternoon wandering through the fields and along the dyke, trying to convince himself that the girl had not told on him. Now he had two reasons to avoid home: the fear of his father, and the fear that others would seek him out there. Finally, tired and hungry, he had decided to take his chances, cautiously studying the trailer as he approached it. When he had seen only his father's truck parked on the dyke, he had decided it was safe to sneak inside the trailer, if only to find something to eat and then to leave again.

Inside, he discovered his father drunk, with a naked woman on his lap. The scene was not unusual. The boy knew that his father used prostitutes when he'd had an especially good opening on the river, and the night of the scabbing had been highly profitable.

The boy did not want to risk being seen, so he did not watch for long. Instead, he crept into the kitchen, took some chicken from the refrigerator, and ran outside.

The smell of the river and the oppressiveness of the sky only increased his excitement. He looked quickly around him, as if stricken by the absence of everything but his own thoughts. The clouds hovered like burnt ash, the tide seemed about to burst with burning embers.

Five minutes later, he was running along the dyke, upriver toward town, heading for his stash under the cannery in the harbour. He had to pause only once, when he saw a large man walking rapidly toward him, his head down. The boy made a wide detour, dropping from the dyke to the road, then climbing up again and continuing on his way. As he ran, a voice told him it was too soon after the failure of the last fire, too soon after he'd been seen by the girl. But another, stronger voice urged him on, assured him he would never be caught as long as he paid attention to the fire at the end of his hands.

By the time he crawled across the muck between the pilings, his heartbeat was exploding over and over in his ears. He grabbed the burlap sack and crawled through the reeds up the bank. Before now, he had always set fires after dark. He felt especially vulnerable in the full daylight, though the sky was dark and heavy as dusk and the streets and wharves were silent. He peered over the bank and then, terrified, he exposed his body to the air, rising up and racing across and down the dyke.

In ten seconds, he was kneeling in the tall grass of the vacant lot, fumbling with the sack. Hardly able to use his hands because they were trembling so much, he spread some newspaper on the ground, struck a match, and touched it to the paper. The orange flame leapt from his fingers and devoured the words and images. The boy panted over the heat, his eyes widening as the flame climbed toward his face; it felt as though it was rising from inside his body, the sudden ebbing of his own blood. He watched amazed and frightened as the fire grew, and then gradually he began to breathe more evenly, despite his continued fear of being caught.

When he glanced around again, and saw no sign of anyone, he added more paper to the fire, hoping eventually to set the whole field ablaze. Soon the flame almost reached the level of the grass, becoming a wide orange blade among the green. The boy experienced a mingled sense of wonder and control that grew stronger as the heat intensified and clumps of black ash rose over the field.

After a while, noticing the ashes, he panicked, realizing that someone might see the smoke. Still kneeling, he quickly undid his pants and urinated on the fire, which hissed and sizzled but did not go out completely until the boy smothered it with the sack.

Exhausted but relieved, he was about to rise and return to his hiding place under the cannery when he heard sneering laughter behind him. He looked back over his shoulder just as a kick landed in the middle of his back and sent him face forward over the doused ashes. The boy didn't have to look to know who it was. He started to cry into the burnt ground, understanding that his secret had extended beyond the circle of a small girl's keeping, and that his nights would be longer and more terrifying now than they had ever been.

The butcher walked for an hour before deciding that he'd had enough. He couldn't just keep going. For one thing, he would run out of land to the west and would have to circle back toward town eventually, and for another, he was hungry. As always, the exercise sharpened his appetite, and he had never been a man to forego the satisfaction of that basic need. Eating, at least, was something to which he could give himself fully.

But he didn't have the heart to face anyone, so he chose not to eat at the restaurant, but to go home and fry up a nice cut of steak. After that? More of the same, he realized, the tension in his body still building, the sense that he could not walk it off making him move even faster. He thrust his strides into the weighted air and sank from the dyke into the tall grass of the vacant lot.

All day in the Gulf, hovering around the mouth of the river, the sockeye waited for the perfect tide and for the rain to fall, driving them upriver. They massed together, shivering as the current slid over their scales. Their fierce eyes, open as keyholes, stared through the murk and silt and saw only gravel beds spumed with milt and roe, only their own beautiful endings in the clear waters of origin. They stared through the human filth and the neon shadows of the world that hardly knew they existed; they stared through the heavy meshes and the claws and the ten thousand years of icelessness that gave them their long swim home; they gaped without fear or pity or joy at the imminence of their own extinction.

By dark, when the tide had slowed, they thrummed like a huge tuning fork, poised to receive the first vibration of the rain, which would not come. It maddened them; they butted their hard, silver heads as the water streamed through the small, fine teeth in their slung jaws. The banks of the river trembled, the rushes waited to be lit, even the hunting owls turned their eyes back to the west as they flew, feeling the weight of an equal gaze on their wings. The whole edge of the Gulf waited to crash in, like a snow-covered mountain slope. The lower coast was suddenly layered and fragile. A footstep on a wharf, a wharf on a delta, a delta on water, water on a plate, a plate on a planet, a planet in endlessness: it was all essential and insignificant. The sockeye massed in their own cold constellation, as the hands that would kill them hung in the coal-oil light, and the ears that would hear them die filled with an angry and impassioned voice.

"I say it's not over," Ed railed, "as long as we say it's not over! Let the bastards make their backroom deals!" The yellow light caught his full height and made his body shine in the surrounding gloom. "I'll say it again. Damn the union. If you break this strike, no matter what they say, you're a scab. That's it! A scab! And if one man thinks you're a scab, you can't escape it, that's what you are. Go ahead, do what they say, untie your boats no matter how you voted, go out and anchor, then pick the goddamned fish until your wrist bones snap. It doesn't matter how the hell much money you make, you're a scab, and you'll always be one."

He pulled his wallet from his back pocket and removed something from it. The men gathered around him watched intently as he struck a match and held it in front of his glowering face. In his other hand he held a small square of paper.

"Corrupt power isn't power worth having. You voted to reject the offer, eighty percent of you. That means everything. Not what someone else, even your own union, tells you. Not this Jesus Christly card!"

Ed touched the small flame to the square and watched it burn down at the end of his fingers. The men didn't know how to respond. Most of them were stunned, unsure of what their next move should be.

Vic watched the card burn and went over the facts he knew.

The union had disregarded its membership's votes and had accepted the companies' offer. Ed only knew the results of the vote because he had overheard two of the union's executive discussing it. Could it be true? And if so, what were they supposed to do now, go against their union? That's what Ed was saying, but did that make any sense? Looking around him, Vic could tell he was not the only one puzzled by this turn of events. Most of the fishermen just stared at the tiny flame over their heads, and looked away only when the sirens sounded in the distance.

But this time, no fire burned in the harbour except the small one in the raised hand. The fishermen tensed, peering down the channel, waiting for a light to flare in the darkness. But nothing happened and the sirens eventually died out to the west.

The disruption dissipated some of the force of Ed's speech and gesture. Two men turned and walked down the gangway to their boats.

"No choice now," one threw back over his shoulder. "We have to make a living."

Another man followed, and that started a chain reaction. Within five minutes, most of the men had either walked to their boats or gone home to wait for dawn before heading to the fishing grounds. Ed stood in silence on the fish crate and watched them go. One by one, they represented pieces of a past that he was no longer sure he had ever been a part of. He couldn't blame them for going. He felt more sadness than anger, sadness that his world no longer seemed to honour the collective will of its inhabitants.

"Well," he shrugged to the few remaining fishermen, "that's that." He stepped off the crate, but hesitated before he left the wharf. His dark, tired eyes picked out Vic in the coal-oil dimness. Despite his own convictions, Ed did not want this man to feel bad for what he no doubt believed he had to do for the sake of his family.

"We tried, Victor," he grinned. "We did what we could."

Vic shrugged in response. He shared Ed's resignation and fatigue; it was hard to go on believing in certain things when the world refused in every way to be sympathetic. "That's right," he finally nodded. "We put up a fight at least."

"Dinosaurs now, Victor, that's what we are. Old Fraser River dinosaurs. Might as well drag out the linen and the bluestone vats." Ed smiled as he spoke, but there was no real laughter in his voice when he added, "Ah well, I've still got a dozen years before I can call it quits. I guess I'd better drag myself out there for the morning."

Vic sensed Ed's motive and was grateful for it. "Might as well," he admitted, "even a dinosaur's got to eat."

Ed's deep laugh boomed over the harbour. "You've got that right," he chuckled, slapping the crossbeam of the net-rack. "That's about the size of it." He paused again, took in a lungful of the heavy, mud-rich air, and stared over the river. Then he turned back to Vic one last time. "See you out there, then," he said hoarsely, and vanished around the netshed.

Vic stood silent for several minutes, dragging on a cigarette. The other fishermen had left the wharf. Only Troy remained. A few boats started up and idled out of the harbour, their mastlights candling the thick overhang of the sky. Vic did not speak to Troy as they walked to the house, except to mutter, just as they reached the top of the driveway, "Low tide in the morning, a couple of feet, low and fast."

That figures, Troy thought, it can never be easy. He only nodded in response, but his father's bootsteps were already crunching over the gravel. Following slowly, Troy wondered when he'd have to answer questions about Corbett, whether he'd pretend he didn't know where he was or whether he'd mention the hospital against his brother's wishes. Another fucking choice, he scowled, feeling that the whole season had been one ongoing and impossible need to make a decision.

He reached the side yard and stood breathing the scent of apples heavy on the limbed air. The night also hung full and ripe. Troy could almost smell the sockeye's musk wafting up over the banks. Everything seemed to be waiting to move or to fall, the clouds, the salmon, the apples, the rain, everything. He yawned and climbed the steps into the kitchen light.

Downriver, huddled deep in the high stalks of a cornfield, Ling Cod, the boy, and two other wharf-rats watched the old barn crash in on itself as the firemen gushed their hoses in vain over the bone-dry wood.

"Look at that, ho—ly shit!" Ling Cod laughed wildly. He was drunk and ecstatic with it, his eyes bulging out like small planets. He could hardly keep himself from rushing toward the flames. He and his two constant companions formed a capering trio, throwing their heads back under bottle mouths and cursing out their irreverent joy in the liberty afforded them by the darkness. It had been Ling Cod's idea to set the fire; he wanted to get even with the owner of the barn who once told him, in the middle of town, to move off the sidewalk. "You're going to do it," Ling Cod had told the boy, "'cause you're the fuckin' expert. And if you don't . . ." His grin was oily and full. "If you don't, I guess we'll just have to tell the cops on you."

By now, the boy was in a state of constant terror. Setting the barn-fire had excited him briefly, the flames giving him back that giddy sense of power and control, but the excitement soon died and was replaced by the more familiar fear and humiliation. Because he was afraid that they would tell the cops if he ran away, the boy drank with them, desperate to quell his relentless panic. He wasn't tormented only by the fear of being found out, but also by the more immediate fear of what the others might make him do, or what they might do to him, which was always worse when they had been drinking: he still had the scrapes on his palms, knees, and chin from the time they'd stolen a car, roped him to the bumper, and made him run behind all the way from Canoe Pass to the Indian Reserve. Whenever the car sped up, he had to run faster or the rope would tighten and yank him down onto the gravel road. By the time they finally stopped, five separate spots of blood glistened on his body and his neck was chafed raw.

So he drank too, when he could get the alcohol from the others, and tried to convince himself that they were his friends. Who else even paid attention to him? If he disappeared one day, his father wouldn't notice unless he was angry and needed something to hit. But his friends, at least, went looking for him, and much of the time they didn't do anything to him except laugh or blow smoke rings in his face.

The group watched the barn collapse and then they stumbled through the corn, snapping and kicking at the stalks.

A half hour later, they stood in almost complete darkness on the muddied edge of the low tide, halfway between Chilukthan and Pheasant Island. Fifty feet in front of them, the river flowed sluggishly. Thirty feet behind them, the empty dyke stretched darkly away to the east and west, like another horizon; a few fir trees towered along the bank to the east, while farther off to the west, a cluster of squat shacks and netsheds looked no larger than fish boxes.

But Raskin's boy was too frightened to notice his surroundings. The others lurched and slipped around him, giggling and occasionally shouting a curse into the heavy air. Ling Cod had a rope in his hands and sniggered as he directed his two friends to hold the boy tighter against the piling.

"Come on, hang onto him so I can get the rope around." Ling Cod's breath was rye-drenched, as though his insides had been fermenting in the fields. One of the boys hesitated.

"Come on, chickenshit, hold his arms back!" Ling Cod worked feverishly, driven by the same weight of atmosphere that had hovered over the delta all day. "Don't fuckin' worry," he snapped, "I know what I'm doing!" Then he whispered over his shoulder, "We'll come back in time."

The boy went limp as the rope tightened across his stomach. His head fell forward until all he could see was the quick, dark motion of feet sloshing in the mud. In a moment, even that had gone, and he was alone again, the damp wind on his hair and a buzz of vague images in his mind: fire, a woman's breasts, cornstalks, bullrushes, a lifted bottle, Ling Cod's face. He heard the tide running nearby, the rising wash of it against the bank, but he was strangely unafraid. What would the river ever do to him? He had never looked into its depths and found a hostility equal to what he knew at home or elsewhere.

The boy slumped into the rope. His nerves had taken so much punishment that his mind could not grasp the present danger. He knew the tide was backing up, but he also knew instinctively that he had time to let his terror build again, to worry about whether his friends would come back. For now, half-drunk and exhausted, he rested, the laughter trilling off the dyke as faint as the current whispering across the mud at his feet.

Hours passed. The black hands of midnight prayed and broke apart again. The river backed up, the tide spread over the marshes and filled them in, until the rushes worked like gills, opening wider and wider to breathe. Water covered the muddy banks, swelled to the tops of the sloughs, and driftwood and dark shadows of seagrass washed in. On the quiet drifts, anchored gillnetters turned slowly upriver on their chains, as though caught by the same fever that burned in the sockeye's blood. The clouds, the night, and the river were formed of the same heavy substance, a darkness that existed outside of time, that waited for nothing but its own completion.

The tide went slack, held for an hour, started to run out again, slowly, then faster and faster. The gillnetters swung around, the rushes gasped, the driftwood resumed its antlered migration to the sea. On the slack, the schooled Stuarts had burst into the mouth like an earthquake, to shake the silts of south Vancouver and shatter its drugged and pretty lights. Thousands of salmon streamed upriver, unseen and unheard, and poured past Chilukthan, Steveston, New Westminster, turning the human clock back, smashing it, salmon like chips of ice seeking the sides of a dead glacier, like loaded syringes pushed into the province, over and over, on the slack and when the tide turned, still coming in the thousands, the current gagging their hard jaws and washing silt and filth into the blue dream of their gapes. Advance guards for dawn, the next one, the memory of the last one, the ones after, the undreamed of and the forgotten, the sockeye tore the meshes of everything the earth put in their path, wanting only to bring the last curve of the cycle around and complete it with the violent dawn of their own deaths.

The butcher thrust his body into the rising wind that blew in off the Gulf. A little moisture touched his brow, but he did not notice it. He pushed on, leaving the lights of the town far behind, his shoes crushing the gravel dyke, his thick arms muscling the air into submission as he swung them forward in a scything motion. His chest swelled with every huge breath as though he was trying to find in the black night ahead of him some small current that Mrs. Mawson had initiated with a sigh or whisper. Five minutes a week, that would be enough if it was guaranteed. A man could live on that, couldn't he? Yes, he repeated, five minutes, if I can't secure that much, I don't deserve to live.

Suddenly the sky crashed down, the rain flooded through the bank of black clouds now invisible in the darkness and smashed into the river. It pelted so hard into Joe's face that he finally stopped and looked around. The fresh water seemed to wake him into full consciousness. He grinned up into it, his fists clenched with resolve: I will phone in the morning, first thing. Yes.

He stared unblinking into the downpour, letting the rain stream over his skin. The clouds shuddered and split and a sleeve of stars appeared in the slight gap. All the energy in his large frame had suddenly altered and deepened. He pushed westward into the bramble-thick rain, challenging its force with the surge of his own. To think that it had taken so long to find the will to match the simplicity of his desire. But had it really been so long? A matter of months since he'd gone searching in the fog, was that all? He smiled into the faint starlight beyond the rain, and ground the gravel under his feet.

He reached a curve in the river and stopped. The rain fell harder and wafted the rich musk of the tide over the bank. Joe angled his head toward the smell, but couldn't see anything. He was about to turn back to town when the full moon muscled out of the clouds and sent a long rippling beam along the bank in front of him. The light shone for thirty seconds on a small wharf jutting downriver toward a pistonhead of pilings, the rotting remains of an old cannery. Joe squinted in disbelief at the head and neck of a body. Then the moon snapped off, swallowed by the roaming clouds.

Joe ran to the broken gangway and started down. He slipped twice on the wet mossy planks before he reached the wharf, which was so small that it rocked slightly from side to side as he turned and lumbered downriver along its twenty-foot length. He stopped abruptly at a sudden slosh of tide his weight had brought over the edge of the planks. Now he could just see the outline of the body; it was attached to one of a half-dozen decayed cedar pilings clustered together and pointing up at different angles, like tombstones in a neglected graveyard. Only a foot or two of wood stuck above the small head which hung forward with the angle of the piling, upriver toward the wharf. "Hey!" Joe shouted into the wind and rain. "Hey there!"

Only the river seemed to respond, slapping and sucking at the pilings as it tore past. "Jesus," Joe whispered, looking up at the sky, praying for the moon to reappear. When it didn't, he knelt on the edge of the wharf, and leaned as far forward as he could, close enough to the body that he could see the water swelling and beating at its throat. He could not tell if the boy was alive, but he did not even think of the alternative. He stretched carefully out to the piling but could not reach it while on his knees. As he hesitated, the moonlight flashed again, held the boy's face for ten seconds, then shrank back as though ashamed. Joe pulled away with it.

That face, he had seen it before! But the boy groaned suddenly and Joe's heart leapt. He leaned forward again, trying to calm himself by speaking. "It's all right," he said. "I'll get you down. It's going to be all right."

Because he knew little about rivers and tides, he did not connect the direction of the river's flow to its height. He saw only the surface of the black water collaring the boy's throat and swelling up toward his chin. Joe believed he had precious few minutes to act.

He lay flat on his stomach and plunged his hands into the river, touching the slimed wood of the piling and searching until he found the rope. Then he quickly released it and pulled back to study the situation. If he undid the rope, and the body fell, he would not be able to grab it from the water before the tide pulled it away. The only solution would be to undo the rope with one hand while holding onto the body with the other. Joe knew he was strong enough to support such a light weight, but still, he was breathing heavily as he immersed both arms in the water again.

The knot wasn't tight, but it was hard to undo because of its position. Joe struggled and pulled at it, his eyes inches above the blur of the river. The rain crashed around him and merged with the rising thrum of the tide and the blood in his ears. The knot held.

A knife, he cried inwardly, pulling back. Or something sharp. There might be something on the wharf. He rose to his feet and turned quickly. His weight suddenly shifted, and he staggered backward, desperately windmilling his arms to regain his balance.

The motion was just enough to right himself. His heart thumped against his ribs as he bent over and scanned the planks. Nothing. He dropped to his stomach again at the edge of the wharf and reached farther toward the piling, his hands yanking at the knot. Just a little more, he gasped, his head and chest inching toward the piling, the black sheen of the river slapping at his dropped jaw.

Suddenly the boy twisted away. Startled, Joe looked up and saw the boy's eyes blink open, his mouth widening as if to scream. But no sound came. Instead, the boy twisted away again, kicking out in the same motion.

Joe jerked forward. In a panic, he grasped at the rope around the boy's body, but missed it. His weight shifted over the rippling black, and he dropped heavily into the current, head first, the cold water biting at his skin and lungs. Within seconds, the river had carried him beyond the cluster of pilings.

The current gripped him around the waist as he flailed his heavy arms and legs upward, pounding with clenched fists at the sinewed water. But trying to surface was like trying to peel a shadow from the earth. His body was a slab he could raise only because he was strong enough to ignore the fact that he could not swim. The black muscle in the tide clenched around him, but he kicked above it, his lungs bursting, the surface a thin membrane that seemed it would never break.

He managed to lift his head out of the water just once, his eyes rolling across the rent clouds and glimpsing a faint row of stars. He reached for it, but it broke like a frosted twig in his tight clutch, and as he opened his mouth to cry out, a swell of rain-pocked darkness flooded in and smothered his final sound. His body sank into the main drag of the current. Salmon flashed by like flung knives in the silted gloom, nicking his cheeks and throat, hitting his torso with a dull thud, then falling away. Down and down, his body boned the black flesh closing around it, finally thumped into one of the girders of the bridge, snagged for a second, then spun off and was swept out to the Gulf.

chapter twenty-six

At daybreak, a fisherman heading to Canoe Pass took the boy down from the piling. Cold and disoriented, numbed by his night's long ordeal, he found his way home just in time to be put back to work. He would spend the rest of the summer grasping the salmon's flesh and setting gas fires along the riverbanks. Until he was caught, his acts of arson dominated the front pages of the local paper and deflected attention away from all other stories, including the disappearance of Joe Meers.

No one saw anything strange in the butcher's absence until well over a week had passed. Customers came to the shop every day, peered in, shook their heads in mild surprise, and went away. Or else they called the shop and let the phone ring ten times, hanging up with the same indifferent shrug. That's odd, many of them thought. But since no one was close to Joe Meers, no one took his absence seriously enough to be alarmed by it.

After several more weeks, however, when the shop remained closed and wholesalers and others who had regular business dealings with the butcher began to make inquiries, the police were called in. Their investigation proved futile. No one had seen or heard anything. When residents of Chilukthan thought about the case at all, they concluded that the butcher had simply left town the same way he had arrived, suddenly and quietly. Many assumed that he would return eventually. The possibility of foul play, which the police had to follow up, seemed ridiculous. The butcher? Who could possibly want to harm such an unassuming fellow?

But his disappearance did not really capture the interest of the town. People raised their eyebrows about it for a while, made a few half-hearted speculations, and moved on to more important matters.

The Mawsons had their own pressing concerns. The strike had ended, but not victoriously for the gillnet fishermen. They had not received a decent contract, nor did they have much success in the way of big catches on their return to work. When fishing opened on the morning of the butcher's disappearance, most of the Stuart sockeye had already moved upriver. The fishermen averaged fifty fish for the day, twenty fish more than they would average per opening over the next few weeks. Only the run of Adams River sockeye in late August and early September brought the numbers back up, but by then, the opportunity for a big economic return had been missed.

Vic and Troy scraped along like everyone else, making a little money through August, and then considerably more during the Adams run. Kathleen watched her husband spend an anxious summer and sensed that his ability to remain an independent fisherman while staying close to his family was coming to an end. They would survive another winter, just barely, but eventually Vic would be forced to choose between following the winds of commerce or going on a payroll. At fifty years old, with fishing as his only significant employment record, he would struggle with the choice each year, finally taking odd jobs as a manual labourer to supplement his income.

As for Kathleen, she would continue to manage the household, damming up her emotions for the sake of the family. She would not allow herself to listen to the past for fear it might consume her, and so she lost the ability to hear the voices of her parents and her dead son, and with it, the ability to enrich her life with a full and human complexity. Turning outward to her family, she survived, but at the expense of the deep knowledge that exists only in the smell of the earth and rain. Her eldest son's situation, in particular, shocked her into ending the inward journey on which she had embarked.

Because of his injuries, Corbett could not fish the boat he'd been offered, so he spent a miserable month recovering until he was fit enough to deckhand for his father again. Vic and

Kathleen had accepted the lie about a bar-room fight, only after they realized that the boys, for whatever reason, were not going to deviate from the story. For once, it seemed that they had allied for the same cause. As far as their parents were concerned, knowing the truth about the injuries would not help them to heal any faster.

Troy and Corbett had grown closer because of the incident at the netshed, but only for a while. The differences between them were such that, before long, the brothers had assimilated them completely into the nature of their relationship. Love remained between them, and loyalty, but they had lost the ease of affection they had once known.

But before their relationship weakened again, while they could still remember the intensity of feeling that had existed at the hospital, Troy made a decision to protect his older brother that Corbett would never know about.

On the weekend after the beating, as Troy was getting out of his car at the ballpark, Margo Petrovich approached him. She hurriedly took an envelope from her jacket, and asked him to give it to Corbett. Troy did not say a word to her; he only stared at her coldly until she lowered her eyes, repeated her request in a hoarse whisper, and walked away.

Troy stuffed the letter in his duffel bag, and thought about it only after the game. He finally concluded that no matter what it contained, the envelope would bring nothing but more misery to his brother. It didn't make much difference whether Margo was still trying to continue the relationship or writing an end to it. Either way, Troy could not see any benefit; she was married, and as long as that fact remained, Corbett was better off with her out of his life. Still, despite his best intentions, Troy was too curious not to read the letter. As he had expected, Margo apologized for everything that had happened and made it clear that the affair was over. She was going north immediately and wouldn't be back until the fall. She hoped that Corbett would understand, and said that she was sure he would have moved on with his life by the time she saw him again. Troy tore the letter into pieces and dropped them in the river.

As for Corbett, it took him a long time to understand that his life would not always move in perfect accord with his desires. But the beating had already served to distance him from Margo, so that by September, what with all the attention women gave him because of his cast, he had recovered from the worst of the emotional fallout. Nevertheless, despite his carefree manner, he would not easily file his first serious romance in the past. Though he would move on with his life, as Margo had predicted, he would not do so with the same unwary recklessness as before. Some of the lightness had gone out of him, replaced not by cynicism or fear, but by a sort of guarded caution.

Some of the same lightness had seeped out of the town as well. The strike had brought a hundred years of history to a climax, and when it was over, and the union had been weakened, a parallel weakness slowly began to show itself in the community. There were no immediate or dramatic changes, but the feeling in Chilukthan was never quite the same. Over time, the crimson August sun would fall onto fewer and fewer hands immersed in blood and tide for more than just profit. The thrum of the ineffable that had comforted John Mawson and others as they strode along the dyke would be heard only by the great blue herons balanced like Ming vases in the reeds. And though the same forces would go on ploughing the years back under the same stars, the dominating presence of the land and the river would turn into a mere backdrop for a speedier and more sophisticated world. Soon, only an earthquake threat would remind the rushing millions of the south coast of the delicate balance on which they lived.

Chilukthan had possessed such knowledge once. It had always survived by watching the tides and by understanding the gift of the rain; its children had climbed into the fragrant attics of rotted orchards and had learned to read through all their senses what was written there; its elderly could remember the river when it carried the whole interior of the province on its black shoulders, when it howled with the unending sound of the void between planets and threatened to pour over the dykes like an army from the trenches.

Chilukthan still possessed the knowledge that September when Vic Mawson, tired from fishing the Prairie Drift and picking out hundreds of Adams River sockeye, tied his boat up in the harbour and walked dejectedly home. It was nearly two o'clock in the morning and a cold wind blew the rippled moonlight in front of him as he moved slowly down the side yard to the garden. As quietly as possible, he found his wheelbarrow and pushed it back up the empty street to the wharf.

Once there, he worked quickly, careful not to wake Corbett asleep in the cabin. He bent under the drum and began pulling sockeye out and laying them on the wharf. Five, ten, fifteen, twenty. He finally stopped and stepped back on the wharf. Then he loaded the salmon into the wheelbarrow and pushed it up the gangway to the dyke.

He paused and looked downriver over the thick trowels of moonlight on the water to the dim shapes of the cottonwoods on the harbour island. Only the wind disturbed the silence. In the west, the moon shone bright and full against the dark clouds, but was smeared with craters and resembled a stained smock. It was hard to believe such a ragged object could spill so much light.

Vic raised the wheelbarrow again and felt the strain in his arms and shoulders as he descended the other slope of the dyke to Laidlaw Street. The weight of the salmon pulled hard at his muscles until he reached the pavement and stopped under the branches of the cherry trees. Behind him, all the way back to his boat, a trickle of blood that had seeped out of a hole in the wheelbarrow stained the ground and shone stickily in the moonlight. A tomcat crept out of the tall grass to lap its rough tongue against the line. But Vic did not see the long trail he had left in his wake. He only noticed the heap of fish in front of him. They looked like the shards of a mirror. He continued toward the house.

Once in the garden, he stared at the fish for a long time before he began to dig a hole to bury them in. The moonlight reflected off their scales and made the blade of the shovel gleam as he squelched it deeper into the soil. When the hole was deep enough, he stopped and studied the salmon again. As always, their eyes were wide open, as if they were still intent on getting home, as if they would start to swim again once they'd been returned to the earth, thrashing down into the darkness until they broke through to the tide that never stopped calling them.

Vic lifted one from the wheelbarrow and held it in the full moonlight. The fish weighed about seven pounds, and had a slight hump to its back and hook to its nose. One more week, and it would have carried its tarnished silver into the mountains and exchanged it for a brilliant scarlet and green. But it was dead. Blood was smeared over its scales and Vic could feel it cold against his fingers. Sadly, he tossed the fish in the hole. Too ripe, the companies had said, the meat is too far gone, can't be canned, can't be sold. And the media had spread the lie so that it was impossible for the fishermen to sell the sockeye privately, or even to give them away. Vic lifted another one from the pile. Maybe Kathleen would can a few more? No, she was already overworked and behind; there were just too many fish. He'd have to stop going out. What was the point? It was obvious by now that the companies had control of the situation and that the fishermen would have to wait.

In the meantime, Vic figured he might as well fertilize the garden. He threw the sockeye in the earth and heard it slap against the other. Then he got behind the wheelbarrow and tipped it up. The fish slid out in an oily beam and sloshed into the hole. Vic grabbed the shovel again and began to throw dirt over the stiffening silver, the gaping eyes.

The salmon began their slow sink into decay. Every ounce of them picked up the familiar route and the scent, every bone longed for its particular place. The moonlight fell in with the dirt and there was no difference; everything was the same obstacle. They had somewhere to get to, they had a death that meant as much as life because it was life, they swam down despite the weight on their scales and the judgement of human eyes. They were dead, but the river and the earth still worked them, the stars still fired the banks. Dead, but their flesh seeped out in a thousand directions to keep the one path sure for the living, their flesh cracked open and released its cold sparks to burn deep into the clay, their eyes would not stop seeing the gravel and the clear stream and the devouring air.

And in the Gulf they kept coming, through the nets and currents, into the rush of silts, over the wavering seagrass on the ocean floor, down with the crabs and the whale bones and the spent light of the sky, down too with a lost human stare that seemed sorry it could not join them, that looked back over its own sinking temple toward the river, over its finger bones slowly turning and turning in the earth, as though its fleshless mouth would ask a question of the salmon's urgency, as though still seeking an answer to the long stillness it had found.